Shadows on the Shore

By the same author:

THE SPOILED EARTH
THE HIRING FAIR
THE DARK PASTURE

THE DRUMS OF TIME
THE BLUE EVENING GONE
THE GATES OF MIDNIGHT

TREASURES ON EARTH
CREATURE COMFORTS
HEARTS OF GOLD

THE GOOD PROVIDER
THE ASKING PRICE
THE WISE CHILD
THE WELCOME LIGHT

LANTERN FOR THE DARK

JESSICA STIRLING

Shadows on the Shore

St. Martin's Press
New York

Library of Congress Cataloging-in-Publication Data

Stirling, Jessica.
    Shadows on the shore / Jessica Stirling.
        p.   cm..
    ISBN 0-312-10546-0
    1. Scotland—History—18th century—Fiction.
    2. Mothers and daughters—Scotland—Fiction.
    3. Women—Scotland—Fiction. I. Title.
PR6069.T497S69   1994
823'.914—dc20   93-42102
                                                CIP

First published in Great Britain by Hodder and Stoughton.

First U.S. Edition: March 1994
10 9 8 7 6 5 4 3 2 1

4/94

Contents

Book One   Strangers from the Sea   1
Book Two   The Serpent's Egg   71
Book Three   A Covenant of Salt   139
Book Four   The Guardian Angel   237

Book One

Strangers from the Sea

Headrick House, 15th January, 1802

My Dear Cousin Andrew,
I have not delayed so long to write to you because I thought nothing of your New Year gift. My tardiness is attributable only to that most merciless of taskmasters – time, time and the lack of it. The tea was of excellent quality. It greatly enhanced the small festivities which I shared with Dr Galloway and the Reverend Mr Soames whose cheerful company helped relieve the melancholy that invariably arises at this gloomy season of the year when sentiment is so much in the air.

No particular crises of fate have attended my affairs this past six months but there is, as you predicted, an infernal busy-ness to being both master and mistress of Headrick. I do not find my new responsibilities burdensome, however, for in them I have discovered such a change from sequestered domesticity that I feel quite refreshed by the challenge.

Since autumn was fair for the most part, salt production continued until the 12th day of December. I was much occupied with finding best markets for Headrick salt and in learning to deal with accounts made complex by excise duty and taxation. In this aspect of management I admit to certain inadequacies and frequently feel that I am being taken advantage of because of my sex as well as my inexperience.

Now that I have finally emerged from the shadows of the past I regret having spurned the folk who offered friendship and support when first I appeared here in Ladybrook as Donald's wife. There is, however, no easy mending of that state of affairs. My ways and the ways of Ayrshire society are far too set to change overnight. So, dear Andrew, as this is the first letter of yet another year, you have my gratitude for standing by me during that period in our lives when you had every reason for never wishing to see or hear from me again.

However much it embarrasses you I refuse to take your generosity of spirit for granted and I will continue to remind you of it now and then until we are separated by something more tangible than Mrs Purves's disapproval. As to our Mutual Acquaintance, I have heard nothing of him and begin to doubt that I ever will.

Alas, Headrick news will have to wait. If I do not put this letter into Pratie's hands within the half-hour it will never make the post and may lie unfinished for a week or more. I will write again soon, I promise.

3

My affectionate regards to Dorothea and also to little Margaret who I hope will soon be well again.
For the meanwhile, dear cousin, Adieu!

Clare Kelso Quinn

One

The clanging of the lodge bell in the town a half-mile below the house drew Clare from sleep. Though muffled by rain and distorted by the big wind that clawed against the bedroom window the sound was so persistent and penetrating that for an instant Clare fancied her husband had returned from the dead to ring and ring again the impatient little handbell with which he had tormented her during the last long months of his illness.

Dazed, she sat upright, groped across the bed-cabinet for flint and tinderbox and gathered them to her. Leaning on the pillow, she struck frantic sparks in the darkness until she realised that it was not the shade of Mr Quinn that had disturbed her but less demanding sounds from far away.

"Mama, are you awake?"

"Yes, dear."

"I hear a bell."

"I hear it too," Clare assured her daughter.

A thud, a scuffle of bare feet upon the boards and Melissa was a sudden presence by Clare's side, as if the child, at eight, had not unlearned the trick that babies have of seeing everything, even in the dark.

"Mama?" Melissa's breath warmed Clare's cheek. "It isn't Papa, is it?"

"No, darling. How can it be? It's the bell from the Neptune."

"What does it mean?"

Clare had a notion that the tolling bell might signify the close of a lodge meeting. She could not understand why a secret brotherhood would choose to announce itself so publicly, however, and at that hour she lacked the mental agility to explain the irony to her daughter.

She said, "A ship in difficulties, I expect."

"A wreck?"

"Perhaps. The weather's certainly wild enough."

Huddled together in Clare's broad bed, mother and daughter listened to the wail of the wind which had raised the seas off the Ayrshire coast and by mid-afternoon had so shaken Headrick's gables that Clare had ordered supper served in the small back parlour where the din of the storm and the threat of injury from imploding glass were greatly reduced.

"Poor sailors," Melissa said. "I hope they are saved. Mr Harding's boat will save them, Mama, will it not?"

"If it can be put to sea," Clare said, "but I fear the waves may be too heavy to allow a launching."

"Then the poor sailors will be drowned." Melissa spoke in a solemn little voice. "All drowned – like last time."

Clare remembered the last time only too well. Some two years ago a timber-laden brig of three hundred tons which had just completed a crossing of the Atlantic had been hove-to off Ladybrook awaiting a pilot when she had been caught by a sudden north-westerly. About three o'clock in the morning the vessel had plunged her anchors and the crew, unfamiliar with Scottish waters, had sought to ground her on a sandy shore. Instead she had ploughed into a saw-toothed ridge of rock, the Nebbocks, that stood out from Ladybrook's harbour, had been gutted on impact and sucked under in seconds.

Come daylight what a windfall there had been for scavengers on the beach, more timber than anyone had ever seen, great heaving rafts of pine, cedar and mahogany, and not a sailorman alive to claim the cargo for the owners or insurers. For days the shapeless wreck had wallowed in the breakers and sodden corpses had floated into Headrick Bay, tide after tide, until the tally reached eleven and the manifest was satisfied.

Clare had taken Melissa to the beach to view the wreck, which had made a deep impression on the six-year-old and brought into her little head all sorts of interesting questions, both comical and profound. Mr Quinn, though, had not been amused by his daughter's interrogations. He saw no trace of the hand of God in the circumstances of the disaster but, rather gloatingly, had tallied the cost of the brig's encounter with the Nebbocks at upwards of two thousand pounds and had thanked his stars that he did not have a stake in her.

There had been other wrecks since, of course, but none had occurred so close to home or had cost so many lives. Besides, spurred by the loss of the timber-ship, the Sons of Apollo had subscribed the building of a rescue boat and the erection of an onshore beacon to mark the position of the Nebbocks. From the same collection had come money for the brand new bell which hung on an iron tripod behind the Neptune's yard.

Fisherfolk and inshore traders had reason to be grateful for the lodge's charity. Several boatmen, usually drunk, had already been plucked from the mighty deep, but the rescue craft had yet to be tested in a winter storm and Clare questioned if it would prove robust enough to withstand a battering by strong seas.

Melissa scrambled into a kneeling position.

"*Shall* we pray for their souls, Mama?" the little girl asked cheerfully.

Clare did not reply. She continued to scratch with steel and flint and regretted that she had not kept a nightlight floating in a water-dish as she had done when Melissa was very young and again when Mr Quinn was ill.

"Mr Soames prays for those in peril," Melissa prattled on. "He says it is something we all should do."

"I'm sure Mr Soames is right, dear," Clare said, as patiently as possible.

At that particular moment she had no desire to hear her daughter's discourse on the minister's Sunday sermons. She required a light less spiritual to shine upon her darkness.

Propped against the pillows, she flaked at the flint and cursed beneath her breath the absence of a flame.

She did not know why the bellowing wind roused such apprehension in her tonight. She had experienced tyrannical storms before now and had thrived on them. Rough weather had made her house seem tighter, her marriage to Mr Quinn less disappointing, more secure.

Since Donald's departure, though, she had become unusually superstitious and irrational and was often filled with dread that she might lose all she held dear – Melissa – as once, fifteen years ago, she had lost her infant son, not to wind and wave but to accidental poisoning.

At last the teasel in the blackened tin took fire. Clare leaned hastily from the bed to transfer flame to candle but was brought up short by imperious rapping on the bedroom door. Frozen, she stared at the door as if she expected it to swing open of its own accord.

Melissa sighed indulgently. "It's only Pratie," she said, and called out for the housekeeper to enter.

The servant was clad in a dun-coloured day-dress and bulky flannel petticoats. A voluminous shawl, fastened at the

7

throat with a bone clasp, was draped over her shoulders. Her square-jawed face was dominated by a starched cambric mob cap tied below her chin with a straight lappet.

Only a few wisps of coarse ginger hair springing from the cap-band and a certain red flecking in her hard grey eyes indicated that the imperturbable Pratie was close to being harassed.

"Did you not hear it?" Pratie demanded.

Clare slid the tinderbox on to the table to burn itself out.

"We heard the lodge bell, yes, of course."

"I heard it first," Melissa chimed in.

Pratie stepped stiffly into the room with the dining-room's three-branched candlestick blazing before her. Darkness gave way to light and Clare, sweeping back the clothes, stepped resolutely out of bed.

She might nurture a fear of many things but she refused to be intimidated by her dour and disapproving housekeeper. She reached for the quilted robe which she had appropriated from Mr Quinn's wardrobe one bitter winter long ago, and hugging it about her turned to confront the Irish woman.

"What has happened? Tell me."

"Gowrie's in the hall."

"Gowrie himself or Gowrie's lad?"

"Gowrie himself."

"What is the hour?"

"Five past midnight," Pratie said. "Did you not hear him thumpin' on the front door?"

"No," Clare said. "If I had heard him I would have come downstairs at once. Come along, Pratie, out with it. What does Bob Gowrie require at this ungodly hour of the night?"

Clare had inherited the Irish woman along with a full complement of domestic servants. Many had been let go when times were hard but those who remained had owed allegiance to Mr Quinn and still regarded the notorious young woman who had stolen the ageing widower's heart away as an interloper. Even now, fourteen years on, Clare was unsure quite where she stood with Pratie Kerrigan and Mrs Shay, the cook, or if they would extend their loyalty to the last of the Quinns – not her, of course, but Melissa.

Pratie said, "From what I can make o' his blethers Gowrie wants you to accompany him to the beach."

"What? At this time of night?"

8

"So it would seem."

"Has the salthouse been damaged by the storm?"

"He wouldna tell me," Pratie said. "He asked for yourself specific, so he did. Insisted on speakin' with the mistress o' the house."

Clare searched for her stockings and under-drawers, seated herself on the edge of the bed and, as modestly as possible, tugged on the garments. Her apprehension had returned though there was nothing alarming in what Pratie had told her. Bob Gowrie was her employee and it was quite natural that he would consult her if the saltpans were threatened with damage.

The wild January weather was probably the cause of her unfledged fancies for, with the door open, everything in the room seemed suddenly animate, curtains, bedclothes, fire-ashes all stirred into motion. Even the pages of Mr Quinn's Bible, open on a stand on the dressing-table, fluttered as if touched by an unseen hand.

Melissa kneeled by her, one plump little hand upon her shoulder, curls golden in the candlelight, blue eyes bright with excitement.

"I'll come with you, shall I?" she suggested.

"No, you will not."

"I do so want to see Mr Gowrie," Melissa wheedled.

"No."

Melissa flung her arms about Clare's neck.

"I'll be frightened, Mama." She whimpered convincingly. "I'll be so frightened up here all by myself."

"Is Lizzie out of bed?" Clare asked the housekeeper.

"They're all out o' bed," Pratie said. "Wake the dead, would Gowrie's hammerin'."

Clare disentangled herself from Melissa's arms and pressed a forefinger lightly against the child's lips to still her protests.

"I'll send Lizzie up to keep you company," she promised. "Now snuggle into my bed. Be quick."

Melissa contemplated further argument, thought better of it and with a vigour that almost dislodged Clare from her perch on the edge of the mattress, burrowed, giggling, under the bedclothes.

She tugged the sheet up to her chin, peeped wide-eyed over it and asked, "Shall I pray for the poor sailors now, Mama?"

Buttoning the bodice of her day-dress, Clare glanced enquiringly at Pratie, who shrugged and, a moment later, led Clare downstairs, leaving Melissa's ingenuous question hanging unanswered in the air.

*   *   *

Bob Gowrie was a broad-cheeked, broad-nosed, plump little man of about fifty, full of his own importance and as bumptious as a beadle. Mr Quinn had once told Clare that Gowrie still regarded himself as a bond-serf, enslaved by articles of employment which had long since been revoked by parliamentary acts of emancipation; reason enough, perhaps, for Gowrie's resentment of the fact that, with the master gone, his fate and his family's welfare had fallen into the hands of a woman.

As Headrick's master salter Bob Gowrie might behave as he wished in his seashore domain. Like it or not, though, Clare Quinn was Gowrie's employer and he was obligated, more by habit than contract, to bow the knee to her wishes and answer to her for his wage.

It was disconcerting to find the salter in the front hall at that hour of the night.

As a rule Clare met with him in the small back parlour where, much to Gowrie's chagrin, she would study his sales ledgers and demonstrate rather too much knowledge of accounting for the salter's liking. Clearly, though, the midnight visit had nothing to do with coal allocations or skimming fees and, it being winter, no salt had been drawn from the pans for weeks.

Gowrie had not taken time to shake out his best clothes. He had flung on a tattered black pea-jacket, cracked black-leather wading boots and a coal-heaver's stiff billed cap which he had churlishly neglected to remove on entering the house. Freckled with spray, his tiny half-moon spectacles clung to the tip of his nose as he rocked agitatedly on the wooden footboard that Pratie had put down to protect the hall's polished floor.

Clare paused on the half-landing to smooth her skirts and adjust her hair then, giving every appearance of command, glided down the last few steps to the hall.

Lurking in the kitchen passageway were Mrs Shay and Jen, the scullion, and, rushing past them like a limb of the gale, came Lizzie, all hair and stays and wrinkled stockings. She bobbed a curtsey to her mistress and galloped away upstairs to keep Melissa company.

Clare did not invite the salter to step down from the board nor did she offer him her hand in greeting.

"Well, Mr Gowrie, this is an unexpected call. Am I to take it that the wind's blown you here at this late hour?"

"After a fashion."

"Damage to my property?"

"No, a boat."

"Wrecked?"

"If it had been wrecked I'd have sent Billy to the Neptune for assistance," he answered.

"If there's no wreck why, not ten minutes ago, did I hear the sound of the lodge bell?"

"I'm not the one to ask that of," Gowrie said. "It may be that a ship's lights were seen, though I myself saw nothing of the kind."

There was something different about the salter tonight. He seemed even more sly and edgy than usual and even before she asked the question Clare sensed that he did not intend to favour her with the whole truth.

Before Clare could speak, however, Pratie thrust the candle-stick close to the salter's nose and snapped, "Well, what is it then? Are you goin' to be keepin' us freezin' here all the night long? Out with it."

Gowrie had always been in awe of the Irish woman and her directness caused him to stammer.

"It – it's a k-k-keelboat, Mistress K-K-Kerrigan, washed up in the b-b-bucket pot."

"So there is a wreck?" Clare said.

"She's not wr-wrecked. She's intact."

"Is there a cargo in her?" Clare said.

"None that I can see."

"Have you secured her?" Clare asked.

"Aye," Gowrie answered. "She was bobbin' in the shallows below the salthouse when, about an hour ago, we found her."

"Does this keelboat have a name?" Clare said.

"The *Midas*."

"Then she will be registered."

"Maybe she'll not," Gowrie said. "She's only a coastin' boat, Mrs Quinn, light enough to be used by lobstermen."

"Do you not recognise her?"

11

"That I do not."

"And you say she's empty?"

"As a maiden's promise."

"Have you searched the pool for survivors?"

"The breakers are frightful heavy, Mrs Quinn. I'll not be riskin' life and limb for strangers."

"Leave her high and dry until morning," Clare said, "and then report her to the harbour master at Saltcoats or, if you prefer it, send word to Cabel Harding."

"She's too good a boat to hand over to Cabel," Bob Gowrie said. "Begging your pardon, Mrs Quinn, but I was thinking we could keep her."

"Keep her?"

"If that's your wish."

Headrick's salters had had more than their fair share of the plunder from the wrecked timber-brig. Clare had no notion where the mahogany beams and lengths of maple had been hidden. But Donald had known, Donald had approved, Donald had profited without getting his shoes wet or his hands dirty. Now, it appeared, Bob Gowrie expected her to behave with the same lack of scruples or regard for the letter of the law.

Clare was tempted to send Pratie to the cottage on the Leddings to fetch Norman Tannahill, or Dr John Galloway. The doctor lived on Cedric's Road, almost two miles away, however; and in the matter that Bob Gowrie had put before her she did not dare shift responsibility on to Tannahill, a hireling whose rank in Ladybrook stood no higher than that of a farm labourer.

Scornful of her indecision, Gowrie rocked on the creaking board and squinted at her through his smeared spectacles.

Clare sucked in a deep breath.

"Pratie," she said, "I'm going down to the shore to see this boat for myself. Please be good enough to fetch my cape and boots."

"An' a lantern?" Pratie asked.

"Yes," Clare answered, "a lantern too, if you will."

*　　*　　*

Clare followed the salter down the side path from the house and across the Linn by the rustic footbridge, the lantern dancing on its ash-pole like a will-o'-the-wisp.

Even in the sheltered glen the wind was strong enough to

12

make Clare stagger. When they emerged from the trees Gowrie grasped her arm and, slanting the pole before him like a lance, supported her across the turnpike and on to the steep sandy shoulder above the beach.

It was just as well that Gowrie was with her. Clare was daintily built and the sudden unimpeded force of the gale might have knocked her to the ground.

She put an arm around Gowrie's waist, leaned against him and peered across the dunes.

Salt spray and stinging sand rendered the air as opaque as German glass and the big wind seemed older than earth and sea, a novel element altogether. She was, however, surprised to discover just how easily she could glide through it once she had gained the relative protection of the sandhills, but as she stumbled after Gowrie glimpses of the roaring sea tempered her excitement and caused her to bury her face in her hood.

She did not look up again until the salthouse was reached and she flung herself behind its sheltering gable.

Gowrie mouthed something unintelligible.

Clare thrust her face close to his stubbled chin and yelled, "Where is the keelboat?"

"Front, beached high."

"Show me."

"Mrs Quinn, I – "

"I did not come all this way in this weather just for the sake of my health," she shouted. "Now show me the blessed boat."

Still he hesitated. His reluctance to obey her was incomprehensible. The look in his eyes, distorted by wet lenses, was curiously pitying. At length he gave himself a shake, dipped the lantern low to the ground and groped for Clare's hand.

"This way, Mrs Quinn," he said.

Two

The Grand Order of Apollo was a good deal less grand than most fraternal institutions. It could boast among its members not a single baronet or earl, let alone a prince of the blood royal. Its provincial branches, where they existed, were petty and discreet, none more so than that which convened in the over-room of the Neptune Inn on the last Tuesday of every month to celebrate certain secret rituals and, afterwards, enjoy convivial fellowship without fear of interruption.

The Neptune was a rambling building of no architectural pretension whatsoever. It occupied the north side of the square that gave heart to Ladybrook's inadequate harbourage and bottom to the more respectable parts of the town.

In the course of half a century the original tavern, a long, low, lime-washed cottage, had been extended upwards and sideways until all but two little mullioned windows had been lost in an assemblage of crow-stepped gables, eaves and awkward corners fashioned from stone and mortar and topped by weathered clapboard.

Corinthian pillars and a Euclidean arch did nothing to dignify the edifice for their rigid geometry served only to show up the ramshackle nature of the rest. But as far as the members of Lodge Ladybrook were concerned the Neptune, with more entrances and exits than a Shakespearean play, was a perfect haven and an eavesdropper might wander about for half an hour before he found the little staircase that led up to the locked door of the temple where the Sons of Apollo forgathered.

The tolling of the tripod bell that windy Tuesday night had no relevance to weather or ships in distress. The bell was simply a signal that the last catechetical toast had been drunk, the last prayer uttered, that the Scribe had closed the Minutes and brothers Ordinary and Scrupulous had been ushered out by the Key-keeper before the hall reopened for business of another, less solemn kind.

14

Uninitiated gentlemen who had been obliged to cool their heels in the Neptune's salon during the main meeting, sighed with relief and trotted off to find the steep staircase in the depths of the inn building.

At half-past midnight the hall door was closed and all those who had lacked the pith to brave the elements were shut out for ever.

Below stairs, doors and gates were locked and bolted and the Neptune's maids and potboys, as well as the landlord and his family, melted into the shadows as if even casual knowledge of what was going on in the temple upstairs might bring down punishments too horrible to contemplate.

The little *ex officio* gathering was in any case complete.

Brock Harding lolled like an old lion in the carved oak chair by the fireside. Relieved of official duties he had discarded the tasselled apron and rosettes but still wore about his neck the chain and Jewel of Apollo as if to remind incomers of the power he wielded here.

Brock Harding was by trade and profession a humble blacksmith, though he claimed to be a genuine descendant of old Tubal Cain himself and was certainly no ordinary monger of horseshoes and wrought-iron gates.

By the sweat of his brow and a flair for nefarious dealing Brock had elevated himself into the ranks of the bourgeoisie and currently owned several properties in town, including the Neptune, the smithy and the row of cottages in which he dwelled with his second wife, his sons, daughters and grandchildren.

In keeping with his station he wore a riding coat of dark brown velvet with huge gilt buttons, a striped waistcoat and a silk cravat. His hair, a great curly mane of it, glistened like silver in the lamplight that illuminated the dais to the right of the fireplace. The passage of time had mellowed his brutal good looks and made him seem less threatening, but none of the real gentlemen present were yet willing to claim him as one of their own.

Brock's eldest sons, Cabel and Daniel, had been appointed stewards for the evening. Muscular, large-limbed and coarse, they looked not unlike their father but had managed by good grooming to achieve a degree of poise that made them seem more like Edinburgh advocates than country blacksmiths.

Cabel, at thirty-seven, had even acquired a certain oratorical polish which, his rural accent notwithstanding, fitted him out as a man destined to rise above his station.

He climbed confidently on to the wooden platform and raised his arms for silence.

"Gentlemen, gentlemen! We all know why we've gathered here on such a blustery night so I ain't a-goin' to squander precious time by speechifyin'."

"Thank God for that," cried Calum McIntosh, agent for the owner of a colliery at Damaris, a dozen miles away behind the Ardeer hills. "I've had enough spray blown into my face tonight to last me a lifetime."

Cabel grinned at the waggish Mr McIntosh and Brock even favoured him with a chuckle.

"As you know," Cabel went on, "tonight is the first sale of the year and I can promise you a display the likes of which you ain't never seen before, not even on these premises. I observe no strangers here, so I won't trouble you with the rules. Suffice to remind you you're hirers not buyers. Sign the papers, pay your cash and keep everything legal and above board."

A canvas curtain screened the hall's long wall. Behind it a side door opened and admitted a swirl of cold wind and the shuddering boom of the sea from the beach nearby.

Beneath the curtain's lifting skirts several pairs of little bare feet were exposed.

The members of the audience paid no more attention to what Cabel had to say and concentrated their interest entirely upon the feet as if, like horse-copers, they believed that the quality of an animal could be judged just by the shape of its hoof.

Cabel paused until the feet came to rest, each pair in position, heels against the wall.

Brother Daniel, who was herdsman to the cargo, slammed shut the small side door.

"To allay your fears," Cabel continued, "I can assure you that the produce is fresh in from the country."

"What country?" McIntosh interrupted. "What treats do you have for us tonight, Cabe? French prisoners?"

"Nothin' quite so exotic. The usual country. Ireland."

"Are they orphans?" asked Oscar Jaynes, laconically.

"Guaranteed without kith or kin," said Cabel.

"Charity brats?"

"That's it, Mr Jaynes."

"May one enquire from which Irish workhouses they were purchased?"

"One may enquire, sir, but one will not be told," said Cabel

16

smoothly. "I mean, I don't go askin' where you buy *your* butcher meat, do I?"

Oscar Jaynes laughed. "Damned if I'd tell you."

"There you are then," said Cabel.

"The point is are they clean and healthy?" Robertson Blyth managed Cairns' colliery on behalf of his father-in-law, the fearsome Lord McCracken.

"'Course they're clean and healthy, Mr Blyth," said Cabel. "Do you think my brother don't pick 'em carefully? Daniel knows what you're after and makes sure the stuff is right. Never had much cause for complaint so far, have you, Mr Blyth?"

"None at all."

"What about the females?" said Oscar Jaynes.

"What about them?"

"Do you guarantee their purity?"

"If you mean what I thinks you mean, Mr Jaynes, no, it's up to you to discover if they're 'guaranteed' – but only after you've squared your bill."

Under cover of the laughter that greeted Cabel's remark Brock whispered to his son to move the proceedings along then he settled back in his chair and eyed his clients speculatively. He knew them all, and all their little foibles.

Colliery agents were only interested in "hiring" boys to fill the niches in their pits that damp, disease and small disasters regularly emptied. Bull Thompson from the high farm at Mossgrove preferred girls and was willing to pay a good price to satisfy his appetite for untouched innocence. When he wearied of the new piece he would pass her on to one of his tenants to use for field labour and would return to the Neptune to buy himself another toy.

To stock his city brothels Oscar Jaynes would take either girls or boys, provided they were pretty, though to Brock's way of thinking there was no scarcity of footloose females and lost lambs to be found in Glasgow.

It was Robertson Blyth who had first put the idea of trafficking in live cargo into Brock Harding's head. The venture had turned out to be profitable and a deal less hazardous than running untaxed rock salt from Liverpool, an exercise in free trade which had cost Brock's brother, Jericho, his life.

Labour was scarce in the Scottish coalfields and trained hewers could name their price. On the other hand Ireland's workhouses and charity schools overflowed with unwanted children who might be bred and bonded to the underground

17

trades. It was not that the Irish as a race were particularly cruel to their offspring or sought to be rid of them, but the French wars and distracting internal struggles kept the peasant class in constant penury and in almost every family there were more mouths to feed than food to feed them. In consequence Daniel Harding, with two or three trips a year, had little difficulty in matching supply to demand.

Tonight eleven youngsters cowered behind the curtain. They had been purchased on the cheap from workhouses in the north, shipped by coalboat from Ballycastle two days ago and kept out of sight in the Hardings' old stable since their arrival in Ladybrook. They had been well enough fed and not, so far, ill-treated. That afternoon, though, each of the darlings had been scrubbed spotless, had their nails pared and hair combed and had been dressed in short sarks to show off their limbs.

Brock was particularly pleased with one acquisition, a girl whose name was recorded as Eleanor Antrim. She was three or four years older than the others, a raven-haired, dark-eyed beauty who, Brock was sure, would fetch a tidy sum. When Cabel had finally finished his harangue and the curtain was drawn to expose the tearful children it was, as Brock had anticipated, Eleanor Antrim who attracted all the attention.

"Start with her, Cabel," Brock murmured. "Start with the dark beauty."

"Aye, Dad," Cabel answered and, winking at his eager audience, brought Eleanor forward by the hand.

*   *   *

Robertson Blyth was a gentleman of uncommon severity. He seldom smiled and never laughed. He had precious little to laugh about, really. As son-in-law to Lord McCracken and husband to the formidable Sarah, he was committed to keeping the colliery at Cairns in profit by every means in his power. He had a reputation for being a hard taskmaster and not thought any the less of for that. But several lodge brethren considered him a prig for his refusal to drink himself insensible and for his swift departure from late meetings when the talk turned bawdy.

As an elder of St Cedric's kirk, though, he was perhaps entitled to be a bit stand-offish. It was also undeniable that his presence added moral ballast to proceedings that often got out of hand. Certainly he had no stain on his character and, although only forty-two, he had already acquired the air of glum sagacity that usually accompanies late middle-age.

Robertson Blyth had no interest in girls. There were women aplenty among the riff-raff that his managers employed, colliers' daughters, say, or the widows of pressed seamen who were only too willing to haul creels and pick coals for a shilling a day. He had no need of female domestics either. His house overflowed with cooks, maids and scullions, a hierarchy so complex in its distinctions that only his wife could keep track of it.

Robertson Blyth's purpose at Neptune's sales was to find boys to haul waggons, operate vents and shovel dross, nothing more nor less than that.

"What you see before you, gentlemen," Cabel was saying, "is a fine young Protestant girl of about fifteen summers. She can write a fair hand but she ain't no scholar and she is, so she tells me, unversed in the ways of the world."

"Will she do what she's told?"

"She'll learn all the lessons you wish to teach her," Cabel Harding said. "Look at her, gentlemen. Ain't she a peach? If you can't find a use for her yourself why not take her home for your wife?"

"I'll give you three pounds for her."

"She's worth twice that, Mr Jaynes."

"Five."

"Good for you, Mr Thompson."

"Six."

"I'll spring seven."

"Pounds or guineas, sir?"

"Guineas."

Until that very moment, just after midnight on a wild January night, Robertson Blyth had considered himself immune to corporeal temptation.

It shocked him considerably when he heard himself call out, "Ten pounds," and felt his right hand rise to register the bid.

Brock Harding's greedy yellow eyes slid in the coalmaster's direction. "Was that you, Mr Blyth?"

"It was, Mr Harding."

"She's a female, you know?"

"I have observed that fact, Mr Harding."

"Ten it is then." Cabel shrugged. "Mr Jaynes?"

"She must have charms invisible to me," Jaynes said. "Still, I'll keep the pot boiling. Make it twelve."

"Fifteen," Robertson Blyth said promptly.

Necks craned, heads swivelled. Too late to retract. He would lose face by withdrawing now. Besides, the young girl's gaze was upon him, pleading with him – so Blyth imagined – not to let her fall into the clutches of a man like Jaynes or Thompson.

"Twenty, damn it," said Oscar Jaynes.

A tinker's child could be bought for five shillings on the quays of Ardrossan, a charity brat for next to nothing, but tinkers' brats and workhouse waifs seemed like flotsam compared to the beautiful Irish girl.

"Oh, God, what *am* I doing?" Robertson Blyth thought. He was engaged in an act of sheer, extravagant folly yet he seemed powerless to call a halt. The girl's breasts rose and fell against the shift and when he appeared to hesitate she clapped a hand to her lips in horror.

"And five," Robertson Blyth announced.

"That's five-and-twenty, Mr Blyth."

"I know, Cabel. I know."

"Mr Jaynes?"

"I wouldn't pay that for a duchess," Oscar Jaynes declared.

And there being no more bids on Eleanor Antrim, Cabel cried out, "*Done*," and signalled to his brother to take the prize downstairs.

*   *   *

Clare's initial impression was that the boat had been hauled an impossibly long distance from the edge of the pool. The pond itself was too flurried by wind and wave to reveal much and beyond it only surging breakers were visible against the black night sky. She had no alternative but to accept Gowrie's word that the craft had indeed been found floating in the pot and somehow dragged close to the shelter of the salthouse.

Its mast was intact, its sail neatly furled, oars still roped to the rowlocks. Crouched by the bow, she gestured to Gowrie to dip the lantern and by its light saw that the vessel had shipped very little water and showed no signs at all of damage.

"Where's Billy?" she shouted.

"Indoors with the others."

"I want you to search the beach."

"What for?"

"To make sure that the occupants of the boat haven't been washed ashore."

20

Gowrie seemed to shrink from her. "Wait until mornin', Mrs Quinn. It's too dark tonight."

"No," she told him. "Fetch Billy and do it now."

"Very well," said Gowrie. "If you insist upon it." She had expected him to put up an argument and was taken aback by his sudden capitulation. He wiped his chin with his hand, nodded, then headed off into the salthouse without another word, taking the lantern with him.

She wished that she had spared time to send for Norman Tannahill or John Galloway. There was something very odd and sinister about the appearance of the boat, and in Gowrie's behaviour. Filled with apprehension she hurried towards the the panhouse and, struggling against panic, pushed open the heavy wooden door and stepped quickly inside.

The panhouse's stout stone walls reduced the volume of sound to a piping wail and Clare, relieved to be indoors, shucked off her hood. Rakes, skimmers and shovels were racked against the wall like muskets and the metal-lined pans loomed like medieval tombs in the half-light. She peered up the steep wooden staircase which led via a trapdoor to the Gowries' living quarters.

"Gowrie?" Clare said. "Gowrie, are you there?"

She loitered by the foot of the stairs, weary now, cold and irritable. She was impatient to have this silly stramash over and done with and to be back warm in bed with Melissa.

Footsteps on the boards overhead; Clare tilted her head to call out to the salter once more. "Gow – "

A hand closed over her mouth. She was snatched back into the gloom beneath the staircase. Gloved fingers smothered her cry of alarm. An arm snared her waist. She felt herself being lifted, swung round and, before she could resist, drawn into an embrace.

"Hush," an almost forgotten voice told her. "Hush, my love, not a sound if you please."

The kidskin grip slackened.

Astonished, Clare uttered the name of the man who had fathered her first-born child, who by selfishness and neglect had brought about that same child's death.

"Frederick?"

"Yes, dearest. I've come back."

"But – but why?"

"To marry you, of course," Frederick Striker said.

Three

The confessions that Clare had made in letters to her cousin had always been sincere. She had not intentionally deceived Andrew Purves when she'd informed him that her hatred for Frederick Striker had waned.

Marriage to Mr Quinn and Melissa's birth had diminished her obsessive desire to make Frederick suffer for his part, however coincidental, in Peterkin's poisoning, though at one stage she had supposed Frederick to be guilty of the crime, not merely a rogue but a monster.

For months after her acquittal and release from Glasgow's Tolbooth in 1788, Clare had been possessed by an overwhelming desire for revenge and had done everything in her power to track down Frederick with the intention of killing him. In the end she had failed to run him to earth and in the autumn of that nightmare year she had drifted back to Scotland and had learned from Andrew Purves the real facts behind Peterkin's death. She had wept then as she had never wept before, wept until there was nothing left to weep for and no feeling left within her.

Soon thereafter she had married Mr Quinn, who had been one of Frederick's victims too, and had abandoned her search for her former lover.

As the years had piled one upon the other she had thought less and less of Frederick Striker until whole weeks would go by without his name being raised. Only an occasional enquiry in a letter from Andrew would bring Frederick to mind and lead to speculation as to what fate had finally made of him.

Nonetheless, Clare had clung to the belief that her rage was impermeable, that if ever she met with Frederick again it would burst forth like fire from the earth.

Now that the moment had arrived, however, she was dismayed to discover that far from exploding with fury she was pleased to hear his voice again and, for a split second, to rest easy in his arms. When he endeavoured to kiss her, though, common sense prevailed.

She twisted her face to one side, placed her hands upon his shoulders and pushed him away.

"How much did you pay him?" she asked.

"Who? Pay who?"

"Gowrie. How much did you pay Gowrie to lie to me?"

"A guinea."

"Pah! You could have bought him for a shilling."

"I wanted to surprise you."

"Be assured, Frederick, you succeeded on that score."

"I did not deem it wise to appear on your doorstep unannounced. I was afraid you might swoon."

"How you flatter yourself," Clare said. "I'm not the timid little mouse you left behind in Glasgow, you know."

"You were never that, Clare, never timid." He laughed softly. "But yes, on reflection, I agree. You are not the swooning type."

"How long have you been in Ladybrook?"

"I was washed ashore in the storm."

"Indeed?"

"On my way to Greenock, a passenger on a trading brig," Frederick said. "When the brig ran into heavy seas I thought it prudent to cut myself loose before she foundered."

"So you stole a keelboat which happened, by chance, to be on board the brig?"

"I suppose I did."

"And by a stroke of providence happened to be washed ashore right on my doorstep?"

"That's the way of it," Frederick said. "May I kiss you now, please?"

"No, Frederick, you may not."

"Have you no mercy? Can you not imagine how I've longed for this moment, this meeting – "

"*Did* the brig founder?" Clare interrupted.

"I really have no idea. It was very dark and I was hard pressed to keep my own small vessel from sinking."

"God must have been with you, Frederick."

"I like to think He was, yes."

"Working a miracle on your behalf," Clare said. "Are you sure that you did not walk here on the tops of the waves?"

"Clare – "

"How else could you arrive with every stitch bone dry?"

23

"Ah!" Frederick exclaimed. "Yes! I think perhaps I should begin again."

"Do not trouble yourself with explanations on my account, Frederick." Clare swung on to the staircase and called out, "Gowrie, fetch me a lantern."

Scuffles and thumps. Kate Gowrie appeared in the trap. She was Gowrie's elder daughter, a child-woman of eighteen who in shape and size seemed barely half that age. Her only redeeming feature was a pair of luminous grey eyes which stared owlishly down at Clare through a tangle of hair.

"Are you too ashamed to show yourself, Bob Gowrie?" Clare shouted. "Indeed, so you should be. I will deal with you tomorrow, sir, be certain of that."

No response came from the loft. Clare snatched the lantern from the girl's grasp and clambered downstairs again.

Curious to see what changes time and circumstance had laid upon Frederick she raised the lantern above her head and shone its rays into the panhouse.

Frederick had hoisted himself on to the rim of one of the pans and, balanced like a boy on a field gate, drummed his heels on the brickwork.

For a moment it seemed that he had not changed at all, but that impression was instantly dispelled as soon as the light fell full upon him.

"My! What a termagant you have become, Clare," he said. "Bullying your poor salters."

"I'm mistress of Headrick now, as I expect you well know, and I will not be treated like a fool by my servants," Clare said. "Make no mistake, Gowrie will be punished for his disloyalty."

"You mustn't blame old Bob," Frederick said. "Don't forget, I've known him much longer than you have." He reached out a hand to her. "Be that as it may, come closer and let me look at you."

"You may look all you wish from where you are."

She lowered the lantern. She was afraid that he would detect in her the same signs of decay that she saw in him, crow's-feet, crab-claws, sorrowful wrinkles, patches of rough skin. She felt old in Frederick's presence, old and faded.

She was, after all, almost thirty.

"You've changed hardly an iota, Clare," he said. "You are, if anything, more beautiful."

Once she might have been taken in by his flattery but now

24

the honeyed phrases struck her as not only insincere but positively perverse.

"Why do you stare at me like that?" Frederick said.

"Like what?"

"As if you'd seen a ghost."

"I have seen a ghost."

"How can that be? Did you suppose that I was dead?"

"I supposed nothing of the kind."

"Are you afraid of me?"

"Certainly not."

His greatcoat was fashionably long, with two broad falling collars, the upper faced with otter skin. He fanned it open with his elbows so that Clare might admire a frock-coat of Dunsinane velvet and a froth of lace crowned by a cravat stuck with a large pearl pin.

What Clare saw, though, was not style but that which style could not adequately conceal – the lineaments of a man grown old. His hair had been recently barbered but the locks, blackened by lampwick, had been bow-curled to disguise their scantness.

It was not Frederick's thinning hair that disturbed her – in a man nearing fifty such a thing was to be expected – so much as his haggard features.

"Why do you insist on staring at me?" Frederick said.

"Because I cannot believe you are here."

"Well, I am."

She had quickly lighted upon a weakness. For someone as vain as Frederick loss of looks must be a bitter pill to swallow. Clare experienced a little wriggle of triumph when he hopped down from the rim of the pan and, to evade her scrutiny, ducked out of the circle of light.

"Perhaps we should begin again," Clare said. "How long have you been here?"

"I came ashore the day before yesterday."

"And stayed where?"

"Here, with the Gowries."

"And where did you come from?"

"From Ireland."

"Dropped off a trading brig?"

"In a manner of speaking, yes."

"A collier brig?"

"Why, yes!"

"One of Robertson Blyth's vessels, perhaps?"

25

"I suspect it may have been. Come to think of it, yes, it was."

"In that case I will see to it that the keelboat is returned to the coal pier at Malliston as soon as the weather settles."

Puzzled by her calmness, Frederick protested, "Here I am, washed back into your life, Clare – here *we* are together again – and all that concerns you is the craft that brought me."

"I presume," Clare said, "you do not wish me to inform the Shore Master or the Excise Officer of your arrival?"

"I would prefer it if you did not."

"I thought as much," Clare said. "The truth now, Frederick, why *are* you here? What *do* you want in Ladybrook?"

"I told you, darling, I came to see you again."

"Hah!" Clare said. "To marry me?"

He appeared out of the shadows behind the saltpans. In suffused light he was almost as handsome as he had been at the time of their affair. An odd little pang of longing caught Clare momentarily off guard.

"That was simply an idiotic remark on my part, a jest in poor taste." Frederick cupped his elbows with his fingers, a gesture so distinctive that it seemed to make the years fall away. "I trust you did not take me seriously?"

"I used to trust your every word," Clare said.

He raised an eyebrow. "But not now?"

"No, not now," Clare said. "Not ever again."

"Is that where we stand?"

"It is."

"What of Eunice, the trial – the rest of it?"

"What of it?" Clare said.

"I can explain, you know."

"No doubt you can," Clare said. "Particularly as you've had fifteen years in which to practise your story."

"Clare, I did not murder Peterkin."

"I know that you did not."

"I would not have harmed the little chap for all the world." He spoke softly. "Do you recall the last time we were together, the three of us?"

"Vividly."

"I have been to see his grave, you know," Frederick told her. "I put flowers upon it. I freely admit that I knelt and wept, there by the little bare stone."

Sentiment drew Clare like a vortex. She resisted it with less ease than she had resisted his flattery. She had forgotten how deadly Frederick's manipulations could be. She would not share her tears with Frederick, however, and wrenched the memories of her son from her mind.

"We'll talk again tomorrow, Frederick," she said, "if, that is, you have not fled from Ladybrook in the interim."

He was taken aback by her abruptness.

"Where are you going, Clare?"

"Home, to my bed."

"But we have so much to discuss."

"Remarkably little, I suspect," Clare said.

She lifted the lantern and brought it close to her eyes to see if the candle would last her back to the house.

"Permit me to accompany you." Frederick began to fasten his greatcoat as if her acceptance could be taken for granted.

"I prefer to go alone."

"In this weather?"

"I'm not made of straw, Frederick."

"Let me, at least, fetch Gowrie."

"Damn Gowrie."

"Clare, wait."

"Goodnight, Frederick."

"Clare – "

With the lantern held before her she stepped out into the wind and was lost to him in darkness before he could think what to say to fetch her back.

*   *   *

Discarding his customary concern with "face" Robertson Blyth had left the auction early and turned up at the door of Harding's stable to collect his purchase in person.

As a rule he dispatched a foreman with a waggon to fetch the new apprentices. But tonight he had made only one purchase and he was too consumed by guilt to delegate collection to an underling who might bring his authority into disrepute by gossip or, worse, alert Sarah to his indiscretion.

The wind bullied him across the angle of the square and into the lane which led to the Hardings' stables. He could see the phosphorescent shimmer of breaking waves swarming on to the town beach and the air was alive with flecks of foam and particles of debris whipped up from the shore.

The coalmaster steadied himself then pounded upon the stable door with all the authority he could muster.

27

In due course the door opened to reveal the ferrety features of Brock's youngest son.

"What d'you want?" the boy shouted.

"I've come to collect my purchase," Blyth shouted back.

"Gotta receipt?"

"Do you not recognise me, young man?"

"No receipt, no goods, Mr Blyth."

Robertson Blyth thrust the scrap of paper at the boy and waited, seething with impatience, in the wind-swept lane until the door opened again and, without ceremony, the girl was shoved out at him.

"Is that it?" the juvenile Harding shouted.

Instinct told Mr Blyth that the creature under the plaidie shawl was indeed Eleanor Antrim but he had not slipped so far out of character that he would accept goods without check. He gestured with his forefinger and when she obeyed and lowered the shawl he saw dark eyes, full red lips, a heart-breakingly perfect face.

"Well, Mr Blyth?" said Joey.

"Yes."

"Good luck to you then," said the little Harding and, with a grin and a wink, hastily closed and bolted the stable door once more.

Robertson Blyth had ridden into Ladybrook on his horse, Pranzo. The gelding was liveried in one of the Neptune's outbuildings. Taking the girl by the hand he led her there and by lantern light inspected his purchase closely.

The tawdry cotton frock and patched skirts could not disguise her rarity. Never before had he seen a girl so beautiful and desirable.

He had no notion of what he would do with her, where he might hide her. He did not dare take her back to the servants' quarters at Cairns for one or other of Sarah's maids would be sure to tell her mistress and he would be on the carpet without, as it were, a leg to stand on.

The stalled horses were restless but their stamping had not roused the ostlers who slept in the loft above. Robertson Blyth glanced upward, saw nothing but dusty straw and cobwebbed rafters.

He peeled off his gloves, tucked them in his belt and placed both hands against the girl's cold cheeks.

"Do you know who I am?"

She shook her head.

He brushed a lock of heavy black hair from her brow. Except within the guidelines of common courtesy he had never in all his years touched a woman other than his wife. But this girl demanded to be touched. Her creamy skin and glossy hair were irresistible.

"I am Robertson Blyth, your new master," he said. "I am the owner of the colliery at Cairns." Sudden alarm in her eyes caused him to add, "But you will not be put to the pickings, I assure you. You have been hired for another purpose altogether. To be a house-servant, probably. Do you have anything to say against that?"

"I'm cold, sir."

Surprisingly her voice was not reedy and uncouth but warm and drawling. It reminded him incongruously of chocolate beaten in a cup with egg yolk and fresh milk.

"Is that all you have to say?"

"What'll you be doin' to me when you get me home?"

What did she expect him to do to her? What, he suddenly wondered, had been done to her before? She was surely too beautiful not to have attracted the attention of other men.

"Can you ride a horse?" he asked.

"I've ridden a donkey often enough."

"Very well, that will have to do," Robertson Blyth said. "It's too rough a road and too wild a night to expect you to walk. You may ride before me on the saddle."

"Ride where, sir?"

"To Cairns." Robertson Blyth could think of no suitable alternative offhand. "Where I live."

"How far is that, sir?"

"Four miles."

"I'll walk if you wish."

"That will not be necessary."

He moved into the stall, untied Pranzo from the rail and, a minute or two later, rode out along the beach track with young Eleanor Antrim perched before him on the saddle.

*　　*　　*

Clare was deadly calm during the trail back to the house. Pratie had waited up for her and opened the front door as soon as Clare rattled the brass knocker.

The housekeeper stood back as the wind blew the young woman into the hall then closed the door, relieved Clare of lantern and cloak and led her directly to the small back parlour where the fire had been built up and a decanter of brandy and a kettle of hot water set out.

As a rule Clare was no tippler but she had been so shaken by Frederick's reappearance that she accepted the glass that Pratie held out to her and gulped at its contents.

"There was no wreck, Pratie," she told the housekeeper. "Gowrie deceived me. I shall have a few choice words to say to that gentleman tomorrow, believe me."

"What did he want of you then?"

"He was persuaded to fetch me by a – a visitor."

"A visitor, at this hour?"

"An old acquaintance."

Pratie's pink cheeks seemed more prominent than ever. Her hard grey eyes were filled with suspicion. Clare had not forgotten that by dint of his partnership with Mr Quinn Frederick had penetrated this household too.

Clare moistened her lips.

"Perhaps you remember Mr Striker?"

"Jesus an' Joseph!" Pratie fashioned a sign in the air and completed the superstitious gesture with a twist of the head and a dry spit over her shoulder. "God's curse on that man, if ever there was justice."

"Apparently Mr Striker has been in our neighbourhood for two days," Clare said. "I'm rather surprised that you haven't heard gossip to that effect."

"If I'd had heard anythin' of the kind sure I'd have informed you first thing. Have you got such a low opinion of me, Mrs Quinn, as to think I'd have dealin's behind your back with a devil like Frederick Striker?"

Since the day of Clare's arrival on Headrick, Pratie Kerrigan had remained dumb on the subject of Clare's guilt or innocence and her notorious relationship with Frederick Striker.

Now that shock had unlocked the housekeeper's tongue, though, she ranted on with a degree of heat that Clare had seldom witnessed in her.

"So he's come back, has he? That smarmy English devil!" Pratie cried. "Damned if I don't wish it had been his bloody corpse had been washed up on the shore, not him alive at all. What does he want of us, Mrs Quinn?"

"That is something I have yet to discover," Clare said. "It would appear, though, that whatever mischief Frederick plans he already has Gowrie on his side."

"Oh aye, he's in thick wi' Bob Gowrie. Always was. Him an' Gowrie plotted things together poor Mr Quinn knew nothin' of, not until it was too late." Pratie dumped the lantern on to the table, flung Clare's cloak to one side and leaned so close that Clare could make out each of the little ginger whiskers that bristled on the woman's chin. "Mark me, Mrs Quinn, it's no coincidence Striker's turned up now, not with Mr Quinn dead and gone. Sure, we can all take a fair stab at what Striker'll be after."

"What might that be, Pratie?"

"You, of course, now you're widowed."

"The thought had entered my mind," Clare admitted.

"He'll marry you to get his claws on Headrick."

"Yes," Clare said, "that would be typical of him."

Taken aback by Clare's coolness,the housekeeper stepped away from the table and stared at her mistress. "You wouldn't be thinkin' of takin' him on, not after all he's done to us in days past?"

"I might," Clare said without a trace of levity or mischief. "Yes, Pratie, I might at that."

"Jesus an' Joseph!" Pratie Kerrigan exploded in disgust and snatching up the lantern swept out of the parlour and kicked the door shut with her heel.

Four

The gelding was used to hard riding, for Robertson Blyth had
no taste for carriage travel and could not always wrest the use
of the gig from his dear lady wife. But even the sturdy Pranzo
balked at being nosed into the bruising wind along the shore
road and Blyth soon turned and headed inland.

The girl was firmly braced against his thighs. He had
insinuated an arm around her waist and held her as tightly
as he dared. On a fine summer night it would have been a
pleasant, not to say amorous, experience but January was no
month for travellers let alone lovers and Robertson Blyth had
too much on his mind to enjoy the casual dalliance.

Pranzo picked his way along the lanes for the best part of
a mile and had almost put Ladybrook behind before a vague
scheme began to take shape in Robbie Blyth's brain, a possible
solution to the problem of what to do with the beautiful stranger.
Before he could refine the plan, however, the weather took a
sudden turn for the worse and a fierce, cold squall of rain
drummed down upon them.

Isolated villas surrounded by large rambling gardens flanked
the old high road to the north-east of Ladybrook. Several worthy
citizens had residences here, including John Galloway and the
Reverend Mr Soames. In fact, Pranzo had just trudged past the
manse when the heavens opened and released such a torrent of
rain that within seconds the riders were wet through.

The girl curled over her master's arm. She wriggled close
against him and tried to protect herself with the flapping
shawl.

"I'm cold," she moaned. "So cold."

The manse was hidden behind a beech hedge and a row of
dwarf conifers but even if it had been open and welcoming
Robertson Blyth would not have dared seek shelter there.

Randolph Soames might be one of the New Light moderates
but he was also an opponent of the Grand Order of Apollo and

would have barred its members from worship if it had been within his power to do so. Robertson Blyth had no wish to add fuel to the minister's fire by showing up on the manse doorstep in the dead of night with a strange Irish girl tucked under his plaidie.

He would have to seek shelter somewhere, though, for Eleanor, slithering on the wet saddle, had wrapped her leg about his calf with such a degree of dependence that it was all Robertson Blyth could do to hold any sort of seat.

"Sit still, can't you?"

"Oh, sir, I'm wet. I'm wet an' I'm cold."

"Yes, yes," said Robertson Blyth.

"What's that buildin' there?"

"The kirk, St Cedric's kirk."

"Could we not be shelterin' there, sir?"

In days long past, when Robbie had been a boy, Ladybrook had been rife with rumours of unholy conventicles in the kirkyard and covens invading the church itself. Auld Nick in person was reputed to ride abroad among the gravestones from time to time, scouring for acolytes. But no sensible witch or warlock, let alone the Fiery Fiend, would be caught dead out of doors on such a miserable January night and Robertson Blyth steered Pranzo towards the kirk without a qualm of worry on that score.

He trotted to the small side door and, with the rain pounding against his back, slithered from the saddle.

He held Eleanor in place with his shoulder and fastened Pranzo's reins to the rail that guarded the step.

Fortunately Reverend Soames had insisted on the small side door being left unlocked as an invitation to pilgrim worshippers and the sore at heart. Robbie Blyth doubted if he fell into either of those categories but he was too harassed to care.

He slung both arms about the girl and gathered her to him all of a piece.

She was as heavy as a sugar sack but the smell of her wet hair and the feel of her body under her wet clothes shrunk his irritation to a tiny hard point and gave him strength.

Grunting, he hoisted her into his arms, kneed open the vestry door and carried her bodily into the kirk.

The girl, thank God, did not protest.

*   *   *

33

Nothing so far had gone according to plan. For one thing, he had seriously misjudged Clare's reaction to his reappearance. For all the effect his charade had had upon her he might have saved himself the bother of borrowing a boat and the expense of bribing Gowrie to fetch her to the salthouse at dead of night.

He might have created a better impression if he had ridden up from Irvine in a hired fly with trumpets blowing and servants running before him with carpets and parasols and his baggage roped, towering, behind him.

He realised his error now, too late.

He had imagined Clare as she had been fifteen years ago, had thoroughly miscalculated the effect that marriage to dull-dog Quinn might have had on her. He had felt quite meek and humble in her company, in fact, as if the hectic pleasures he had enjoyed in the intervening years had been less mature and gratifying than a quiet life spent in Ladybrook.

Frederick was not in the best sort of mood when, stripping off his gloves and greatcoat, he clambered up the staircase, pushed open the horizontal door and hoisted himself into the salters' loft.

The long room provided spacious accommodation for five people. The leeward wall was partitioned into stalls by buckram curtains slung from hooks on a brass rail. Each cubicle housed a cot, a cupboard or tallboy, a single rush-bottomed chair and those appurtenances which were required for hygiene, a jug, a bowl and a porcelain chamberpot. The rest of the loft was given over to communal quarters, the oblong space between the gables broken by a deep-throated fireplace upon which the cooking was done. When salt boiling was in progress the atmosphere in the loft became unbearably foul but on a windy January night there was no haze in the room and the smell was fresh.

Salt-making was a profitable enough trade for Bob Gowrie to furnish his nest tolerably well and, by dint of sums made in dealings with Mr Striker many years ago, the family had been lifted well above the high-water mark of poverty. Frederick had spent two or three nights here on those unfortunate occasions when an ebb in the tide of his affairs had necessitated a keeping down of heads.

The Gowries were all wide awake and watching him. Even the youngest, fourteen-year-old Annie, had managed to stave off sleep and squatted upon the floor by her grandfather's chair, thumb in mouth, her gaze fixed upon Frederick.

Annie was more attractive than her sister but just as slight and spare, and perhaps a little wanting in wits. If she had been more attractive Frederick might have shown more interest, for calculations indicated that Annie might be the fruit of his loins, the result of a single passionate mating with Bob Gowrie's wife, Flora, who had been carried off by the same outbreak of fever that had made Donald Quinn a widower.

Bob Gowrie did not know that Frederick had cuckolded him and he was as eager to please Mr Striker as he had ever been. Frederick was less sure of support from Gowrie's father-in-law Matt Pringle. Pringle had never approved of the salt-smuggling venture and it did not seem as if age had leavened his distrust of Englishmen.

As for the rest of the family, Billy and Katy, Frederick spared them hardly a thought. The girl was too ugly to interest him, the boy too stupid.

"Did the widow not invite you to stay up at the big house then?" Gowrie asked.

"I am to go tomorrow," Frederick said.

"For breakfast?" Matt Pringle enquired.

"The arrangement is left open," Frederick said. "I am free to come and go as I wish."

"Until Brock finds out you're here," said Matt Pringle, "after which you'll only be free to run for it."

"I'm not afraid of Brock Harding," said Frederick, airily. "He's not the sort of chap to hold grudges."

"I wouldna be so certain of that if I were you," Matt Pringle said.

Pringle was long past his prime and almost blind. He still did a stint with measures and scales but, according to Bob, he was useless as a pan-worker.

"I'll inform Brock of my return in my own good time," Frederick said. "Once he learns what I've brought him, he'll not reject me."

"I doubt if Brock will forget what you did to his brother," Matt Pringle said.

"Jericho Harding murdered a King's man. It was for that crime they hanged him. It had nothing to do with me."

"Aye, but you were there, were you not?" said Pringle.

"I was in Liverpool but I was not in the jail."

"I'm sure Brock knows the truth of it." Bob Gowrie was seated at his writing desk. He had taken off his wet outer garments and Katy had draped them across a pine rack to dry. "It was just fortunate for us that they hanged Jericho Harding before he could blab out the whole story."

Annie had wandered to her father's side. She rested against his shoulder, thumb stuck foolishly in her mouth, like a calf at teat. Frederick could hardly bring himself to look at her. He pulled out a stool, seated himself upon it and began to undress.

He was angry at having wasted his finery. He'd even had his nankeen breeches laundered especially to impress Clare. He had bungled their first meeting badly. He had been left confused by it. He could have coped with Clare's anger, even revulsion, but he was dismayed by her self-control, a quality in women which he considered immodest and unfeminine.

"Mr Striker, did you really see Mr Harding's brother hanged?" Billy Gowrie, cross-legged upon the floor, asked.

Frederick sighed. He had been through all this before and was bored with the history. "Yes."

"I never seen nobody hanged," Billy said. "Wisht I could see somebody hanged."

"It's not an edifying sight, I assure you," Frederick told him, "particularly when the victim is an old friend."

"Well, Brock's no friend," Matt Pringle reminded him. "Whatever you think, Brock still blames you for puttin' Jericho behind bars and peachin' on him to save your hide."

"I'm no traitor to my own kind," Frederick said indignantly. "Do you really believe I would inform the King's officers what we were up to? What possible reason could I have for blowing the gaff?"

"You owed Jericho money," Matt Pringle said. "Some folk might think that was reason enough for wantin' him out of the way."

"Hold your tongue, old man," Bob Gowrie said. "Mr Striker doesn't want to listen to your clack."

"Better my clack than Cabel Harding's strap wrapped round his throat."

Frederick kept silent. He did not wish to give too much away at this stage. He knew more of Brock Harding's current circumstances than he cared to admit. He had calculated his return to Scotland with care and had deliberately delayed until his other arch-enemy, Lord Drumfin, had passed away.

"I'm sure Mr Striker's got good reason for comin' back to Ladybrook," Bob Gowrie said and glanced enquiringly at his guest. "Uh?"

"Indeed, I have," Frederick agreed. "Very good reason."

"Can you not tell us what it is?"

"All in good time, Bob. All in good time."

The salter pursed his lips in pique at being kept in the dark, then he snapped his fingers. "Katy, serve Mr Striker with some o' that skink."

The draft in the chimney had kept the coals glowing and the pan of fish soup bubbled and brothed.

At her father's command Kate scrambled to her feet, gripped the pan with a pair of wooden pincers and lugged it to the table. Frederick detested the gummy stuff. He had had his fill of the Gowries' hospitality at supper and the evening's adventures had irritated him further. He was careful not to be too short with the Gowries, though, for he did not wish to offend them.

"Why, thank you, yes. I believe I could manage a mouthful just to see me off to bed."

The girl ladled skink into a bowl and placed it on the table directly in front of Frederick. He paused, scooped up a spoonful of the pungent soup, sipped it, managed somehow not to grimace. He eyed the girl furtively while he ate. If only she had been as fair and full-figured as her mother had been. As it was he felt not the slightest twinge of desire for her in spite of the fact that her charms were amply displayed through the scant material of her shift. He finished the soup manfully, smacked his lips and pushed away the empty bowl.

"More, Mr Striker?"

"No, no, Kate. I am satisfied, thank you."

"What about your friend, sir? Would the French gentleman like some, d'you think?"

The girl gestured towards a ladder-back chair in the corner where, bolt upright and oblivious to the commotions around him, Henri Leblanc slumbered peacefully.

"I believe, Kate," Frederick said, "that we will leave my friend as he is. He looks too comfortable to disturb, don't you think?"

"Aye, Mr Striker," Kate said and, favouring Frederick with a smile, flirted away to the fire again to save the remains of the skink for breakfast.

*   *   *

St Cedric's church had been erected in an age when Ladybrook's population was small and scattered. Now the edifice seemed

37

embarrassingly deficient in scale and grandeur and the Presbytery had been dinning the heritor, Lord McCracken, to replace the little building with one more suited to a thriving township. McCracken, however, would not bite and declared the kirk to be more than adequate for the size of the community.

If Lord McCracken had ever attended worship there perhaps he would have changed his mind. However solid St Cedric's appeared from the outside it was a ramshackle mess within. Its passages were few and narrow and its entrance hall so cramped that there was, every Sunday, a most un-Christian-like struggle to exit the sanctified interior and escape home for an early luncheon.

To Robertson Blyth on that stormy January night, however, the interior of St Cedric's kirk seemed as vast and mysterious as a cathedral.

He shivered as he groped for the candles which were stored beneath the pulpit and scratched out a light. He lit three candles, stuffed each into a holder and placed them along the edge of the table.

On entering the kirk he had set Eleanor on her feet by the high pews. When he turned round after his light-bringing exercise, however, he found her lying faint and exhausted in a puddle of wet clothing, one arm bent under her cheek, the other flung out in a pose that, had it been intentional, would have seemed like one of abandon.

Hands on hips, the coalmaster stared nervously down at her. The kirk was obviously empty at that ungodly hour yet he could not shake off the feeling that his every move was being watched. He was tempted to blow out the candles again but was more afraid of the darkness than of the light.

Unbuttoning his greatcoat, he knelt beside the girl and touched her brow with his forefinger. Her hair was like black moss, her skin like swansdown. A pronounced pulse fluttered on her neck above the pin which held her collar fast. Tentatively he touched her neck. Her flesh quivered like the flank of a mare pricked by a horsefly.

At that moment she was completely at his mercy and the realisation frightened him.

He tried to imagine what Bull Thompson of Mossgrove would do to her, what rough treatment the farmer would mete out and how Eleanor's squeals of protest and cries for help would add spice to the grappling. Surely he was no less a man than Farmer Thompson? Impulsively he kissed the girl's neck and touched the tip of his tongue to the throbbing little pulse on her throat.

She stirred but did not waken. She was like the maiden in a fairytale that Nursey had told him long ago, long before he knew what coal was or had embarked on his mineral destiny. He had loved Nursey as he had loved no other since. From Eleanor Antrim he caught the same warm-bread aroma that Nursey had brought with her to his little bed on those nights when she had slept with him to give him comfort.

Spurred by that childhood memory he untied the handkerchief that crossed the girl's bosom. Once started he could not stop. Quickly he unpinned her bodice and was abruptly confronted by her breasts veiled only by a thin cotton chemisette. Cautiously he pressed his mouth against the fabric and sucked each of her breasts in turn, then he trailed his lips across the membranous cotton until his nose touched the waistband of her petticoat and he breathed in the smell of her.

Her shoes were water-curled, her petticoat grubby, her mulberry-coloured stockings, gartered just above the knees, were wrinkled. But none of that mattered. It was as if he had never experienced a woman's body before. Everything about her seemed dark and mysterious; and for an instant he was afraid that, when broken, she might release secrets which it was better for him not to know.

Flinging back the skirts of his coat and tearing at the tie of his breeches, he straddled her and peered inquisitively into her face.

Her eyes were open, lips parted.

Her compliance was more disturbing than resistance would have been, less expected, less natural. She was as passive as grain awaiting the scythe.

He sat back and then, alarmed by a faint sound from the shrouded pews, called out, "What's that? Who's there?"

"It's nothing, sir," Eleanor Antrim told him. "It's no one," and, before he could escape, wrapped her white legs about his back and drew him down.

*   *   *

The bracket clock on the mantle told Clare that it was almost two o'clock. Pratie, a determined sleeper, would be in bed, stretched out on her back like a log, hands folded upon her flat bosom. Clare was all alone in the back part of the house and would not be disturbed.

She went to the chest in the corner, opened it, lifted out a japanned box, placed it upon the desk and unlocked it. She removed the items that it contained, arranged them on the polished wooden surface, pulled out a chair and seated herself upon it as if to play a hand of Solitaire.

All that remained of her former existence was spread out before her. Donald had never pried into what the box contained. He had no need to do so. He had known most of what there was to know about her within an hour of their first meeting.

Collusion, not rapport, had drawn them into marriage. They had exchanged vows of revenge against Frederick Striker if ever his path crossed theirs again.

Clare picked up the New Testament that Mrs Rossmore had sent in to comfort her in jail. She held it fondly to her breast for a moment before she put it to one side and turned her attention to Andrew's letters which were arranged in sequence year by year.

Andrew's letters had been her salvation, a lifeline to a family which, though she was no more than distantly related to the Purveses, she continued to regard as her own.

Of Peterkin she had no memento at all, not so much as a little shoe or a ribbon or a curl of baby hair, nothing to evoke a memory of the son she had lost because of Frederick Striker's selfishness and greed.

She could not bring Peterkin to her rescue. He had no place here in this house at this time. Her first-born was little more than a sentimental memory, as incomplete as a rhyme remembered from childhood or the fragment of an air that has no end.

The japanned box contained one more article; a long document in an unsealed packet. Frederick's "confession".

Frederick had left the document in Andrew Purves's safe some months before he, Frederick, had disappeared from Glasgow. It detailed all Frederick's illicit dealings with the Hardings, the Gowries and Donald Quinn and its contents were to be made public only in the event of his death.

All Clare's powers of persuasion had been needed to coax Andrew into giving her the document. Once in her possession, however, it had served as a guide to Frederick's progress and, using it thus, she had followed him from place to place throughout the long summer of '88. She had been well aware of the confession's value and the fact that its revelations of salt smuggling on a grand scale could send all those involved, including Donald Quinn, if not to the gallows at least to prison.

She read through the yellowing document in its entirety then, with memory refreshed, rose and locked it away along with the other papers.

She felt better now, more in control of herself, and quite prepared to square up to Frederick without conscience or remorse.

Calmed and determined, she carried the candlestick through the darkened house and upstairs to the bedroom where, in the large bed, Melissa lay asleep in the crook of Lizzie's scrawny arm.

Clare did not have the heart to disturb them. She made her way to the little bed and peeling off her clothes slid gratefully between the sheets.

She blew out the candle and lay down.

She tried not to hear the wind that chivvied the trees and battered the gables and brought the roar of the sea drifting inland, into her house.

She could not keep it out, though; not the wail of the big wind or thoughts of Frederick, close to her again, or the feeling of wistful longing that had possessed her when he took her in his arms once more.

Five

Parisian born and Parisian bred, Monsieur Henri Leblanc had no love for the countryside. In his muddle-headed way he associated fields and pastures with the *sans-culottes* who had so rudely disrupted his valuable work at the Institut de Science Chimique where, under the auspices of the Compte de Lazenberg, he had been engaged in unravelling the tangled secrets of the universe before nemesis caught up with him.

M. Leblanc had not been deaf to the thunder of the revolutionary forces which had torn his country apart. He had in fact been arrested early in the purge but had managed by shabbiness and loquacity to convince his captors that he was no friend of the detestable Compte but merely his lackey.

After promising to manufacture a quantity of gunpowder to assist the work of the *Enragés*, M. Leblanc had been released. Having nowhere else to go he had returned to his rooms in the Institut, an ugly old building in the rue de Poissy, where for the next nine weeks he had kept his head down and his nose clean and had as a result been ignored by the *comités de surveillance*.

On the 3rd of September, 1793, however, the ventilation holes of the Institut's half-cellars, which were set on a level with the street, had afforded M. Leblanc a first-hand view of what was being been done to the malefactors who had been dragged screaming from the Monastery of Bernardins just across the way. Even he had recognised a massacre when he saw one and, because he had a faint inkling that chemists might suddenly have tumbled into the same undesirable category as gentlemen in holy orders, Henri had evacuated himself *tout de suite* through a grill above the concierge's latrine and had escaped into the Boulevard St Germain.

And thus, armed only with his laboratory notebooks, three stale loaves and the clothes he stood up in, M. Henri Leblanc had been let loose upon the world.

"What is your impression of Ladybrook, Henri?" Frederick Striker enquired. "Is it not ideal for your purpose?"

"No, my friend, it is far from ideal."

"Adequate?" Frederick suggested hopefully.

M. Leblanc's accent no longer buzzed with *zees* and *zoes*. He had mastered the Anglo-Saxon idiom very well and answered Frederick's question with a phrase that was both economical and obscene. Frederick had been acquainted with M. Leblanc long enough not to be nonplussed by his Gallic candour.

"But does it not have everything that you require?"

"It has nothing. It is a dungheap worse than Dublin. In truth, I have seen nowhere more despicable since I left the Low Countries."

"I concede that a salthouse attic is not as grand a lodging as you're used to," Frederick said, "but I hope to remedy that state of affairs in the very near future."

"I need only a place to do my work."

"Ladybrook *is* that place, Henri," Frederick said. "Ladybrook will be your laboratory."

"Where is my glassware? Where are my pipes? Where is my furnace? Frederick, you made to me promises – "

"All in good time." Frederick gripped the Frenchman's arm a little more tightly as if he was afraid that Mad Henri would stalk off in high dudgeon and never be seen again. "I promised you I'd provide investment to buy you what you need. And I will. But even I cannot conjure money out of thin air."

"What of these wealthy *patrons* of yours, this Brock Harding, for instance? How soon am I to be introduced to him?"

"One thing at a time, Henri," Frederick said. "First I must prepare Mr Harding to accept you at face value."

"Why? Does he imagine all Frenchmen are at war with England? Has he not heard of *émigrés*?"

"Brock Harding's no easy mark, believe me. The prospect of starting chemical experimentation in Ladybrook will be new and startling. He will take some convincing that there's profit to be made from it."

"I will convince him."

"Perhaps it would be more prudent to let me make the running."

"But you do *not* run, Frederick. You *walk*."

"Henri, Henri! Would I have brought you here if I did not have faith in you? Would I have gone to such a deal of trouble and expense to transport you to Scotland if I doubted your talents?"

For the time being the Frenchman was placated.

He extricated his arm from Frederick's and walked on, wrist arched against his hip in a manner that most Scotsmen would consider effete. It was no more than a mannerism, though, for Henri Leblanc, while confused about almost everything else, was not confused about gender.

Frederick did not much care how Henri walked. He had witnessed Leblanc's scientific demonstrations in Dublin and was willing to take Leblanc's word that, given congenial conditions and a little of the wherewithal, Henri might very well advance the cause of human knowledge and line his, Frederick's, pockets at one and the same time.

Frederick had already made one small fortune here in Ladybrook and, however much the world had changed since those heady days, he was convinced that he might yet make another.

The fact that Leblanc was French added a minor complication but with negotiations for a peace of sorts already underway in France, questions of treason hardly entered the reckoning.

"Where do you take me, sir?" Henri Leblanc asked.

"Nowhere in particular," Frederick answered. "I thought you might appreciate a breath of fresh air, that's all."

"Air? Pah!" Henri glanced witheringly at his sponsor. "Show me instead the house where I will be entertained."

They had taken the shore track south of the town. All Ladybrook's industries were crowded upon the community's north-eastern fringe, in hillocky country around the glen of Cairns. Laid out before the visitors were fertile headlands and pastures with hardly a wisp of smoke to spoil the purity of the calm January morning.

Taking Henri by the elbow, Frederick turned him about and pointed inland. "There it is."

"What is it called?"

"Headrick."

"Who resides there?"

"I've told you a dozen times – a friend."

"Ah, yes!" Henri Leblanc allowed himself a smile. "The widow whom you will seduce."

To his surprise, Frederick experienced a twinge of annoyance at the Frenchman's suggestive simpering.

44

He looked away towards the trees where rooks cawed in the beech boughs and gulls hung pale against a silvery sky.

"Each man to his trade, Henri," Frederick said grimly.

"How long will the process take?"

"Not long," said Frederick. "Not long at all."

*   *   *

Even in January the whins that screened the Tannahills' cottage remained green and sappy and the gorse was prone to flower yellow long before spring was due. Between the shrubs, circles of grass remained unaffected by the biting winds that rendered Ayrshire's other pastures dun and unproductive.

There was no apparent reason why the Tannahills should flourish in a lush wilderness and why across the Leddings nature should be so uncontrollably abundant.

Dr John Galloway, a pragmatist to the marrow, believed that a subterranean spring brought unusual warmth to the subsoil, nourished the ground with sulphurs and carbons and protected the roots of growing things against the winter's chill. When asked for her opinion on the matter, however, Rose Tannahill merely shrugged as if she was too old and too simple to comprehend such primitive mysteries.

The Tannahills had been Headrick's tenants for as long as anyone could recall. The cartulary of the estate, going back seventy years, contained no reference to any other occupants and Clare had heard from Donald, who had had it from his grandfather, that Rose had first appeared in Ladybrook when he, the grandfather, had been young. How that could be, and how Rose could have borne four sons when she was already forty or fifty years old, were questions that nobody, not even Donald, ever dared to ask.

The cottage itself was nothing grand. It hunkered in a narrow glen through which the Linn ran trout-brown over a gravelly bottom, its privacy so guarded by blackthorn, bramble and scrub alder that little more than chimney reek was visible from the top of the rise.

There was no evidence of deliberate cultivation yet nature, left to her own devices, seemed to provide everything that the Tannahills required.

Some folk believed Rose Tannahill's blessings came from God, others that she was in league with the devil.

In more rigorous times, perhaps, she would have been flung

off the rocks at Trotter's Point or burnt at the stake in the Hardings' yard. Fortunately such barbarous punishments had no place in the lives of civilised men, men who devoted themselves to the worship of Promethean gods and kept account of their pacts and sacrifices in cash-books and ledgers.

For all the scurrilous gossip, Rose Tannahill was friend to many a girl, and many a wife too. Her remedies for stubborn ailments, from infant's colic to a broken heart, ensured that the path to the Leddings carried much female traffic and no woman ever spoke ill of her visit or called curses on Rose Tannahill's head.

Only one of Rose's sons remained at home. The others had departed to find their fortunes many years ago.

Norman Tannahill was a large man, handsome but silent as stone. In exchange for free rent upon the cottage and a piece of ground in the Leddings, Norman tended Headrick's kitchen garden and stables and the only mysterious thing about him was how he managed to put in so much labour with so little apparent effort.

It was not Rose's healing talent that had attracted Clare to the cottage. Rose had other gifts too, gifts which enabled her to penetrate the future and the boundless realm of the unknown.

Many years ago Clare had endeavoured to persuade Rose to use her clairvoyant gifts to trace Frederick and use a spell to summon him back to Ladybrook. The old woman had refused. She had informed Clare that while destiny could be predicted it could not, without danger, be altered.

Thereafter Clare had had to be content with brief readings of the crystal and the handing down of advice that was more practical than occult.

In spite of her late night Clare had wakened early, for she had a great deal to do that day.

First she had written a note to Mr Striker inviting him to take supper with her at the hour of six o'clock. She had dispatched Lizzie to the salthouse to deliver the note directly into Mr Striker's hand. Next she'd instructed Mrs Shay to prepare a menu suitable for a gentleman and to accompany Pratie in the gig to Irvine to purchase whatever delicacies were necessary for the feast.

Clare had even acceded to Melissa's piping demands that she be allowed to accompany the servants to town and be given a penny to buy ribbon.

Much as she loved her daughter, Clare would be glad to be

46

rid of her for half a day. She had too much on her mind to give Melissa her undivided attention.

She could not deny that she was eager to see Frederick again. She was consumed by curiosity as to how he had fared over the years and what he really wanted here in Ladybrook. She did not expect him to divulge the truth on either score and, for her part, was perfectly prepared to vie with him on exactly those terms. She did feel in need of a little advice, however, advice best obtained not from John Galloway but from the old woman in the cottage across the backs.

Smoke from the Tannahills' chimney twisted like worsted thread in the remnant of the previous night's wind. Four tortoiseshell cats lounged on the slab before the open door. They did not dart away at Clare's approach but followed her, purring, into the cramped kitchen.

"Rose, are you there?"

"Come along in, my dearie."

A long oak table filled much of the kitchen. Earthenware pots and quaint glass jars littered the table-top and the old woman was briskly beating at a mixture in a china bowl.

Without pausing in her task, she glanced up at Clare and smiled her welcome.

"Am I intruding?" Clare asked politely.

"No, lass. I expected you to call this mornin', after the sort of night we had."

"Has there been damage?"

"Aye, there's been damage. But not on the Leddings."

Rose Tannahill wore a blue serge skirt, and a short-sleeved jacket bared her forearms to the elbows. Her flesh was wrinkled but the muscles were not wasted and she beat at the stuff in the bowl with a vigour Clare could only envy.

"I'll be done in a trice, Mrs Quinn, then we'll have our conversation undisturbed."

The kitchen was lined with shelves and strewn with sheets and blankets, snug as a linnet's nest. Beyond the doorway a curtain which closed off the beds and a short steep stair led to the attic where Norman slept.

Every nook and cranny contained an assortment of found objects. Shells, stones, roots and fragments of polished glass rubbed against the bleached skulls of seabirds, hares and field mice. From the overhead beams dangled bunches of herbs and dried flowers whose aromatic scents mingled sweetly with the smell of wood smoke.

Because it seemed natural to bless bounty with bounty, Clare never came empty-handed to the Leddings.

She placed upon the table a generous wedge of cheese that Mrs Shay had cut from the round in Headrick's larder and wrapped in muslin for the carrying.

Rose glanced at the cheese, nodded her thanks, and continued to whisk the stuff in the bowl until she judged it to be of the right consistency. Carefully she poured the mixture into a glass jar which she sealed with a cut cork.

She wiped her hands on her skirts, moved to the hearth and seated herself on a wicker chair and beckoned Clare to occupy the high-backed chair opposite her.

"I can see you're eager to tell me news," Rose said. "I have something to show you too, Mrs Quinn, but we'll put that off for a bit." She paused. "He came last night, did he not, the man you've been waiting for?"

"Did you see it in the crystal?"

"It's no great feat to see shadows on the shore. It is him, is it not?"

"Yes."

"And the other one?"

"What other one? I met only with Frederick. He's lodged with the Gowries at the salthouse. Did he not come alone?"

"I saw two."

"The second person, was it a man or a woman?"

"A man, but not one of us."

"An Englishman, do you mean?"

"No, from a foreign country."

"What country?"

Rose Tannahill could not say.

"Are you sure they came together?"

"Aye, I'm sure of that."

"Is it their intention to harm me?"

"The harm's already done, I fear."

"What should I do for the best?" Clare asked. "Should I send Frederick packing?"

"Do what your heart tells you to do."

"I do not know what that is," Clare said.

Rose picked up an iron poker from the hearth and stirred the birch logs that burned and blistered in the grate.

Clare had long ago learned the value of patience. She said nothing while the old woman released from the logs a column of pure grey smoke that rose into the chimney like a vine. Clare did not doubt that what Rose Tannahill had told her was the truth. But she wanted more, wanted the future laid out for her so that she might be on guard against it.

At length the old woman said, "The Englishman will stay with you."

"I'm not sure I want him to."

"There's no help for it. You've never been rid of him," Rose said. "And you never will be again."

Never before had Clare been frightened by one of Rose Tannahill's predictions but she was frightened now.

"What have you seen, Rose, what have you seen in the clouds?" she demanded. "Tell me so that I can protect myself against it."

"Nothing in the crystal is clear."

"Fetch out the egg," Clare said sharply. "Perhaps it will speak to me."

"No."

"Throw salt for me then."

"No."

"Why not? You do it for others."

"Nay, but I do not. I throw salt for no one."

"The egg then. Fetch out the serpent's egg, Rose. I'll pay you well for a reading."

"I've no need of your money," Rose said. "You're more head than heart, Clare Quinn. It's up to you to decide what you want from this man. I'll tell you this, though, if you do take him into your house he'll never leave Ladybrook again."

"I don't believe you saw anything at all. I think it's invention, something you made up."

"Think what you like," the old woman said. "This I can tell you, Clare Quinn, strange things are happenin' in our town. Your man was not the only arrival from the sea." She reached out her hand and took Clare's arm. "You must not doubt me, lass, not at this time. Now, come, I've somethin' to show you in the room next door."

"What?" said Clare.

"See for yourself," said Rose.

*   *   *

The girl lay fast asleep in a wooden cot which hugged the cottage's outer wall.

49

Even in the dim light Clare could see that she was extraordinarily beautiful, with a proud chin, moulded cheeks and a fleshy high-bridged nose. It was her mouth that Clare found most fascinating. The full underlip was the colour of blood and two square white teeth glinted upon it as if, even in sleep, the girl was ready to bite.

"Who is she?"

The girl stirred. She had thrown the patchwork blanket from her shoulders and Clare noticed with a twinge of envy the heavy blue shadow of her breasts as she turned upon her side.

"She was brought here last night," Rose said.

"By Frederick?"

"No, no."

"Where is she from?" Clare whispered.

"From Ireland."

Clare had heard rumours of child sales in the Neptune. Several of the boys who rode Mr Blyth's waggons or attended his heavy horses were Irish and they seemed none the worse for being apprenticed to the coal trade. John Galloway and Mr Soames were angered by Brock Harding's sales but Clare saw little harm in them. Given the state of the poor ragamuffins who hung about the quays and salt cadgers' children so skinny they hardly seemed human at all, Clare supposed that these little Irish waifs could hardly be worse off.

She was not so naive, however, as to suppose that the girl in Rose Tannahill's bed had been hired to crawl along a coal seam or labour in the fields.

"Is she one of the strays that Daniel Harding fetches across the water to work in the pits?" Clare asked.

"Aye."

"Where are the others?"

"Sold, I expect."

"To whom does this one belong?"

"To a man who should know better," Rose said. "Robertson Blyth brought her in late last night."

"Robertson Blyth! But he has a houseful of servants and more places to put a girl than tongue can tell. Why did he bring her here to you?"

"Because he does not know what else to do with her."

"If that's the case why did he hire her?"

"He did not 'hire' her," Rose said. "He bought her."

"But why?"

"Is the reason not obvious?"

50

"I did not think that Mr Blyth was so venal."

"All men are venal if you scratch them hard enough."

"Do you think he will try to – to take her?"

"He has taken her already," Rose said.

"What? Are you certain?"

"The girl told me as much," said Rose. "Blyth was himself in a great state of agitation last night."

"Did he fear he had hurt her?"

"Hah!" Rose said, scornfully. "His only fear is that he'll be found out by his wife."

"How long will you keep her here?"

"For as long as I can."

"Surely Mr Blyth will want her back?"

"Aye, when his lechery overcomes his conscience," Rose Tannahill said. "But he shan't have her. He brought her to the Leddings and now she's mine."

"But who is she? Where does she come from?"

"The egg will tell me, if she will not."

"But what will you do with her, Rose?"

"Give her to Norman," the old woman said.

"To be his mistress?"

"To be his wife."

Six

Clare's visit to the Leddings had thoroughly unsettled her. In spite of Rose's denial she could not rid herself of the suspicion that the beautiful waif in the Tannahill's cottage was connected in some way with Frederick's arrival in Ladybrook.

She had been stern with herself all afternoon and had gone about preparing for the supper party with apparent efficiency. When Pratie called out to inform her that "he" was at the front door, though, Clare was caught unprepared and, heart pounding, flew nervously downstairs like a silly young thing.

"Open the door, Pratie. Open the door, please."

"Open it yourself." Pratie stood resolute, arms folded, ginger hair bristling. "It'll not be my hand that lets that devil into this house again."

"I'll have words with you about this, Pratie."

"Have all the words you like, Mrs Quinn. You'll not be makin' me change my mind."

The knocker clacked once more.

Clare grasped the handle and whipped open the door.

"Frederick!"

"Delivered as requested."

"Come in, please."

"I trust I'm not late?"

It was on the tip of her tongue to tell him that he was fifteen years too late but instead she answered, "Not at all," and invited him across the threshold.

Clare had no hope of regaining her composure. She felt as coy in his presence as she'd done all those years ago in the banking hall in Purves's Land.

He beamed and held out his arms. "How lovely you look, Clare, how youthful. I can hardly credit the evidence of my senses. How do you do it? By magic?"

Pratie snorted at such blatant trumpery, swung on her heel and stumped off down the passageway to the kitchen.

"I don't think your housekeeper cares for me," Frederick said. "But then, she never did."

"Pratie Kerrigan is not the forgiving type."

"Are you?"

Clare's initial excitement had receded and a certain wariness had taken its place.

"Since my domestics are disinclined to wait upon you," she said, "allow me to relieve you of your hat and gloves."

Tonight Frederick was dressed in a brown frock-coat and a double-breasted waistcoat that seemed out of kilter with Clare's image of him as a dashing young man about town. She glanced at his stockings which were undarned, at buckled shoes polished like ebony and firm at heel. By whatever means Frederick had been transported to Ladybrook he had not travelled lightly.

Frederick laughed at her scrutiny. "No, Clare, I'm not down upon my uppers. On the whole fortune has favoured me these past few years."

"Why, then, have you returned to this poor corner of the world?"

"I told you. I dropped in just to see you," Frederick said. "Why do you continue to doubt me?"

"Because you are just as glib as ever you were," Clare answered. "Come along, let me judge for myself whether or not you're starving. Fine feathers do not always make fine birds, as any poultry-keeper will tell you. Lizzie, stop skulking in the corner. Come out and take Mr Striker's things."

Scowling, the little servant darted forward, snatched the hat and gloves from her mistress's hand and scuttled away out of sight.

"Good Lord!" Frederick said. "Are they all hostile? Surely that one isn't old enough to remember me?"

"No doubt she has heard Pratie's tales about you."

"Calumnies," said Frederick, jocularly. "All lies."

"Perhaps not *all* lies," said Clare, and led her guest into the drawing-room where supper had been laid.

Frederick glanced around the room in astonishment.

"Well, I declare," he said. "Headrick has certainly changed for the better."

"Did you expect me to inhabit a barn?"

"No, but I admit I did not expect Quinn to have such excellent taste."

"He had taste enough to marry me," Clare said.

"Well, indeed. I intended to ask why you – "

"I thought you might want to kiss me first," Clare said. "But, no, of course you have too much respect. It will not have escaped your notice that I am still in mourning."

"Clare, I – Yes," Frederick said, "how remiss of me not to offer my condolences immediately. I do so now, most sincerely."

"Thank you, Frederick," Clare said. "Now, if you will be seated at table, I will endeavour to find a servant willing to serve us supper."

"And then?"

"Then, Frederick, we will discuss business."

"Business? What business?"

"The business that brought you back to Ladybrook."

"What makes you suppose I am here to do business?"

"It's written all over your face, Frederick," Clare informed him, then, politely excusing herself, left him to ponder her last remark and adjust his strategy accordingly.

* * *

The herbal infusion that Rose Tannahill had administered to help the girl sleep had had no lingering after-effects. Eleanor had wakened, refreshed, soon after noon. She had been given tea, bread and cheese, dry clothes and then allotted certain small tasks to do about the house, tasks she had completed quickly and thoroughly. She had asked no questions concerning her whereabouts and had made no reference to Robertson Blyth or her experiences of the previous night. She had been so passive and compliant, in fact, that Rose Tannahill had begun to wonder if beauty was nature's compensation for lack of brain.

As afternoon waned into dusk, however, the girl's demeanour had changed. She had become more sure of herself, sure enough to ask questions about the objects on the shelves and what Rose did with them. Before darkness had enclosed the cottage and Norman returned from the fields, Rose Tannahill had become convinced that her prayers had been answered, that young Eleanor Antrim was exactly what she needed to secure the Leddings' future and protect her son against a lonely old age.

About a quarter past five Rose invited Eleanor to seat herself on a stool before the fire. She combed and plaited the girl's lustrous hair into two braids which she tied back with a white cotton ribbon.

She found a clean gingham apron and a muslin cap and when the girl had put them on gave her a little hand-mirror and watched, amused, while she preened.

"Is it really me, Missus?" Eleanor glanced round. "I never saw myself look so wholesome before."

"Aye, it's you," Rose told her. "If you are very well behaved you may have the glass to keep."

"To take away if he comes back to claim me?"

"Oh, he'll be back, lass," Rose said. "Make no mistake about that."

"Am I not to be yours then?"

"No, you are his, at least for the time being."

The girl primped at a braid, brushed a finger over her brows, touched her tongue to her lips to wet them.

"I shan't really mind being his," she said, "provided he treats me right."

"Would you not rather stay here with us?"

"Sure an' I would," the girl said. "But if I am to be his it'll be no great hardship. He's a weak man. I'll see to it he does me no harm."

"What do you know of men and their differences?"

The girl hunched her shoulders as if she nurtured secrets which could not be shared on short acquaintance.

"Enough, Missus Tannahill. Enough."

"Enough it is," Rose said. "Now put the glass in your pocket and help me fill the tub."

"For what?"

"For my son Norman, who will soon be home."

*　　　*　　　*

The poplars that stood guard on the great house of Cairns swayed in the dark wind. The sight of their lofty elegance brought back the gnawing anxiety that he had managed to hold at bay for most of the day.

He reined Pranzo to a halt and tried to compose himself for the ordeal of greeting his wife. He had not slept in almost forty hours and had driven himself through the long afternoon by sheer power of the will but now, with home in sight, guilt and exhaustion in equal measure were finally catching up with him.

By the time he had left Rose Tannahill's cottage there had been no point in going home. He had ridden directly to the colliery offices and had scrounged a bite of breakfast there before meeting with a Greenock engineer who had been engaged to estimate costs for the installation of a steam-engine capable of raising loads from a depth of four hundred and forty feet. He had even accompanied the engineer underground, swaying downward in the bucket and creeping along the tunnel to inspect a virgin seam. Activity had whittled away the spiky edges of his guilt but now, in sight of the swaying poplars, it came prickling back.

Soon a groom would lead Pranzo away, Fingal would relieve him of his coat and boots, a footman would fling open doors and he would be confronted by Sarah as she stood, a pillar of indignation, by the hall's arched fireplace.

"And where, sir, have *you* been?"

"The engineer – "

"Do engineers work in the dark?"

"Well, actually, as a rule they – "

"Are you not the employer of this engineer?"

"Sarah, the business had to be con – "

"I have been ready to dine this good half-hour."

"Dine?"

"Sup, if you prefer the vulgar term."

Generally he was indifferent to his wife's sarcasm. He knew his worth and drew consolation from the fact that, through competence and character, he had turned the colliery into a thriving enterprise. The unpalatable truth remained, though; he was merely Lord McCracken's daughter's husband, little better than a hired hand.

"Very well, Sarah, you have my apology. If you will permit me a few minutes to wash my hands, I'll – "

"Have you been underground again?"

"Sarah, a pit is not a piece of clockwork which will operate without supervi – "

"Were you underground last night, too?"

"I was in Ladybrook, as you know, at a lodge meeting."

"What took place at this lodge meeting that kept you from me all night long?"

"That I cannot tell you," Brother Blyth said.

"You mean that you will not."

"As you wish – will not tell you."

"And after the Sons of Apollo had gone home to bed – all except the coalmaster, apparently – what happened then?"

"Nothing happened then."

"You were inebriated, were you not?"

"No, I – well, yes, to be honest I did have a drop too much claret."

"Slept it off in some filthy stable, I expect."

"I slept in a room at the Neptune."

"Alone?"

"Yes, quite alone."

"Now you've come traipsing home with your tail between your legs, have you?"

"I've come home," Robertson Blyth sucked in a deep breath, "to dine. And that, Sarah, is precisely what I intend to do."

"Wash first."

"Of course, my dear," Robertson Blyth said, and clumped upstairs to his dressing-room where Fingal, his valet, had laid out hot water and towels.

*　　*　　*

As soon as supper was served Clare dismissed Lizzie to the kitchen. Frederick was perfectly capable of dishing out goose, slicing a veal pie and uncorking a wine bottle and it gave Clare pleasure to watch him perform the functions of host at her dining-table.

She could not help but recall the first daft days of their courtship when Frederick had walked her out to dine in the Duck Club on the banks of the river Kelvin. How grand she had thought it all, how colourful and romantic. She had gone willingly to bed with Frederick in the Duck Club's upstairs room and, at the time, had thought love-making romantic too.

Age, however, had deprived him of smoothness and there were hairs where no hairs should be, and Clare could not imagine what his skin would feel like now against her cheek.

She watched him slip a pickled herring on to his plate, crush it with a fork and devour it in three mouthfuls.

"There's beer if you would prefer it," she said.

"I may have changed, Clare, but I have not changed so much as all that. No, I will leave the drinking of beer at supper to lesser mortals." He plucked a bottle from the basket, drew the cork and sniffed. "Hock?"

"Did you expect a Portugal?"

"Quinn did you well, I see."

"I lacked for nothing."

Frederick poured wine and as casually as if he was discussing the time of day said, "Why did you marry such a man?"

"He asked me to."

"Was that reason enough?"

"At the time, certainly."

"But Donald Quinn! Such a dull fellow."

"Dull perhaps, but reliable," Clare said. "Mr Quinn made me a generous offer of marriage which, in the circumstances, I had no hesitation in accepting. He was not, you see, in the least daunted by the fact that I had been in prison and had stood trial for murder." She paused. "We had more in common than you might at first imagine."

Frederick attended to his plate. Clare noticed how he blinked, a strange flickering motion of the lids, a habit of which he seemed unaware.

She said, "We had you in common, Frederick."

"A mutual acquaintance. Quite!"

"You almost destroyed us, you know, both of us."

"I think you exaggerate."

"I do not believe that I do. If you had landed into Ladybrook ten years ago, Frederick, my husband would have shot you dead."

"Would you not have prevented him?"

"No, I would have put the loaded piece into his hand."

"Ah!" Frederick said. "In that case it's as well I did not land into Ladybrook a decade ago."

"Donald may be gone but Brock Harding is still here."

"What do you know of Brock Harding?"

"A great deal."

"Just what *did* Donald tell you?"

"Everything that I did not already know."

Frederick lifted a heavy silver fork and held it pinched between finger and thumb.

"I did not poison our son, Clare. I swear on my life."

"I know now that you did not. You have Andrew Purves to thank for supplying me with the truth. Andrew Purves and the Edinburgh lawyer who was appointed to my defence."

"Adams, was it not?"

"He is a judge now, did you know?"

"No, I had not heard."

"He was not a judge then, however. Drumfin was the judge. It was Drumfin who saved me from the gallows, Drumfin and Mr Adams between them." Clare helped herself to a slice of goose breast and poured upon it a trickle of blackberry sauce.

"If you were innocent of the crime, Frederick, why did you not come to Glasgow and speak out in my defence? It should not have been left to other men to attend to my welfare and save my neck from the rope. Where were you?"

"Clare, believe me, I could not attend you."

"You knew of it, of what had happened to Peterkin?"

"Of course I knew of it. Damn me, I wrote volumes in letters to the advocates. I kept nothing – very little – back from those legal vultures."

"You were, however, too engaged with business to bring the truth with you in person."

"It wasn't business that kept me away, Clare."

"What was it then?"

"Fear."

"Fear?"

"Do you suppose I did not suffer over the death of little Peterkin? Was he not my flesh and blood too?" Frederick set down the fork. "I knew *I* was innocent of the crime and that *you* would never destroy the thing that you loved most in all the world. I did not know precisely who had killed Peterkin but – mistakenly, as it happened – I thought I knew the reason for it."

"In God's name, what reason could there be for murdering an innocent child?"

"Revenge," Frederick told her.

"Revenge against an infant?"

"Revenge against me," Frederick said.

Clare sat back, astonished.

"I thought Brock Harding had arranged the murder of my son in revenge for what he believed to be my part in his brother's arrest."

"Did you betray his brother?"

"I had no need to do so. Jericho Harding was his own worst enemy. Indeed, my neck was as close as this – " he held up his hands, palms an inch apart "– as this, Clare, to the hangman's noose. I did not sell Jericho Harding to the King's men. Jericho understood it but Brock did not; or, if he did, would not accept it."

"Did you really imagine that Brock Harding had had Peterkin poisoned?"

"Yes."

"Why did you not declare it in your letters to the court?"

"How could I?" Frederick spread his hands. "It would have been construed as a confession of guilt to other crimes. Dear God, Clare, do you not appreciate how dangerous my situation was?"

"And mine," Clare said, "was not?"

"I was confident that you would not be found guilty."

"There are those who still believe I did it."

"Then they are fools. Evil, malicious fools."

"They say that I killed my son to protect you."

"Well, that's a motive that might just hold water, I suppose." Frederick paused then said, "At least we understand the truth of it now, that fate and nothing else took poor little Peterkin from us."

"With Eunice as its instrument."

"Poor woman. My poor, benighted sister. Yes."

"Do you still think of her?"

"Constantly."

"How do you think of her?"

"Fondly, and in sorrow."

"She tried to kill you, Frederick. She tried to poison you. It was only by accident that Peterkin died instead."

"No, Clare, I cannot accept that Eunice would seek to do me harm. It was pure mischance that the medicines, the blue bottles, became confused. Eunice would never willingly have done me harm."

"Why did she take her own life, Frederick?"

"Because she gathered unto herself the blame for Peterkin's death. She adored Peterkin too, you know."

"I would not for a moment deny it."

"She blamed herself for the – the accident."

Frederick's voice was strident, fists bunched on either side of his plate. He might, Clare thought, have been crying to be fed, not pleading innocence.

"Fifteen years haven't eased your conscience," she said. "Eunice's death still pains you, it seems."

"Of course it pains me."

"What of the years between?"

Frederick let out a breath and sat back. After a moment he helped himself to a slice of roast goose. "Oh, I have done well enough. I have, one might fairly say, rubbed along."

"Where have you 'rubbed along'?"

"Here and there."

"Liverpool?"

60

"For a time, yes. London, too." Frederick chewed, swallowed, speared another slice of goose breast with his fork. "Trading, quite profitably for the most part, in small parcels of commodities."

"In salt, for instance?"

"Oh, no. I'd had my fill of the salt trade." He swallowed once more. "Did well from salt, though. No doubt Quinn told you just how much profit came our way from running cargoes of Cheshire rock salt under the noses of King's officers."

"Do you have a wife, Frederick?"

"No, no wife."

"Do you intend to stay in Ladybrook?"

"For a time, certainly."

"Have you made your peace with Brock Harding?"

"That feat will be accomplished very shortly."

"How will it be accomplished?"

"By sensible agreement," Frederick said as airily as he could manage through a mouthful of buttered cabbage. "I'll not hide from Harding, Clare. My days of hiding are done."

"Harding's not the same man that you knew. He wields a great deal of power in this part of the world."

"Yes, I have heard rumours to that effect."

"Our blacksmith's gone up in the world. He owns a number of small properties, as much as McCracken will allow, and his ambition is not yet satisfied," Clare said. "Old Brock has aspirations to be a gentleman."

"Old Brock will never be a gentleman."

"He is keen to purchase Headrick, you know."

"Is he, indeed!"

"He made several offers to Donald and has recently made advances to me."

"Why has he set his sights on Headrick?"

"Because it is the only seat of any worth which isn't entailed to McCracken."

"Is Headrick profitable?"

"No, it is not," Clare lied. "The land's too poor for cultivation. The west portion was sold off to pay debts some years back and the rent book is not substantial. Truth to tell, Frederick, I'm gravely concerned about Headrick's future."

"Surely the salt revenue keeps you afloat?"

"Barely."

Frowning, Frederick pushed his plate away. "I had not

61

expected to hear this, Clare," he admitted. "I thought Headrick was flourishing."

Clare's supper lay untouched. Beneath the linen tablecloth her fingers were laced tightly together. "I had not expected to have you here to listen to my woes."

"Woes? Are you not happy?"

"Widows are not expected to be happy."

Frederick stroked his chin thoughtfully. "Perhaps I might be able to offer assistance."

"What manner of assistance?"

"Candidly, Clare, I had not anticipated that you would be so forgiving. I expected you to send me packing." He pressed his forefinger against his lips as if the finger was a valve designed to deliver truth in minute quantities. "I regret what happened between us. Hardly a night has gone by that I have not thought of you. And felt contrition." He released the forefinger and smiled. "Perhaps now I may be permitted to make amends."

"How?"

"Although I've not traded in salt for a dozen years I have kept abreast of the markets and, of course, I've an intimate knowledge of how salters do their work."

"I trust you're not suggesting – ?"

"Smuggling? Good God, no."

"What then?"

"I'm suggesting that you appoint me to be Headrick's salt factor."

"*What!*"

Clare managed to make her astonishment seem genuine. She was less surprised than she pretended to be, however. She had intentionally navigated the conversation towards this issue and was surprised only that Frederick had fallen so readily into her trap.

"Listen," Frederick went on, "I have not been entirely honest with you. You see, I did not know where I stood in your affections – or lack of them. Clare, I *do* have business here in Ladybrook."

"How fortuitous."

"Is it not?" Frederick said. "But it will not occupy me greatly. Surely it would be advantageous if I were also empowered to act as your salt factor."

"Advantageous to whom?"

"To both of us."

"What," Clare said, "will it cost me?"

"Not one penny piece."

"I could not allow you to work for nothing, Frederick."

"Provide me with lodgings then."

"Having you live under my roof would not be discreet."

"It would certainly set tongues wagging," Frederick said. "Do you care about the opinion of such stuffy folk?"

"Yes, I rather think I do."

"Look," Frederick moved on hastily, "I've seen every trick a salter can contrive to withhold profits from an employer. Gowrie's no worse than any other, but he's no better either."

"He skims," Clare said. "He falsifies the tally. I know that. Skimming's a perquisite of the trade."

"He also bribes the exciseman."

"Common practice." Clare shrugged. "The point is, Frederick, that Gowrie invariably delivers his quota."

"But not one ounce more."

"No, that's true," Clare conceded.

"Two pans. Five salters. Salt at one shilling and two pence across the counter to the cadgers. Ten percentage less for bulk purchase." Frederick shook his head. "If you allow me the opportunity, Clare, I can double your income from the saltpans within, say, a six month."

"By smuggling salt from Cheshire?"

"No, no, no. By increasing production."

"I refuse to run to windward of the law, Frederick."

"Absolutely not. You have my solemn word on that." He placed his right hand upon the tablecloth, palm uppermost. "What do you say, Clare?"

"I do not know what to say. It has all happened so quickly." She touched her brow with her wrist. "I must sleep on it before I give you an answer."

"Sleep on it, dearest, by all means."

"And perhaps take advice on the matter."

"Advice?" Frederick said. "From whom?"

"Friends."

"Do you mean Purves?"

"Andrew?" Clare laughed. "No. As soon as I married Mr Quinn I ceased to be Andrew Purves's responsibility. I have not heard from Andrew in many a long day."

"If not Purves, who then?"

"Dr Galloway."

"I've never heard of him."

"Hardly surprising," Clare said. "He has only been resident in Ladybrook for the past four years. He was a particular friend of Donald's, a great source of comfort during Donald's last illness. He was, in fact, Donald's appointed executor along with Mr Greenslade. He remains punctilious in his concern for my welfare."

"How old is this fellow?"

"No older than you are," Clare said. "If, indeed, he is quite so old."

"Where does he reside?"

"He maintains a small practice nearby."

"Where? Irvine? Kilmarnock? Where?"

"In Ladybrook."

"A small practice, to maintain his family?"

"Dr Galloway is a bachelor."

"I see," Frederick said, thinly.

"Obviously I am obligated to consult him on all matters pertaining to the management of Headrick," said Clare, "if only in his capacity as executor."

"If he is such a fine fellow," said Frederick, "why has he allowed you to fall into such desperate straits?"

"I did not say my straits are desperate. Only that I am concerned about Headrick's future. After all, if the French decide to invade our coast – "

"Pshaw!" Frederick exclaimed. "Precious little likelihood of that happening. Napoleon is far too canny to challenge the British navy. In my opinion the French will sue for peace before the summer's out."

"I know little of these matters," Clare said, "only what I have learned from John."

"John?"

"Dr Galloway. And from Mr Soames."

"Who, pray, is Mr Soames?"

"Pray indeed, Frederick," Clare said. "Mr Soames is the minister of St Cedric's and a close family friend."

"Also a bachelor?"

"For the time being," Clare said. "I do believe that Randolph would marry if he could find a suitable candidate."

"Someone," Frederick said, "like you?"

Clare feathered her eyelashes and, bringing a hand from beneath the table, rippled her fingers as if Frederick's suggestion had embarrassed her.

"La! La! I'm not on the marriage market."

"You do, however, appear to have attracted quite a number of possible suitors."

"Do you grudge me my friends?"

"I am in no position to grudge you anything," Frederick said, huffily.

"In any case," Clare said, "I'm not in need of a husband, only, it seems, of a salt factor."

"I would be happy to fill that latter post."

"But not the former?" Clare said.

"What do you mean?"

"I haven't forgotten your first words to me, Frederick, even if you did not intend them to be taken seriously."

"Do you mean to say – "

"I mean to say nothing," Clare lifted her glass. "To our fortunes, Frederick, together or apart."

He held his glass out, hesitated, then asked, "When will you give me a decision, Clare?"

"Oh, tomorrow," she said, "or the next day. Meanwhile, when you have finished supper, I have someone I would like you to meet."

"And who might that be?" Frederick asked, suspiciously.

"My daughter, sir," said Clare.

*   *   *

It had always seemed to Rose Tannahill that a scrubbed skin and washed hair were more important than a chalked doorstep and polished brasses. She had no good word to say for the rancid housewives of Ladybrook whose notion of cleanliness was to rub a little wintergreen into their eyebrows and sprinkle flea-powder on their petticoats.

Even in straitened days, when the boys were young, Rose had made soap from herbs and washing sponges from moss and had set her lads an example by bathing daily in the Linn in all but the coldest of weathers. After Benjamin, Robert and Peter had left, however, she had warmed the water for her morning bath and had taken it before the fire in the kitchen and in the evening had extended to Norman the same comfortable privilege.

Rose had not seen her son since breakfast time. He had been up early to put in a long day's stint with a shovel on the coalhill at Malliston, for the storm had delayed loading of several collier vessels and casual labour, paid by the piece, was there for the asking.

Norman could turn his hand to anything, but whatever the nature of his labour he would put all of his day's wages directly into his mother's hand the moment he returned home. He had no interest in money. He would not even watch her slide the tin box from its hiding place behind a stone in the fireplace to add his earnings to the savings that were already there.

Kettle singing on the hob, Rose would make her son tea. He would drink a cup while his mother peeled off his coat, vest and shirt and, kneeling before him, eased off his boots and heavy stockings, a ritual that had gone on for years.

On that cold January night, however, Rose had changed the order of things. She did not put Norman's earnings into the tin box but slipped the money discreetly into her apron pocket. She did not pour Norman tea or stand behind him to strip off his jacket.

She signalled to the Irish girl to perform the little ritual instead.

Norman, of course, had been roused by Roberston Blyth's arrival in the wee small hours of the morning but had kept in the shadows while the coalmaster had struck his strange bargain with Rose and had gone riding off again, leaving the girl behind him. He had drunk tea with the visitor, had watched her fall asleep at the table and, on instruction from his mother, had carried the girl to the bed behind the curtain before returning to his own bed in the attic.

At breakfast the following morning Norman had said nothing whatsoever about the night's unusual occurrence and had gone off to work as if nothing untoward had happened.

If he was surprised to find the girl still present in his mother's house when he came home that evening he gave no sign of it. He took the teacup from the girl's hand, downed its contents and handed it back to her as if it was the most natural thing in the world to be served by a total stranger.

When she tapped his shoulder he held out his arms and let her peel off his jacket and shirt. Next the girl ladled hot water from the copper pan into the wooden tub and handed him a rag and soap.

Norman hesitated for a second then returned the soap and rag to the girl and quietly indicated that he wouldn't object if she washed his shoulders and broad, bare back.

Norman's skin steamed. The wash-rag steamed. The girl's cap bobbed. Her breasts bobbed under the apron bib. She scrubbed away. Norman's expression throughout was as matter-of-fact as the girl's. She rinsed him off. She poured away the water. She mopped up the floor while Norman put on a clean shirt and stockings and, with a tiny sigh of contentment, seated himself by the fire.

Norman was forty-four years old. Nature had already begun to lay cruel marks upon him. His shoulders were less square than they had been a year ago, his neck less columnar. The rime of hair on the razor with which he shaved was grey, and silver strands lurked among his dark brown curls.

If Rose could have prevented her son from growing old she would have done so willingly but that miracle was beyond her fragile powers. She could no more set Norman free than she could liberate herself from an inevitable return to the earth. In the meantime, though, she must do what she could for his future, even if it meant giving him up.

The beautiful young Irish girl could do what she could not. The girl would bring nature, fresh as dew, to the Leddings and would breed children to ensure that some of the old flourish remained to stand against encroaching coalpits, steam-engines and the waggonways' rigid geometry.

"Are you hungry?" Rose asked.

"Aye, Missus," Eleanor answered. "Famished."

"Sit then and I'll serve."

Rose crouched by the hearth. She dipped the ladle into the stewpot and fished for onion, potato and fat pink gobbets of mutton to fill the young folks' bowls.

When she turned round again it was to find Norman and the girl seated side by side at the table, each with spoon in hand, each looking at the other in that matter-of-fact way which Rose did not quite understand.

Her son spoke for the first time that day.

"What's your name, lass?"

"Eleanor, sir, from Antrim."

"I'm Norman," Norman said and, reaching for the barley loaf, broke bread enough for both of them.

*   *   *

"Mama, who is that man?" Melissa said.

"Someone your Mama used to know."

"Is he very important?"

"Not at all important."

"Why did you serve him goose then?" Melissa asked.

"Because he was our guest and I wanted him to go away with a favourable impression of Headrick's hospitality."

"*Has* he gone away?"

"No, he's lodging with Mr Gowrie for a time."

"Is he a salter too? He does not *look* like a salter."

"Oh, and what does a salter look like?"

Because it had been such an extraordinary day, because Frederick had gone off earlier than expected, because Melissa had not been asleep when she'd come upstairs, Clare, for the sake of peace, had taken her daughter into her bed.

Melissa was not thrown by the question. "Like Mr Gowrie."

Clare had restored a nightlight to the cabinet by the bed. The wafer's tendril of wick burned clear within the bulbous dish and made her daughter's blue eyes shine like porcelain. The wind had died and the night had a dead, cold feel to it as if frost was stealing down from the moor. It would be bitterly cold in the salters' loft tonight.

She wondered if it had been callous of her not to invite Frederick to stay at Headrick. No. Frederick would have misconstrued the gesture, would have imagined his cause to be more advanced that it really was.

She must not allow herself to be deceived by his grey hair and haggard appearance, to be tricked into thinking that he had lost his sting.

She must move cautiously against him.

She drew Melissa closer, fitted her daughter snugly into the crook of her hip. Melissa put her cheek upon Clare's breast.

"Like Mr Gowrie," she said again.

"Come now, dear, not all salters resemble Mr Gowrie," Clare said. "Mr Striker certainly doesn't."

Melissa giggled. "Frederick told me he was a saltmaster."

"Frederick? Do you not mean Mr Striker?"

"Mr Striker told me I may call him Frederick and that we would be firm friends."

"When did he say such a thing?"

"When you went out to visit the appointments."

Melissa was exceedingly skilled in evading topics that might bring a reprimand and Clare put an arm about her so that she could not escape under the bedclothes.

Clare had been gone from the drawing-room for no more than five minutes. She'd had no qualms about leaving Melissa with Frederick for she recalled how fond he had been of young children, how much at ease with them. She remembered how he had soothed the teething pains of Andrew Purves's youngest, how cleverly he had put the insufferably spoiled Willy Purves in his place, how tenderly he had played with Peterkin on that last afternoon.

"What else did Mr Striker tell you?" Clare asked.

"He has brought a friend with him."

"What sort of friend?"

"A Froggie, Frederick said." Melissa, who apparently had nothing to hide, sat up, letting cold air flood the bed. "Not a *real* froggie, Mama, not a puddock. A man friend, who is from France. *We* call French people 'Froggies'. But I'm not to tell the gentleman that because it isn't polite."

"Where is the Fro – Mr Striker's friend?"

"Lodging with Mr Gowrie too. Did Frederick not tell you about the French gentleman, Mama?"

"No, he somehow neglected to mention it."

"Perhaps he thinks you do not like French people. Because of Nappie." Melissa sighed. "I do not like Nappie but Frederick says I will like his friend. He speaks English quite properly, you see, like us."

"I think that's quite enough conversation for one evening, Melissa," Clare said. "Put your head down beside mine and hide your eyes from the light."

"I've said my prayers."

"Good."

"I prayed for the sailors, even if there weren't any. And for Mr Galloway. And Papa in heaven. And for Mr Soames. And for you." Melissa paused. "For Frederick too."

"Melissa, you really must not call him Frederick."

"He says – " Again a pause. "I like him, Mama. Do you not like Mr Striker?"

"I am respectful towards him, as you should be."

Melissa sighed once more, kissed Clare's chin and snuggled against her mother's hip.

"Mama?"

"What is it now?"

"Have you said your prayers?"

"I will, dearest, I will."

"When?"

"Before I go to sleep."

"Do not forget now."

"No, darling," Clare promised, "I won't forget."

69

Book Two

The Serpent's Egg

My Dear Andrew,
In my last letter I promised you news from Headrick. I had not anticipated that I would have such astonishing news as I have for you now, an event of such magnitude that it has quite stood me on my head.

Our Mutual Acquaintance has returned. Frederick Striker is back in Scotland and here on Headrick, presently lodged with my salters. What's more it seems he has brought a Frenchman with him, a mystery man who, according to Gowrie, is possessed of some wonderful secret process in which Frederick has a share. How Frederick hopes to exploit the Frenchie I know not. Gowrie himself does not know or he would tell me as he is being very ingratiating since I put him under threat of dismissal.

Although we often used to discuss Frederick's return, you and I, neither of us actually stated what we intended to do when the day came. I do not believe we can seek redress against him on legal grounds. It seems unlikely that the Board of Revenue would be still interested. In any case, how can I pitch evidence against him without implicating my late husband and inviting the risk of having my coffers drained by fines and unpaid taxes. This seems to me like folly.

Frederick is not the same man we knew. He is older and, I believe, wiser. Ah, you will say to yourself, my cousin is about to make a fool of herself again. Not so. I believe I have his measure now.

I confess I am intrigued to learn what Frederick has in store, though, and how he intends to use the Frenchman. Before that, of course, he will have to win over Brock Harding which will be no easy task. In the meanwhile I have asked Frederick to act as my salt factor and he has promised to increase my profit from the pans. I think he hopes to win my favour and to be invited to lodge in my house. If so he will be doomed to disappointment.

I know I should have sought advice before reaching my decisions but the rapidity of events swept away that possibility, for John Galloway is presently out of town and not even Mr Soames can say for certain when he will return. I would ask, though, that you keep an ear to the ground in the hope that you might pick up some information on the history of the mysterious Frenchie whose name, so Gowrie tells me, is Henri Leblanc.

For the moment I am safe and really quite entertained by what has come to pass. I wait impatiently for Sunday when Frederick has indicated that he will attend the morning preaching at St Cedric's and confront Brock Harding.

Frederick has asked me to accompany him but of course I will not do so. I will go, as always, with my daughter and my servants.

I will, however, pen you a letter immediately afterwards to let you know what transpires.

In haste, Adieu.

Clare

Seven

The citizens of Ladybrook were not all agog with news of Frederick Striker's return. The general ruck of weavers, rope-makers, sailcloth repairers, candle manufacturers, brewers, millers, fisherfolk and colliers did not care tuppence what jiggery-pokery Brock and the Englishman were up to this time.

There was no mass exodus from cottage and croft that cold, grey Sabbath morn, no storming of St Cedric's doors. The majority did their customary bit for the Lord by staying in bed as long as possible, leaving worship to children and wives and those who were, or aspired to be, genteel.

Into this last category Brock Harding and his clan had gradually transformed themselves.

In his prime Brock would have died before darkening the door of a kirk. Only the influence of Soames's predecessor, the Reverend Angus McGonigle, Grand Master of Lodge Ladybrook, had persuaded Brock that the purchase of a family pew was an upward step and that a chap in his position need no longer fear the opprobrium of local squires and merchants whose beneficial influence upon the community was nothing compared to his own.

Two years after the Hardings joined the church Angus McGonigle was struck by a fatal seizure of the heart, which, some said, was no more than he deserved. The Hardings, however, did not abandon St Cedric's. On the contrary, Brock took great delight in taunting Mr Soames by exhibiting himself at Sunday preaching with the Jewel of Apollo worn in plain view and his inattentive family, babies included, spread along the benches directly beneath the minister's nose.

Something in the dissolute appearance of the Hardings spurred Reverend Soames, not by inclination a ranter, to heights of oratory that would have put the great Dr Knox to shame. Soames was, in fact, a gentle soul who liked nothing better than to crack a bottle of Madeira with his friend John Galloway and discuss matters far removed from doom and damnation. He was well versed in literature, agriculture and politics, as well as local gossip.

Rumours that something was brewing in Ladybrook reached Mr Soames during the course of his parish visits but, with John Galloway out of town, he did not learn the ins-and-outs of it until it was too late.

It was a cold, dull Sabbath morn but dry. Fewer carriages and carts than normal piled up behind the kirkyard wall, for quite a number of folk had chosen to walk to service.

The kirk had been heated by the lighting of a log fire in the iron grate which nestled under the gallery but the old building had absorbed most of the warmth into its bones. Breath hung in clouds about the mouths of worshippers so bundled in shawls and scarves and topcoats, so brown and dense that Reverend Soames might have been addressing a congregation of Russian bears, not pious Scots men and women.

The elders who met in the vestry were not their usual sober selves. They seemed to share a need to nudge, whisper and chuckle at the expense of Robertson Blyth who, Reverend Soames noticed, did not participate in the levity.

"Are you quite well this morning, Mr Blyth?" Soames asked, a polite enquiry which brought a stifled guffaw from Mr Millar, Ladybrook's grain merchant, and a positively ribald giggle from Mr Ormiston, the Shore Master.

"I am very well, thank you, Minister."

"I am glad to hear it."

"Toned up, Mr Blyth?" said Millar.

"Fit as a fighting cock?" said Ormiston.

Spots of red the size of sixpences glowed on Robertson Blyth's cheeks and his mouth hooked down like a piece of wire. He kept silent, however, until the Guidance Prayer was over then swiftly dismissed himself to his station below the prow of the pulpit. Randolph Soames stared long and hard at Ormiston and Millar but wrung not a blush from either of them let alone an explanation.

A few minutes later Soames went into the passage that led from the vestry to the church and peeped curiously through a gap in the curtain. He did not quite know what he expected to see but the church was just the same as it always was on wintry Sundays, dank and stony and grey. He could discern the Harding wives with toddling children attached to their arms by

76

tapes; then he noticed Brock, Cabel and Daniel standing in the aisle with their faces turned towards the kirk's main entrance, and realised that it had grown eerily quiet as if, on a signal, all servants and labourers in the gallery and all the fine ladies in the oak pews had stopped gabbing at once.

Reverend Soames had heard much of Striker and the origins of his blood feud with the Hardings. He had also heard of Striker's unfortunate connection with Clare Quinn and had, in the past few years, developed his own image of the man.

The reality was disappointing. He had expected something more imposing than the stiff, swaggering beanstalk who walked, all alone, down the aisle towards the Hardings.

It was deathly still in the church now, except for some coughing and the crying of an infant in the gallery.

When Striker spoke everyone could hear him.

He said, "Glad to see you still in the land of the living, Brock."

"Aye," Brock answered, "I heard you were back."

"Nothing escapes you, does it?"

"Nothing worthy of notice," Brock said. "I've waited a long time to meet up with you again, Fred Striker."

"Well, here I am," Striker thrust out his hand. "Will you not give me a proper greeting?"

For a long moment Brock contemplated the proffered hand and then, frowning, shook it reluctantly. As he did so his attitude altered. The belligerence drained out of him. His head jerked up and his eyes narrowed. He was, Soames thought, startled. Something in the handshake, some unusual pressure or position of the fingers had conveyed a special meaning to Brock Harding, a sign that could not be ignored.

Releasing Striker's hand Brock stepped back and said, "Daniel, give Mr Striker your seat."

"But Dad – "

"I want Fred right here by me," Brock declared and, a moment later, the Englishman and the blacksmith were seated side by side, like brothers lost and found again.

*   *   *

Robertson Blyth was possibly the only person in St Cedric's who was not wholly intrigued by the meeting of old enemies. The coalmaster had more to worry him than ancient history. He had spotted Eleanor in the gallery; Eleanor, Rose and Norman Tannahill prominent in the front row behind the rail.

The beautiful Irish girl had already attracted a fair share of attention and comment and Robertson Blyth could not escape the feeling that he, not Frederick Striker, was the focus of every eye. To add to his torment his wife was positioned directly below him and by a tiny rolling motion of the eyeballs he could glance from Sarah to Eleanor, Eleanor to Sarah and be drawn into the making of comparisons that were both invidious and dangerous.

By many a man in Ladybrook, not to mention Ayr, Sarah Blyth, with her parchment skin, fine chiselled features and regal bearing, was considered the epitome of beauty. She was certainly at her most luminous in the kirk's motley gathering and yet that morning seemed beaten into second place by the young stranger in the gallery.

Robbie Blyth, seated in full view of the congregation, cudgelled his brains to come up with a strategy by which he might safely claim Eleanor Antrim for his mistress.

If half the men in Ayrshire envied him his wife the other half coveted his position as McCracken's son-in-law and manager of Cairns.

The truth was that he had no real power at all. He was bound into that noble family by fear and responsibility. If he had not been McCracken's lackey, the taking of Eleanor would be easy. He would simply send his valet, Fingal, to fetch her whenever the fancy took him. But he did not dare do so for he could trust no one, not even his own valet, not to blow the gaff to Sarah.

Chilled and embarrassed Robertson Blyth endured the preaching as best he could and, at the end of the service, having found no solution to his problem, he meekly followed the minister back into the vestry and allowed Eleanor to go home again with Rose.

*　　*　　*

The carriage was a deep four-wheeled boat with whalebone springs. It had been in the McCracken family for many years, a quaint old heirloom which, when his Lordship had been young had prowled the streets of Edinburgh and had cradled on its brown cowhide upholstery more than a few of the Netherbow's luscious *jeunes filles*; if, that is, Lord McCracken's tales of a reckless youth were to be believed.

The carriage had been brought back from the capital for Sarah's wedding, had transported bride and groom from their nuptials to the great feast at Cairns House and since then had been trotted out, like uxorious devotion, for Sarah's use whenever the whim took her.

The sons were stuck in the back. Sarah and Robertson rode in front, with a driver in a red coat perched before them and a horse-boy, nimble as a lizard, clinging on behind.

"Who is that girl?"

Little knots of worshippers hung about in the grey, hazy air, some by the gate, some by the kirkyard wall. The coalmaster glanced behind him. He stared up at the track that curved around the hillock beyond the kirkyard where Rose, her son and Eleanor were wending their way back to the Leddings.

"What?"

"Has the cold affected your hearing, Robertson?"

"I'm sorry, I – "

"The girl with the witch-woman?"

"I really have no idea."

"Do you not find her pretty to look upon?"

"I cannot say that I noticed her."

"You stared at her hard enough."

"I was not aware that I – of her."

"Were you 'aware' of the gentleman who was invited to sit with Harding?"

"Why, Sarah, did you not recognise him?" said Robbie Blyth, relieved to be on safer ground.

"It was Mr Striker, was it not?"

"Certainly, it was. Heaven knows, Sarah, he supped with us at Cairns often enough."

"Supped with you," Sarah said. "If you will cast your mind back you may recall that I was seldom invited to those masculine soirées which seemed principally to be concerned with the drinking of too much claret."

"Huh! I'd forgotten about the claret," said Robertson Blyth. "However, I did not indulge in supper-taking with Striker all that often, Sarah. In fact I hardly knew him well enough to call him friend; which is perhaps as well in the light of what happened later."

"Why do you say that?"

"Say what?"

"Cast aspersions on Mr Striker's character."

"Clare Quinn, the trial. I mean to say – "

"I do not believe Mr Striker was charged with any crime."

"No, come to think of it, he wasn't. But – "

"Whereas she was."

"That's true. On the other hand, she was acquitted without a stain on her character."

"Without a stain?" Sarah sniffed. "Now that is a matter of opinion, not to say interpretation. Father – although he is too polite to tell me the whole sordid story – Father claimed that she allowed Drumfin to engage in intercourse as part of the price of her acquittal."

"She was the accused and Drumfin was the judge. Obviously he had to have intercourse with her."

"Intercourse, intercourse."

"Oh!" said Robbie Blyth. "Did your father tell you that in so many words?"

"Do you suppose I made it up?"

"No, but – "

"Do you think so highly of Donald Quinn's widow that you believe it to be impossible?"

Robertson Blyth sighed. "Truth to tell, Sarah, I hardly think of Donald Quinn's widow at all. What does it matter if she did or did not have relationships with Drumfin. Good God, Sarah, if you were given a choice between swinging on a rope's end and bedding a judge – "

"I'd swing."

"Yes." Robbie sighed again. "Yes, my dear, of course you would."

*   *   *

Broad-bottomed and lumbering, Brock went before him up the narrow staircase. Behind came Cabel and Daniel. Frederick felt as if he was a prisoner of the Hardings and the Neptune their jail. He had, however, deliberately contrived to make their first meeting as public as possible and even Brock Harding would hardly be rash enough to do away with him now.

Brock unlocked the door and preceded Frederick into the gloomy over-room. The younger Hardings came crowding after.

One of them locked the door behind them.

"Do you know what place this is?" Brock asked.

"The Lodge of Apollo," Frederick answered. "I have been in many similar."

"Where?"

"I undertook my first oaths in Liverpool," Frederick said. "But it was at the hands of the brethren of Cranstown Lodge near Belfast that I had the honour of learning the language required for my final testing."

"How do I know that what you say is the truth?"

"By the application of the Third of the Seven Sciences," Frederick answered promptly. "It is Dialectic which teacheth a man to distinguish Truth from Falsehood."

"Are you not then a Deceiver?"

"Apollo has but one Deceiver."

"That being?"

"The Malevolent Moon," said Frederick.

"Daniel," Brock said, "put a light to the fire and wick the candles. It seems we are entertaining a brother rather than an old acquaintance."

"I hope that you may consider me to be both."

"All in good time, Fred," Brock told him. "All in good time."

*   *   *

"I know where we're going," Melissa said. "We're going to see if we can find the Froggie."

"Nothing of the sort," said Clare. "Since the day is dry I thought we would take a short walk before we returned home. It will allow Pratie and Mrs Shay time to prepare dinner. Are you not hungry?"

"I am, Mama."

"Cod in custard, I think," said Clare.

For once Melissa did not wrinkle up her nose at the prospect of being forced to eat fish.

She was very pert and bright in a new coat and bonnet but, Clare thought, rather too grown up. Spring, summer or winter, the season did not seem to matter to Melissa, who was indomitably gay and curious.

"Are we going to walk about the shore, Mama?"

"Where it is not wet, yes."

"Past Mr Gowrie's?"

"If inclination leads us that way."

"I *knew* we were going to see the Froggie."

"Melissa – "

"Will Frederick be there too?"

"I think not, no."

"I saw Frederick with Mr Harding. What was Frederick doing with Mr Harding? They were being very naughty, Mama. They talked all through prayers. Mr Soames did not like it at all. He was 'cowling at them so hard. I think he would have put them out if they had not been grown up."

Melissa was at times too observant for her own good. It would have been even more entertaining for the little girl if she had been acquainted with the facts of life that lay beyond her present understanding.

Melissa held on to Clare's hand as they picked their way along the shore track. Sandy soil had carried away all traces of rain and a steady ocean breeze had dried the overnight dew. The sea was dark as blueberry juice, gulls poised above it stark white against the clouds.

"Mama." Melissa tugged at Clare's sleeve and whispered. "There's a man behind the bushes. Watching us, I think."

Unlike Melissa, Clare had not been bobbing up and down and consequently had missed the tell-tale glimpse that the child had had of a pair of polished brown boots and a tall beaver hat peeking under and above a tangled gorse bush.

She saw the hat now, though, and experienced a sudden little pang of panic.

"Sir, you sir, why are you lurking there?" she called out shrilly. "Show yourself this instant."

The bush rustled and from behind it a man appeared.

He was clearly flummoxed at being caught out and, Clare guessed, had been answering a call of nature when Melissa and she had hove around the corner.

"Mama," Melissa whispered, round-eyed, "I do believe it's the Fro – "

With a sharp tug Clare pulled her daughter against her skirts to stifle her indiscretion.

The man was certainly of foreign appearance. Long breeches tied below the knees with tattered rosettes seemed foppish, the tightness of his frock-coat too. His wig was a mass of wiry curls, his shirt front frilled. He had a round, bilious sort of face with hairy black eyebrows that curled like ladies' lashes above eyes of old amber.

"Larking, Madame? Larking?" he blustered. "I have you to know that I am not the sort of person who larks."

His accent was a fusion of French and Irish with plummy vowels added to the mixture as if he did not want to be caught out as a playhouse foreigner. In this deception he was unsuccessful. He was too much a perpetual emigrant to wander undetected amid the alien corn.

Clare drew Melissa deeper into her skirts to smother the possibility of giggles.

"I did not accuse you of 'larking', sir," Clare said, "I accused you of lurking. That *is* what you were doing. And on my property too."

His hands fluttered then froze in mid-air, one forefinger held aloft. "*Ah!*"

"Ah?"

"She you are," the Frenchman said, "but of course."

Melissa crouched low, face buried in Clare's sleeve, shoulders shaking.

"The child is she ill?"

"Prone to fits," Clare said. "But this is not one of them. What, sir, are you doing on my property?"

"I am a resident here, Madame Quinn."

"You have the advantage of me, sir?"

"Henri Leblanc." He swept off his hat, restrained the impulse of his wig to follow it, and bowed deeply. "I am to be soon a guest at your house, I believe."

"Are you, indeed, M. Leblanc?" said Clare. "On whose invitation?"

"On the invitation of Frederick Striker."

"Did Mr Striker tell you that?"

"He said it would be an arrangement quickly made."

"Well, M. Leblanc, I regret to inform you that Frederick Striker has no authority to promise hospitality on my behalf. In fact, Mr Striker has not yet seen fit to inform me of your existence. Am I to assume that you are also lodging in the salthouse?"

"*Phoufff!* It is regrettably yes."

"We are going in that direction now," Clare said. "Perhaps you would care to accompany us so that we might converse upon the way."

"To your domicile?"

"To the salthouse. And no further than the salthouse."

"Madame, I would treat even such a humble favour with delight." M. Leblanc bowed again and rather to Clare's chagrin winked one amber eye at Melissa. "*Vous aussi?*"

"*Oui, Monsieur,*" Melissa replied. "*Moi aussi.*"

"She converses like a born *Parisienne.*"

"Only a few words as yet," Clare said. "My husband taught her to the limit of his capacity."

"I have capacity immeasurable. I will teach her more." M. Leblanc cocked an elbow out from his hip like a teapot handle. "You will take my arm, perhaps, Mademoiselle?"

"Mama?"

Clare nodded and watched with guarded amusement as Melissa slipped her hand through the Frenchman's arm and, matching him in strut and style, started out along the sandy track again as if it were the road to Versailles.

"Now, Madame Quinn," said Henri Leblanc. "What is it you wish to converse about with me?"

"Frederick Striker," Clare said, and saw at once from the stranger's changed expression that she had struck a chord of sympathy.

*   *   *

Frederick said, "Yes, Brock, I admit that I went to the hanging. It was not mere idle curiosity that took me there."

"How did he die?"

"He died well," Frederick said. "I thought you might have come down at the last. I looked for you in the crowd."

"A large crowd?"

"A very large crowd."

"Did Jericho please them?"

"Indeed, indeed! Everyone in the Square was on Jericho's side, even though he was a Scotchman. They cheered him to the echo when he appeared from the gate of the Tower in the executioner's cart."

"I wisht I had been there," Brock said.

"Why were you not?"

Brock shrugged. "Prudence."

"I stayed," Frederick said, "because he was my friend."

"You stayed," said Brock, "because you were afraid he would blab."

"Jericho? Never!"

"What happened to the ship?"

"Confiscated, of course, along with the cargo," Frederick said. "Small price to pay for the thousands we skimmed from the Treasury."

"Jericho paid with his life."

"If only I'd been in Liverpool at the time of Jericho's arrest," said Frederick. "I'd have kept him calm.. We would have lost the ship and cargo, yes, a fine of some proportions would have been imposed upon us but – "

"Are you blamin' my brother for what happened?"

"No, no, most certainly not. But if the ship hadn't grounded at the mouth of the Mersey – " Frederick hesitated then courageously said, "Jericho was drunk, you know."

"My brother was drunk?"

"Yes, Brock, blind, red drunk," Frederick said. "In spite of what you may think I didn't peach to the Γ cise. Hand upon my heart I swear to you by the Solemn Oath of Apollo that I wasn't to blame for what happened to Jericho."

On an October morning in the year of 1788 Jericho Harding had been brought from the gate in the wall of Liverpool's Tower, chained upright in a dung cart. It had been clear from the first that he intended to make the most of his moment of glory. He had leaned back against the chains and the wind had filled his calico shirt and imparted a false impression of sturdiness.

Frederick said, "If Jay hadn't lost his temper and throttled a King's officer with his bare hands he would still be with us today."

Brock nodded. "Always did have a bit of temper, our Jericho."

Shantymen and river rats had roared loud and long when Jericho had been led to the platform. A parson in a black robe had intoned the funeral service while Jericho, bare-breasted, pigeon-chested, had stared out across the ocean of faces.

Brock said, "Did he see you there?"

"No," Frederick answered. "No, alas, I do not think he did. Perhaps it would have been a comfort to him to spot a friendly face in the crowd."

Although his hands had been tied Jericho had jerked his shoulders violently and had snarled at the executioner. The executioner, a mild, insignificant fellow clad in brown leather, had consulted with the governor who had consulted with the sheriffs who had indicated that it mattered not what the prisoner did at this stage in the proceedings and that if he did not wish to be capped then it was no skin off the community nose.

"Did he utter any last words?" Brock asked.

"He did not."

The bell of St Nicholas had tolled slow and solemn and pigeons and a gull or two had burst from the spire and had soared away on the wind. The crowd had fallen silent when

85

Jericho had stepped on to the trap. He had squinted up at the overhead beam and had nudged the noose with brow and shoulder, like a cat currying favour. Tucked away on a corner of Brunswick Street, a safe distance from the gallows, Frederick had been much affected by that gesture.

"I tell you, Brock," Frederick said. "It was all I could do not to weep."

The executioner had settled the noose daintily beneath Jericho's calico collar but Jericho had hardly seemed to be aware of the hangman's final ministrations. He had craned forward and scowled at the crowd with such ferocity that even the roughest ruffians had stopped jeering.

"Was it – was it quick and merciful?"

"Very quick," said Frederick. "Very merciful."

The executioner had skipped down the steps to the iron lever beneath the pedestal. Jericho and the parson had been left alone upon the board. The bell had tolled. The parson had chanted. Jericho had stretched out his neck like a fighting cock. Only at the very last second had he picked out Frederick's face in the crowd.

"STRIKER," he'd bellowed. "I SEES YOU, FRED STRIKER. I'LL SEE YOU AGAIN – IN HELL."

He'd started headlong towards the edge of the board as if he'd intended to throw himself upon the multitude.

From beneath the pedestal – a resounding clang.

Beneath Jericho's heels the trap had opened.

"I could not look," Frederick said. "Swift though it was, Brock, I had to turn my eyes away."

"Where did they bury him?"

"Somewhere," Frederick said.

"The limepit?"

"I expect so, yes."

"Without stone or ceremony," Brock said.

"That's the way of it," Frederick said.

"Poor old Jericho," said Brock. "What did you do then?"

"Stayed on in Liverpool for a while."

"Doin' what?"

"Playing billiards for the most part."

"Profitably?"

"It kept body and soul together," Frederick said.

He had spent so much of his money on the Glasgow house, in setting it up for Eunice, that he'd had precious little left. With Eunice dead and Clare lost to him he'd had no inclination to work at schemes to raise his fortunes. It was not in his nature to mourn for ever, though. As soon as he had seen Jericho safely off he'd felt within him familiar stirrings and an urgent need to move on to something new.

"It took more than billiards to put those clothes on your back," Brock said. "Is what you told me in the kirk true?"

"I would not lie to you, Brock."

Brock's sons were both on guard by the door.

Cabel had placed one brilliant, buckled shoe upon a tilted chair and displayed an arrogant indolence.

Frederick remembered the pair as boys, swearing and brawling with the best of them. To all appearances they had changed into gentlemen. Frederick was not deceived.

"'Course you'd lie to me, Fred," Brock said, "if it suited you. I ain't surprised to see you here. I always thought you'd drift back eventually. Only thing is, I expected you to arrive broke and beggin' favours."

"Why should I beg for favours?" Frederick said. "If anything it's you who should be doing the begging."

"Now then, now then," Daniel Harding warned.

"If you're not interested in my proposal," Frederick said, "I'll take it elsewhere."

"What's he talkin' about, Dad?" Cabel said.

"Money," Brock answered. "So listen."

"More money, young man," Frederick said, "than you ever dreamed about."

"We don't mess with cheap salt traders no more," Cabel said. "We don't want to go a-windin' up on a rope's end like Uncle Jericho."

"Let's hear what Mr Striker has to say before we condemn him," said Brock.

"Aye, let him tell us exactly where all this money's a-comin' from," said Daniel.

"And why he'd want to share it with us," said Cabel.

"Oh, I don't want to share it with you," said Frederick. "Unfortunately I can't finance the venture unaided."

"What venture?" said Cabel.

"Aye, what's the money for?" said Daniel.

"To construct a laboratory," Frederick said.

"To do what?" said Daniel. "Turn lead into gold, eh?"

"Last charlatan who tried that chestnut on us wound up swimmin' off the Nebbocks," Cabel said, "with his so-called Philosopher's Stone tied round his neck."

Frederick sighed. "If I were to tell you that I have engaged the services of a Frenchman who can produce all sorts of wonders with chemical substances what would you say to that?"

"Commercial wonders?" Brock said.

"He can manufacture soda out of sea-water."

"Soda! Nothing new in that," said Cabel. "What else?"

"He has gone some way to developing a universal solvent," Frederick said.

"Is it under patent?" Brock asked.

"Not yet."

"What else?"

"A gun which can produce a beam which can pare through metal as easily as a knife cuts cheese."

"How is this beam produced?" said Brock.

"By the interaction of gases."

"What gases?"

"That I cannot tell you," Frederick said, "for the simple reason that the Frenchman will not tell me. I have, however, seen it done. What's more this beam can also be adjusted to make metals fuse together."

"By varying the temperature?" Brock asked.

"That is the principle, yes."

"How large is the device?"

"Not large," Frederick replied. "Quite transportable, in fact."

"If such a machine already exists why do you need invest-ment?" said Cabel.

"To produce the gases in sufficient quantity to make the device marketable," Brock said. "Isn't that right, Fred?"

"On the nail, old friend."

"Have you really seen it done?" Cabel asked.

"Yes, in Dublin."

"More than once?"

"Oh, yes, several times."

"Was there no investment to be had in Dublin?"

Frederick had prepared his answer. "Investment, but no craftsmen capable of making the necessary equipment."

"And you thought of us?" said Brock with a hint of sarcasm. "How considerate!"

"I have other reasons for wishing to return to Scotland."

"May we enquire what those reasons are?"

"Matters of the heart."

"The heart?" said Brock. "I didn't know you had one."

Frederick feigned embarrassment. "Well, when I read notice of Quinn's death in the *Gentleman's Magazine* – "

Brock laughed. "By God, Striker, do you mean to say it's love of the widow Quinn brought you back?"

"I do not regard it as a laughing matter."

"No, oh no, it's certainly not that," Brock said. "Tell me, how were you received at Headrick House?"

"Warmly enough to suggest that my cause may not be entirely in vain."

"Can your Frenchman not invent a chemical to melt female resistance?" said Cabel.

"I'm not quite so long in the tooth," Frederick said, "that I have forgotten how to do that for myself."

"Clare Kelso." Brock shook his head ruefully. "Clare Kelso Quinn. Well, well, well!"

"I'm to serve as her salt factor."

"Is that so?" Brock said. "Would that have anything to do with the fact that Mrs Quinn has a shed available for conversion into a chemical works; a shed that wouldn't require a manufacturing licence from the Parish Board?"

"The thought," Frederick said, "had crossed my mind."

"By God, Freddie, you've been fast off the mark."

"If things fall rightly I hope to lodge with Mrs Quinn."

"Lodge what with Mrs Quinn?" said Daniel.

"Now, now, son," said Brock, "that's no way to talk of a respectable widow lady."

"What transpires between Clare Quinn and me is no business of yours," Frederick said loftily. "What of the other matter, though? Are you interested?"

Brock spread his hands on his thighs. "What would it cost to put on a chemical demonstration for us at the lodge?"

"I can't say exactly."

"If I was to arrange it with the brothers would you put up half the cost of such a demonstration?"

Frederick didn't hesitate. "Yes."

"On that condition," Brock said, "you can take it I'm interested. First, though, I'll need to meet your Frenchie and hear from his own lips just what he thinks he can do."

"Of course."

"If he lives up to your billin', though," Brock said, "you can take it we'll come to some arrangement to provide you with funds."

"You won't regret it, Brock," said Frederick.

"I know I won't," said Brock.

*   *   *

Clare had read of the charm of French men but she could not honestly say that she found M. Henri Leblanc particularly captivating. She was amused by his stiff manners and preening arrogance. It seemed that M. Leblanc had such a high opinion of himself that even the simple gestures of friendship appeared as condescension and it took half a fish custard and a full bottle of Bordeaux to make him unbend.

Clare had permitted Melissa to dine with them. Melissa did not let Mama down. Seated at table she matched each of the Frenchie's mannerisms as they related to the eating of food and the wiping of chops as if she had been born by the banks of the Seine.

M. Leblanc was much taken with Melissa. He did not seem to regard her questions as impertinent. At first Clare was content to let her daughter lead the conversation and to chip away at her visitor's reluctance to say what he was doing in Scotland and how he had become the friend, if friend he was, of Frederick Striker.

It was not until they had repaired to the drawing-room and M. Leblanc had imbibed two tumblers of whisky that, metaphorically, he loosened his trouser strings.

"I am the greatest chemist who has ever come out of France," he began, without preamble. "I should not be rolled from post to pillar like a block of wood. I have sat at the right hand of the great Lavoisier, who would have made me a tax-farmer if I had not disagreed with his opinions in front of the *Académie*. What does the digestion of a guinea-pig matter?" He fixed his gaze upon Melissa who was seated on a stool by the pianoforte. "Hah?"

Melissa touched her tongue to her upper lip. Clare had not yet explained to her daughter how real questions differed from rhetorical ones.

M. Leblanc sipped whisky. "Hah?"

"I think," Melissa said, "it might matter to the guinea-pig, sir."

Clare knew that Melissa had not intended to be insolent but before she could think what to say to cover her daughter's gaffe a strange honking sound filled the drawing-room.

90

M. Leblanc was laughing.

"It matters to the guinea-pig," the Frenchman said, gasping with amusement. "Naturally, naturally it matters to the guinea-pig."

He rose unsteadily to his feet and advanced upon Melissa, who barely had time to quail against the keyboard before Henri Leblanc reached her and patted her curls with a sticky hand.

"Lavoisier did not think of such a thing," he said. "If Lavoisier had thought more of the guinea-pig perhaps he would not have had his head chopped off. I should have told Antoine to think more about the guinea-pig, no?"

"How did you escape, M. Leblanc?" Clare asked.

"They did not know what I was doing. If they had known what I was doing they would have marched me to the guillotine behind the tax-farmers." He continued to pat Melissa's curls while the little girl sat rigid with astonishment. "I kept my head, yes, but I lost everything else. My baggages, my books, my relatives, my friends. But now," he honked again, "now I have found new friends, no?"

"Do you mean Frederick?" Clare asked.

"I mean you, Madame."

"Oh!"

Henri swayed, steadied himself, placed his hands about Melissa's waist, lifted her from the stool and, before Clare could prevent it, rattled up the keyboard cover.

"Now," he announced, "I will play the music for my new friends, no?"

Rippling his fingers over the keys Henri Leblanc coaxed from the old instrument, a melody which Clare recognised, with strange *frisson*, as an air that Eunice Bates had often played in Frederick's house in Glasgow while Peterkin, in Mama's arms, had laughed and clapped his tiny hands in appreciation of his aunt's musical skills.

Clare rose, crossed to the piano and placed a hand on Henri's shoulder. "What is that piece called, sir?"

"Ah! Let me think of it? It has the title 'The Lass of Malton', I believe. A trifle Frederick used to whistle when we lodged together in Dublin."

Clare laid her fingers across the keyboard.

Surprised, Henri stopped playing. "Do I not play well?"

"I think that you play very well, M. Leblanc. I would be pleased to hear another piece – but not that one."

He inclined his head. Haughtiness gone, he seemed to be

shrewdly aware of what Clare really required of him. He sat back on the padded stool.

"Do you not care for it because it was taught to me by Frederick?" he asked.

"That is part of the reason," Clare said, "Where did you first meet Frederick?"

"In Dublin."

"In the house of a lady, by any chance?"

"Why, yes!"

"Frederick's lady?"

Henri struck a sharp little chord. "Frederick's wife."

"His wife! Frederick told me he was unmarried."

"The lady is deceased. He is, like you, a widower."

"Was she a widow when Frederick married her?"

Henri nodded. "She was not young. He brought her happiness for only a brief time before their joy was cut short by her death."

"Did Frederick inherit her property?"

"There was, I think, a disputation about the will. The lady's children – " Henri shrugged "– they did not take to Frederick from the first."

"Of what age was Mr Striker's wife?"

"It is not a question a gentleman asks."

"M. Leblanc, please."

"Older than you, much older. About sixty years, I think."

"How long was Frederick married to her?"

"Twenty months."

"How long is it since she died?"

"One year," M. Leblanc replied. "After his wife's decease Frederick came to meet again with me in Belfast and provided me money for my work."

"What is your work, sir?"

"I am a chemis "

"An apothecary?"

"I do not make pills for the bellyache, Madame, no."

"What do you make, M. Leblanc?"

"Whatever is required by the gentleman who pays me. If he wishes lime to strew upon the fields I will make it more cheap than the market can supply. If he requires soda for bleaching I make that too. Turkey dye to stay fast in water – *phooph!* – simple."

"What do you hope to manufacture here in Ladybrook?"

"Fluid heat."

"Can you do it?"

"I have done it."

Clare hesitated. "M. Leblanc, what did the lady die of?"

"The lady?"

"Mr Striker's wife?"

Henri spread his hands. "A sickness."

"She died suddenly, did she not?"

"I believe it to be so, yes."

"And," Clare asked, "what was her name?"

"Her name, Madame, was O'Neill," the Frenchman said, "Eleanor Antrim O'Neill."

"Eleanor Antrim, do you say?"

"That was her name, yes."

"Well, well," Clare murmured, "what a coincidence. What a very odd coincidence."

"What is?" said Henri.

"Nothing, sir, nothing," Clare said. "Will you not play for us again?"

"With pleasure, Madame," Henri said and, after solemnly cracking his knuckles, broke into a rousing chorus of *Le Joyeux Petit Berger*.

Eight

John Galloway had long ago learned that when spinster sisters govern a household a degree of compliance with the wishes of servants becomes not just civility but necessity. He could not, for instance, make a request directly to Ishbel, younger by a year than her sister, for Ishbel had been trained to subjugate herself to Eppie who, though small and soft as a quail, had a rigid spirit that even the good doctor, for all his love of order, could not match.

It would be a case of enquiring of Ishbel if Eppie would be kind enough to allow him to take chocolate for breakfast instead of tea, if he might have a glass of whisky before dinner or if she, Ishbel, thought Eppie would consider him justified in asking for a woollen undervest, given the state of the weather. Message duly delivered, Eppie would appear from the kitchen, would study him gravely and would mutter confidentially into her sister's ear. Only then would Ishbel come forward, drop a creaky curtsey and tell him, "That'll be all right then, Doctor Galloway," as if one of them, God knows which, was conferring a tremendous favour upon the other.

John Galloway had not inherited the Ramsay sisters. He had gone to an Easter market in Kirk Street in Ayr and had hired them himself. He had no one else to blame. In spite of their eccentricities, however, he preferred Eppie and Ishbel to the Talbots, the joyless husband and wife who looked after Randolph Soames's manse.

The doctor had been back from Glasgow for less than four hours when Randolph Soames arrived at his door and, given permission by Eppie, was shown by Ishbel into the long first-floor room which served Galloway as both library and dining-room.

Galloway had just washed down a crusty pie of rabbit and pickled pork with a second glass of claret and was not in the least put out at the prospect of having to share his pudding with his friend from the manse.

There was no formality between the men. It was off with his coat and up with his sleeves for Randolph Soames. He was seated at the table in no time at all and wasted little time in small talk.

"I cannot say that I am anything but relieved to see you back," he began.

"I'm flattered, Randolph," Galloway said. "I had not realised that you would so much miss my company. Will you take a dish of Eppie's excellent apple and ginger?"

"No, I have eaten my supper already."

"A glass of wine?"

"If you insist."

The doctor poured from the bottle, handed the glass to the minister, who sipped politely before allowing agitation to overcome him once more.

"There are strangers in our midst, John," he blurted out. "They turned up two weeks ago."

"Strangers?"

"What's more, the lodge has had another sale."

"Calm yourself, Randolph," John Galloway said. "Am I to take it that the two pieces of news are connected?"

"There is that possibility."

Galloway finished his pie, pushed the plate away and dabbed at his lips with his napkin. "Kindly explain."

"Do you recall the name of Frederick Striker?"

"Of course I do."

"Before our time in Ladybrook," the minister said, "but we've heard so much about him. It came as a shock to see him march into the kirk last Sunday."

"So Frederick Striker's back, is he? Does Clare know?"

"How could she not? Striker is lodged in the salthouse."

"How peculiar."

"You do not seem unduly surprised, John."

"Few things surprise me these days."

"Brock Harding and this Striker fellow met at St Cedric's last Sunday. At first they squared up to each other like two fighting cocks."

"And then?"

"They shook hands."

"Peace and brotherhood?"

"More of the latter than the former, I suspect."

"Oh, yes," Galloway said. "Brotherhood would do it, would it not? Did Striker arrive with the Irish cargo by any chance?"

"Apparently not," the minister said, then launched into an account of the events he had witnessed, embroidered by acquired gossip. He concluded with a question. "Do you not think we should call upon Clare as soon as possible?"

"For what purpose?"

"To make sure she has come to no harm."

Galloway lifted a spoon and dug into the bowl of apple and ginger pudding that Ishbel had put out to cool some ten minutes before.

"Are you just going to sit there munching as if nothing has happened?" Soames said. "Haven't you heard a word I've said?"

"I heard you fine, Randolph. I just do not see what action you expect me to take at this late hour."

"It's only half past nine o'clock."

"Too late to go calling."

"I'm sure Clare would not object."

"I would not be so certain of that," Galloway said. "Hasn't it occurred to you that Clare may be entertaining Striker at this very moment?"

"What?"

"I doubt if she'll let him languish in the salthouse for long."

"What do you know of this affair?" Soames asked suspiciously.

"No more than you do," the doctor said. "How can I know more when I've been incarcerated in Glasgow University for the past fortnight, examining candidates for a testimonial granting of degrees?"

"Profitably?"

"The fee is niggardly, the business tedious," said John Galloway curtly, "but it's a necessary chore if I'm to continue to support myself in idleness here in Arcadia."

"I still think you're wasting your talents."

"My talents, such as they are, are long ago exhausted. I would be delighted to complete the process of retirement if I did not need an income to supplement my pensions."

Both Randolph Soames and John Galloway were the youngest sons of large families.

Galloway had been born and raised in Inverness where his father and brothers, physicians of the old school, still bled, purged and blistered the highland lairds and ladies who could afford their exorbitant fees. Young John had elected to leave the nest to study surgery at St Bartholomew's Hospital in London where he had specialised in the practice of obstetrics.

In due course, he had found himself an appointment in Manchester Infirmary where, over the years, he had gained a reputation for neatness and dexterity as a surgeon and accoucheur and was much respected for his gentleness and strict purity of morals. He had, however, also taken on the duties of surgeon to the Royal Manchester and Salford Volunteer Corps and had been sucked into ministering to those who were sick from no disease but poverty, an epidemic disorder which not even his skills could cure. Depressed and disillusioned, he had eventually resigned his Manchester posts and, at the age of forty-four, had returned to Scotland and the peace and quiet of coastal Ayrshire.

"Tell me about the orphans," Galloway said. "Have you heard how many were brought and to whom they were sold?"

"The brothers will not talk to me. They take refuge behind their dreadful oaths of secrecy. However, I believe Rose Tannahill has one of them out at the Leddings."

"A child?"

"No, a young woman, extraordinarily beautiful to look upon. She came with the Tannahills to the preaching on Sunday and I strongly suspect that she is one of the Hardings' imports."

"What's Rose Tannahill doing with her?"

"Another mystery Clare might be able to solve," Randolph Soames said. "We could be knocking on Clare's door in twenty minutes, you know."

Galloway grinned, "Aye, and be beaten about the head by Pratie Kerrigan's broom-handle."

"Why are you so shy about visiting Headrick? Is Clare Quinn's welfare no longer your concern?"

"If Clare needs my advice she'll ask for it," Galloway said. "I'll call on her tomorrow, or the next day."

"Why not tonight?"

The doctor dabbled at the remains of his pudding and said nothing.

"Great heavens!" the minister exclaimed. "Surely you do not suppose that she is actually *with* Striker."

"I suppose nothing of the sort."

"Oh, Galloway, Galloway, you cannot lie to me. I've known you too long to be deceived. You're afraid we'll discover Clare in this English fellow's arms. But does she not loathe and detest him?"

"Remember, Randolph, Striker was once her lover," John Galloway said. "First loves are not so easily put aside. I'll see what I can find out tomorrow."

"Do let me know what you uncover."

"Of course."

"First thing?" the minister asked.

"First thing," the doctor answered and, patting his friend on the shoulder, rose to ask Ishbel to ask Eppie if he might open a second bottle of claret.

*   *   *

It was late when Clare quit the drawing-room for the back parlour. Light in the kitchen indicated that Pratie and Mrs Shay were still up and about and in all likelihood discussing the scandalous events of the week and speculating on why their mistress had taken leave of her senses.

The little servants, like Melissa, would be sound asleep. Henri Leblanc had also been put to bed and lay, snoring volubly, in the larger of the vacant bedrooms.

The information that Henri had imparted had set Clare's mind into a whirl. But he had also entertained them most royally by playing a medley of songs, French, English and Irish, with words simple enough for Melissa to imitate.

It had been many years since the drawing-room had rung with such merriment. It had not escaped Clare's attention, or Melissa's, that the increase in M. Leblanc's jollity was related to the level of whisky in the decanter.

"Mama, is M. Leblanc drunk?"

"Perhaps just a little."

"Mama, I think he's falling off the stool."

"In that case I think we should find somewhere for him to lie down."

"In our house?"

"M. Leblanc is in no fit state to walk, dearest, let alone find his way to the salthouse."

"Will he have Papa's room?"

"No, the big room at the corridor's end."

Henri had boozily acquiesced to Clare's suggestion that he be escorted upstairs.

Cheerfully aware of his condition, he had chuckled to himself as he'd tottered up the staircase and along the passageway, "I am drunk. *Mon Dieu!* How drunk I am! Heh-heh-heh," and had fallen upon the old oak bed with arms akimbo and, still smiling, had fallen asleep instantly.

Now that she was alone in the back parlour Clare knelt before the fire and watched the little blue and yellow flames trickling through the coals. She was disappointed that Frederick had not come scurrying to Headrick, resentful of the fact that she had taken Henri into her house and apprehensive lest the Frenchman revealed things that she, Clare, was not supposed to know.

How long she sat there brooding Clare had no notion.

She was eventually disturbed by a knock upon the parlour door and, thinking that it might be Frederick come late, scrambled hastily to her feet.

"Who is it?"

"Me, Mrs Quinn." Pratie threw open the door. "Can I be havin' a word with you?"

Although it was only about ten o'clock Pratie was already in her night attire, her red face framed by a cotton bonnet.

"It's not right," the housekeeper said.

"If you're going to berate me, Pratie, the least you can do is close the door first."

Pratie Kerrigan slammed the door behind her and folded her arms ominously.

"It's not good enough, Mrs Quinn. First it's the foreigner, next it'll be Striker."

"I'm not sure I understand your complaint," Clare said.

"If you're not careful Striker will have his foot in the door, the rest of him will follow and before you can say 'knife' the devil will be in your bed."

"How dare you?" Clare snapped. "If you think so little of my manners and my morals you are at liberty to seek another position without waiting for quarter-day."

Pratie was taken aback by the threat of dismissal. Her tone became peevish and wheedling.

"You may think you know this Striker mannie," she said, "but take my word for it, Mrs Quinn, you don't know the half of what went on under this roof last time he was here."

"If you are about to tell me how Mr Striker persuaded Mr Quinn to invest money in smuggling salt and then – "

"Not the salt," the housekeeper said, "the women."

"What women?"

"Every woman he could leech upon."

"Servants, do you mean?"

"Other mens' wives," Pratie said. "My mistress among them."

The information was new to Clare but somehow it came as no surprise. "Was Mr Quinn aware of what was going on?"

"How could he be otherwise? The mistress was daft with yearnin' for Frederick Striker. She would have run away with him if he'd given her half a chance."

"How do you know, Pratie?"

"She confided in me. She wept in my arms."

"What did you do?"

"I told the master, o' course," Pratie said. "I told him he should throw her out. But he was too generous for his own good was Mr Quinn. He forgave her."

"Well, what you've just told me comes as no great surprise," Clare said. "Mr Striker has always nurtured a reputation as a ladies' man."

"A ladies' man! He was a devil, Mrs Quinn, a devil and a despoiler. He seduced Bob Gowrie's wife too."

"Who told you that?"

"She told me herself, not long before she died." Pratie scowled and nodded. "She thought the last bairn, the daft lassie, might have been Striker's."

Clare said, "I cannot say this information pleases me, Pratie, but it does not shock me. May I point out that all of this happened years ago and that Frederick has changed."

"The devil doesn't change," Pratie said. "He's wicked through an' through. I couldn't stand by silent-like and see you deceived by him again."

"I thank you for your concern, Pratie," Clare said. "But you have my word that you will never spy Frederick Striker creeping out of *my* bedroom. If I bring him here to lodge it will not be out of love."

"Why do you want him here at all?"

"To keep an eye on him."

"Huh!" said Pratie. "Do you really think he's changed?"

"He has certainly grown older."

"He's the same man, Mrs Quinn, the same wicked man he always was. He'll get what he wants – regardless."

"But what *does* he want, Pratie?"

The housekeeper opened her mouth to reply, thought better of it and stubbornly shook her head.

"Frederick Striker may not have changed, Pratie, but I have."

"Keep him away."

"No."

"Do you intend to bring him here to lodge?"

"Yes, and the Frenchman too," Clare said. "If you wish to leave then I will not stop you. I'll see to it that you are paid for the half-year and have excellent letters of recommendation. But I would much prefer you to stay, not just for my sake but for Melissa's."

"Huh!"

"I don't expect you to be friendly to Frederick Striker. I ask only that you attend him as diligently as you would any guest of the house," Clare said. "To cope with the extra work I'll see to it that another servant is employed."

"No call for that," said Pratie. "It's not the extra work that worries me."

"Do you really wish to leave Headrick?"

"That I do not."

"Then stay," Clare said. "And help me."

"If that's what you want, if you're sure."

"I'm sure," said Clare.

"What about Bob Gowrie? What will you do about him?"

"Let Frederick take care of him," Clare said and saw Pratie Kerrigan grin as a glimmer of understanding dawned.

*   *   *

It would have been a simple matter for Robertson Blyth to slip away to visit Eleanor during daylight hours but somehow the urges which drove him to the Leddings were things of the night. Besides, he felt more obligation to the colliery than he did to his wife and while he might possibly bring himself to betray the latter, to the former he would always be true.

He still had not decided what to do with the Irish girl or if it would be possible to fit her permanently into the intricate pattern of his existence for she was too beautiful and original to be hidden from sight and comment for long. It was not then to remove her but to enjoy her that Robbie Blyth stole out of Cairns that calm, cold February night, with the excuse that Mr Soames had requested his attendance at a Session meeting in the manse.

The night was clear, the sky sprinkled with stars and the

coalmaster was roused by the prospect of lying with a fresh young girl under the wide night sky. He expected no resistance from Rose Tannahill. He would slip a guinea into the old woman's hand and take the girl out for an hour and lie with her on his plaidie among the whins in what the poets were wont to call "bucolic reverie".

He dismounted at the cottage, tied Pranzo's rein to the trellis and rapped on the door.

Rose Tannahill appeared instantly, as if she had been lying in wait for him, her wrinkled face as sour as a crab-apple, not welcoming but defiant.

"I wish to see the Irish girl," Robertson Blyth said. "Fetch her to me, please."

"She's fast asleep."

"Waken her."

"Have you come to take her away?"

"No," Robertson Blyth said, "only to – to have converse with her for an hour or so."

"You can converse in our kitchen," Rose Tannahill said. "I'll see to it you're not disturbed."

"I prefer to converse with her privately," said Robertson Blyth. "I'll take her for a walk by the burn."

"And have her freeze to death?"

"Do not argue with me. Fetch her immediately."

"Very well, Mr Blyth," the old woman said. "But will ·· not step inside and wait in comfort while I see her dressed to please you properly."

The coalmaster was reluctant to enter the cottage. He had heard so many strange tales about Rose Tannahill.

Angus McGonigle had even barred her from the kirk but Mr Soames had dismissed as pagan cant the elders' suggestions that she was in league with Auld Nick and had restored her to membership of St Cedric's.

At the time he had sided with the minister's rationalist stance but now he was less sure of his ground. He did not believe that Rose Tannahill was actually in cahoots with Lucifer but her gifts of divination and her sympathy with girls who got themselves into trouble were legendary.

Apprehensively Blyth followed the old woman into the cluttered kitchen.

He looked about for Eleanor, saw only garlands hanging from beams, jars and skulls, stones and pans, cats skulking under worn wicker chairs.

"Where is she?" he said.

"In bed, next door," the old woman said. "Show me your paper, Mr Blyth."

"Paper? What paper?"

"The document Harding gave you. The false contract."

"I – I do not have it upon my person," Robertson Blyth said. "What right have you – Look, where is Eleanor?"

"Safe," Rose Tannahill said. "Unless you can show me a document that names you as her master, Mr Blyth, I canna give her over."

"In God's name, woman, what drivel's this?"

The old woman did not answer. She swung away and swung back, holding in her hand a heavy leather pouch. The coalmaster flinched, as if she had offered him a snake or a live coal.

"What is that?"

"Thirty pounds," the old woman said. "More than the price you paid for her. Take it, sir, an' go."

"What trick are you up to now?"

"I wish to keep the girl here."

"Did she put you up to this?"

"She wishes to stay with me."

"Damn it! Let me speak to her."

"She doesna wish to see you, Mr Blyth."

"Where is she? What have you done with her?"

"I've done nothing with her."

"Why will you not let me speak with her?"

"Because she's afraid of you."

"Afraid?" said Robertson Blyth. "Afraid of me? Good God, woman, have you not told her who I am? Come along, fetch her out."

"Have you found a place for her at Cairns?"

"I have – have the matter in hand."

"What place have you in mind for Eleanor, Mr Blyth? Is she to serve as your wife's chambermaid, maybe? Is she to take over Mr Fingal's duties an' bathe you an' dress you?"

Robertson Blyth's lips were frozen. He could think of nothing to say. The girl had told the old woman everything.

"Perhaps I should take her to Mr Soames and see if he can find a place for her," Rose Tannahill suggested.

"No, I – "

He felt . . . demeaned. The sensation was so familiar that he recognised it instantly but his response was violent, not meek.

He cuffed the purse from the old woman's hand and fastened his fingers upon her aged throat.

"Stop that, Mr Blyth." The coalmaster was lifted and swung in the air as if he had no more weight than a feather pillow. "Don't dare touch my mother again."

Norman Tannahill wore a nightshirt of coarse linen, plain as a priest's vestment. The sheer size of the man was intimidating but Robertson Blyth fought to control his fear by reminding himself that he owned the souls and bodies of a dozen men bigger and stronger than the cottager's son.

"I want to see Eleanor," he said. "I'll not leave until I do."

Rose gave a signal of assent. Norman pulled back the dividing curtain and beckoned Robertson Blyth to step to the threshold of the little room next door.

A nightlight burned in a bowl, yellow as a daffodil. By its light the coalmaster looked down on Eleanor Antrim. She sat upright in the narrow bed, a sheet gathered to her breasts, head tilted, eyes upon him. She was clad in a simple linen gown. Uncapped, her hair fell in ebony rivulets about her white shoulders.

"Girl, do you wish to stay here?" Robertson Blyth said.

"Aye."

"I'll take you away if you wish it."

"I do not wish it."

His desire was stronger and more obstinate than ever.

He should have been relieved at being rid of his guilty burden; instead he was filled with anger.

He experienced a wild urge to strike Tannahill down, to tear the sheet from the girl's body, to fling her across the bed and enter her, to have her draw from him once more the great coarse cry of release that had echoed among the empty pews of St Cedric's church that night last month.

He held out his hand. "Then pay me."

The purse dropped into his palm.

He regarded the girl he had owned and lost for one long icy moment, said, "Stay here then, and be damned," and, turning, stepped out into wintry darkness once more.

*   *   *

"Has he gone?" Rose Tannahill said.

"Aye, Mam."

"Are you not cold, Norman?"

"No."

104

"Come in, though. Close and bar the door."

"Bar it?"

"In case he comes back."

"He'll not come back," Norman said.

The girl was up and in the kitchen. For the sake of warmth, not modesty, she had draped a blanket about her shoulders and had seated herself on Rose's chair by the fire. Her eyes were watchful.

"Did you hear, lass?" Rose said.

"I heard."

"The money I paid to Blyth doesn't bind you to us. If you wish to leave we'll not stand in your way."

"Why would I be wishin' to leave? Where would I go?"

"Back where you came from," Rose said.

"What's behind me is far worse than anythin' here."

"What is behind you?" Rose Tannahill asked.

Norman remained by the door. He seemed enormously tall in the low-ceilinged kitchen but in spite of the half-length gown not in the least comical.

"I was born to a high lady in Dublin." Eleanor drew the blanket tightly about her. "She couldn't keep me, though, for I was not conceived to her husband. She put me out before I was weaned but the nurse in the house had no patience and when I was old enough she flung me into a Brat School. I was servant to the Superintendent but when he died his wife would have none of me, since she had her eyes set on a new husband. She found me a place on a boat to Scotland where I was supposed to have a position in a house to go to – but did not." Eleanor paused, then added, "That's all there is to me, Missus, I swear."

"Where's the lady who gave you birth?"

"Dead."

"She left you nothing?"

"Only her name."

"Eleanor Antrim?"

"Aye."

The story was a familiar one, Rose Tannahill thought, but surely the high-born lady had bequeathed Eleanor more than her name. No doubt the girl's beauty was descended from fine, pure, cultivated stock, quite suitable for a Tannahill to marry.

"Let's see now what will become of you, Eleanor," Rose said. "It's time to see what the serpent's egg can tell us about your future."

105

A faint expression of alarm, undetected by either of the Tannahills, passed over the Irish girl's face as Rose turned to the dresser in search of the crystal.

It was contained in a stout wooden box and wrapped in thick black velvet to protect it from destructive light.

The sphere had been handed on to Rose by her grandmother, a far-sighted woman, a famous scryer and clairvoyant.

She had told Rose that the crystal was the egg of a sea-serpent which had lived once in the depths of the ocean. It had been carried to the Isle of Skye by a servant who had stolen it from a wizard at the Court of the Russian kings. And this servant had given it to his island wife who had the power to see in its icy depths visions of past and future events. And that gifted wife had been a Tannahill. And so the egg had been passed on along the female line until it had come down to her, to Rose.

Eleanor appeared to listen with rapt attention while Rose placed the egg upon the table and folded the cloth around it to make a soft dark sort of nest.

She beckoned Eleanor to sit herself at the table.

Nervously Eleanor obeyed.

Norman moved behind her, a large brown-skinned hand resting upon her shoulder. He kept back from the crystal, though, for he had no wish to distort its emanations and when his mother instructed the girl to lift the crystal Norman broke contact with her.

Rose said, "Hold the – "

"I know what to do," said Eleanor.

She closed her eyes, lifted the crystal and pressed it against her breast.   Once or twice Rose had consulted the crystal on her son's behalf and had seen the birth of the world in the dark glass and a great olive-green serpent coiled in a sea-cave, flame bubbling through it and ice like a lid overhead. She had seen good things and bad things but she had refused to tell him what they were lest she corrupt him with knowledge that no man should possess.

Watching the Irish girl now Norman felt that at last he had an inkling of what those mysteries might be.

Two or three minutes passed in silence before Rose eased the crystal from Eleanor's grasp.

She took the egg into her own hands and peered into it as into a pool. Her features softened as she gazed into the liquid blue core and she appeared to sink at once into a state of waking abstraction.

106

Eleanor glanced at Norman.

He touched her reassuringly.

"What do you see there, Missus," Eleanor asked. "My future or my past?"

Rose gave a little cry of distress. "Nothing."

"Clouds?"

"Nothing."

"Colours?"

"Nothing."

Eleanor released her breath, then, almost with levity, said, "Do you not see a ship? A waxing moon? The sun high over the horizon?"

"I see neither dark nor light, green nor orange," Rose said and, before the girl could ask more of her, let the sphere roll from her fingers on to the velvet cloth.

"Perhaps it's too early," Eleanor said. "Perhaps we should try again at the evenin' hour on the next rising moon."

"What do you know of risin' moons?" Rose asked.

"I've seen crystal readin' done before. The old wife who attended the Superintendent was far-sighted. She used a jet-black crystal, though, and saw all sorts of queer things in it. She told the master when he was like to die."

"What did she find when she read for you?"

"Nothing – just like now," Eleanor said. "Let me hold the crystal again. Perhaps it'll work if I hold it longer."

"No, no, enough for one night," Rose said. "I'm tired."

Hastily she wrapped the crystal in its cloth and locked it away in the box.

The absence of aura disturbed her. She had known it happen only twice before, with a woman of low morals, and with a man who was no better than a brute. She had expected Eleanor Antrim to light up the egg like a lantern and now she was obliged to take the girl on trust.

"Go now, son," Rose said. "I'll sit up awhile."

Eleanor leaned towards the old woman and, in a low voice, asked, "Is it him you want me for? Is that it?"

Rose Tannahill studied her beautiful face for a long moment before she answered, "Aye. For him."

"I thought as much," Eleanor said and, gripping Norman's hand in hers, led him to the little staircase and up the stairs to his bed.

Nine

The long garden behind the breast-high wall that fronted his villa was John Galloway's pride and joy. He was in constant competition with Randolph Soames in matters of cultivation and poured scorn on the minister for the fact that he, Soames, employed the services of a man and a boy to do his spade work.

The minister, of course, had the Glebe to contend with for the Glebe came as an addendum to his stipend and provided extra income from what could be grown or pastured there. Even so, John Galloway played mercilessly upon the minister's advantage and was forever rubbing it in that any ninny could toddle round the beds with a little watering can and that the art of the cultivator lay in trenching, strewing, weeding, pruning and plucking, skills which separated the genuine gardener from the mere dilettante.

Reverend Soames did not take kindly to being called a dilettante. He was forever thrusting great bunches of Agrippinas or Picta-Formosismas at the doctor, dahlias raised from slips, armfuls of untinged tulips or bouquets of China roses as large as cauliflowers.

In return he would receive baskets crammed with shallots, elephantine stalks of rhubarb and brilliant nosegays of parsley and carrots, the latter sweet as saccharin and, even Soames had to admit, far too good to waste on horsefeed.

Throughout the dreary winter months an amnesty existed between the rivals.

They would huddle round the fire and put their heads together over seed catalogues and lists of apples and peas and, like women shopping amid a sea of calicoes, become thoroughly confused by the number of varieties on offer.

Clare left the care of Headrick's plots entirely to Norman Tannahill. Only her position as a friend to both gentlemen entitled her to arbitrate on the fragrance of flowers and the edibility of the vegetables and fruit that were showered upon her. She was careful to bestow praise even-handedly although, on balance, she thought John's garden showed the better of the two even on a dull February morning.

When the gig drew up at the doctor's front gate Clare was pleased to see her friend upon the doorstep, although she had sent no word of her intention to call. He was dressed in a plain tweed waistcoat and striped shirt, sleeves rolled up as if it was already summer. His breeks were fastened about his calves not with tapes but with neat horn buttons. Hands in pockets, legs spread, he was surveying the manure-strewn flower beds and the quiet little orchard of fruit trees with an air of satisfaction.

When he saw Clare, however, he hopped from the doorstep and strode, beaming, to the wicket gate that opened to the road. So pleased was she to see her doctor friend that Melissa would have been over the side of the vehicle if Clare had not held on to her skirts.

"Dr Galloway, Dr Galloway," the little girl called excitedly. "We're going to Irvine. We're going to Irvine. Are you coming too?"

John Galloway vaulted the gate without opening it and, reaching up, lifted Melissa into his arms and admired her bonnet and curls and the patterned cashmere shawl that Mama had pinned about her.

"My, how you've grown, young lady!" he said. "An inch at least in height and several pounds avoirdupois." He lowered her to the ground. "Where are you off to at this early hour? Irvine, d'you say?"

"To buy ribbon," said Melissa.

"Yet more ribbon?" John Galloway said. "Gracious!"

"Are you coming too?" Melissa said again.

He glanced at Clare. "Am I invited?"

"Most cordially," Clare said, "if, that is, you have no engagements with patients and can spare the time."

"I have one engagement," he said. "I must call in upon Mrs Patterson, the brewer's wife at Skelty. She's due in twenty days. Since this is her first child she's heavy and uncomfortable. I've a relieving medicine for her, to help the water. The call will not take long."

"Skelty is on our way," said Clare. "We can stop there for as long as is necessary."

Clare wore a blue cloak with a fur-trimmed hood. The

morning air had rouged her cheeks and brought a bright, almost girlish glitter to her blue eyes.

"I've need to talk with you, John," Clare said. "Have you heard what has happened? Has Randolph told you?"

"He has told me as much as he knows."

"Tell Dr Galloway about the Froggie," Melissa put in. "We've a Froggie stayin' in our house, Dr Galloway."

"Hush, Melissa," Clare said. "Will you accompany us, John?"

"Of course," the doctor said. "Allow me to change into my shoes and find a suitable coat and I'll be with you directly."

He did not vault the gate a second time, Clare noticed, but unlatched it and hurried away up the path, calling out for Ishbel to fetch his buckled shoes.

Melissa leaned upon the gate and swung forth and back, making the hinges creak. She seemed to put the question not to Clare but to the garden and the trees.

"Why are we taking water to Mrs Patterson? Are there no pumps in Skelty?"

"It isn't water, it's medicine."

"Is Mrs Patterson ill?"

"She's expecting a baby, Melissa."

"Today?"

"No, but quite soon."

"Oh!" Melissa said and, curiosity appeased, went back to swinging gently on the gate.

*　　*　　*

The pony had excellent road manners and John Galloway had little to do to hold the gig to the brow of the road. Skelty was the most southerly of his ports of call. Beyond the brick-built brewery lay territory to which Irvine's three practitioners laid claim.

Galloway's mind was not on medical matters, however. He was far more concerned with Clare's account of Striker's reappearance in Ladybrook.

"As you see," Clare said, "I've already embarked upon a course of action. I hope that I might enlist your support, John, in seeing it through."

Melissa was tucked safely in the little seat behind Mama where she chattered quietly to the wooden-headed doll that he had brought as a gift from Glasgow.

"What do you propose, Clare – a voyage of discovery or a familiar crossing by another route?" Galloway asked.

"More of the former than the latter," Clare said.

"Are you still attached to Frederick Striker?"

"No."

"Are you sure you're not deceiving yourself?"

"I want him where I can see him," Clare said, "that's my only reason for inviting him to lodge at Headrick."

"Along with the Frenchman?"

"Yes."

"I'm not sure what you hope to gain by the association."

"Profit, for one thing," Clare said. "Frederick will, I'm sure, fulfil his part of the bargain and increase my takings from the saltworks."

"That's all very well, but why have you undertaken to support the Frenchman? You've seen nothing to suggest that he might produce a patentable device."

"Brock Harding believes in the Frenchman's experiments."

"Harding? Have you discussed the matter with Harding?"

"Certainly not," Clare retorted. "Nonetheless I have every reason to believe that Harding is impressed by Frederick's proposals."

"What leads you to such a conclusion?"

"The fact that Brock has not murdered him."

John Galloway laughed. "Give him time, Clare."

"I'm perfectly serious," Clare said primly. "I don't think you realise how vicious Brock used to be or how much he hated Frederick."

"Brock's certainly not a fellow I'd wish to cross," John Galloway said. "Tell me, Clare, why are you so intent on binding Striker to you?"

"Is it so obvious?"

"To me it is."

"I do not intend to harm Frederick, you know."

"It's you who might come to harm, Clare," the doctor said. "Please be careful."

"Rest assured, I will," Clare said.

"Now," John Galloway said, "perhaps you'd be good enough to inform me why we are travelling to Irvine?"

"To call upon Mr Greenslade."

"The lawyer. Why?"

"To have him alter the terms of my will."

"And my part?"

"To witness it," said Clare.

* * *

"What, in God's name, did you tell her?" Frederick demanded.

"Very little, very little," Henri croaked. "I played upon the pianoforte and sang to make amusement for the child."

"And drank more than was good for you?"

"Ahhh! How my head does pain."

"Put your feet in the water."

"Frederick, I am dying. I do not wish to become a corpse with feet of ice."

"Do it, Henri. It'll uncloud your brain."

The pair were perched on the barnacled rocks that enclosed the Headrick bucket pot. The pond itself was calm but a brisk little breeze from the sea slopped wavelets up towards the men and caused Henri, barefoot and bare-calved, to cling frantically to Frederick's arm, groaning all the while.

Impatiently the Englishman elbowed his suffering companion closer to the edge then, with a final nudge, unbalanced him. Crying out, Henri projected his cringing feet into the ocean and when the waves curled up to clasp his ankles and calves, fell back upon the rock like a sacrifice to old Poseidon.

Frederick pinned a forearm across the Frenchman's chest and, taking care to keep his own clothing dry, held him down. "Did I not tell you immersion would clear your head?"

"*Auuugh!*"

"What exactly did you say to Clare Quinn, Henri, to make her change her mind about us?"

"I t-t-told t-to her ab-b-bout m-my exp-p-eriments."

"On the strength of which she offered you capital, premises and a place in her house?" said Frederick sceptically.

"B-both of us, Frederick. B-both of us. L-let me up, I b-beg of you," Henri pleaded. "S-something is eating on my f-feet."

"Mullet, I expect."

"Mallet, what is mallet?" the Frenchman yelled.

Taking pity on his companion Frederick hauled him back on to the rock. Henri peered bleakly at his toes. "I am eaten. How many am I eaten?"

"Your toes are perfectly intact. Here, dry yourself with your stockings." Frederick watched the shivering Frenchman chafe at his legs and feet. "Don't you realise that Clare Quinn plied you with drink simply to loosen your tongue? God, Henri, sometimes you act like a simpleton."

"S-simpleton I may be, F-Frederick, but it is me that you should thank for our new lodgings."

"Did she ask about me?"

Henri shook his head.

"I trust you didn't tell her that I had been married?"

"But certainly not."

"*Did* she ask about me?"

"She asked only about what I would do here."

Frederick was silent for a moment or two while Henri buckled on his shoes and got shakily to his feet. He was still shivering but had lost the fuddled look of a man hung over with whisky fumes.

"I do not understand why she's being so generous and co-operative," Frederick muttered.

"She was not your lover?"

"Yes, of course she was."

"Perhaps she still cares for you, Frederick."

"I think she asked questions, which you answered. In a word, Henri, I think you're lying to me."

"I am not lying. I told her what I hoped to do, about my experiments and she offered to support me. Also to give the fish-shed for a laboratory."

"The fish-shed is smelly and dilapidated, you know."

"It is a roof and walls. It is all which I need."

"Are you sure Clare didn't ask about me?"

"Frederick, I tell you the truth."

"We'll see." Frederick got to his feet. "Come along. We'll pack our belongings and transport ourselves to Headrick House in style. How do you feel now, by the way?"

"F-frozen," said Henri Leblanc.

*　　*　　*

It was after six before Clare and Melissa returned from Irvine. Melissa had slept much of the way home. She had been cross when wakened and crosser still to discover that Dr Galloway had not been invited to Headrick for supper.

The plum-coloured ribbon that had been bought for her in Irvine offered no comfort from the grim February cold and she grumbled and groused to the wooden doll, which she had named Jane, during the final mile to the house.

113

She soon cheered up, however, when she discovered that her other friends, M. Leblanc and Frederick, had come to stay and were busily unpacking in rooms not far from her own.

M. Leblanc had Papa's room. Frederick was in the old part of the house in a room where Papa had kept his fishing rods and gun and where Papa's dog, Ming, had had his basket. Ming had been dead for a long time but the dog-smell lingered.

It was funny to look along the passageway and see flickers of firelight where she had never seen firelight before, the glimmer of a candle and Frederick's shadow passing like a ghost beyond the half-open door.

Melissa did not like Frederick's room. She was much taken with M. Leblanc's apartment, however, which already had lots of bottles and jars on the cabinet and on the long table. It reminded her of Mother Tannahill's cottage except that it had a different smell.

When Mama went off to talk to Mr Striker, Melissa showed Lizzie her new doll and let Lizzie try her new ribbon. Then Mama, a little red in the face, came back and Pratie arrived and there was a bustle to get dressed for supper. And when they were ready Pratie went off downstairs and rang the little handbell that Papa had used when he was ill.

It sounded different now, quite jolly. She heard the pleasant sound of men's voices in the passageway, a heavy manly tread upon the stairs.

Mama brushed her hair with the tips of her fingers and told her to behave herself and not talk too much.

Mama sounded breathless tonight and Melissa felt that Mama was as excited as she was about having strangers in the house to stay.

"Now, Melissa, let us go down," Mama said at last.

Off they went, like two fine ladies, swishing down the staircase and into the drawing-room where the gentlemen, standing, waited to greet them.

*   *   *

Clare Kelso had never been conventionally beautiful but her daintiness and colouring had made her immediately attractive. The quality had not diminished as she'd grown older. There was no swelter of desire in Frederick, only a wistful longing to have Clare for his own.

The child, however, was a problem he could not ignore,

a little marker which separated Clare past from Clare present.

Henri stepped forward. He fashioned a deep bow, took Clare's hand and kissed it, then did the same for the child, as if mother and daughter were equals.

"Madame, it gives me pleasure to be a guest in your house."

"It gives me pleasure too, Clare," Frederick said but without the Frenchman's affectation.

Perhaps he had been wrong to come here. Clare was too much in control in this comfortable, well-ordered house. She was protected by her child, her servants, by the very "virtuousness" of her situation.

"Please, do be seated," Clare said. "I've instructed supper to be served in a quarter of an hour. Before that I have something to say to you."

She bent from the waist and murmured into Melissa's ear. The child nodded and went out of the room, closing the door behind her.

Without the presence of the child Clare, to Frederick's relief, suddenly seemed more accessible.

Frederick flicked up his coat-tails and seated himself in the armchair by the fire.

"As M. Leblanc has no doubt informed you, Frederick, I have agreed to act as M. Leblanc's patron and sponsor," Clare said. "I will finance such experimental work as M. Leblanc wishes to undertake for a period of not less than one year. If in that time M. Leblanc's inventions prove of commercial value I shall, under our contract, participate in all profits that accrue from the lease of patents and shall be assigned a share of such patents for their fourteen-year term. In short, I will become an equal partner."

"I have already signed a partnership agreement of sorts with Henri," said Frederick.

"Is that true, M. Leblanc?"

"Madame, it is."

"In that case it will be rendered void by the signing of a new agreement which my lawyer, Mr Greenslade, will present to you within the week."

"Am I to be excluded?" Frederick said.

"Of course not. I will honour the original agreement but will see to it that Mr Greenslade adjusts the terms and percentages accordingly."

"An even division, I trust?" said Frederick.

"Perfectly even," Clare said. "M. Leblanc, do you find my proposal satisfactory?"

"Yes, Madame, I do."

"Frederick?"

"I'll have to study the documents before I agree."

"I would expect no less of you," Clare said. "In addition to meeting bills for apparatus and chemicals I will provide M. Leblanc with the use of the building which lies south of the salthouse and which, I believe, you have already inspected. Also, I will lodge you both under my roof for the period of one year. I will charge nothing for lodging and will make sure that you are adequately provisioned. Small beer and ale will be served as you desire it but if you wish wine or spirits you must purchase them for yourself."

"How much, in financial terms, are you willing to put towards stocking the laboratory?" Frederick said.

"M. Leblanc assures me that two hundred pounds will be sufficient to that end."

"I was led to believe that you were short of funds."

"Increased salt production and sales will ensure that I do not fall into debt," Clare said. "I'm depending upon you to keep your promise, Frederick. Now, do you wish to dispute the conditions of our agreement?"

Frederick's forehead was beaded with sweat. He touched his wrist to his brow. Why was Clare seeking to hedge him round with lawyers' contracts? Why had she leapt to assume the burden of patronage for Leblanc when, surely, she hadn't the least idea what Henri could produce? She was so cool and practical that he could not begin to believe that she was doing it out of love for him.

"M. Leblanc?" Clare said.

"I have no dispute, Madame Quinn."

"Frederick?"

"I – your generosity – "

"Overwhelms you?"

Already she had granted him almost everything he had come to Ladybrook to acquire and by her rapid acquiescence had negated every one of his plans. That, he suddenly realised, was what he resented.

"Yes, I am overwhelmed," he said.

"My servants will attend your household needs but if you require your clothes brushed or boots polished I suggest you reward the maids with occasional small emoluments." She

116

seemed to be finished and moved towards the door when she was struck by what appeared to be an afterthought. "By the by, I've employed an extra day-maid. Fortunately I was able to find a local girl in search of a position. Now, gentlemen, will we seal our agreement in a traditional manner with handshakes and whisky?"

"An excellent suggestion," Henri said.

Frederick's hands were trembling slightly. He tucked his elbows to his sides to hide the frailty.

Even before he heard Clare call out her name, before the girl appeared in the doorway, he had a sudden presentiment of what was about to happen.

Demure and deferential, Eleanor Antrim carried in a wooden tray with a decanter and glasses upon it.

Her jet-black hair was hidden by a neat muslin bonnet, a bib covered her bosom. No one could possibly have guessed by her appearance that not so long ago she had been his mistress and, before that, a common Dublin whore.

"Thank you, Eleanor," Clare said. "Put it upon the oval table, if you please."

The girl slid the tray carefully on to the table and turned. "Will that be all, Missus Quinn?"

"That will be all, thank you."

Eleanor bobbed a curtsey and, without so much as a glance at Frederick, glided out of the room.

"Is – is that the new day-maid?" Frederick said.

"Yes," Clare said. "Why do you ask?"

"She's exceedingly pretty."

"Ah yes, of course. I'd almost forgotten what a fast eye you have for beauty, Frederick," Clare said. "Whisky for you, M. Leblanc?"

"A small one, if you please."

"Frederick?"

"With water," Frederick answered and, still trembling, crept forward to take the glass.

Ten

It took M. Leblanc the best part of an hour to dispose of the Phlogiston Theory and the composition of the colourless, odourless and still mysterious gas called oxygen.

Oxygen, Henri explained, had replaced "Phlogiston" as the focus of chemical attention as a result of Antoine Lavoisier's experiments at the *Académie Royale*, experiments in which he, Henri Leblanc, had been privileged to participate.

By this time half the Sons of Apollo had entered into combination with Morpheus and the other half were beginning to wonder what miracle process the Frenchman thought he had developed that hadn't been known to iron founders for umpteen years. At this point in the proceedings, however, Henri's manner changed from one of droning pedantry to that of a mischievous schoolboy. Grinning, he produced from beneath the table a huge wooden box and plucked from it, like a conjurer, the proper tools of his trade. Dishes of glazed porcelain were dealt out like playing cards, rubber bladders snapped between finger and thumb, chemical jars rattled like dice.

"Oxygen," Henri went on, "is a simple substance, an element composed of single atoms. It is the most common of all elements in the three kingdoms of bodies. It demonstrates caloric affinities which, when separated, can be reformed in gaseous conditions, an instantaneous union which produces fiery matter and, in consequence, heat."

On uttering the word "heat" Henri shovelled a spoonful of greasy-grey powder into a porcelain dish and poured upon it a few drops of water from a wine glass. The *whaff* of flame which shot from the dish awakened even the determined sleepers and caused more consternation than admiration.

"Do not sniff, my friends," Henri cried, "for gunpowder you will not smell. No smell. Only heat. Heat and light."

"How much heat?" Brock Harding asked.

"Sufficient heat to render metal malleable."

118

"Can't you demonstrate that wonder for us?"

"I have been invited here to demonstrate." Henri held up a forefinger which the audience stared at as if expecting it to shoot sparks. "Therefore I will do so. But I cannot give you more than a – a – "

"Peep," Frederick prompted.

"Yes, a 'peep' at the powers of elastic fluids."

"Why?" said Brock.

"Because it's a trick," said Mr Ormiston. "Damn it all, I've made more of a fire with coal-oil on straw."

"No," said a voice from the rear of the room.

Everyone turned to stare at Robertson Blyth.

"We're being unfair to our visitor and, dare I say it, a bit obtuse," the coalmaster said. "If minute quantities of materials produce a small effect then surely we must expect greater effects from greater quantities."

"Eh?" said Daniel Harding.

"Greater quantity of materials is not a necessity," said Henri. "It is the manner in which the combination of materials is delivered which increases effective heat."

"What will the raw materials cost?" Brock asked.

"At the first, much money," Henri admitted.

"Seems to me," said Cabel Harding, "materials should be cheap enough since it's only air you're usin'."

"No," Robertson Blyth interrupted. "Don't you see, Cabel, it's not air as we breathe it but *dephlogisticated* air. That's the difference. Brock, we should listen to this man."

"I am listening," Brock Harding said. "But right now I'd prefer to see what these fancy theories add up to."

"With pleasure, sir," Henri said. "If you would care to gather round the platform I will make assembly of my parts."

Charcoal panniers were lighted beneath two copper retorts and the vessels filled with liquids measured from special flasks. Water was added. The necks of the retorts were sealed with cork to a pair of rubber bladders which hung on from a wooden clamp.

The charcoal burned slowly and evenly and, in due course, the bladders began to expand.

During the process Henri explained the principles of gas separation but would not reveal the nature of the substances which the vessels contained.

That, he declared, was his secret.

At length the bladders were plump enough to do the job.

119

Henri dived a hand into his box and brought out an iron tube like a stout little gun barrel. On one end of the tube were two nippled apertures, on the other a metal bulb and a brass nozzle. The metal parts, Henri said, had been made to exact specification by a Dublin gunsmith.

He called for the doors to be closed and asked that he be given a piece of metal. An old key was found and handed up to the chemist who attached it to a clamp placed an inch or so from the brass nozzle.

It was very quiet in the over-room.

The brothers glowered apprehensively at Henri's accumulation of apparatus which seemed not at all Euclidean but, candidly, little more than an untidy mess.

Frederick had seen the demonstration many times before and had no fear of its consequences. The experiment did not become dangerous until the volume of gas was greatly increased.

He glanced at Robertson Blyth. Stiff with concentration, the coalmaster wore a high-browed, lofty look as he watched Henri attach the bladders to the nipples, align the nozzle with the key and casually lean a hip upon the table.

"My friends, are you prepared?" Henri asked.

"Aye, damn it. Get on with it, sir."

"Do not look away, I beg you," Henri said, "because I cannot repeat the event or its outcome."

"All right. We're a-watchin'."

Softly, almost sensually, Henri placed his hands around the bladders and palpated them for a moment, then squeezed them firmly.

Leaning across the table he lit a wax taper from the charcoal and wafted a trail of strong black smoke in the air.

"*Attention!*" he cried, touched the tiny brass tap with a fingertip and flicked the taper towards the nozzle.

There was an abrupt fierce roar, flame jetted out and, in the blink of an eye, dissolved the key to a blob of molten metal.

Henri turned off the tap.

The jet died away but what remained of the key continued to drip and splash, cooling, on to a tin plate.

"Good God!" said Cabel Harding.

"Astonishing!" said Robertson Blyth. "Astonishing and amazing."

"Did you see it?" said Daniel. "Did you see it, Dad?"

"I saw it, son," Brock Harding said. He stepped to the

120

platform's edge and offered his hand to the Frenchman. "You, sir, are to be congratulated."

Henri preened and bowed.

And Frederick knew that, not unexpectedly, he had trouble on his hands with a vengeance.

*   *   *

She tried to lose herself in sleep but she could not shut out the violent sounds of love-making from the bed upstairs.

In distraction she paced the kitchen while creaking joists sent down little rains of dust, the girl squealed and giggled and Norman, her Norman, groaned and grunted in painful ecstasy. She covered her ears with her hands and sank helplessly into the fireside chair, rocking and rocking forth and back, forth and back, as if she was nursing him still.

She was not entitled to be so distraught. Her son and his lover were doing nothing wrong. Their selfishness was indicative of a fertile passion. And as she rocked her old body in the chair by the fire Rose consoled herself by imagining the sturdy child that would surely result from such a mating.

"Mother?"

She had fallen asleep with head bowed, back bowed, chin on chest. She felt dazed and sore.

"Mother, Mother?" He shook her gingerly. Did he suppose her to be so old and mortal that she would slide away from him in her sleep?

She opened her eyes. "I'm here, son, still here."

The nightgown clung wet to his chest and thighs. She could smell his sweat.

Behind him, in shadow, the girl waited, arms crossed over her breasts, hair tangled like thorn.

"What time is it?" Rose said.

"It's late," Norman told her.

She raised herself a little in the chair.

"Mam," Norman said, "I wish to marry Eleanor."

"Aye," Rose said. "It might be just as well."

"I think we should be wed soon," Norman said.

"Are you sure she's the one for you, son?"

"I'm sure."

"Will she have you?"

From the shadows Eleanor murmured, "Aye, Missus Tannahill, I'll have him."

121

"Do we have your blessing, Mam?"

"Aye, son," Rose said, "you do."

*   *   *

The meat came slabbered with greasy gravy and the potatoes were burned. Henri was less than impressed by the Neptune's *haute cuisine* and contented himself with a slice of bread and a glass of claret while the brothers tucked into beef augmented by something that had once been cabbage.

Supper had been brought up to the over-room and served upon a table by the fire, as far away as possible from Henri's flasks and bladders.

The men who had been invited to stay for supper were all keen to learn more about his experiments and Henri had difficulty in parrying their questions about costs and applications without seeming too vague or defensive.

Henri had facts and formulae coming out of his ears but they related mainly to complex chemical structures and not to pounds and pence. He was, however, no fool. He was well aware that Clare's offer of a partnership had placed Frederick in a difficult position and that the spectacular success of the evening's demonstration had only made matters worse.

Brock stuffed a forkful of beef into his mouth and tapped Frederick impatiently on the sleeve. "Come on, Freddie, stop bein' so damned coy. You came to us in search of money and money's to be had. You don't have to scratch for it. Blyth and me will shell out for a share of the patent."

"I tell you," Robertson Blyth put in, "I have seldom been so impressed. With a larger model of your device, M. Leblanc, one could cut waggonway tracks in no time at all. One could – "

"Put blacksmiths out of business," Daniel Harding said. "I ain't so impressed by that prospect."

"It's progress, son," Brock said, "and since somebody's got to build the devices it might as well be blacksmiths."

"If it's a question of capital," Blyth said, "I would certainly be prepared to put forward a substantial sum to enable M. Leblanc to develop his invention and secure a patent upon it."

"Hadn't you better ask your wife first?" Cabel said. "McCracken might not like you throwin' his money around."

"I'm not without funds of my own," the coalmaster said. "In fact, I would insist that the shares were assigned to me, not to the McCrackens."

"There you are, Fred," Brock said. "Partners galore. Now all we've got to do is settle how much it's a-goin' to sting us to buy in."

"Unfortunately – " Frederick cleared his throat, " – the shares in the patent are no longer for sale."

"What? I thought you were desperate for partners."

"Ah, no. The partnership is, alas, closed."

"Watch out, Dad," Cabel said. "This johnnie is tryin' to boost the price."

"No," Frederick said. "It's not that."

"Give us a taste then," Cabel said.

"I can't. For the time being at least the partnership is closed."

Brock drummed his knuckles on the table. "If you didn't have anythin' to sell, Freddie, why did you lead us on?"

"I thought you might be interested in the scientific aspects of – "

Brock's fingers gripped Frederick's arm.

Cabel and Daniel got to their feet and Henri discreetly closed his fist about the handle of a beef knife.

"It is not Frederick who you must blame," Henri said. "It was me who took on the other partner."

"Just who is this other partner?" Brock demanded.

"Clare Quinn," said Frederick.

Brock laughed and playfully buffed Frederick's chin with his knuckles. "You devil," he said, admiringly. "You intend to have it all, don't you, Freddie? If you can't have the whole piece you'll strip it from the lady pound by pound."

Frederick allowed a smile to twist the corner of his mouth. "No pulling the wool over your eyes, Brock. You've hit the mark first time." He placed a forefinger to his lips. "But mum's the word. Promise me, gentlemen, mum is the word."

"Depend on it, Fred," Brock said and with laughter rumbling in his chest raised his glass to honour Brother Striker and the gullible Mrs Quinn.

*   *   *

From the window at the corridor's end Frederick peered down into the yard. He had kept vigil yesterday but had somehow missed her. She had been in the kitchen when he'd come down for breakfast and she had served him without a sign of recognition. Today he'd been up long before dawn and had watched her emerge from the darkness that shrouded the Leddings. She had been accompanied by the cottager's son, a sullen fellow, and in the kitchen yard they had parted with, to Frederick's chagrin, a kiss.

Frederick had first encountered Eleanor on the Dublin quays when she had been plying her trade for less than six months. From the moment he'd clapped eyes on her he had known that his luck was on the turn and that he had found what he was looking for at last.

He'd paid thirty pounds to the bawd who'd kept her and had at once begun to groom Eleanor to take her place in polite society. His plans had changed, however, when he'd discovered that the girl's tale of bastardy and abandonment was more than banal invention. By some miracle Eleanor had clung to her birth name, her mother's name, and was able to direct him towards the elderly, wealthy widow O'Neill, who still lived in a mansion in Chalmers Street.

Frederick's mission had been charitable, perhaps even sentimental, in its intention. He'd hoped only to bring mother and daughter together again. If a small price was attached to the service – well, the widow O'Neill could certainly afford it. When he'd found the poor old dame susceptible to his charms, however, he'd changed his plans for a second time, had wooed her and wed her all within a three month. He'd said nothing to the old lady about the existence of a long-lost daughter but had set up Eleanor in a house in the Liberties while they waited for the poor old dame – now legally his wife – to dwindle and die.

How could he have known that her sons would challenge the will, contest the legality of the marriage, pry into the manner of her death?

A similar disaster had occurred before, years ago in Shrewsbury, and Frederick's experience had told him that the game was up, that he had better make himself scarce before the sons' suspicions turned to accusation and he was visited by an inquisitive arm of the law.

He had fled, with Eleanor, to Belfast where he had taken up again with Henri Leblanc and, sore pressed for money, had cobbled together a scheme that would bring all three of them, separately, to Scotland.

Eleanor's compliance with his hare-brained plan had been unexpected.

She had agreed to be sold for cash, sold again, and transported to Scotland like a slave so that she might still be near him. Of course, he had promised her that when he'd skimmed a sizeable sum from the gullible citizens of Ladybrook they would run off together to London town, none the worse for their experience. But somehow Clare had altered the pattern and Frederick had an uncomfortable feeling that since the instant he'd stepped ashore he had lost control of his destiny.

When Clare had ushered Eleanor into Headrick's drawing-room two evenings ago it was as if she, Clare, had deliberately and cruelly brought the separate halves of his life together. He was convinced that Henri had colluded with Clare but Henri strenuously denied it. And Frederick was left nursing the oppressive fear that the shades of his past were being given new shape and dimension and that he might very soon be trapped in nets not of his own making.

He hastened down the narrow back stairs and caught Eleanor just as she entered the passage from the yard.

From the kitchen came the clatter of pans, sleepy voices, Pratie Kerrigan's commanding bark.

"Eleanor?"

"Oh, it's yourself, is it?"

"We must talk."

"I've work to do."

"No," Frederick whispered. "Come into the parlour, just for a moment."

"I can't."

He caught her arm and drew her along and, passive and unresisting as always, Eleanor allowed herself to be led into the little back parlour.

Frederick had no real desire to kiss her but realised that it would be expected of him. As soon as the door was closed he took her in his arms, pulled her against him and caressed her breast through an armour of winter clothing.

She did not smell the same as she'd done in Dublin. She smelled of salty air and astringent spices. Her lips were cold. When he pushed her back against the door she gave a little yap and, to Frederick's dismay, thrust him away.

"I've missed you, dearest," Frederick said. "I cannot tell you how relieved I am to find you situated here, close and convenient for our meetings."

She kept him at arm's length. She might appear to be soft and female but her youthful muscles had an animal strength that Frederick could no longer counter and she fended off his half-hearted attempt to fondle her with ease.

"Where have you been?" he whispered. "I thought you were with Blyth, the coalmaster."

"He sold me to Rose Tannahill."

"Sold you? But why?"

"I was too much for him, I think," Eleanor said. "No matter. I'm better where I am."

"It hardly seems to be your style of thing, Eleanor. Never mind. I'll have you out of there soon."

"I've no particular wish to be out of there."

"You're confused, Eleanor. You knew very well what arrangements had been made. I didn't have to force you."

"We needed the money, aye."

"We did, we did. And you got paid."

"How much will you pay me now?"

"What?"

"Against the door. How much?"

"Eleanor!"

"It'll be the last you'll have, Freddie."

"Eleanor, what's wrong with you?"

"I've found a man."

"Surely you can't mean – "

"Aye, I do mean. Norman will do just fine for me."

"But he's a peasant, Eleanor."

"And what am I?"

"You're Eleanor Antrim's daughter."

"And a fine lady *she* was to be sure," said the girl.

"Eleanor, what's possessed you?"

"Not you, Freddie, that's for certain."

"Listen, I gave you my word I'd take care of you and take care of you I will."

"Huh! I've heard that tale from half the tars in Dublin," Eleanor said. "I never believed them an' my one mistake was believin' you."

"If that's how you feel, would Blyth not be a better prospect than Tannahill?"

"Oh, if I'd been a plain thing Blyth would have rode me to my knees like Hennessey's donkey. But plain I've never been, Frederick."

She was crouched against the door in the gloom. If he had not been able to make out her profile in the steely dawn light from the window, he would have taken her for a stranger.

She said, "I've been paid for so many times I've lost count. But I won't be bought an' sold no more."

"Do you intend to waste your life in a dank cottage on the moors?" Frederick said. "You're too good to squander yourself on the likes of Tannahill."

She laughed. "Well, I tell you, Freddie, he's twice the man I've ever had before."

"I thought you were long past caring about that?"

"Twice the man in other ways."

"What other ways?"

"He intends to marry me."

"Have you not also heard that tale from half the tars in Dublin town?" Frederick asked.

"Sure an' I have," Eleanor answered. "But none o' them ever posted banns or set a date for the wedding."

"Has Tannahill done so?"

"He's with the minister now," Eleanor said. "On the first day of March I'll become Norman Tannahill's wife."

"Does he know what you are, Eleanor?"

"He thinks he does," Eleanor said. "Are you goin' to tell him different?"

"No, I'll do nothing to spoil it for you, Eleanor. But I do think I'm entitled to request a fair exchange," Frederick said. "My silence for yours."

"Why?"

"Because I might take a bride myself quite soon."

"The widow Quinn?"

"Who else is there for me?" said Frederick.

"Will she die on you too?" Eleanor asked.

"Only God can answer that question," Frederick said. "In the meantime let us agree to act like strangers."

"Not meantime," the girl said. "For always."

"Even when I'm master of Headrick House?"

"Always," Eleanor Antrim said and, ducking beneath Frederick's arm, escaped to her duties in the kitchen.

Eleven

In all her years in Ladybrook Clare had never been asked to take tea at Cairns. The invitation, therefore, came as a complete surprise. It was delivered mid-morning by a liveried servant who waited in the yard while Pratie carried the sealed letter to Clare who, as it happened, was in the drawing-room with an instrument-maker from Kilmarnock who had been summoned to tune the piano.

Clare read the letter there and then and, excusing herself, repaired to the back parlour where on a sheet of her very best paper she penned an acceptance.

She sealed the reply and returned it via Pratie to Sarah Blyth's courier who rode off with it in his satchel.

"Pratie, I will be visiting this afternoon at half-past two o'clock."

"A far journey?" the housekeeper asked, though she knew perfectly well where the courier had come from.

"Tea," Clare said, "at Cairns."

"Will the child be goin' too?"

"I think not," said Clare.

"Will you be takin' the gig?"

"I will."

"Who'll drive it?" Pratie asked. "Tannahill?"

"I'll drive it myself."

"That isn't how it should be done, Mrs Quinn," the house-keeper pointed out. "When the first Mrs Quinn went callin' she always had a carriage wi' a driver."

"I will not require a driver," Clare said. "I will, however, take a maid to accompany me."

"Lizzie?"

"No, the new girl," Clare said.

*   *   *

It seemed odd that in a house as large as Cairns no snug apartment could be found in which tea might be comfortably served. A table had been put out in the centre of the great hall along with two gilded chairs which, so Sarah Blyth informed her guest, had once graced the bedroom of John Churchill, Duke of Marlborough, and had been willed to her paternal grandfather in gratitude for service rendered. Sarah Blyth did not specify the nature of the service but if the hall's display of armorial bearings and edged weapons was anything to go by it was something rather more military than prompt delivery of a shipload of domestic coals.

The octagonal teapot, pear-shaped cream jug and boat-shaped sugar bowl, even the kettle perched on its brazier, apparently all had fragments of McCracken history stamped into them like hallmarks and Clare had to endure pointless anecdotes about each vessel in turn. In fact she would have traded the whole collection for four or five logs to throw upon the puny fire that cowered in the fireplace fifty feet from where she, shivering, toyed with a teacup and a thin slice of bread meagrely spread with salted butter.

Fortunately Clare hadn't pandered to fashion but had bundled herself into a warm round robe with sleeves which came down to her wrists. Even so, she was numb with cold and could not understand how Sarah Blyth could survive the stone cold chill in a delicate muslin that would have been scant cladding even on a summer's day. But Sarah Blyth was so slender, so pale-skinned that she seemed almost luminous in the hall's gelid light, so brittle and icy that any degree of warmth might damage her constitution and induce decay.

The tea itself, Sarah Blyth managed to inform her guest, was Fifty Shilling China which her father imported directly by schooner from Canton.

It was on the tip of Clare's tongue to enquire if the cream had been drawn from a sacred cow on the Ganges and flown over from India by hot-air balloon. But she restrained herself and waited primly for Lord McCracken's daughter to explain the motive for such a splendid exercise in hospitality.

"We have seen so very little of you since you came to Ladybrook." Sarah Blyth snipped at a finger of seed-cake. "It was quite remiss of Mr Quinn not to entertain more. In the old days Headrick House was always a seat of jollity."

Clare swallowed a crust and washed it down with tea so weak that it had no taste at all.

"As he grew older," Clare said, "and wiser, my husband preferred to indulge in less public pleasures."

Sarah Blyth laughed, at least Clare supposed it was laughter. The sound was not unlike a pebble being rattled in a cup and there was no accompanying movement of the lips.

"I hear that you have guests at Headrick." Sarah had come to the point at last. "Gentlemen who may not be so retiring as the late Mr Quinn."

"I do have guests, Mrs Blyth," Clare said, "but they are mature men who know how to behave themselves."

"Must say, it's exceedingly courageous of you to furnish accommodation for *two* gentlemen simultaneously."

"Courageous?"

"Brave of you to flout convention."

"I have never cared o'er much about convention, Mrs Blyth."

"Has Mr Soames spoken to you on the matter?"

"Why should it concern Mr Soames?"

"He is, after all, guardian of our community's moral welfare."

"Mr Soames knows me well enough to realise that my moral welfare is not at risk."

"But does Mr Soames know the gentlemen in question?"

"No, he does not," Clare said. "He will meet them very shortly."

"At church?"

"At supper."

"One of the gentlemen is, shall we say, an old acquaintance of yours – is he not?"

"And of yours too, Mrs Blyth, if I'm not mistaken."

"I beg your pardon."

"I presume that you refer to Mr Striker," Clare said.

"I do," said Sarah Blyth. "I hardly know the man, of course, and I doubt very much if he remembers me at all."

"Oh, but he does," said Clare.

"Has he – has he spoken of me then?"

"Frequently."

"Indeed?" Sarah Blyth uttered the pebble-in-cup sound again. "What, pray, does Mr Striker have to say about me?"

"He asked if you were as beautiful as you used to be."

"What reply, if one may enquire, did you make?"

"I told him I had seen too little of you to judge."

Sarah Blyth let that sink in then, after a silence, said, "What of the Frenchman? Is he amusing?"

"I certainly find him so."

"My husband seemed impressed by his knowledge."

"M. Leblanc is undoubtedly skilled in his profession."

"Have you seen his demonstration?"

"Not as yet."

"Is Mr Striker a Freemason?"

Clare was caught off guard. "What?"

"Is Frederick a member of a lodge? Associated, say, with the Sons of Apollo?"

"I really have no idea."

"Oh, do you not?"

"It is hardly the sort of thing that Frederick would discuss with a woman."

"I wonder," said Sarah Blyth, "what goes on there." She paused then added, "If, dear Mrs Quinn, you happen to hear any rumours or receive information about the workings of the lodge I would be grateful if you would inform me."

"If Frederick *is* a member of the brotherhood," Clare said, "he will be bound by its oaths and customs which, I believe, are very strict and severe. I doubt if I will hear anything at all about doings at the Neptune."

"But if you do, if, in a moment of intimacy, say, Mr Striker happened to let slip some crumb – "

"I am not given to trading in gossip," Clare put in so curtly that Sarah Blyth retreated from the topic in haste and glanced down the long hall towards the doors that led into the vestibule.

Within the hall, just to the left of the doors, her maid and Clare's were seated side by side on a mahogany settle. They had been served with tea but did not appear inclined to engage in conversation. Sarah's maid was a young woman but plain and dressed in dowdy brown.

Clare had put Eleanor into an old scarlet dress of her own and, being good with a needle, had quickly let out a seam, here and dropped a hem there to make it fit.

Sarah leaned over the historical silverware and in a sibilant little whisper asked, "Is she, by any chance, 'the one'?"

"I do not know what you mean, Mrs Blyth."

"The one who was brought in from Ireland last month."

"She is Irish, yes, but she has not been long in my employment. I know nothing of her origins, only that she has recently become betrothed to Rose Tannahill's son, Norman."

"Come to think of it, I did hear banns cried from the pulpit on Sunday. How strange that love should blossom with such rapidity," Sarah Blyth said. "I suppose that is how it is with such people. When do they plan to consummate the affair?"

"In three or four weeks' time."

"Will you keep her on at Headrick?"

"I see no reason why I should not."

"In my opinion she is too forward to be a lady's maid." Sarah Blyth leaned forward again. "My husband was much surprised to hear the banns announced. I cannot think why, since he claims he does not know the girl."

Clare said, "Norman Tannahill is now and then employed at Cairns. Perhaps your husband recognised his name."

"I would not care to have the Tannahills as tenants," Sarah said. "All those stories one hears about the old woman must have some truth to them. But then you have so few tenants on Headrick, my dear, I suppose you cannot afford to lose a cottage rent."

"In fact I can't afford to lose the Tannahills' services," Clare said. "Norman Tannahill is worth his weight in gold. He does the work of four men. The rent of a cottage is little enough to exchange for his labour."

Sarah glanced towards the doors once more.

"The girl has an overheated look," she said. "No doubt there will be children sprawling all over your yard in no time at all."

"I do not object to children."

"Not to one's own, of course," said Sarah Blyth, "but servants' children are such noisy and offensive brats."

Far off in the depths of the house a clock chimed.

Echoes slithered through the chill atmosphere to reach the ladies in the great hall.

Clare seized on the opportunity to make her excuses and rose to take her leave. She had had more than enough of Lord McCracken's daughter who reminded her of Glasgow's commercial nobility, particularly of Edwina, Andrew Purves's wife. Sarah Blyth had less apparent vitality than Glasgow's tea-table wives but beneath her parchment skin was the same vulgar addiction to gossip and sexual scandal.

The maids stood up as the women approached but while they were still out of earshot Sarah Blyth touched Clare's arm and halted her progress towards the doors.

"I wonder," the woman said, "if you would be kind enough to pass on a message to Mr Striker?"

"Do you wish me to deliver a letter?"

"No, a message by word of mouth."

"I'll do so with pleasure, Mrs Blyth."

"Tell him – No, ask if he would be good enough to call upon me," Sarah Blyth said. "Any weekday afternoon would be convenient."

Fifteen years ago Clare would have been horrified if a daughter of the nobility had tried to steal Frederick from her. Over the years, though, she had learned so much about Frederick Striker's conquests that she was not particularly surprised by this latest turn of events. She could not imagine what Frederick had ever found attractive in the tall, bloodless woman but she doubted if he would find the lady Sarah at all appealing now.

"Will you grant me the favour, dear Mrs Quinn?"

"Why, of course," Clare said. "I have no doubt that Frederick will be eager to comply with your request."

"Do you think so – Clare?"

"I'm sure of it – Sarah," said Clare and, by way of farewell, was treated once more to the pebble-in-cup sound which Lord McCracken's daughter confused with laughter.

*　　　*　　　*

The drone of wind under the eaves and a stirring in the dry, dark air reminded Clare that winter would soon be over.

Spring was already crouched in seed and tuber and soon it would be time for peewits to nest, ewes to lamb, cows to drop calves, and all the din of nature would drift into her bedroom along with the scent of wild flowers and the warm shine of the sun. She felt restless and impatient for the season's change and could not bring herself to sleep.

The nightlight by Melissa's bed gilded the child's hair and lashes. She had that settled, soggy look which indicated deep sleep when Clare stole out of the bedroom into the passage in the hope that Frederick too might still be awake.

She had selected a pretty nightgown frilled at yoke and sleeves and had loosed her hair. She had no cheval glass in which to inspect herself for the long mirror remained in Donald's room where Henri now snored his Gallic snores.

Buoyed by a deep breath Clare headed for the door at the passage's nether end and knocked so lightly upon it that she was surprised Frederick heard her at all.

He spoke from just behind the door, as if he had been waiting for her.

"Who is it?"

"Clare."

He opened the door and peered out at her.

She recalled the days, which did not seem so long gone by, when Frederick would have recklessly flung the door open, but now he seemed almost reluctant to acknowledge her, let alone admit her to his bedroom.

"What is it?"

"Were you asleep?"

"I had only just got into bed," he answered in a tense whisper. "What do you want, Clare?"

"To talk with you."

"At this late hour?"

"I cannot sleep."

He opened the door barely wide enough to admit her and quickly closed it behind her.

She expected him to take advantage of the darkness but he was already groping towards the embers in the fireplace. She heard him grunt as he stooped to light a taper, grunt again as he rose, matched wick to wick and lit the candles at each end of the mantelshelf.

He wore a striped nightshirt and a tubular nightcap whose shredded tassel hung over his shoulder like a plait. He looked not unlike old Mr Purves, Andrew's father, who had been prone to doddering about the banking hall in night attire. An ugly bandage bound one of Frederick's kneecaps and Clare could smell the odour of liniment.

On the ledge above the fireplace were six or eight small jars, two glass flagons, a gin flask and a half-filled water glass. Frederick's remedies! Clare had forgotten how agitated Frederick could become over trivial ailments and afflictions. It was too late to hide the jars from her and Frederick did nothing to prevent her stepping forward to examine them.

Clare lifted one between finger and thumb and tilted it towards the light.

A little mound of powder shifted within the glass.

"Sulphur?" Clare asked.

"Yes."

"Not arsenic?"

"No, not arsenic."

She angled the bottle this way and that.

Frederick seated himself upon the edge of the bed.

"It isn't the same bottle, Clare," he said.

"How could it possibly be?" She replaced the blue jar exactly where it had been. "That particular object was left behind in Glasgow. I returned it to Eunice and she, I believe, destroyed it."

"If I had known what it contained," Frederick said, "if it had occurred to me that arsenic had accidentally replaced medicinal sulphur, I would not have left it with you."

"Frederick, I know what happened," Clare said. "There's no mystery to it. Besides, the episode took place so long ago that I have all but put it from my mind."

"I wish I could."

"What do you dose for now, Frederick?" Clare said.

He pulled a wry face and shook his head. "It's nothing. A rheumatic twinge here and there. Nothing that will hinder me in my duties." He forced a smile. "The best remedy for all my ills is to be here with you."

She had positioned herself in such a manner that the candle-light shone upon her. Frederick cocked his head and rubbed a hand across his jaw, stubble rasping against his palm.

"Is Melissa asleep?" he said.

"Fast asleep."

"Come, Clare, sit by me."

She hesitated then seated herself by his side on the mattress. He leaned his shoulder against her and when she did not resist put an arm about her waist.

"What wakened you, Clare? A bad dream?"

"Yes."

"Is your sleep often troubled?"

"Often," Clare said. "I imagine I'm in prison. In my mind's eye I can see the cell window and fancy I can smell rotting straw. I know I'm waiting for Hanging Johnny and no matter how desperately I struggle, how loudly I cry out, this time there will be no escape."

"Horrible."

"Then I imagine I'm stepping on to the gallows in front of the Tolbooth – "

"Please, Clare, no more."

"– with a rope about my neck, a rope so tight I cannot draw breath."

"Tell me how the dream ends." Frederick hugged her close. "Surely you waken before the – the drop?"

"No. The trap yawns open. I fall. I hear the roar of the crowd like the roar of the sea and a dreadful rushing in my ears. Then it's all darkness."

"And you waken?"

"No, the darkness endures, an interminable, eternal darkness in which I am completely alone. I scream and scream but nobody hears my cry, nobody responds."

"Good God!"

"Only Donald knew how to soothe away my fears."

"What did he do?"

"He took me in his arms," Clare said, "and held me until I had recovered."

"Did you suffer that dream tonight?"

"Yes."

"Is that why you came to me?"

His hand was spread across her stomach.

Her mouth was dry with lies, the heat of Frederick's caress simply another fabrication.

He had been her first love, her first lover: *I love you with all my heart, Clare Kelso. Let me show you how much I love you, Clare Kelso. Do you think that you might learn to love me too?* He had kissed her behind the ear. He had put his tongue into her mouth. He had pressed her voluptuously on to the bed in the upstairs room in the Duck Club all those years ago.

"Clare? Is it?"

He eased her on to the bed, his damaged knee placed carefully across her hips.

He lowered his mouth to her breast and kissed it. She felt her nipple swell. The rapid ebb and flow of tension began in her belly. He slid his hand to where his mouth had been, his mouth upon her mouth, his tongue – still expert – teasing her lips apart.

"Is that why you came?" His fingers stroked the soft flesh of her thighs. "To let me soothe away your fears?"

She did not close her eyes. She no longer had a need to please.

She jerked her head to one side and thrust her hands against his shoulders.

Startled, he hoisted himself from her.

"What is it? What's wrong?"

"Nothing's wrong, Frederick."

"Do you not want me to . . . Ah, is it – inconvenient?"

She had no fear of him. He was too dependent to take her against her will, to force himself upon her. She slipped from under him, pausing only long enough to kiss him by way of consolation.

"It's not in the least 'inconvenient'," she said.

"Will you not lie down with me, Clare?"

"No."

"Why then did you come?"

"To bring you a message."

"What sort of message?"

"A message of love."

"Ah!"

"From Sarah Blyth," Clare told him.

"Sarah Blyth?"

"The coalmaster's wife," Clare said. "She invites you to call upon her. Some afternoon when, presumably, her husband is not on hand. That is the message."

"*She* asked *you* to tell me *that*?"

"Precisely that."

"God in heaven!" Frederick said angrily. "What right has she to suppose that I'm at her beck and call."

"It was a perfectly polite invitation, Frederick. I do not understand why you are so upset by it."

"I'm upset because she used you as her – "

"Perhaps she thought I'd understand."

Frederick leapt to his feet. "Damn me! No, I will not attend her. What there was between us is dead and buried. I've no desire ever to see the woman again, let alone – let alone consort with her."

"Write and tell her so."

"Will you not tell her?"

"No, I will not."

"Clare." He caught at her arm but she was too quick for him. "Clare, please allow me to explain."

"I am not your wife, Frederick. It is not my place to approve your friendships."

"Do you not care about me?"

"I care about Headrick."

"Clare, what *am* I to you?"

"My salt factor."

"Is that all?"

"What there was between us is also dead and buried."

He stared at her incredulously. "How can you say that?"

He looked so lugubrious, so helpless that she felt almost sorry for him.

"Do you want to take me to bed?" Clare said.

"Of course, of course I do."

"Then you must woo me," Clare said. "You must woo me and win me and convince me you'll make a decent husband."

He laughed uneasily. "How can I do that?"

"I'm sure you'll find a way."

"What if I made you rich?"

"That would be a good beginning."

His eyelid twitched, a tic appeared at the corner of his mouth. Abstractedly, he rubbed at the nerve with his thumb.

"It will not be easy," he said.

"To make me rich?"

"To convince you of my sincerity."

"No, Frederick," Clare agreed. "It will be exceedingly difficult."

"Is this a stratagem?" he asked.

"No stratagem, I assure you," Clare answered.

"What about the others?"

"What others?"

"Galloway, for instance?"

"John Galloway is a friend, not a suitor."

"Are you certain of that?" Frederick said.

"Quite certain."

"Then I have time on my side?" Frederick asked.

"All the time you need," said Clare.

Book Three

A Covenant of Salt

Dear Cousin Andrew,
I am pleased to learn that ratification of the Treaty of Peace & Friendship between the Consuls of the Republic and our own King George has resulted in a surge of borrowing and that the bank is consequently flourishing. It must also be a relief to you to know that Willy is safe in his naval commission and has nothing further to fear from French gunners. I think you were wise to send Margaret to stay with Frances and Mr Malabar in Cardross. Bracing air and cheerful company will surely be the best medicines after a winter of illness.

All here is thriving. M. Leblanc was much amused by the terms of the French Senate's Act of Amnesty. The notion of presenting himself at a Republican Commissary in Brussels and denouncing practically everything just to be readmitted to the list of the Public Treasury made him laugh aloud. Somehow I do not think Henri will be returning to the land of his birth. He declares himself happy here. None of us has much idea what it is he works upon with such devotion. John Galloway insists on being admitted to Henri's laboratory once or twice a month to take stock on my behalf and is of the opinion that Henri is indeed striving towards an objective and that not one penny of my investment is being wasted.

Melissa and I have been but once to the laboratory which was as clean and scrubbed as a warship's deck. Henri has done much of the work himself but the Hardings have been contracted to build a furnace and some special metal cylinders. Melissa and I were both impressed by Henri's glass-blowing and the dexterity with which he pulled tubes and globes from the molten mass.

Very strange this business of furnace heat and freezing mixtures. If I had time to spare I would insist upon being party to Henri's experiments in defiance of Frederick's claim that a laboratory is no place for a woman. I am more at home, though no more welcome, in the salthouse. Gowrie does not seem to have forgiven me for putting Frederick above him. I suffer no remorse for doing so. It is no more than Gowrie deserves.

So far it has been an excellent season for salt. True to his word, Frederick has increased my income threefold and a year's output of five thousand bushels no longer seems unattainable. Cadgers queue daily at the scales and Messrs Boag & Macallister, the mercantile company of

141

Greenock, have ordered four hundred bushels of third-water salt, at 3s 2d the bushel, for the pickling of pork. Frederick has also negotiated a new discounted price per load on pan coal which has reduced the making cost per bushel to 1s 1d which is the reason for the increase in profits. I am not yet entirely trusting of our Mutual Acquaintance, however, and need no reminding to be circumspect in my dealings with him.

I do not see as much of Dr Galloway or Randolph Soames as I would like to do. We are not, of course, estranged but our communions are somewhat strained. It is perhaps unavoidable that old friends should feel themselves ousted by the new.

In general, though, I am content to let the summer run its course until such times as Henri makes a king's ransom for us all. When that day comes, dear cousin, I will hire a barge of burnished gold and a retinue of oarsmen and sail to Glasgow to attend on you in person – and let your good wife make what she will of it.

In the meanwhile, and more soberly,
Adieu!

Clare

Twelve

There were times when John Galloway wondered why the current of human energy ebbed and flowed with the seasons and if there was in him, as in all men, a closer affinity to the brute kingdom than was justifiable in a creature shaped in the likeness of God. It was not a point he dared debate with Randolph Soames for it smacked too much of heresy. But John Galloway had seen miracles enough not to nurture doubt that all was quite so pat as the Good Book declared it to be.

After twenty years as surgeon and midwife he knew only too well that whatever joy awaited one in Paradise, earthly life, for saint as well as sinner, began and ended in mess.

Two days ago he had been at the bedside of Peggy Bridgestone, the young wife of a Malliston weaver, who, worn and wasted by consumption, had died in a final fluxion which medical skill could not staunch.

Last night he had attended the lying-in of Cabel Harding's wife and had delivered her of a male infant. Out the boy had come, all slithering and eager, and had wailed lustily when carted off by female kin to be bathed with whisky and swaddled like a tiny Pharaoh. From each event Galloway had scurried home to his garden where, kneeling behind pillars of sweet peas, he had kneaded the loam between his fingers as if to be rid of the taint of blood, or simply to anneal his own poor flesh in contact with the fertile earth.

This morning, after an hour among his rose beds, he had washed at the pump, had eaten breakfast and, with the sun growing hot overhead, had started out for the beach in the hope that he might find Clare Quinn alone upon the shore road or, failing that, some other company to take his mind off more ponderous matters.

The day was going to be hot. Already he could smell tide-weed frying in the sun and Arran was hazed almost to invisibility. Alas, he did not encounter Clare upon the shore path and strolled on alone towards the salthouse.

He had been long enough in Ladybrook to tell smoke from a domestic hearth from the wavering pall of heat released by a pan and, to avoid disturbing the salters' labours, he headed through the gorse to come across the rocks to the Headrick pool.

He frequently visited the pond in the course of solitary rambles. He liked to sit upon the rocks and peer into its tranquil depths. The pond, however, was not tranquil or deserted this weekend morn and there was a good deal of activity in the lane to the girnal where cadgers came to buy their measured "pocks" to resell around the farms.

Cautiously Galloway clambered over the rocks and squatted by the edge of the pool and from there, unnoticed, watched young Katy Gowrie work.

What hard work it was too, up to her belly in cold salt-water. Fishermen went wrapped in woollens and thigh boots but the girl was condemned to labour half-naked as she raked in weed to prevent it choking the panhouse's pipes and pump.

The doctor shielded his eyes from the sun's glare and observed the young girl with a mixture of pity and respect as she dragged in the laden net and hoisted the dripping burden on to her skinny shoulder. He thought of Peggy Bridgestone, dying before her time, and fat Evelyn Harding, heaving and sweating to give birth while the men of the household slept. It was impossible to reconcile the fishy smell of ailing womanhood with this slim young girl, lithe as an eel, as she dabbled in the sunshine in the sea.

"Katy," he said at length, "how are you today?"

"Fine, sir." She staggered. "Fair busy, though."

"Yes, I can see that," Galloway said. "Is it the new factor who's got you going so hard at it?"

Too ingenuous to lie, she answered, "Aye, it is."

She cinched the rope across her breast, unintentionally showing off the buds of maturity which pressed upon the fabric of her shift.

She seemed well enough, the doctor thought, coddled by hot summer weather. It took no great feat of diagnosis, though, to recognise in her an inherent constitutional weakness. The Gowries were not sanguine like the Harding clan. The Gowries would never know what it was to tear at life like dogs at meat and the strain would soon die out, leaving hardly a dimple on the waters of history.

144

"Have you seen Mrs Quinn today, by any chance?"

"No, sir, she hasna been down here t'day."

"What of Mr Striker?"

"He's gone for to fetch coals, I think."

John Galloway looked away over the gorse to the tops of the trees which was all he could see of Headrick.

Nothing to stop him going to the house. Clare would not object. If Striker had indeed gone to Cairns he would, perhaps, have Clare all to himself for once. He had been in love with her almost from the first hour of meeting and could prescribe no remedy to cure his condition. He could hardly claim that his love went unrequited for he had been far too courteous to announce his true feelings to the lady and had cultivated her friendship as patiently as he had cultivated his roses.

"How long has Mr Striker been gone, Kate?"

The Gowrie girl shook her head, and shivered.

How callous of him to keep her waiting with the great tentacled bundle of dulse and bladderwrack hanging from her thin shoulders.

Rising, he said, "Come ashore. I'll help you land your catch, lass."

The weed was piled on rocks to dry out, then sold to a grower from Kerse to fertilise his rows. The shillings that the load fetched would be pocketed by Bob Gowrie and not so much as a penny of it would find its way into young Kate's purse to buy cloth or slippers or lace.

John Galloway took the rope from her hand, dragged the bundle across the sand to the mound and shook it out. The crackle of the old weed and the drone of the black flies that buzzed over it reminded him how hot it had become in the last half-hour. He returned the empty net to the girl in the pool. She had been in the water too long, even for a warm day, and her skirts, hitched into a broad leather belt, were soaked through.

"Can you not come in now?" John Galloway asked.

"Nah. I've to wait until I'm told."

It was pride not humility that governed her, he realised, when she shook her head obstinately.

"Will he beat you, Kate?"

The net was slung across her shoulder and she clutched the rake like a trident.

"Frederick willna beat me," she declared. "Frederick loves me."

She had, of course, misunderstood. He had meant Gowrie not

145

Striker. He was too taken aback to correct her. Did she mean to imply that Striker was her lover? The barbed question stuck in Galloway's throat and he heard himself mutter, "Well, Kate, I'm sure Mr Striker does care for you, but – "

"He loves me."

"Well, that's – that's very nice."

"An' I love him."

She shook the net and cast it upon the water and then, angry at being doubted, poked the rake deep into a tangle of bladderwrack, her back turned to him.

John Galloway retreated to the beach.

*　　*　　*

It was difficult to believe that Striker would take advantage of the scrawny child's infatuation but then he had no sure knowledge of what warped moral attitudes might be woven into Striker's character to balance the gift of fatal charm. Brooding on the matter, John Galloway trudged up the soft sand by the pipe.

He would have been past the salthouse and safe away if the panhouse door had not flung open and Billy Gowrie, as red as a boiled lobster, had not blundered into the simmering morning air.

Sweat drenched the young man's body and plastered his hair to his skull.

"Hot in there, Billy, is it?" the doctor said.

Billy fanned himself and grinned and winked.

"Hotter'n hell, Mr Galloway. By God, though, we're earnin' our lick in premiums."

"How much are you paid, Billy?"

"Four shillin' for every boll done over the 'taught'."

Familiar with salters' lingo John Galloway was gratified to learn that Striker, whatever his other vices, was no mean exploiter of labour.

He stood aside as Billy strolled past him and plunged his head and shoulders into the freshwater cistern that jutted from the sandy slope.

Galloway watched the boy fling back his wet hair then dip again to slake his thirst. Thin steam rose off him in the June sunlight. His vertebrae were as prominent as cockleshells, his neck thin as a pipe-stem.

Billy leaned on the rim of the cistern and wiped his mouth with his forearm.

146

"We've dug out the big pan," he boasted. "We'll scrape it this afternoon, fill an' start a first boilin' before dark."

"When will you sleep?"

"When we're deid, Mr Galloway," Billy said, grinning. He cocked his head. "Hey, listen. I think I hear the carts comin'."

The doctor barely had time to scramble up the sandy slope before the first four-wheeled cart rolled down the track. It was mounded with coal, pulled by two horses and driven by a hireling from the coalhill at Malliston. Billy Gowrie whooped at the sight of the cart and danced along with it as it swung past the salthouse followed by two similar vehicles. Galloway found it difficult to make a relationship between coal heaps, lathered horses and money. Credit notes, tax invoices, ledger transfers and big papery banknotes were so clean and particular, so distilled and refined, yet this was what they represented; Ayrshire's edifice of commerce built on crops and cattle, coal and salt.

Panhouse coal was stored in two iron-lined bins fed via a hatch in the seaward wall. Galloway observed the unloading from behind the cistern, the cool smell of hill water tickling his nostrils.

He did not recognise Frederick Striker just at first for he hadn't expected the factor to be smocked and booted like a common collier.

"Good morning to you, Galloway," the Englishman called out. "Have you come to take a turn with a shovel?"

"Not I, Striker," John Galloway replied. "I'm not well enough muscled for that task."

"Prefer the trowel to the shovel, do you?"

"That I do, sir, that I do."

Striker laughed, showing teeth in a coal-blackened face, a red leather tongue, like a mummers' dragon.

"Come out of hiding, Bob," Frederick shouted. "I've brought you some extra fuel."

Bob Gowrie appeared in the doorway of the panhouse. Like his son he was flushed and sweating and clouded round with caustic steam. The odours of a saltpan in full production wafted into the hazy air and coiled away like cottonseed across the pond.

Bob Gowrie glowered at the carts. "*Three* loads?"

"Sufficient for the quota, plus fifty more."

"I've no record of an order for three loads."

"Enter them later, after they're in the bins."

"We don't shovel coal," Gowrie declared. "Loads are purchased to include labour."

"Not on the terms I've negotiated," Frederick told him. "Now, where are the shovels?"

Factor and salter glared at each other for half a minute before Gowrie yielded. "Annie," he yelled. "Shovels."

The area around the panhouse was suddenly crowded.

Matt Pringle and Mr Bartholomew appeared from the girnal, and Kate was summoned from the pond to skim the pans while the menfolk unloaded the carts.

Frederick Striker worked side by side with the labourers.

Something's different about him, John Galloway thought, something's changed him over the course of the summer, adding vigour and robustness and a certain unbearable arrogance.

John Galloway had no need to strain his imagination to reckon what that something might be and what part Clare played in it.

After five minutes as an idle spectator the doctor slipped quietly away and, a half-hour later, was seated safely in his rose garden, sipping tea and brooding once again.

*　　*　　*

Horse and pony had been released into the strip of pasture that looked out over the Leddings. Having eaten their fill of meadow grasses they lay muzzle to tail, ears flicking, under the shade of a crab-apple tree. Although the heat was oppressive larks still sang, pigeons crooned and half-grown lambs blethered in the fields beyond the dyke. Shearing would soon begin on those farms where sheep were kept and, here and there, hay-making had started early.

Norman had scythed the lawns a week ago and had mown the terrace that fronted the house so that, on that hot June morning, the grass had the texture of cambric.

Clare had had Pratie carry out a chair and a carpet and had strewn cushions here and there for Melissa to lounge upon while, in a listless sort of way, she heard her daughter's lessons.

There was, however, something unnatural about schooling in the out of doors. Book covers curled in the sunshine. The slate was annoyingly squeaky. Chalk sticks crumbled and dust seemed more grainy than it did indoors in the parlour.

Melissa, of course, was distracted by butterflies and dawdling bees and even Clare found concentration difficult. Her inclination was to sit idle, to sit and *not* think.

The servants were also enjoying the sunshine.

Laughter floated from the kitchen yard behind the house. Clare guessed that they would be chattering about the Feast of St John the Baptist which was only four days away. As usual, the lodge had laid on a fair.

Some Old Light diehards, Pratie among them, considered the midsummer celebration too pagan but that wouldn't stop them turning up to wonder at the acrobats and jugglers or cheer the parade of lodge brothers who, in full regalia, marched through the town behind a band of fifes and drums.

Rain had spoiled the event for the past couple of years. Farmers had been too concerned about their crops to make the journey into town, the lodge parade had looked like a funeral procession and the afternoon sports and evening bonfire had been cancelled altogether.

This year, however, the weather seemed set fair to last until the weekend and excitement was rife in the shire.

Last summer Clare and Melissa had been accompanied by John Galloway. It had been Clare's first public excursion since Donald's funeral. She had enjoyed the day enormously in spite of the rain for John had laid on a supper at his house, with singing, dancing and reciting afterwards so that, as Randolph put it, dear old John the Baptist had had due recognition after all.

Clare rather regretted having promised the day to Frederick and Henri. She knew that John and Randolph were "put out" but there was no help for it. Henri, it seemed, had been roped in to provide a special entertainment, though not even Melissa could wheedle out of him what it was.

Stirring herself, Clare took up the chalk and applied it to the dusty slate.

"I am going to draw a line, Melissa," she said. "What is this sort of line called?"

Clare was not entirely steady in her understanding of Geometry but had grasped enough of the subject from reading to guide Melissa in its rudiments. In spite of Frederick's warning that the female brain was not constructed to absorb too many facts, Clare was determined to give her daughter something better than a drawing-room education.

Melissa tutted. "A straight line."

"Yes, but it is up-and-down, is it not?"

"Per-pen-dic'lar."

"Perpendicular. Also called?"

"A vertrical."

"Ver-tic-al," Clare corrected. "Say it, please."

Melissa repeated, "Ver-tic-al."

"And this sort of line?"

"Horry-zont-tal."

"What is special about such a line?"

Melissa rolled on to her tummy and looked past Clare towards the trees that crowded the little valley of the Linn. "It's flat, like the horizon," she answered, adding, "but Henri says the horizon isn't flat. Henri says if we could see more of it we would detect that it's curved like the top of an orange. Do you think the horizon is curved, Mama?"

"I do. Have I not shown you pictures of it?"

"Henri says that's why storks stand on one leg."

"M. Leblanc is making a joke."

The little girl giggled. "I know, Mama. I know."

Clare put down the chalk, blew dust from her fingers and gravely enquired, "Why *do* storks stand on one leg, Melissa?"

The blue eyes flickered, the little chin jutted out.

Clare did not know whether to be amused or annoyed by the fact that she had finally engaged her daughter's attention with a frivolous question.

"Mama," Melissa said. "Someone is watching us."

"What?"

"In the trees. Someone's standing there. A man."

Clare straightened her shoulders and slowly turned her head in the direction of Melissa's gaze. She could hardly make out the figure in the fretwork shadows. He had come up, apparently, from the bridge over the Linn but how long he had been there Clare had no idea.

A little cold shiver travelled down her spine. Here, even here, in her own garden on a breathlessly hot summer's morning she was not entirely free of the irrational fear that her past and her present would meet and meld and somehow bring harm to Melissa.

She got up and called out shrilly. "You, sir, who are you? Show yourself or I'll have my servant release the dogs."

"Dogs, Mama?" Melissa whispered.

"Hush, dear." Clare put her hand down by her side and drew Melissa close against her skirts.

"No, no, Mrs Quinn." Robertson Blyth stepped from under the boughs, hat in hand. "No need to be alarmed. I am not a footpad or a gypsy, as you can see." He advanced across the lawn. "I'm sorry if I startled you, you and the child. Did you not hear me approach?"

"No, Mr Blyth, I did not."

He was dressed unpretentiously in a loose cream-coloured shirt, blue breeches and fine cotton hose, coat folded over his arm. The hat was not his usual black narrow-brimmed beaver but a floppy fantail with a cock's feather in the band. He wore no wig. Clare was surprised to see that his cropped hair was almost white.

"The heat, Madam, the heat," Robertson Blyth said, as if he had read her thoughts. "I cannot abide the heat."

To the best of Clare's recollection Robertson Blyth had never before set foot upon Headrick's lawns, not during her tenure. He dawdled nervously by the carpet's edge, fanning himself with his hat.

"Where is your horse, Mr Blyth?"

"I came on foot. Walked."

"Then there can be no urgency to your business." Clare did not invite him to be seated. "Is it a religious matter which brings you here?"

"I am not your appointed elder, Mrs Quinn, a privilege which falls to Mr Millar, I believe."

"Little enough we see of Mr Millar," Clare said.

The coalmaster hardly appeared to be listening. He fanned away with his hat and squinted past Clare towards the house, dazzling in the glare of the noonday sun.

"Hot," he murmured. "So hot."

Clare said, "If you are in search of Mr Striker, I must tell you that he's not here."

"Oh, no, I saw Mr Striker earlier this morning," the coalmaster said. "I just happened to be in the vicinity of Headrick and I thought – " He shifted his weight from one foot to the other. "It's such a time since we've conversed, Mrs Quinn, I thought – "

"Melissa."

"Yes, Mama."

"Go to the kitchen yard and tell Pratie that we have a guest. Ask her to send Lizzie with a chair. Also to bring my parasol and – " before Melissa could rush off "– a jug of lemonade. Will you remember all of that?"

"I shan't forget anything, Mama," said Melissa and lifting her skirts set off up the slope of the lawn towards the gable.

"If you care to be seated on the carpet, Mr Blyth," Clare said, "you may support yourself with a cushion until a chair arrives."

"Thank you."

He lowered himself gingerly on to the rug, propped one of the big cushions under his right arm and, as if to restore a little dignity, placed the fantail hat square upon his head.

"Are you comfortable?" Clare enquired.

"Perfectly."

"Very well, Mr Blyth," Clare said. "Converse."

*   *   *

Ordinance of war had never seriously engaged Henri's attentions in spite of his interest in air-guns. He was, however, thoroughly familiar with the action of combustible compounds and in a series of drawings in his laboratory notebook soon devised interesting variations on the Rocket, the Martyr's Wheel and that noisy little squib which Paris urchins dubbed *Le Coup de Tonnerre*.

Initially Henri had been indignant at Frederick's suggestion that he manufacture fireworks to entertain a gathering of mule-headed peasants on a stupid feast day.

Once he'd calmed down, though, and allowed the concept of explosive projectiles to infiltrate his more profound philosophies he became quite intrigued by the subject. Besides, Melissa would appreciate a good, gaudy firework display and anything that pleased Melissa Quinn pleased Henri too.

Cabel Harding was not surprised to find the Frenchman engaged in mixing black powder and filling wax-paper tubes. Almost everything the Frog did was, to Cabel's way of thinking, bizarre.

Cabel understood the reverberatory air-furnace that the Hardings had been called upon to construct and he admired the ingenious variations that Leblanc had incorporated into the design. The furnace was clearly intended for the roasting of ores and the cupellation of metals – and that, for Cabel, was fine and well.

What was less fine and well was the complicated apparatus

of copper spheres, gum-elastic tubes, glass bells and brass stop-cocks in which Leblanc hoped to collect and measure quantities of the invisible gas.

What was not well at all was the weird instrument which occupied a rack along one whole wall of the fish-shed.

The container was constructed of baked wood lined with lead sheeting. It reminded Cabel of a coffin. Inside were one hundred preserving jars filled with unspecified liquid, each jar connected by wires to a brass globe, all the little globes connected in turn to a large sphere which hung, hauntingly, above the rest.

The device, Henri deigned to inform his workman, was a Leblanc version of a voltaic battery from which, if you knew how, electrical fluid could be wrung and collected.

The number of violent explosions of the collecting jars, and Leblanc's accompanying oaths, did nothing to soothe Cabel's fears, however, or incline him to wander too close to the demonic-looking instrument.

Cabel and his apprentices, Harry and Will, were crouched on the shed's earthen floor, busily occupied in bolting flanges to the base of the furnace. That done, they would bracket the perpendicular stack to the fish-shed's interior wall and, God be thanked, be shot of the commission once and for all.

Cabel was not happy.

As he kneeled under the rim of the furnace and tapped away at the stout little rivets Cabel could hear the Frenchman humming a strange little tune and he had the horrible feeling that if the humming should cease he and his offspring would at that moment be blown to kingdom come.

When, out of the blue, Henri said, "Harding, look here," poor Cabel's first reaction was to burrow himself head and shoulders under the iron plate and let his backside take the brunt of it.

"Dad, Dad. It's all right, Dad," Harry assured him.

Cabel peeped out from under his armpit.

The Frenchman stood behind him, arms extended like a fisherman showing off a prize salmon, to display a long pasteboard cylinder with a pasteboard cap and a bamboo cane for a tail.

"Wha – what is it?" Cabel asked.

"It's a rocket, Dad. Ain't it, Mr Leblank?"

"The first of several." Henri nodded. "Built to my own special design."

"Wha – what's it do?" said Cabel.

"It flies, Dad," said Harry, hopping with excitement.

Cautiously Cabel inched his shoulders from under the furnace. "What else?"

"Ain't that enough, Dad?" said Will. "By Jove, I never seen such a big 'un before. How high will it fly, sir? Higher'n the roof?"

"Higher than the sun, I'll wager," said Harry. "Won't you show us, Mr Leblank?"

Henri had no liking for the Hardings but they had proved to be able craftsmen and had done all that he had asked of them. He was aware that they were charging Mrs Quinn a tidy sum for their efforts and that Brock was very curious as to the progress of his experiments, but Cabel's lads were simple souls, too young to be deceitful.

"Very good," Henri said. "It is well to test the first of them. I will do it now."

"Hurrah!" Harry cried.

"Can we watch, sir, can we?"

"You may also cheer and make applause if you wish," Henri said. "Come, we will step to the beach."

The chemist, the boys, the blacksmith and the rocket were soon assembled upon a tongue of sparse grass that ran from the fish-shed to a sheltered corner of Headrick Bay. Out in the roadstead four brigantines steered in convoy for the tip of Trotter's Point. Closer to shore a flock of gannets dived spectacularly along the dark blue line of a cold current.

The boys had no eyes for brigs or seabirds. They were agog at the rocket which M. Leblanc was setting up to fire.

First Henri dug a shallow pit in the sand.

Next he consulted his notebook, measured an angle of elevation, drew a line in the sand and placed the rocket along it. He inspected the missile in profile. He made an adjustment.

Finally he produced a burning glass from his pocket, focused the rays of the sun on to a twist of paper and, without hesitation, touched the resulting flame to the rocket's stringy little pigtail.

Cabel had less faith than his sons. He cowered behind the sand-pit with his hands to his head while the boys chanted and pranced excitedly.

The coronet of smoke vanished into the tube.

"Wait," Henri, watch in hand, announced.

Three seconds passed, four, then five.

Suddenly the butt of the rocket spurted red fire, the bamboo was yanked from the sand and the missile, roaring, shot up in a huge, high arc towards the hazy disc of the sun.

Gannets and gulls spun away from the smoking object.

The brigantines seemed to bob as if all the tars on board had ducked in alarm at the same time. Off the rocks, the oars of a lobster skiff flashed blade-up in the sunlight as the occupants fell backwards in astonishment.

Up and up went the rocket until it was hardly visible at all and only a faint fluttering ribbon of powdery air connected it to the gaze of the boys and men on the ground below. Then, at its zenith, the head split open and shot a scarlet fireball higher still.

"The sun, over the sun, I told you," Harry shouted while his father, mouth open, gaped.

"A satisfactory experiment?" Henri asked.

"Oh, aye," said both boys together. "Oh, aye."

"In which case," said Henri, clicking shut his watch, "may I suggest we all now go back to our works."

The boys obediently returned to their rivets and iron bolts. But Cabel Harding, stunned by what he'd seen, lingered on the beach, staring up into the heavens where the last remnant of the fireball had slid like a burnt petal down to the distant sea.

*   *   *

"I admit," said Robertson Blyth, "that I am curious as to what the Frenchman is up to and what stage he has reached in his experiments."

"I am not the person to ask, Mr Blyth," Clare said.

"As his partner, I assumed – "

"I am a partner on paper only, not his apprentice."

Blyth frowned. "Have you not then been shown what Leblanc can do?"

"No, sir, I have not."

"And yet you are willing to advance a substantial sum to promote his endeavours?"

"Willing to take M. Leblanc on trust, yes."

"On the strength of Mr Striker's recommendation?"

"You are labouring under a misapprehension if you suppose that Mr Striker has any influence over me," Clare said. "Oh, yes, Mr Blyth, I'm all too well aware that certain sections of Ladybrook society think I'm Frederick Striker's paramour."

"Madam, no such thought crossed – "

"Let me assure you, sir, that I am not so close to Frederick Striker as all that. He is my salt factor. And I am neither his dupe nor his puppet."

Blyth struggled to rise but the soft cushion defeated his efforts. He clasped his knees with his forearms and rocked awkwardly on his tailbone for a moment or two.

"You are very plain-spoken, Mrs Quinn."

"I am 'conversing', Mr Blyth, on a subject of your choosing. Would you have me discuss the price of dimity?" Clare did not pause, not even for breath. "How is Mrs Blyth these days?"

"Mrs Blyth?"

"Your wife, is she well?"

"In so far as I know she's in excellent health. Why do you ask about my wife, Mrs Quinn?"

"She also seems interested in my relationship with Mr Striker," Clare said. "I thought perhaps it was a matter of universal concern at Cairns."

"I do not know what you mean."

"And I do not know what *you* mean, Mr Blyth," Clare said. "You appear uninvited upon the edge of my lawn in the mid-morning and expect me to believe there's purpose behind the visit?"

As intended, she had thoroughly upset the coalmaster.

Glancing over her shoulder in the direction of the house Clare watched Pratie advance across the lawn with a wooden chair from the hall. The housekeeper placed the chair upon a level spot and Mr Blyth seated himself upon it.

"Lemonade, Pratie?" Clare said.

"It'll be but a minute."

"Make sure that it is cold."

"That'll take longer."

"So be it." Clare gave her housekeeper a sign that she did not wish to be disturbed. "And please to keep Melissa with you until the refreshment is ready."

"I will, Mrs Quinn," said Pratie and, hiding her curiosity, stalked off across the lawn and left her mistress and the master of Cairns to get on with it.

"Since it is not church business that brings you to my doorstep, Mr Blyth," Clare said, "I assume the purpose of your call has to do with money or perhaps with the welfare of a young woman in my employment."

The coalmaster's face flushed as if it had been scorched by fire. "Young woman? What young woman?"

156

"The Irish girl who was – albeit fleetingly – your hireling. Do you not know the girl I mean?"

"I know the girl," said Robertson Blyth. "What lies has she been telling you?"

"Do not be alarmed, Mr Blyth. Your secret is as safe with me as with any of your lodge brethren. Indeed, probably safer. I have too much regard for Eleanor Tannahill – for, as you know, she is now the wife of one of my tenants – to challenge you with irresponsibility on her behalf."

"I – I hired her only because she looked so forlorn. I'm delighted she has settled so quickly into our small community and has found herself a husband."

"Do you wish to speak with her?"

"No, no."

"Are you aware that she's already with child?"

"I remarked upon the fact last Sabbath."

"It's difficult not to remark upon it," Clare said, "as she is already so large."

The coalmaster cleared his throat. "As a matter of interest, when is the child due?"

"October, I believe."

Blyth rocked unevenly on the wooden chair. Arithmetical calculations hovered on his lips and a vague speculative glaze came over his bleak grey pupils. "Has Galloway been called to attend her?"

"Rose Tannahill will not countenance the attentions of a medical gentleman, not even our own Dr Galloway," Clare said. "Now, are you quite sure that you do not wish to see Eleanor, Mr Blyth?"

"I trust you don't think I called upon you just to look over some Irish waif," the coalmaster said. "Whatever the girl may have told you, I – I deny it."

"In that case," Clare said, "shall we embark upon another topic?"

"By all means, Madam, please let us do so."

"How much?" Clare said.

"How much?"

"How much are you willing to contribute towards Henri Leblanc's experiments?"

Robertson Blyth let out an audible whistle of astonishment then said, "Excuse my impoliteness, Mrs Quinn, but your question caught me off guard. Am I to take it that the present subject of discussion and the last are not unconnected?"

"No, sir. You may take it that they are in no way connected. We have changed the subject completely."

"I see," Blyth said. "Do pardon me. I'm not used to dealing with ladies who are quite so astute as you are showing yourself to be."

"Is your wife not astute, Mr Blyth?"

"Oh, indeed!" the coalmaster conceded. "Sarah is a very model of astuteness." He dropped his hat to the grass by the chair and, more at ease now, leaned forward. "No, Mrs Quinn, I'm not averse to plain-speaking when it comes to matters of finance."

"I'm glad to hear it."

"How much do you suggest I should contribute towards the cost of M. Leblanc's experiments? How much does he, in fact, need?"

"It's not a question of Leblanc's needs," Clare said. "It's a question, rather, of how much it will cost you to purchase a share of *my* interest in the Leblanc process."

The coalmaster's laughter was ungrudging. "By God, Mrs Quinn, you've been in our midst for fourteen years and I had not suspected you of such guile."

"I think, sir, you mistake caution for guile."

"Take the compliment how you will, Madam, for a compliment was intended," Blyth said. "I would pay one hundred pounds – no, *two* hundred pounds – to participate in the purchase of a patent for Leblanc's device."

"What if he does not succeed in obtaining a patent?"

"I will absorb the loss without complaint."

"In short, you're willing to share the risk with me?"

"Yes."

"Do you not wish to consult with your clever wife?"

"It would be my commitment, not Sarah's," said the coalmaster curtly. "Indeed, I would insist upon our transaction remaining confidential and the matter being quickly settled."

"You are very eager, Mr Blyth. Is it because you've seen what Henri Leblanc can do that makes you so?"

"The demonstration was limited in its scale," Blyth informed her. "Even so, it's my belief that if it could be expanded it would prove invaluable in many trades and industries, provided costs are kept to manageable levels."

"Very well," Clare said. "For two hundred pounds, Mr Blyth, I will assign you a one-third share in my share of the patent. On payment you will immediately be entitled to participate in all profits which may accrue during the patent's fourteen-year term. Precise details of the agreement will be drafted and delivered to you by my lawyer, Mr Greenslade of Irvine, and the matter will remain entirely confidential between us."

"I did not expect this," Blyth admitted.

"Are you displeased with my offer?"

"On the contrary."

"Was it worth the effort of a walk from Cairns?"

"In every way, Madam."

"Good," Clare said, rising. "Now, Mr Blyth, before you melt completely do allow me to fetch you some lemonade." She smiled and touched his shoulder. "Or shall I have it served by my new servant, Eleanor Tannahill?"

"No, Mrs Quinn," said Robertson Blyth, firmly. "I would prefer it served by your hand, please."

"Business before pleasure, Mr Blyth?"

"A sound principle, don't you think?"

"Oh, quite definitely, sir," said Clare.

*   *   *

If his tryst had been with any other woman, even a herdsman's wife, he would have washed in the Linn and changed not only his linen but his grubby breeks too. He did nothing of the kind for Sarah Blyth, though, for she deserved no special treatment and, Frederick suspected, might even derive stimulation from the small humiliations that he heaped upon her.

He despised her; and he despised himself for succumbing to her blandishments. But inability to resist an easy opportunity had been his lifelong failing and might yet prove to be his downfall.

If only Eleanor had not married Tannahill he would have found solace in her arms. But Eleanor was already transformed into a big-bellied, contented, unapproachable wife and he could hardly bring himself to look on her now, not out of distaste for her condition but from envy of it. It reminded him of how Clare had been sixteen years ago, and of what comfort might have been his if only he'd kept his side of the bargain.

Thinking of Clare and aware of the risk, he continued to climb uphill through the briars and stunted pines that topped the cliff above the cove at Croyne to keep his sullen rendezvous with Sarah Blyth.

It was about half-past three o'clock. The sun slanted

bluey-green shadows through the old pines and spore-heavy ferns. Too hot for birdsong. Even the ring-doves were silent. As he paused for breath Frederick could hear no sound at all except the pulse of blood in his head and the drone of flies in the undergrowth.

He could see Sarah through the trees. She seemed out of place in the woodland setting. She loitered in a little velvety dell sprinkled with wild flowers. Out of sight below the knoll a lady's maid, a trusted servant, would be waiting in a cocking cart or hooded gig to drive her home again.

For a woman in Sarah Blyth's exalted position discretion was relative.

Frederick paused to knot a red bandanna about his sweating forehead and to brush his thinning hair over it and then he softly called her name. She spun round to face him as if he had caught her not by arrangement but by surprise.

On the grass was a silken plaidie with tassels like weasels' tails, and a folded white linen napkin. Her dress was of pale blue Japanese muslin, slippers and stockings of similar hue. Frederick would be willing to wager that her garters, clasped tightly round her thin white thighs, would match in shade too.

She took off her turban before he reached her and placed it fastidiously upon the napkin, its blue glass jewel glinting in the sun.

Frederick stepped over it, caught her up in his arms and carried her before him until she was propped against the rough bark of a pine tree, her spine pressed against his fists.

"Frederick, look at you! How dare you appear in such a state. Where have you been, sir? Have you no manners? Do you think I'll let you fondle me in that filthy condition?"

"Oh, yes," Frederick said. "You'll let me do much more than fondle you."

"A kind word first, please. I'm not one of your Dublin trulls, sir. I'll not be treated as if I'm for hire."

"Lie down."

He pulled her away from the tree. He held her by the waist and pointed to the shawl upon the grass. Its fabric was speared by spiky little stems so delicate that the weight of silk had broken them already.

"Do you want me so badly, Mr Striker, that I am not to be courted at all?"

"I'll be the judge of that," Frederick said, "when you prove yourself worth my attention."

She settled primly upon the silk, legs straight out before her. Frederick was amazed that she could maintain poise even in that position. He did not invite her to expose her breasts which were as flat as lozenges. He stood above her and confidently unfastened the drawstring of his breeches for in that respect at least the years had not diminished him.

"Do you want me to undress you?" he said.

Pale blue eyes fastened upon him.

She shook her head.

"Do it then," he said.

She lifted her skirts and displayed stockings, garters, thighs and hips, her belly lily-white.

The sun beat down upon Frederick's neck, squeezed sweat into the rough red cloth that bound his brow. He felt dizzy with the brackish odour of pine-kernel and damp sand. The pain of wanting someone else was almost unendurable.

"Frederick, I'm waiting."

God, how he despised the frigid nymph, so still, so placid, so ultimately paralysing. He sank to all fours. He pushed her knees apart and slithered on top of her.

She lay back like a swan, tilted her hips to meet him and, just as he entered her, said, "Be careful of my dress, Frederick, please."

"Damned if I will," said Frederick and, for the first time since he'd known her, made the lady cry aloud.

Thirteen

Clare had no notion why St John the Baptist deserved an Ayrshire celebration. The feast had no particular significance in the Protestant calendar nor, as far as she could gather, in the lodge book of the Sons of Apollo. She was inclined to agree with Pratie that the fair was nothing more than a pagan relic and an excuse for an extra holiday.

Whatever its origins the fair of 1802 was memorable for all sorts of reasons. The sun beat down, the air was balmy, the sea calm and everybody who was anybody turned up for the longboat race which marked the beginning of the afternoon's card of events.

The Neptune was packed. Hard-drinking farmers, colliery managers, independent weavers, boat-owners, corn dealers, fish merchants and salt traders happily rubbed shoulders and filled Brock Harding's coffers with their hard-earned bawbees. In other ale-houses and dramshops the lines of social distinction were more firmly maintained. Colliers kept themselves apart from sailors, sailors from fishermen, house-servants from field-hands, horse-copers from cattle drovers. Even poor peasants got to lord it over the tinkers who, smelling silver on the breeze, had come skiddling early into Ladybrook.

On the stroke of half-past two Lodge Ladybrook's finest, arrayed in all their glory, trooped out from beneath the Euclidean arch.

The Hardings were out in force. Even Cabel's brand new son, blind to everything but the breast, was carried from the cottage and passed round to be handselled and admired, while the brothers, some none too steady on their pins, assembled behind Brock for the walk to the quays.

The quays and harbour wall were thronged by the time the solemn procession arrived and Brock and Cabel led the parade to the barrelhead where the Reverend Braintree, in cassock and robes, waited. Braintree, a dedicated Freemason, had been co-opted from the Auld Parish Kirk at Malliston to replace Mr Soames who had point-blank declined to do the honours.

Betting had been a main occupation over the dinnnertime and even when the minister bowed his head, raised his arms and chanted a sober prayer on the virtues of self-denial the chink changed hands and final odds were calculated.

Five boats in the race this year: Ardrossan coal-whippers had put out a crew and Mr Saunders, owner of a Saltcoats' boat yard, had staked his employees to a row. The fishermen's eight was still favourite but those in the know had wagered on Lodge Ladybrook's rescue team which had been training practically every evening throughout the month.

The race began with a flying start from a line adjacent to the Rescue Bell.

The boats scudded around a buoy, followed the inside line of the Nebbocks and would finish at the harbour wall where the first bowsman to pluck a pennant from a floating keg was declared winner.

Clare had little interest in the outcome of the race.

For Melissa's sake she pretended to support the boat that Frederick had put his money on.

She was, however, decidedly taken aback when her daughter screamed like a parrot from her perch on Henri's shoulders and as Ardrossan just pipped the Lodge on the line, thumped poor M. Leblanc's head in frustration and bitterly condemned the losers as "lazy sons of dogs".

During the course of the race Clare's attention had been directed not towards the boats but at Brock Harding.

The elderly blacksmith had been aware of her interest and, touching the Jewel of Apollo that hung about his neck, eventually deigned to favour her with a salute to which Clare replied with a curtsey and a faint, not unfriendly smile. The gesture did not escape Frederick's notice.

"I thought you could not abide the man?" he said.

"You've made your peace with him," Clare answered, "why should I not do the same?"

"It isn't peace," Frederick told her, "only a truce of sorts which could end at any time."

"When Brock Harding finds you out."

"Finds me out?" said Frederick. "What gives you the impression that there's anything *to* find out?"

They were pressed together in the crowd, his chest brushing her shoulder, his hand laid lightly on her waist.

163

"I know you too well, Frederick," Clare said. "Things are never as they seem with you."

Frederick laughed but said no more on the subject and, a second later, took her arm for the walk uphill to the common where, at half past four, the trials of strength were scheduled to begin.

*　　*　　*

Old habits died hard. It was all Eleanor could do not to return the glances of the males who eyed her up and down and to engage with them in a moment of promise and invitation.

She recognised several of the men who had been in the upstairs room in January and others who had ogled her less openly during Sunday visits to St Cedric's. But it hardly mattered. All men were the same to her now that pregnancy had made her a level wife.

She clung resolutely to Norman's arm and, with her stomach thrust out before her, tried not to skip glances at the men who stared at her or to show her teeth to the women who glowered and drew their children out of her path as if she might deliberately step on them or knock them to the grass. She was no Dublin brass heel now. She was the regular wife of Norman Tannahill, kirked and cradled, for better or worse. She deserved their respect.

She watched Frederick from the corner of her eye. How attentive he was to Clare Quinn, how charming.

Once, not so long ago, she'd been his pet. They'd eaten beefsteak and oysters and had drunk champagne under the awnings by the Liffey in the tavern yard at Kingsbridge, when he was married to her natural mother, before the poisoning.

"I'll find a shady corner by the trees, dearest, where you can rest," Norman said. "Mother'll join us in a while."

"Aye, that would be nice," said Eleanor.

The old woman had taken a stall in the market square to sell her ointments, cordials and fragrances. Eleanor had offered to accompany her but the old woman would have none of it and had left her behind to help Norman milk the cow and feed the calves. Rose Tannahill's attitude to her had changed over the past months, had become somehow resentful. Now and then, in dead of night, she would hear the old woman shuffling about in the kitchen and would wonder if that damnable serpent's egg had finally revealed the truth.

Norman spread a shawl on the grass and Eleanor lowered herself down on to it.

He had not chosen a good spot. Blackthorn bushes gave little shade and cattle spats among the roots encouraged a cloud of black flies. The other Headrick servants, she noticed, had carried their baskets of food towards more open ground.

Norman looked anxiously towards the line of cottages that bounded the common.

"Go an' find her if you want to," Eleanor said.

Norman shook his head. He was as protective towards her as if they were bound by blood and his devotion was stifling.

Soon after this baby was born the Tannahills would expect her to breed again at once, again and again and again. Love-making had always had a price but now she was the one who would be expected to pay it.

"She'll need help with her baskets," Eleanor said. "I'll be fine here by myself 'til you come back."

Norman hesitated. Not for the first time he was torn between devotion to his wife and obligation to his mother.

Eleanor was not the only one with a stubborn streak. The old woman had staggered off that morning with the pannier of remedies roped to her back like a creel and had refused to let Norman carry it into town for her. What need was there to sell herbals in any case? There was more cash stuffed behind the fireplace stone than she could earn in a year on the streets. Rose Tannahill's pretence of poverty had been put on just to embarrass her and make Norman feel guilty.

"She said she'd be here by four o'clock," Norman said.

"Business might be brisk," said Eleanor.

"I should go an' see."

"Go then, for God's sake."

"And you?"

"I'll sit here an' not be movin'. But find her an' bring her back quick," said Eleanor. "I'm hungry, an' wantin' my dinner."

"Aye, that's what I'll do."

Norman kissed her on the brow and set off across the common for the town, walking with giant strides.

165

Eleanor watched her husband's departure. Only when she could see him no more, not even his hat, did she hoist herself to her feet and, with a little grunt of discomfort, propel herself in the direction of the coalmaster's party, to seek out Robertson Blyth.

*   *   *

The Blyths, quite naturally, had staked claim to the best position in the field and had possessed it by glamour and weight of numbers. No need for staves or wickets. Ten or a dozen servants, gathered about Sarah's carriage, saw to it that the gentry from Cairns were suitably protected from the *hoi polloi.*

The carriage had been hauled across the field from the gate with Sarah, her sons and her maid still in it. Although rugs and white tablecloths had been squared upon the grass, little stools and even a chair set out for her comfort, Lord McCracken's daughter preferred to remain on the carriage's padded seat and look down on the revelry from that vantage.

She looked as cool as well-water in a sprigged muslin dress, with a great soft cartwheel of a hat shading her head and a silk parasol in her lacy hand.

She had refused to travel through the town's dusty streets to watch the longboat race. Her sons would have gone if she'd allowed them but the harbour and its inns were vulgar, contaminating places and no amount of pleading by or on behalf of the boys would change Sarah's mind.

Sarah Blyth had been on show for twenty minutes and betrayed not the slightest interest in what was going on about her.

She was blind to the motley gatherings about the marked oval in the centre of the field, to ale tents and beer stalls, to the vendors of fresh mussels and oysters, pork ribs, mutton broth, pies, pastries, sugar cakes, watery fruit concoctions and little pats of jelly that melted swiftly in the children's hands.

She had no interest in the wrestlers, harriers and throwers who had journeyed from farms and hamlets round about to pit themselves for prize money against sporting professionals; or in the urchins who scampered about the horse ring where tinkers made their trades; or in the muzzled bear, the doleful camel, the acrobats, sword-swallowers and jugglers who displayed their skills wherever an odd corner could be found.

Lord McCracken's daughter was there not to see but to be seen and she received homage with a frosty grace that took heed of nothing but precise social distinctions.

She nodded to colliery managers, bowed discreetly to the wives of land-owners, dipped the rim of her parasol to kirk elders and inclined her head in response to an old schoolmaster's greeting. She ignored the Hardings completely and once, only once, smiled.

"Mr Striker, sir," she said.

"Good afternoon to you, Mistress Blyth. Are you in good health?"

"I am, sir. How kind of you to enquire."

"If I may be permitted to put politeness aside in favour of truth, you look, Madam, quite exquisite."

"I thank you for the compliment, Mr Striker."

"It is my pleasure to give it."

Sarah watched him move away from the line of rugs and tablecloths.

She admired his height, his arrogant swagger and, without the flicker of a lash or a blush on her bloodless cheek, wished that the whole field might suddenly empty so that she could summon him back to make love to her right here on the common ground.

"Mrs Blyth?"

Sarah lifted her chin and peered down her nose at the girl who stood below the carriage.

She knew perfectly well who the girl was. She had seen her in kirk and, on one occasion, in the hall at Cairns. If it had been any other girl, any other servant, Sarah Blyth would not have stooped to give reply.

"Yes?"

"Is Mr Blyth not here?"

"What do you want with Mr Blyth?"

"Is he not with you?"

"Do you see him here, girl?"

"Sure an' I do not."

"Are you not Mrs Quinn's servant?"

"I am. Mr Tannahill's wife too."

"What business do you have with my husband?"

"I've a message for him."

"A message? From Mrs Quinn?"

Smiling, the girl shook her head.

She was no less striking than she had been a couple of

167

months ago but her figure had gone, absorbed by pregnancy.

Sarah recalled the humiliations of her own pregnancies but felt no pity for the Irish girl, only a callous satisfaction that indiscriminate breeding would quickly rob her of her looks as well as her youth.

"Tell me where he is, lady."

"There he is, with the Hardings." Sarah pointed with her parasol. "Are you acquainted with the Hardings?"

"Oh, aye, Missus, I'm well acquainted with the Hardings," Eleanor said and, without so much as a bob of gratitude, waddled off to join the gentlemen who had gathered at an ale stall by the gate.

*　　*　　*

Although no love was lost between Randolph Soames and the Hardings they were civilised enough, just, to drink a cup of ale together without quarrelling.

Brock was still attired in his topcoat and dripping with Masonic regalia, but his sons had removed their coats and vests to catch whatever whisper of breeze might stray across the field now that evening was on hand.

Soames had drunk two cups of the local brew and John Galloway hoped that he would not have to carry the cleric home over his shoulder or, worse, that his friend would become argumentative and start throwing punches at the black sheep of his flock.

Robertson Blyth was also in the group, dour as ever.

Galloway did not notice the girl approach.

She came at the beer stall from its blind side and emerged suddenly out of a gaggle of high-spirited servants and farm labourers.

"Hullo!" said Cabel Harding. "If it ain't the Irish beauty. Lookin' for your master, lassie, are you?"

"I'm thirsty. I've come for a drink."

"Strong ale ain't good for females in your condition," Daniel Harding said. "Shoo away an' bother your husband."

"Mr Blyth," the girl said, "won't you give me a cup to keep me goin'?"

The men were silent. None of them moved.

John Galloway offered her his cup.

"Here, take mine."

168

"It's yours I want, Mr Blyth." the girl said.

She was, John Galloway reckoned, very large for a woman not long married. To judge by the way her bodice strained and her abdomen thrust against the lacing of her skirt the foetus was already well developed.

He had seen the girl several times at Clare's house and had been struck by her unusual beauty. Now he was struck by its deterioration. The sustaining powers that blessed the Leddings had, it seemed, failed to grip the young Irish girl who was, in his professional opinion, unhealthily distended.

"By God, Robbie, she won't have anyone but you," Daniel said. "Ain't supped enough from your cup, I reckon. Give her more, Robbie. It's what she's a-askin' for."

"Get her away from me," Robertson Blyth hissed, his lips hardly moving. "Get – her – away."

"If you won't do it for me, do it for what's inside me."

"I'll get rid of her," Daniel said.

"No." Brock caught at his son's shoulder. "Give her your cup, Robbie, let her drink and be on her way. I don't want no trouble with Headrick."

Robertson Blyth's back was pressed against the beer trestle and he could retreat no further. Eleanor had inched so close that her protuberant belly almost touched him. For a moment he seemed paralysed, then he thrust the cup towards her, crying, "Take it, damn you, take it."

Eleanor seized the cup in both hands.

She stepped back from the stall and turned around. She raised the cup aloft and held it there for two or three seconds before she lowered it to her mouth and drained it dry.

The coalmaster groaned and covered his face with his hands. Galloway could well understand Blyth's distress. Following the line of the Irish girl's gaze he had found himself staring at the lady of Cairns who, from her high vantage point, had witnessed the whole incident.

Without a word Eleanor dropped the cup to the grass and walked away.

"Good God!" Randolph Soames murmured. "How odd!"

None of the others said anything at all as they watched the girl steer her belly proudly past the tablecloths and rugs, past the carriage in which Lord McCracken's daughter sat aloof and upright.

Brock Harding uttered a strange sound, not angry but amused. "Huh! She put us all out there, did she not?"

169

"Insolent bitch!" said Daniel. "I'd have the hide off her backside this night if she was mine."

"She seemed to imply that the bairn's yours, Robbie." Brock said. He paused. "Is it?"

"How can it be?" Blyth said. "I never laid a finger on her, let alone anything else."

"More fool you then," said Cabel.

"But she has a husband. I married them myself," said Soames. "Undoubtedly the child is of Tannahill's making."

"Depends when it arrives," said Cabel.

"She's not due until the end of October," Blyth said.

"So you've enquired, have you?" said Cabel.

"No, I – "

Brock put a hand on the coalmaster's shoulder. "Aye, aye, Robbie," he said. "Never fear. If you didn't touch her then the bairn must be Tannahill's."

John Galloway was not so sure. He said nothing, though, and two or three minutes later the party broke up and he drifted away with Soames to watch the wrestlers limbering up for the first bout of the evening.

*　　*　　*

It was still daylight in the streets of Ladybrook. For those with long journeys home, though, the evening was wearing on and at a signal from Brock Harding the bonfire had been lighted and, at seven o'clock, Henri's battery of fireworks had been trundled out.

The missiles' trajectories had been carefully calculated so that burning remnants would not fall upon thatch or tinder. Horses and ponies had been herded from nearby fields and into a paddock further south. Stray dogs and children had been rounded up and returned safe to their owners. And when all was ready, Henri had lighted his smokepot and, outlined against the bonfire's glare, had tipped a straw to the first of the fuses.

Melissa was held between Frederick's knees. He was crouched upon the grass, coat draped over his shoulder, big hands locked securely about Melissa's waist. Clare stood just behind them and Headrick's servants had gathered about their mistress, the Gowries too, all except Billy who had slipped off to visit a dramshop in the town. Strange, Clare thought, how the lighting of a bonfire brought them all together, as if some recollection of twilight persecutions transformed them, without plan or intent, into a clan.

Whoosh: Clare was startled by the violence of the first rocket's explosion.

Henri had failed to warn her what to expect. She might have slipped and fallen if John Galloway had not protected her with his arm. She had been unaware that he had come to join them. She glanced over her shoulder, saw him smile as the rocket burst and shed a trail of russet particles through the rays of the westering sun.

Melissa cried out in delight.

And Pratie snapped, "Jesus an' Joseph, will you be lookin' at that," as if she disapproved of something so unnaturally spectacular as fireworks.

A second rocket shot upwards then a third and a fourth.

Mare's-tails of sparks trickled down the sky.

The bonfire crackled, dry branches blazing.

Clare smelled its hot resins and tasted gunpowder on her lips. She felt odd, as if she were floating. Only John Galloway's hand upon her waist kept her steady, her hand upon Frederick's shoulder.

For three or four seconds she seemed poised between the two and then, as the first of the Martyr's Wheels flung out its fire and Melissa cried, "Look, Mama, look, look," she came to earth again with a bump.

Fourteen

"Fireworks," said Brock Harding. "Do you think I'm so provincial as to be impressed by a mere firework display?"

"No, Mr Harding," Clare answered. "You are, however, one of the few people who've been inside the laboratory."

"Is the work not satisfactory?"

"Perfectly satisfactory."

"What do you have there, Mrs Quinn? Is it my account?"

"It is your account, Mr Harding. I have come to pay it."

"Aye, that's very prompt, Mrs Quinn."

"It is the way I do business, Mr Harding."

"I thought you'd have sent your factor with payment. I hadn't expected to be honoured by a visit from the lady o' Headrick herself. All by herself, too."

Clare placed her reticule upon the inn table, untied its drawstring, drew from the bag a canvas purse weighted with coin and dropped it neatly into the blacksmith's hand.

"I suggest you count it, Mr Harding."

"No need for that. I'm sure you've been most correct and merit-trickulous in your calculations, like your husband was before you." Brock slipped the purse into a pocket of the tattered coat that he had put on over his apron. "He taught you well, did old Donald."

"Have you forgotten, Mr Harding, that I was raised in a banking house?"

"No, I've not forgotten. I was never one of those who thought Quinn married downward. In my book old Donald got the best of the bargain when he took you to his bed."

"I expect that's a compliment," Clare said. "But I cannot agree with you. Few men of substance would have married a girl who'd been charged with murder."

"Don't be too sure of that, Mrs Quinn." Brock laughed, chestily. "By God, I'd have took you on myself if I hadn't had a wife at the time."

"Ah, but I would not have taken you on, Mr Harding."

"Was I beneath you, even then?"

"I knew far too much about you."

"We were all rogues together when we were young," the blacksmith said lightly. "Donald, myself, my poor brother Jericho."

"And Frederick Striker?"

"The biggest rogue of all."

"We've changed, however, have we not, Mr Harding? We are none of us as we were in those days."

"Aye, well, Jericho's changed and Quinn too, since the both o' them are dead." He shifted his weight, making the oak bench creak. "Nor can I say I'm the same man I was fifteen years ago. Then again, Mrs Quinn, I can't say I've done too badly."

It was four days after the Feast of St John the Baptist. The weather remained warm but the skies had clouded over and a thin, opalescent rain drifted in from the sea, wetting hedgerows and half-grown crops and laying a clean, subtle shine on the town's cobbles. There was no wind, though, and the Neptune at mid-morning was quiet both inside and out.

"Quite the contrary, Mr Harding," Clare said. "You've fared very well indeed, for a humble blacksmith."

The man laughed again.

She amused him, no doubt, but she also made him wary.

Clare had not forgotten that Brock Harding had once been a bullying shadow in her life and that he had played a crucial role in sending Peterkin to his grave.

"Come now, Mrs Quinn. I'll not be accused of humility. That's never been one of my vices. But, aye, I've done well enough."

"Well enough," Clare said, "to wish to do better."

"Have you come to sell me Headrick?"

"Not Headrick, no."

"What then?"

Clare had become so accustomed to seeing Brock only at St Cedric's or strutting about the market that it had not occurred to her that the great Mr Harding would still bend horseshoes or hammer plates for pan repairs. She had caught him at the forge and had watched him from the shelter of the arch, her head shawled against the dripping rain. Shirt open, sleeves furled, sweat had accentuated the scars on his face, neck and arms, pale-edged like tribal tattoos.

When finally Brock had noticed her he had covered himself

at once as if the scars were secrets, not to be seen by the uninitiated. He had called Daniel from the depths of the forge to complete the shaping of the white-hot bar and had walked Clare across the angle of the square into the Neptune's back parlour where he had ordered her cake and sweet Madeira wine and, for himself, a tumbler of gin toddy.

"What is it you have to offer me then?" Brock said.

Clare brought from her bag the deed that Mr Greenslade had drafted to her dictation.

"Just this."

She placed the document on the table. Brock lifted it, unfolded it and held it up to the light from the parlour. He read slowly, brows puckered in concentration. When he had finished he did not put the paper down but slipped it under his armpit and pressed it there as if it was something from which he would not be parted.

He sipped toddy and contemplated Clare thoughtfully.

"Did Fred Striker put you up to this?"

"Certainly not," Clare answered.

"Is Freddie not waitin' round the corner?"

"Frederick, as far as I know, is tallying yesterday's draught of salt for Excise duty," Clare said. "As you will no doubt have noticed, Mr Harding, the deed of partnership is signed by *my* lawyer, Mr Greenslade, who does not share his services with Frederick Striker."

"Freddie could have put you up to it, though."

"I do not blame you for being suspicious but you have my personal assurance that Frederick knows nothing of this matter and has no hand in it at all."

"What's he to you? Striker, I mean?"

"He acts as my salt factor."

"He used to be more than that."

"He used to be *your* partner too, Mr Harding."

"Aye, my partner, but not my lover."

"Do you really suppose that Frederick is my lover now?" said Clare without heat.

"I don't know what he is to you," Brock Harding said. "All I know is that it was Striker who brought the Frenchman to Ladybrook – so I've every right to be cautious, ha'n't I?"

"Perhaps if Leblanc had arrived here with a parcel of Irish waifs you would have been more inclined to accept him," Clare said.

"No comparison," Brock said. "Nor can you threaten me, Mrs Quinn. I make no special secret o' the fact that I supply labour for the pits. I do servants too, now and then. Why, I do believe you've got one o' my poor foundlings servin' in your house right now."

"I do believe I have," said Clare. "I accept, sir, that you can calculate to the penny what a young boy or girl is worth on the labour market but can you not also calculate how valuable Henri Leblanc might be to us?"

"Us?"

"Read the document again, third paragraph. I believe you will see that I have already taken on another partner."

"Who?"

"One of your lodge brothers – Mr Robertson Blyth."

"Huh! Uh-huh!"

"I'm offering you a one-third share in the patent for Leblanc's process, one-third of all profits that may accrue during the patent's term."

"For two hundred pounds?" Brock Harding said.

"Yes."

"It didn't cost you that?"

"What it cost me is no concern of yours," Clare said.

"Aye, I'll admit you were smart enough to beat us all to the mark, Mrs Quinn," Brock said. "I suppose you're entitled to expect the piper to play your tune. Why come to me, though? Why not make this offer to Lord McCracken? Better yet, why not invite your friend Galloway to invest?"

"Because," Clare answered, "you know what Leblanc can do, what value his process will have when it's perfected."

"Well, my lads an' I built his furnace for him," Brock said, "but that doesn't mean we know what'll come out of it. You'll not be offerin' any sort of security." He paused. "Will you, Mrs Quinn?"

"I think you know what Headrick's worth," Clare said. "If Henri Leblanc fails in his efforts then I'll ensure that my partners receive back a fair portion of their investment."

"How will you do that?"

"I'll put a mortgage against my estate."

"In writing?"

"If that's what you wish, sir, yes."

"Does our friend Striker know nothin' of this?"

"Nothing," Clare said. "It's not his concern."

"I fear he'd not approve."

175

"Why do you say that, Mr Harding? Frederick, after all, has great faith in Leblanc's powers of invention."

"How much of his own money has Striker put up?"

Clare thrust out her hand. "I see, sir, that I am wasting my time. Give me back my paper. I'll seek a third partner elsewhere."

Brock extracted the paper from beneath his arm and scanned it once more. "I see no mention of Headrick."

"Does the fifth clause not clearly state that I am the party of first onus for all losses incurred?"

"Still, it says nothin' *specific* about Headrick."

"Do you suppose I'd be able to sustain a loss of almost six hundred pounds without mortgaging Headrick?" Clare snapped her fingers. "My paper, if you please."

"Don't be so hasty, Mrs Quinn. The least I can do is consider it for a while," Brock said. "Can you tell me how long it might be before the Frenchman will be ready to test for his patent?"

"He tells me he hopes to have all his problems solved by the end of August."

"Can you not support him until then?"

"I do not choose to do so."

"You can't, can you?" Brock said. "You're runnin' too close to the rim as it is. Tell you what, let me make you a straight offer for Headrick."

"I see we are travelling in different directions, Mr Harding." Clare got to her feet. "I've told you before, Headrick is not for sale, not at any price."

"And yet you'd risk it all for this Frenchman?"

She had at last reached the moment which she had rehearsed so carefully.

She said, "No, Frederick assures me – "

She bit off the sentence as if mention of Frederick at this point had been unintentional.

Brock Harding was on to her slip immediately.

He stroked his nose with his forefinger and with a soft little sigh spread Mr Greenslade's tidy document upon the table before him.

"How soon do you require the money, Mrs Quinn?"

"As soon as possib . . . as is convenient," Clare said.

"Let me dwell on it." Brock nodded. "I'll give you an answer by noon on Saturday."

Clare let out her breath.

"I wish it to be understood, Mr Harding," she said, "that you will be investing in Leblanc's process and not making a down payment upon Headrick estate."

"Aye, aye, of course."

She could tell by his tone that Brock Harding had fastened on another idea, the wrong idea.

It was all she could do to hide her relief.

Solemnly she offered him her hand.

"Until Saturday, Mr Harding?"

"Until Saturday, Mrs Quinn."

*   *   *

Frederick had promised Clare an increase in revenue and, by God, he intended to deliver. To this end he had set a private salt quota of which Clare had no knowledge.

In the present part of the season he was some one hundred and twenty bushels up on target and, if the Gowries could be kept to scratch, was well set to deliver five thousand bushels of second and third water salt before the year's final tally in November.

Gowrie's bairns were already suffering purple paws and scarlet eyes, however. Even Billy, stiffened half the time by drink, was beginning to creak under the strain of round-the-clock manufacture. What with heat and lack of sleep, Bob had shed a stone or so in weight and looked hardly more robust than his skin-and-bone daughters.

Frederick too was weary.

Managing the affairs of a busy saltworks was no sinecure and kept him occupied from dawn to dusk.

In addition to negotiating new markets for bulk salt he was responsible for the security of the pans and girnal, for paying wages and keeping accurate records. It also fell to him to obtain coal at beneficial terms, fifteen bushels of salt in return for ten carts of coal being the best he could do. And he was required to arbitrate in the Gowries' squabbles, cajole the girls, bully Billy, bribe Bob and listen patiently to Matt Pringle's constant complaints.

Boiling brine kept heat trapped in the panhouse and loft and, in summer months, there seemed to be no escape from it.

In spite of his conservative disposition Frederick could not but share a little of the salters' resentment when he returned to Headrick late of an evening to find Clare in the cool drawing-room, toying with her embroidery and listening to

177

one of Leblanc's recitals on the pianoforte while the Gowries slaved throughout the night to fill her coffers.

Frederick's clandestine meetings with Sarah Blyth did little to relieve his tension, yet his desire for Clare had not diminished, so much so that he feared he might actually be falling in love with her. Factoring seemed to be all that she had left to him and a strange sense of loss clouded his days and nights like a fog. He did not know what to do to be rid of it, except wait it out.

A clearing in the dismal summer rain had brought long strips of sunlight into the sky and the waters of the firth were streaked with it. Frederick had been in the panhouse for what seemed like hours. His lungs felt as if they'd been scalded, his shirt was sticking to his back and his breeches were pasted to his thighs when he staggered, dazed from the fumes, to sniff the healing breeze that skittered over the pond. His body was weighted by accumulations of age, illness and fatigue and he headed numbly for the fresh-water cistern. His brain was foggy with caustic and the din of argument.

He put his hands upon the cistern's rim and, sighing, dipped his head towards the water to drink.

She came from beneath the surface like one of Henri's rockets, trailing water not fire.

Salt scoop in one hand, her shift wrapped wet about her like a fish's skin, her eyes were wide open, her lips drawn back in a grin.

Frederick reared back in alarm. "Kate!"

"Ha-ha, aye, what did ye think, I was a ghost?"

"What – what are you doing inside the cistern?"

"Cleanin' the flume, like ye told me to."

"From under the water?"

"It's how it's always been done."

The salt scoop was coated with mud and sand. Kate pressed her breast against the cistern's edge, casually tossed the debris into the weeds then leaned her elbows against the iron and grinned at him again.

"Are ye wantin' a drink, Mr Striker?"

"No, I think I'll wait, thank you."

"The sediment'll soon settle, y'know."

"Don't let me interrupt your work, Kate."

"It's nearly done."

With her hair plastered to her skull and her slender figure outlined by the shift, a fanciful man might have regarded Kate Gowrie as a nymph. Frederick was not a fanciful man at the best of times and had too many things on his mind to pay her much attention.

"Help me out, Mr Striker."

Frederick gave a little *tut* beneath his breath but, to please her, extended his hand.

She grasped it strongly, planted her feet against the cistern's inner wall and jerked herself up and forward. She looped an arm about his neck, soaking his shirt, before Frederick could prevent it. Strands of wet hair brushed his cheek and then, still clinging to him, she was perched on the cistern's edge.

"I saw you," she said, smugly.

"What?"

"I saw you in the woods wi' the leddy."

Frederick shifted his grip from hand to wrist and pulled her to the ground.

"What did you see, Kate?"

"What you done."

"Do you know who the lady was?"

"Aye – from the castle. The lady Blyth."

"Have you told anyone, anyone at all what you saw?"

She twisted at her arm, the grin gone.

She was petulant but entirely uncomprehending of the damage she might wreak upon him – and upon herself.

To his astonishment Frederick realised that the girl supposed this shared secret would bring her to his notice and oblige him to pander to her adolescent demands. He glanced around to make sure they were alone then dragged her by the arm towards the bushes, flung her into them and followed her.

He thumped his hands upon her shoulders and held her firmly. She was agog, grey eyes huge.

"Are you goin' to – to – "

"No, damn it. I'm not going to do anything to you. I want to know what you were doing in the pine wood? Did you follow me there deliberately?"

"Aye."

"But why, Katy? For God's sake, why?"

"To see where you went."

Thumbs on her throat. Tendons taut beneath cold skin.

She was frightened of him now.

"Did somebody tell you to follow me?"

"Nah. I just – I just done it."

Sunlight flitted across the gorse, bright for an instant and then gone again.

"What exactly do you think you saw, Katy?"

She struggled to find the right words. She did not wish to offend him nor yet to seem naive.

"Love?" the girl said.

He let her go.

She crouched, quivering, face framed by lank wet hair and one hand webbed across her little breasts.

"Listen, Kate, listen to me carefully," Frederick said. "You must tell no one what you saw, not Billy, not your sister. No one. Do you understand?"

"Nah."

"I'll buy you ribbon. I'll buy you cloth for a pretty dress. Would you like a pretty dress, Kate?"

"Aye."

She did not really care about the dress.

She was not deceived by his desperate promises. She obeyed him now only because she was afraid of him – and fear would not last for long.

"Nothing bad will happen to you provided you keep our secret," Frederick told her. "Do you understand what I'm saying?"

"Aye."

She was childishly stupid yet Frederick knew that sooner or later nature, female nature, would assert itself and little Katy Gowrie would begin to realise her power. He touched his fingers to his cheek where her hair had deposited trickles of salt-water which suddenly felt more like blood than tears.

"Get away with you then," he said.

"Aye, Mr Striker."

Kate Gowrie dashed off through the gorse in the direction of the salthouse stairs.

And Frederick stared after her, frowning.

*   *   *

Early that morning John Galloway had amputated a hand.

Twelve-year-old Shaun Sullivan, working the windlass on Malliston's coalhill, had caught his fingers between rope and crank and the bones had been crushed to the consistency of sugar by the grinding impact of the wheel. By the time John Galloway arrived, there was nothing left to sew up save a lump of bloody flesh lathered with black grease.

The boy had been removed to a shed, covered with a

blanket and given neat brandy to drink. He had vomited up the brandy and most of his breakfast and had been in a foul and raving state.

Shaun Sullivan was one of the Irish orphans brought to Cairns by the Hardings a year or so ago. The coal-heaver with whom the boy had been lodged had been angry because the boy, if he survived at all, would need nursing.

The coal-heaver had held the boy down while the doctor had forced laudanum between his teeth. The boy had then been carried to the tackle shed where a table, spread with a tarpaulin, was available.

John Galloway had taken off his jacket, had put on his apron and had rolled up his shirt-sleeves. He had spread out his instruments and without more ado had removed Shaun Sullivan's left hand just above the joint of the wrist. He had arranged the loose tendons so that the nervous flow would be as little affected as possible, and had cauterised the stump.

Mercifully the boy had swooned while the little saw was doing its work and the doctor had been able to complete his task and dress the wound without distraction.

Galloway had been pleased with the job. He would call upon the patient at the coal-heaver's cottage that evening, administer another dose of laudanum and, in the course of the next few days, would rebind the stump to ensure that it remained free of gangrenous pus and to avoid a general poisoning of the bloodstream.

He would also present an account for five pounds to the coalhill foreman who would see to it that he was paid out of the Injury Fund.

What would happen to Shaun after recovery was not John Galloway's concern.

It had been half-past eleven o'clock before the doctor had arrived home. He had unsaddled his horse, fed and watered it, and had washed and polished his surgical knives and returned them to his bag. That done, and looking forward to a glass of ale and a bite of dinner, he had headed down the gravel walk to the villa's side door.

Hardly had he stepped over the threshold, though, than Ishbel had been upon him, wringing her hands as if some great tragedy had fallen upon the house, a tragedy that would probably turn out to be no more than a blocked drain or a mouse in the pantry.

With the prospect of dinner disappearing over the horizon, John Galloway sighed.

"What is it, Ishbel? What's wrong?"

"Eppie says there's a girl in the garden."

"What? A tinker? Is she stealing my flowers?"

"It's Mrs Quinn's new servant, the Irish."

"Tannahill's wife?"

"Aye."

"What's she doing in the garden?"

"Awaitin' for you."

"How long has she been here?"

"An hour or more."

"Did you give her refreshment?"

"She asked for ale. Eppie made me give her tea."

"Did she indicate what she wants with me?"

"She has a message from Mrs Quinn."

For some reason Galloway was suddenly nervous.

He had just removed a human hand without apprehension yet he found himself tense at the prospect of meeting a servant girl in the shadow of the hollyhocks.

Ridiculous!

Grumbling at his own foolishness Galloway backed from the door and strode to the arbour where the dark-haired beauty had made herself comfortable on a rustic bench in the shade of the privet which protected the rose garden.

She did not rise to greet him.

She wore a heavy skirt of emerald green and a huge linen apron which was tied across her belly with three tapes. Her bodice laces were loosened. She had taken off her bonnet and put it on the bench beside a teacup and saucer and a plate with the remains of a buttered bannock upon it. However much his housekeepers might disapprove of the gorgeous stranger they had not forgotten how to be civil.

The fragrance of roses permeated the warm, moist air. He had sprayed for aphids last night and the faint pungency of carbolic mingled with the perfume of the summer blooms. In a less gravid condition, the girl would have been a perfect ornament for his rose garden, as opulent as a Bourbon or blood-red Damask. Now, though, she presented an unwholesome overblown appearance that was anything but attractive.

"I believe you have a message for me?"

"Aye, sir. I do."

She fumbled in her pocket, brought out a little note which was sealed with a blob of the jade-tinted wax Clare favoured for casual correspondence.

The doctor clipped off the wax with his thumbnail and gently unfolded the missive.

Dear John,
If you are free to join me for a luncheon between noon and one o'clock today I would welcome an opportunity to discuss certain confidential matters. If this time is not convenient perhaps you would be good enough to suggest another.

Clare.

He brushed the signature with his fingertip as if to test the density of the ink then dug into his waistcoat for his watch.

Twelve minutes past midday.

"How did you come here?" he asked the girl.

"On foot, sir."

"Are you up to walking back?"

She heaved herself to her feet. The effort was obviously wearisome. She put a hand to her back above the arch of her hip and kneaded the flesh beneath her garments. She looked alarmingly massive. The unlaced bodice was not affectation but necessity. Small wonder she had resisted the temptation to clamp her waist with stays, a vanity all too common among servants and farm lassies.

"I'm fit for anythin', sir," she said.

The doctor studied her carefully for a moment then said, "I think I'll run out the gig."

*　　*　　*

Seated by his side in the light two-wheeled vehicle, the girl had said not a word since he'd helped her aboard.

She had put on her bonnet again and had tucked in her hair and was perched quite primly on the narrow bench now, one hand gripping the rail, the other placed across her stomach as if to cushion the tenant from the roughness of the ride.

John Galloway cleared his throat. "How long have you been married?"

"Five months, sir."

"Are you happy with Mr Tannahill?"

"Happy as I can be."

If she twigged where he was leading the conversation she gave no sign of apprehension. Her eyes were hidden under the bonnet's brim and she had that squat comfortable appearance that heaviness brings.

"After the child is born," Galloway said, "will you continue to work at Headrick?"

"Aye. Missus Quinn says she'll take me back as soon as I'm ready for it. The old woman'll look after the bairn."

Nothing definite, just a touch of coldness at the mention of her mother-in-law. Resentment between two women of different generations obliged to share the same house was understandable.

"When do you expect the child to arrive?"

"Sure an' I don't know."

"Well, if you don't know, who does?" John Galloway said. "Calculate it from your wedding night."

"He tried me out before that," she said without a blush.

"Was Tannahill the first to – to try you out?"

She turned her head slowly. She was not afraid of him or his knowledge. "An early drop runs in my family."

"Your family? I was led to believe you were an orphan."

"I knew who my mother was."

"But not your father?"

"I heard stories."

Galloway tightened the rein until the horse was barely moving forward, hoofs dragging dust from the road. Off to the right the town looked incredibly serene under a clear, calm sky, the sea so blue as to be almost black.

"What stories," Galloway said, "will you concoct when the baby arrives six or eight weeks before it's due?"

"It won't be that early."

"I think it will."

"I'll – I'll keep it in."

"Impossible."

"Norman'll take my word for it."

"He might – but she won't. Rose, I mean."

"I'll deal with her when the time comes."

"How, Eleanor? It may not be so easy to explain why you've presented Tannahill with a child conceived a month before you met him."

184

"Aye, I'm big enough to drop tomorrow, I suppose."

"Too big," Galloway said. "Have you given birth to a child before, Eleanor?"

She shook her head.

"Have you lost one?"

"Lost?"

"Miscarried."

"Sure, how would I know?" She shook her head again.

"Eleanor, Eleanor!" John Galloway sighed. "How in God's name did you hope to fool Rose Tannahill? You were already pregnant when you stepped off the boat from Ireland."

"If I was, I didn't know it."

"Did someone in the Brat School force himself on you?"

"Someone in the Brat School! God, it could have been any one of a hundred men. Sure you're not that wise after all, are you, Mr Doctor?" She laughed. "Maybe you can see into me, sir, but you can't see through me."

"A hundred?"

"Aye, five times a hundred. But not one o' them had the snuff to fill my belly." She laughed again. "What can they do to me here, eh? What's the worst they can do? Cry my name from the pulpit as a fornicator?"

"The Kirk Session has the power to declare your marriage void," Galloway said. "Or the Tannahills might throw you and the baby out."

"Norman would never do that to me."

"Perhaps not," Galloway said, "but the old woman would."

"She's witch enough for anythin'," Eleanor agreed. "She took me in just to use me, you know. It wasn't me she cared about. She just wanted a ewe for her pet lamb, a mare for her stallion."

"If Rose does throw you out where will you go?"

She flashed him a smile, quick and wicked. "Will you not take me in? Do you not want me?"

"I don't think I do," John Galloway said. "No."

"No, it's Missus Quinn you fancy. I'll bet I could make you forget her quick enough if you was to take me in." Before he could protest she waved her hand airily. "Anyway, I'm not in need o' casual charity. If I am flung out o' the Leddings then Pappy'll take care of us."

"Pappy? Your father?"

"The bairn's pappy, not mine."

"But I thought – "

"Did you imagine I came to this country for no reason? Did you imagine I came wi'out a friend?"

"So you do know who fathered your child?"

"Sure an' I do," she said.

"I trust you're not asking me to believe it was Robertson Blyth?" Galloway said.

"Blyth?" Her laughter was genuine and coarse. "God, Blyth couldn't put a whelk back in its shell never mind plant a bairn in my belly."

"Yet, in the field at the fair, you tried to make him believe he was responsible. Why?"

She shrugged. "To pay him back."

"If it isn't Blyth, who is it?"

She put a finger to her lips. "My secret."

"Does he know that the child is his?"

A shake of the head.

"Does he know you're in this condition?"

"Aye, but he thinks since I'm wedded it means our ways have parted for good." She laughed yet again and shook her head. "Silly old devil!"

"Good God!" John Galloway exclaimed. "It's Striker."

"Our secret, Mr Doctor," Eleanor said and, pressing her finger to her lips, stayed silent until he dropped her off in Headrick's stableyard.

*　　*　　*

Although the day had turned fine Clare had ordered luncheon served in the small back parlour.

Broth and beef, new bread, fresh butter, a ripe cheese and a bottle of French wine graced the table and, in spite of his mental turmoil, John Galloway soon found his appetite and ate heartily.

He was tempted to raise the subject of the errant servant girl but he did not wish Clare to suppose that he was malicious or intended harm to Striker's reputation and prudently kept silent on the subject.

Clare looked as well as he had ever seen her.

She wore a dress in the Greek style. Her blue eyes were clear, her hair shiny and her cheeks had acquired a light dusting from the sun and sea air. She seemed just a shade plumper too, as if contentment had brought her into bloom.

For a minute or two John Galloway revelled in the faint,

sagging thrill of unrequited love and all thought of severed hands and vastly pregnant servant girls drifted from his mind. But he knew, somehow, that the mood would not last long and that he would probably soon be drawn into another little crisis of communal or domestic affairs.

"I have seen so little of you lately, John," Clare said.

"It is not my wish." He hesitated. "Circumstances seem to have interrupted our friendship."

"Are you much occupied with your profession?"

"More than I wish to be, really."

She was holding him off by polite questions. With anyone else he would have been blunt. But not with Clare.

"You are a very honest man, John Galloway."

"Thank you," he said, a little disconcerted.

"Along with my cousin Andrew you are one of the few honest men I have ever met."

Oh, God, John Galloway thought, please do not let her tell me that I am "reliable". He did not want to be thought of as reliable. He wanted Clare to regard him as a dangerous influence. Small chance of that, for they were too alike ever to make the sparks fly.

Clare took from the desk a long envelope with the carrier's mark still fresh upon it and passed it to him across the table.

"What, in all honesty, do you think of this?" she said.

He recognised Greenslade's handwriting and seal. His eye travelled down the page, found Clare's signature, then that of James Brock Harding. Brock! In the package was a banker's draft for two hundred pounds also signed by Harding but witnessed by Gilbert Hewlitt, a shifty lawyer from Saltcoats and an erstwhile member of Lodge Ladybrook.

"What have you sold him, Clare? Not Headrick?"

"For two hundred pounds? Hardly!"

"A first payment, perhaps?"

"No, John, not Headrick."

"What then?"

"A share in Leblanc's patent."

"Has the Frenchman completed his experiments?"

"He is, he informs me, smoothing out the blemishes."

"I have never quite understood what value there is in Leblanc's process." John Galloway said. "There! Is that honest enough for you?" He sat back, brows arched, as an inkling of her intention occurred to him. "Oh, wait! Is that it? Have you

187

elected to set off your investment in Leblanc because you regard him as a charlatan?"

"On the contrary. I think Henri is very clever and I am convinced that he will eventually perfect a device for the cutting of metals."

"Do you really understand what he's about, Clare?"

"Other people do," Clare said. "Who better to confirm the correctness of my judgement than a blacksmith and a coalmaster."

"Is Blyth also an investor?"

Clare nodded. "Two hundred pounds."

"What *are* you doing, Clare? What *are* you up to?"

"Blyth and Harding regard themselves as important men in Ladybrook. For that reason they cannot afford to be left out of things. It's as simple as it sounds, John."

"It does not sound simple to me."

"Do you know who I have to thank for putting this opportunity in my way?"

"No, who?"

"Frederick."

"Oh!" Galloway said. "I'd have thought dealing with Striker was something you might wish to avoid."

"You do not approve?"

"No, Clare. I do not approve," John Galloway said. "I mean, you cannot be unaware that Brock Harding will stop at nothing to get his hands on Headrick?"

"I am indeed well aware of it."

"It would not surprise me if Harding hadn't already enlisted Striker's aid in this matter."

"It would surprise me if he had not," Clare said.

"And you are playing into their hands?"

"So it would appear."

"Clare, for heaven's sake, are you so greedy for cash that you'd risk Headrick for a small profit?"

"Four hundred pounds is hardly small profit."

"What have you done with your money?"

"Nothing. Apart from one hundred and eighty pounds expended in furnishing Henri with materials – nothing. In fact the salt revenues have never been better. Frederick is doing very well by me in that respect."

"And in what other respects?"

"Oh, come, John, that remark is unworthy."

"Yes," the doctor said. "You have my apology."

"After all, I've done nothing illegal. I've only traded in a patent for a process which requires development. Blyth is eager to participate because he wishes to achieve something independently of his wife."

"And Harding?"

"Harding cannot believe that Frederick does not have some wily trick up his sleeve."

"Does he?"

"Oh, yes, of course he does."

"Clare, why have you given me sight of this document?"

"In case anything goes wrong."

John Galloway suddenly realised that the bold Mrs Quinn was playing a calculated game of revenge. He contemplated telling her what he had learned from Eleanor Tannahill but a quirky feeling that Clare knew more about the Irish girl than he did stayed him.

"In a month or so," Clare went on, "Frederick will ask me to become his wife."

"Surely you will not accept?"

"Yes, John, I will."

"Oh! So you are still in love with him?"

"It appears that I am," Clare said.

"When – when will you marry?"

"Our betrothal will be announced in St Cedric's in September and the wedding arranged for the month's end. I invited you here today expressly to inform you of my intention."

"In case anything goes wrong?" John Galloway said.

"Yes."

"Before, or afterwards."

"Precisely," Clare reached across the little table and clasped his hand. "Will you continue to be my guardian angel no matter what happens?"

"Of course I will."

Clare paused. "And if, by any chance, I should die?"

"I'll see him hanged for it," the doctor said.

Fifteen

Cultivated raspberries would not be ready in Ladybrook's gardens until the middle of July but the wild fruit on the Leddings had already taken on the deep pink gauzy hue which told Mother Tannahill that it was ripe for picking.

She had persuaded Pratie Kerrigan to let Eleanor accompany her so the girl and the old woman, each with a basket, had gone to the bank above where the Linn ran shallow over gravel and, amid bramble and dog-rose, rasps grew in profusion.

At first Eleanor was pleased to be out of Headrick's kitchens, for the tasks that Mrs Shay considered suitable for a girl in Eleanor's condition were hardly light. She had been absolved from scrubbing floors and lifting heavy pans and, after she had complained how it pained her, from taking her turn at the butter churn. Even so, Eleanor found kitchen duties oppressive and the antics of Lizzie and little Jen wearing in the extreme.

It was hardly better in the cottage of a night. She was still expected to perform the duties of a housewife, to wash her husband's back and serve his supper as if she was a lithe little slave and not a great swollen elephant.

She plucked the fruit and placed it in the basket, ate a berry now and then to freshen her dry mouth. She squinted at the old woman from under her bonnet and wondered if this was just another sort of punishment that Rose had devised to weary her more. It was not until the basket was almost full and Eleanor had begun to stagger that Rose, not a moment too soon, gestured to her to sit and rest.

Eleanor needed no second bidding.

She propped the basket among the bramble roots, shaded by leaves, and lowered her body to the grass. She leaned forward to take the weight of her stomach upon her thighs then, as a burning sensation flooded up into her chest, she lay back on her elbows and let her stomach point towards the puffy florets of pure white cloud which floated across the blue sky. A thin tremulous hum seemed to fill the air and far off a solitary bullock roared in distress.

Eleanor's lids drooped. If only the world could be as she saw it now, pink and soft and comforting. She thought wistfully of Dublin town and the cool brown depths of public houses down by the Liffey, the airy pleasure of the upstairs room in her lodgings where she would lie at ease on hot summer afternoons, waiting for the night-time trade.

"Here, drink this," Mother Tannahill said.

The tin cup had no handle. Burn water beaded its dented rim. The woman held it out and urged her to drink.

"What have you put in it this time?" Eleanor said.

"It's only water from the Linn, clean off the gravel."

Eleanor took it, drank and tasted the acid raspberry pulp that had lingered on her teeth. She felt as if the berries were still stuck above her breastbone.

The old woman squatted on her heels like an Egyptian. She was clad in layers of wool with a huge lacquered black shawl about her from which the sun's rays seemed to radiate outwards in whorls and spirals.

Eleanor's thirst overcame her caution. She drank the burn water greedily.

"She's comin' soon," Rose said.

"Who?"

"Our babby."

Eleanor licked the droplets from the rim of the cup.

"Not for weeks yet, weeks an' weeks," she said.

"You'll burst like a haw before then."

"Sure an' I'm burstin' now," Eleanor said. "I'd be glad if it came early."

"Aye, but how early will it be, girl?"

Eleanor let her lids droop once more.

Her mother-in-law's shadow blotted out the pinkness. Ever since she'd ridden with Dr Galloway and he had accurately defined her term she had lost confidence in her ability to deceive.

"I'm fat, that's all."

"You're a cuckoo, Eleanor Antrim. You're not what you pretend to be. I should have known it by the tricks you played with Norman."

"You were the one who took me in. You nodded me into your son's bed. I'd have been safe with Robertson Blyth if it hadn't been for you."

191

"And do you think the coalmaster can't count?"

"I don't care," said Eleanor sulkily. "It's *my* babby, whatever you say about its pappy."

"My, but you're a wicked one," Rose Tannahill said with a little grunt, not of anger or derision but almost of approval. "I wonder if your past and future will show in the egg now, girl, now you've lost your fire."

Eleanor sat up. "What d'you mean?"

"Tonight's the first night of a rising moon."

"You're not tryin' me with the serpent's egg."

"Then tell me where you're really from."

"From Dublin town. I've told you a dozen times."

"No, there's more. I know there is."

"Norman doesn't think so."

"Norman's a man – "

"You don't have to be tellin' me that."

"Keep your nasty tongue to yourself, girl," Rose said. "And tell me what you're hiding."

"If I was hidin' anythin' do you think my husband wouldn't have found it? God knows, he's searched over every inch of me, long and hard." Eleanor raised herself to her knees. "He's found nothing he doesn't like. Ask him if you don't believe me."

"What's inside you?"

"My babby."

"Who put it .there?"

"God."

"Blaspheme if you will, lass," Rose said, "But when I put the egg in your hand tonight we'll see what tale the babby has to tell, what secrets."

"No," Eleanor struggled to her feet. "I want none o' your witch spells affectin' my babby. I'm not touchin' that serpent's egg again, not tonight nor ever."

"Why are you afraid of a plain piece of glass?"

"I'm not afraid of it. I'm afraid of *you*, you old sow," Eleanor shouted. "Leave me alone. For God's sake, leave me alone."

The burning sensation rose into her throat. She could hear the roar of the tormented beast coming across the moor loud as a brass trumpet now.

"When your time comes," Rose said, "the truth will come out. We'll need no glass then, girl, nor salt nor stars."

"Norman won't let you harm me."

"The harm's already done."

"Your doing then, not mine," Eleanor shouted. "Tell Norman *that* when the time comes. Your doing, your fault."

She raked the basket from the brambles, slung it on her arm and, as fast she dared, laboured up the steep bank away from Rose Tannahill and set off for Headrick through the whins.

*   *   *

In other circumstances Frederick would have found it stimulating to rendezvous with a fine lady in a stuffy room on the second floor of Hunter's Hotel in the heart of Kilmarnock on a bustling market-day afternoon. But the fact that the lady was mistress of Cairns and he had come to bring her news and not pleasure blunted his sense of anticipation and increased his caution.

Farmers and stockbreeders gathered in the coffee room that occupied the hotel's latest extension and the public bars were packed with country folk who carried in from the stockyards the odours of dung, hides, wool and feathers to dampen the effluvia of roasting meats, coffee, whisky and ale. Kilmarnock was a fair piece from Ladybrook but the small town's merchants and dealers were drawn to the larger market like iron nails to a magnet, in search not only of profit but also of convivial company.

In the rumbustious throng were ten or a dozen men who might be classed as friends of Robertson Blyth and five or ten times that many who would recognise the coalmaster's wife on sight. It hardly mattered if Frederick was spotted and identified, for the salt-factoring business took him hither and yon. For the lady of Cairns it was much more dangerous. One glimpse of her, outside of the haberdasher's or calico shop, and questions were bound to be asked and rumours leaked back to her husband.

The braying of males at trough and tap followed Frederick upstairs and wafted him into the second-floor bedroom on a cloud of liquor fumes.

He was surprised to find Sarah's confidential maid still there, the pair of them dining *à deux* from a huge circular platter of cod roe and breaded haddock.

The maid was a sallow Italian-looking woman just past her prime. She had black hair, rather bulbous eyes and a sullen pout that Frederick might once have found attractive. She wore a frock of blood-red silk and was stoutly corseted in ideal contrast to her blonde and slender mistress.

Frederick hesitated in the doorway, frowning, while the maid

193

popped a final forkful of roe into her mouth, washed it down with wine, rose and left the bedroom. Sarah continued to peck at her fish without a word of greeting.

Frederick advanced to the table and kissed the back of Sarah's neck.

She swallowed, shivered, swung round and offered up her lips. One brown breadcrumb adhered to the down, a perfect blemish, as natural as the shared taste of malt vinegar.

Obediently he kissed her again.

Dust rose from the street outside. The room shook slightly with the thunder of brewers' drays. Laughter climbed the stairs from the coffee room, along with the clash of plates and glasses.

Frederick brushed the back of her neck with his lips once more then, breaking from her, seated himself upon the edge of the bed, and propped his elbows on his knees.

Sarah glanced round at him. "Are you so fevered, sir, that you would have me interrupt my luncheon?"

"Eat away, Sarah," Frederick said. "I will not be staying long, in any case."

He had seen high-born London jades riding in the parks and walking in the gardens, the strutting dandies of the Strand, and it had occurred to him then how separate they were from commoner folk, not just in polish but in cruelty, flaunting a selfishness that he could emulate but never hope to match.

Sarah snapped her head round so quickly that he could have sworn he heard the bones crackle.

"Are you ill, sir?"

"I am well enough," said Frederick in a tone that indicated otherwise. "It's not the state of my health that concerns me, Sarah, it's regard for your reputation."

She put aside her fork and turned to face him.

In sunlight from the window her hands seemed almost transparent.

"We've been seen," Frederick told her.

She studied him for a moment, utterly impassive.

"By whom?"

"One of the Headrick salters."

"What is such a person doing in Kilmarnock?"

"Oh no. Not here. Not today."

"Where then, and when?"

"In the pinewood, one afternoon when we – " Frederick

stirred the limpid air with one hand. "You know – when we thought we were *hors de prise*."

"You must pay the fellow off."

"It isn't a fellow," Frederick said. "It's one of Bob Gowrie's girls."

"Buy her off. I'm sure she'll see sense in silence."

"Unfortunately," Frederick said, "she isn't sensible."

"What precisely did she see?"

"Everything."

"How old is the girl?"

"Eighteen, I suppose."

"Did she understand what she saw?"

"Oh, come now, Sarah!"

"Did she tell you this tale herself?"

"She did," said Frederick. "Without prompting."

"What does she want?"

"I think – I think she wants a – a share."

He did not have to explain.

Sarah laughed and clapped her hands together as if to applaud the girl's audacity. She had probably seen Kate Gowrie a hundred times or more but to McCracken's daughter Gowrie's daughter would be nothing but a figment in the grey world of workers who scuffled in the servants' gallery and jostled irreverently at the kirk door.

Frederick doubted if Sarah Blyth understood the damage that could be done by ignorance.

"Give her a share then, if it will keep her quiet."

"Sarah!"

"Did the salter's child follow you here, do you think?"

"Of course not."

"Then why must you hurry off?"

"Sarah, I really don't think I can allow you to become the subject of gossip and slander."

"Allow me? Allow me? I am not under your command, am I?"

"If word of our relationship reaches the ears of the Kirk Session your husband would be humiliated and, more to the point, you would be called to account and rebuked."

"The Kirk Session would not dare rebuke me."

"In any event your husband would be bound to find out."

"And would cut off your supply of coal, hmm?"

"Sarah – "

"Are you intimidated by this salter's brat?"

195

"No, but – "

"Have you, perhaps, invented this ridiculous story just to be rid of me?"

"No, no, no."

"I think you have, sir. I think you are bored with me."

"How could I be bored with such a lovely – "

"It's the Quinn woman, is it not? You are wooing the Quinn woman and you're afraid she'll reject you if she learns about our friendship."

"Yes, I do hope to marry Clare Quinn."

"Does she grant you the same favours as I do?"

"There are no other women in my life, Sarah, at least none like you," Frederick said. "But I have a need for a place and when I marry Clare Quinn I'll be master of Headrick, and secure."

"Will you give her your loyalty, Frederick?"

He looked at her, startled.

She extended one leg towards him, skirt and petticoats hitched up to display a milk-white ankle and calf.

She placed the toe of her slipper on his knee and if he had not caught her heel would have nuzzled it into his lap.

"I certainly intend to give Clare my loyalty. Whether I choose to give her my heart is another story." Frederick lowered Sarah's slippered foot gently to the floor. "Meanwhile I'm disinclined to risk a sacrifice of my one and only opportunity. Consequently I treat the fact that we have been observed in a compromising situation with a deal less aplomb than you do."

"There are no spies here, Frederick, no jealous wretches to disturb us. Will you not stay?"

"Sarah, I can't."

"Frederick, this salter's brat has you dancing like a jacka-napes," Sarah snapped. "You must do something about her, something to stop her."

"I will. I'll see to it, Sarah, I promise."

"What is the creature's name?"

"Kate."

"Kate," Sarah Blyth said, nodding, then swivelled round to the table and attacked the remains of her luncheon while Frederick, dismissed, was left to slink away without so much as a word of farewell.

*   *   *

It was unusual for Blyth's collier brigs to carry passengers. The accommodation was mean, the galley primitive, the crossing slow, and Daniel Harding, a born landlubber, dreaded his voyages on the black and wallowing hulks.

He would invariably succumb to sea-sickness as soon as the vessel rounded Trotter's Point and would disembark at Belfast shaky and wrung out. He was, however, a Harding born and bred. Stoked up with steak and Irish whiskey he would be fighting fit and rarin' to go within hours of putting ashore and would start north in his hired cart to harvest the latest crop of orphans that the parish boards had gathered for him.

Eleven such trips, however uncomfortable, had put four hundred pounds into the Hardings' account with the Greenock Banking Company and had greatly increased the fund with which they would purchase Quinn's estate and become at long last gentlemen.

There was a little creamy smack upon the sea that summer's afternoon when, with the brig gunnelled down and gurgling at the pier's end, Daniel took leave of his father and prepared to carry his valise up the gangplank and, metaphorically speaking, rope himself to the mast for the duration of the voyage.

Brock was in jovial mood and Daniel was amused by the needless instructions which his father had pressed upon him.

"This, son," Brock said, "could be your last Irish jaunt."

"Is that a fact?" said Daniel.

"It's not a proper trade for gentlemen," Brock said, "and I'm inclined to think Freddie will put on his shooting boots as soon as the summer's out."

"Freddie?"

"He'll marry Headrick."

"Has he bedded her already?"

"He has *not* bedded her," Brock said. "But that's only because the lady considers herself virtuous. She may be wary of our Fred but she must be eager or she'd have seen him off by now."

Daniel rubbed his chin. "What if, when it comes to it, Fred won't sell us Headrick after all? I mean, he might decide to stick an' manage the salt, like he's doin' now."

"He'll be deep in my debt by then," Brock said. "He'll not be able to buy his way out of his financial obligations without mortgagin' the estate."

"If Mrs Quinn will let him."

"What choice will she have? She'll be Fred's wife by then and her property will be at his disposal."

"Have we enough in the kitty to buy Headrick right now?"

Brock grinned. "Three thousand, eight hundred pounds is the estimated purchase price. I'll skin Freddie down, though, and we'll have the property for three or my name's not Harding."

"Will there be room for all of us?"

"Room an' to spare," said Brock. "Once we're rid of the witch-woman Headrick will be our place, shared with nobody who isn't a Harding by marriage or blood."

Daniel was not entirely convinced.

He had been listening to his father's tales since he was in swaddling clothes and while he did not doubt the will behind them he had reservations about Striker's honesty and Brock's ability to get the better of the Englishman in the final reckoning.

He knew better than to argue with his father, though, and asked jocularly, "Will you still be in the smithy when I get back?"

"If we're not, son, you'll know where to find us."

"Up the hill?" Daniel said, grinning.

"On Headrick," Brock said and, giving his son a hearty slap upon the back, bid him a fond farewell.

*　　*　　*

For Henri the tar-black, fish-reeking old shed on the foreshore of Headrick Bay was a hermitage divine. It contained everything he required for his work and, at the end of a long day, there was a comfortable billet and friendly company to return to just up the hill.

Small wonder that he had taken to humming while he toasted coke in his nice new furnace, peered at crystals through the eyepiece of his microscope or diligently pinched each of the one hundred and ten wire connections of his voltaic separator.

Pride of place was given to his air-gun, though, a pneumatic masterpiece screwed together from parts forged by the Hardings. Barrels and pistons, cocks, taps and gauges all fitted neatly together, sealed at every seam with cork sleeves and strips of soft leather soaked in olive oil; the device clamped to two huge oak beams which Henri, with block and tackle, had hoisted on a bench as far from the furnace and as close to the door as possible.

Henri loved the air-gun.

It was to him what Melissa was to Mrs Quinn, a lustrous object, more beautiful than the sum of its parts.

In the early morning he would toddle round it and caress its buxom barrels. In the evening he would tuck it warmly under canvas. Throughout the day he would break off from his labours now and then to burnish its edges with a little file and polish its knobs with a cotton rag. He was, in fact, loath to contaminate its pristine beauty with chemicals, to force it to do what it had been designed to do in case the gun, like so many other things in his life, failed to live up to its promises.

Construction of the electrical apparatus which had scared Cabel Harding had cost Henri three months' hard labour but he reckoned he had finally reached a stage where he could safely separate one chemical element from another. He was, however, a shade too impatient to be absolutely thorough. He kept meticulous records, of course, of the strange volatile alkalis and base acids which he had stumbled upon but he did not always pause to examine their properties in full.

If he had been less single-minded, less obsessive, M. Leblanc might have published his results as he went along and have made a great name for himself in the community of science, might have become a centre of controversy and debate and, like many before him, have been driven mad by the sniping of minds less agile than his own. Being French, though, Henri did not have the necessary phlegm to withstand criticism and had consequently fallen into the trap of working mainly for his own satisfaction.

Soon, however, he would be obliged to demonstrate the results of his experiments to Clare, to show her just what his air-gun could do and to that end he laboured on the final problems of synthesis and control of gases in volume.

He had worked all morning, oblivious to the passage of time. It was very warm within the laboratory and the sweetish odour of the gases and coke fumes from the oven had brought beads of sweat to Henri's brow and had caused him to tie a large blue bandanna about his head. A graphite pencil was stuck behind his ear, close to his right hand a sheaf of paper upon which he recorded salient observations. He hadn't noticed the presence of the girls and would probably have remained unaware that he was being observed if one of them, the younger, had not discovered something terribly amusing in the sight of him and let out a giggle.

Henri looked up from the glass retort and caught a glimpse of the pair as they darted behind the open door. One glimpse was enough to identify the children of the salter, Gowrie's daughters. He had frequently observed the elder dredging for weed in the pond; the younger playing with shells or stringing wild flowers on the grass before the girnal.

He pushed himself away from the bench.

For a moment his brain, like his nostrils, seemed to be filled with the smell of gas as he blinked at the band of sunlight that cleaved through the open door. He blinked again and untying the bandanna rubbed his face with it, strolled to the door and peeped outside. He had expected the girls to be gone, to have scurried away like little rabbits into the bushes. But no, they loitered only yards from the door, watching him, cautious rather than timid. The elder had her arm about her sister's shoulder.

Henri hesitated. His initial impulse was to shake his fist and tell them to be off but he sensed their curiosity and, in the elder girl, a defiant boldness which appealed to him.

She said, "What's that you're boilin'?"

Henri smiled.

The girl said, "Is it salt? Are you makin' salt?"

She looked clean, almost bleached, her grey eyes huge in a pinched and furrowed little face. She had no bonnet or scarf upon her head and her hair hung raggedly across her brow and ears. She wore a dress of faded cotton and a tiny apron taped at waist and breast. Her feet were bare; straight feet, delicate and dirty, and quite the prettiest part of her.

"What's 'at smell?" The younger girl addressed the question to her sister, not to Henri. She was thin, pale and pathetic, with weepy pink eyes and a slack mouth. "'At's no' a salt smell, Katy."

"I am not making salt," Henri said gently. "I am making a powder which will give heat."

"Like – like them fire – fiery-works?"

He watched the girls edge forward. The younger one stuck a hand between her thighs and nervously pushed down her dress. He was inclined to laugh but realised that, young though they were, the pair would be sensitive to insult and vain. Besides, he felt quite sorry for these poor, half-grown, dull-witted girls who were bound to this sad stretch of shore for life.

Tucked under the gun bench was fruit in a basket, cheese, oat bread too, a bottle of port wine, the dinner Pratie had packed for him. He had a sudden inclination to be generous, to share his meal with the silly young girls just to show them that he was no ogre after all.

"I am not making the fireworks today," he said.

"What are ye makin' then?" Kate Gowrie said.

"Why do you not come inside and see?"

He held out his hand invitingly and beckoned them into the shed. Rather to his surprise they came quite willingly.

*　　*　　*

The evening was as pink as a rose petal. Along the moorland horizon fine almond-shaped clouds reflected the sunset and the first hot melting of the sea.

Long shadows consumed Headrick's yards and gardens and Frederick, though weary after his ride back from Kilmarnock, had no inclination to go indoors. He wandered to the old breast-high wall behind the stables and gazed across the Leddings to the moorland ridge where the last exalted colours of the day lingered upon rock and heather. He felt a tenuous urge to climb the wall and follow the sunlight before the day ended, before summer turned away.

"Frederick?"

Glancing down he saw Eleanor seated on the grass just beyond the wall. Her skirts were spread out, her legs thrust out like the jointless limbs of a doll, her face turned not towards the sunset but towards the haze of smoke that rose above the dell from the Tannahills' cottage.

Stiffly, Frederick scrambled over the wall and walked the few yards to where the girl, like Humpty-Dumpty, seemed to have fallen. She watched his approach without moving and when he crouched down before her made no attempt to hide her tears.

"Good God, Eleanor!" Frederick said. "What are you doing here? Are you injured?"

"I'm waitin' for Norman."

"Where is he?"

"At the milkin', late."

"Are you hurt? Did you fall?"

"N-no, I'm just waitin' for Norman."

"Why are you crying?"

She swallowed, looked down at her swollen stomach and nodded. Gently Frederick brushed her cheek with his thumb, wiping away tears as lightly as if he was sculpting sand.

"Can I not take you home?"

She sighed, shudderingly. "I can't be goin' anywhere without Norman."

"Are you in pain, dearest?"

"Awww, Freddie, it hurts me so much I don't know what to do to be rid of it."

"It'll pass, Ellie," Frederick said. "Nature will see to it in due time."

"Aye, an' what then?" Eleanor said.

He moved closer, rested his back against the wall and put an arm about her. He did not much care who saw them. If he was spotted he would invent an easy lie, say that Eleanor had stumbled or had been overcome by dizziness.

"In a month or two," Frederick said, "after your baby's born, all this pain will be behind you and you'll be your old self again."

"My old self? Nah, that I'll not be." She laid her head upon his chest and clung to him. "I'll never be my old self again. Frederick, take me away from here."

"I thought you didn't want to see me any more?"

"I didna mean it."

She looked up at him, dark eyes swimming with tears. He had seen her cry at will, to get her own way, but this time the tears were genuine, her frailty without design.

She said, "You promised me, Freddie, promised you'd take care of me."

"What about your baby?"

"I'll leave it with Norman. It isn't me he wants, only the bairn."

"Oh! I was under the impression your husband was devoted to you."

"Aye," Eleanor said, "but when the babby comes I'll be pushed into second place. His old witch of a mother only took me in to breed for her."

Frederick held her to him and looked out at the winey sunlight slipping over the moor's breast, the first pale stars, the rising moon.

Eleanor was shaking and weeping again, an anguish of uncertainty flooding forth.

How could he be sure that it was only her condition which made her volatile, that she was not simply filled with self-pity, marred by frustration and impatience? If she really had changed her mind about Tannahill and Headrick and meant what she said then he would be obliged to do something about it.

202

With or without another man's child, he did not want Eleanor Antrim now for, somehow, she had been spoiled.

Copious weeping gradually reduced to sobs and sighs. She wiped her nose on her sleeve, sniffing.

Frederick continued to hold her tightly.

"Is marriage not what you want, Ellie?" he asked.

"I want out of this place, away from this dungheap," the girl said. "I'm wantin' you to take me away, Frederick, like you promised. We could go to London when we have her money, go to London an' have a high old time."

"Yes," Frederick said. "We will, yes, but I cannot say when it will be, Eleanor."

"Soon," she said. "Sooner than you expect, Freddie."

At almost any other period in his life he wouldn't have given Eleanor's little threat a second thought.

He would have done what he had to do, would have gathered his rewards and slipped away quietly some night without a word to a soul, least of all to Eleanor. That option had been closed to him, however, not by scruples but out of necessity. He would not find another wife as suitable as Clare, not now, and he was determined that nothing and no one would cheat him out of a last stab at happiness.

He handed her a silk handkerchief from his pocket. "Dry your eyes. Your husband will be along soon and he should not find you in this state."

"Did you hear me, Frederick?" the girl said.

"Yes, dearest, yes. I heard," Frederick told her.

After his fashion he had loved her once and remnants of that tenderness remained. Eleanor had chosen another man, however, and would bear another man's child. She had been wayward, impatient, inconsistent and silly and he, Frederick Striker, could not be held responsible for such female flaws.

She said, "Will you take me away with you?"

"I will, I will," said Frederick.

"When, Freddie?"

"As soon as I possibly can."

"After you've done what you have to do?"

"If not before," said Frederick.

*   *   *

About half-past ten o'clock Henri had run out of tunefulness. He had been drinking brandy most of the evening and had passed through a stage of friskiness into a mood which Clare could not fathom.

With Melissa gone, giggling, to bed, the Frenchman had filled his glass to the brim and, while Clare watched in disapproval, had drunk it down as if it had been milk. He had uttered a long sigh, had broken wind by tapping his breastbone, had dabbed his lips with his handkerchief and then, pushing up his sleeves, had played a long, slow, solemn saraband upon the pianoforte.

At length Frederick had grown tired of the grave repetition and, to Clare's relief, had put a hand on the Frenchman's shoulder and had told him to stop.

"*Mais bien sûr, mon ami. J'ai été très discourtois.*" Henri lowered his hands, folded the board across the keys and murmured, "*Je suis ivre encore. Une telle manque de maîtrise de soi est une affliction affreuse, n'est-ce pas?*"

He rose and bowed unsteadily to Clare, "Madame Quinn, *excusez-moi*. It is a moment opportune to make to my bed."

"Goodnight, sir."

"*Bonne nuit, ma chère dame si aimable.*" Henri tottered. "*Frédérique, mon vieil ami, aide-moi.*"

Clare watched the men progress towards the drawing-room door, Frederick leading Henri by the arm.

She was not affronted by the Frenchman's indulgence. She had witnessed much hard drinking in her time and understood that men of all classes and nationalities were drawn to liquor like cattle to a salt-lick. She had been fortunate to marry a man who was abstemious in that respect.

Thinking of Donald a strange, dry wistfulness stole over her. She rose from her seat by the fireplace and wandered to the long window that overlooked the lawns.

It had been such a beautiful day that Clare expected the night to be fine too but no pale powdery light lingered in the night sky and dark consuming clouds had been driven in by a fast and gusty little wind which, even as Clare watched, sprinkled rain against the window glass.

She studied the thickening rain for a time until she realised that she was only waiting for Frederick to come downstairs. She had a sudden inexplicable need for his company tonight, although she could not think what had occasioned it.

Frederick too had been quiet during supper. He too had drunk a quantity of brandy from the bottles he had brought back with him from Kilmarnock where he had been that day. When she'd asked him what business had taken him so far from home, he had shrugged and palmed her off with the casual answer, "Fish business."

After ten or fifteen minutes it became clear that Frederick had gone to bed.

Clare abandoned her vigil, closed the curtains, snuffed out the candles, smoored the fire and, filled with vague dissatisfactions that she could not explain to herself, went upstairs.

The passage was dark. Only a strip of candlelight visible beneath Frederick's door gave it shape and guided Clare to her bedroom. In the apartment next to hers Henri snored and mumbled in French. Clare was no longer charmed by her lodger's Gallic eccentricities. Still thinking of Frederick, she undressed and put on her nightgown.

With Melissa fast asleep there was nothing to prevent her stealing down the corridor as she had done once before, not to taunt Frederick, though, but to tempt him to woo her properly, as a good man will woo a wife.

Donald had been admirable in that respect. He would ask permission to touch her, would thank her courteously, almost formally, after he had taken his pleasure. Donald had not been a passionate man, though, and she had been obliged to trim her temperament to his, to become more modest and mannerly.

She lay upon the top of her bed and put her hands to her breasts. It was warm in the room tonight. Rising wind brought back memories of the January storms, that first unaffected moment when Frederick had appeared to her again. How easy it would be now to use him as wilfully as he had used her. Easier still to go through with the marriage.

Clare swung her feet to the floor and slid off the bed. She fumbled with the tinderbox, lit a candle and, before her nerve could fail, slipped quickly out into the passageway and stole down to the door of Frederick's room.

She knocked softly, waited, heard nothing.

She knocked again.

She turned the handle, pushed open the door and eased herself into the room.

It seemed as if her lungs had folded in upon themselves like moth's wings and she was breathing hardly at all. Her stomach was tense, hard and unfeminine.

"Frederick?" she whispered and held up the candle-dish. The bed, however, was empty and Frederick gone.

*　　*　　*

Among the many disadvantages that age conferred Matt Pringle found the inability to sleep soundly throughout the night the hardest to bear.

He would be up and kneeling at the pot two or three times or would waken, coughing, with a feather in his throat or a cramp in his leg worse than toothache. A considerate man and ashamed of his body's weaknesses, he made as little noise as possible during his fumbling excursions and would lie wide awake, practising stoicism, until he heard young Katy scraping at the fire before he groped for his clothing and climbed gratefully out of bed.

It was not the clang of the kettle that signalled Grandpa Pringle to clamber out of his cot that morning, however, but a sound which he could not immediately identify.

Carefully he wiped away the teary matter that had accumulated on his eyelids and peered into the half-light which filtered through the port.

Early. The day grey. The breeze stiff. Gulls had flocked in from the channel. No stench of salt. No boiling done last night, the pans left to cool. Today, hewing salt-mortar, checking for cracks. Fill, fire, begin another draught.

The sound hardly more than a whisper, made by the barest motion of the lips.

Matt Pringle experienced a queer wee snap of apprehension in his waterworks. He groped for the bedpost, found it, pulled himself to his feet and stepped into the long space of the loft.

"Pa-paaa?"

"Annie? Where are you, sweetheart?"

"Pa-paaa?"

Bob was in the cubicle to the right, Billy beyond that. Exhausted by their recent labours, the Gowries would need to be shaken awake.

"Katy, are you there?"

Matt Pringle lumbered forward and with outstretched hands touched Annie's hair. He gave a start then, stooping, brought his granddaughter into focus.

She knelt beside Bob's desk at the little window in the seaward wall, her thumb in her mouth.

Matt put a hand on her shoulder. He could feel the bones of her spine thin as dulse beneath his fingertips.

"What is it, darlin'?" he asked.

"Katy."

"What about Kate?"

"She's in the pond."

"No, no, lass, it's hardly daylight. What would Kate be doin' in the pond so early?"

"Lyin' down," said Annie Gowrie, and began to cry.

Sixteen

Randolph Soames had on a wintry look which went with his solemn garb of carbon-black jacket and breeches and spotless white stock. He had removed his powdered wig along with his hat, but he did not seem able to relax and fiddled with the wine glass which John Galloway had filled with strong old Oporto in an attempt to cheer the cleric after the dour little noonday ceremony.

Eppie and Ishbel were downstairs busy preparing a dinner-time treat of sheep's-head broth, minced veal and hard-boiled egg yolks and a fresh garden salad. It was hardly a day for salad, though. The sky was sullen and rain had drifted in from the firth to wet the handful of mourners who had followed the salters' cart from Headrick.

Minister and doctor were both well used to burials. For all that, there was nothing perfunctory about the Reverend Soames's committals.

Ten or twenty years ago "religion" had had little part in final send-offs and even now the funerals of the well-to-do were almost indistinguishable from wedding feasts. In the matter of putting away of children and babies, however, Soames had the final say and grief, lacking celebration, seemed much more pure and closer to God.

Soames had attended the "kisting" early that morning and had consoled with prayer the godless salters in the loft above the pans, the loft that looked down on the sea pool where young Katherine Gowrie had met her end.

He had not been in tenure when the woman of the house had passed away and had been surprised at the intensity of the family's grief. He had experienced considerable sympathy for the grandfather and the youngest child who had wept so much that he had feared for their health and sanity.

At the graveside, of course, it had by custom been men only; Galloway, the Frenchman, the salt factor and, for some reason,

Brock Harding, sporting his regalia. The women had watched from a safe distance, lined up behind the lichened wall. Clare and Pratie Kerrigan had had charge of the Gowrie's youngest, Annie, who with thumb in mouth had fallen into an imbecilic trance so complete that she seemed asleep.

"Drink up, Randolph," Galloway said. "It will take the chill out of your bones if not out of your heart."

The minister crossed his legs, twirled the glass, sipped the wine without enthusiasm.

He was seated in one of the big leather chairs that fronted the fireplace. As a rule he found Galloway's library peaceful and soothing in its atmosphere. But today he could not shake the suspicion that Galloway had invited him here to conduct a belated and unofficial post-mortem upon the poor young lass who had drowned in Headrick's bucket pot.

"Dinner will be ready in half an hour," John Galloway said. "Meanwhile, do we prattle about onions and carrots or do we put niceties aside and discuss the mysterious circumstances surrounding the death of poor Kate Gowrie?"

"I thought that was what was on your mind," Soames said. "Are the circumstances mysterious?"

"To a degree, yes."

"Not sufficiently mysterious for you to inform the authorities, however?" Soames said.

"What would I tell them?" Galloway asked "Not a shred of physical evidence exists to suggest that the drowning was other than accidental. The girl was in and out of the rock pool as regularly as the tide."

"Could she not swim?"

Galloway shook his head. "Apparently not."

"So, if she lost her footing in deep water – "

"Quite."

"I suppose that the question remains as to what she was doing in the pool at that very early hour."

"Salters do not keep to regular hours."

"And yet," said Randolph Soames, "you are unhappy with the verdict. Was it something about the body that stirs your suspicions?"

"I did not see the body in the water," Galloway said.

"Gowrie and the grandfather had dragged it from the pool and carried it into the panhouse long before I got there."

"Who fetched you? The boy?"

"Yes, Billy. He arrived on foot about a quarter to six."

209

"Did Billy appreciate that his sister was already dead?"

"Without question," said Galloway. "As you may imagine, he was in a great state of agitation. He kept urging me to hurry, as if he thought I might raise her back to life like Jarius's daughter." Galloway shrugged. "He knew it was hopeless, though, and wept and howled behind me on the saddle all the way back to Headrick."

"What did you find there?"

"The girl had been laid on a board across a corner of the saltpans which, as it happened, were cool."

"Why didn't they take her upstairs to the house?"

"Randolph, I have no idea."

"How was she clad?"

"In night-wear, a cotton shift," John Galloway said. "On the other hand that's all she wore when she raked weed in the pool. I've seen her at it many a time."

"Had she been told to clean the pool?"

"No. Apparently the pool had been weeded only two or three days beforehand."

"What theory, if any, do the Gowries have for the girl's presence in the pool at that hour of the morning?"

"None," said Galloway. "Neither do they think it particularly odd. There is a friskiness, an unpredictability in the behaviour of young girls – boys too, I suppose – that defies adult logic. Perhaps she saw something upon the rocks or in the pool itself that caught her attention."

"What sort of thing?"

"A seal, a gull's nest, a glittering piece of flotsam," John Galloway said. "Something as ordinary as an empty bottle, for all we can tell."

"Did you find any such object?"

"Come now, Randolph, I had better things to do than rake among the rocks."

"She was, of course, beyond your aid?"

"She had been dead, I think, for some hours."

"How carefully did you examine the corpse?"

"Carefully," said Galloway. "I was able to extract a quantity of sea-water from her respiratory cavity. She did die by drowning, of that I'm certain."

"Yet I gather you aren't satisfied that it was entirely accidental?"

"Some contusions about her neck, some small abrasions of the skin had caused bleeding."

"Are you saying she was beaten?"

"I would not go so far as all that," Galloway answered. "Perhaps she slipped upon the outer rocks, bruised herself insensible, fell backwards into the pond and quite simply drowned."

"Surely someone in the house would have heard her cries?"

"Not necessarily."

"If everything indicates that the poor child met with a tragic accident," Randolph said, "why are you so reluctant to accept the obvious conclusion?"

"I'm not sure that I am."

"That is, I admit, a relief."

"Oh?"

"Perhaps I have too fertile an imagination," said Soames, "or lack charity towards my fellow man, but – "

"But what?"

"I had a nasty feeling you were going to tell me that the girl was with child."

"And drowned herself out of shame?" said Galloway. "Come now, Randolph, how many young women can you think of in this parish who would take their own lives out of a sense of shame?"

"Few," Soames admitted. "None probably."

"From rejection, for reason of being spurned, yes," Galloway went on. "Out of pique, an ultimate and irrevocable revenge upon the lover, yes. But from embarrassment?" He shook his head. "It does not seem to me to be in the nature of things."

"She was not, then, with child?"

"I would not be able to tell unless she was far advanced, not without cutting."

"And that you did not do?"

"I had no reason to do so. It would have seemed ghoulish to the Gowries, a dreadful defilement." Galloway paused. "Did it occur to you that little Katy Gowrie may have supposed herself pregnant, even if she was not?"

"Are you implying that she had a lover?"

"She certainly wished to have a lover."

"How do you know?"

"She confided in me," Galloway said, "or, to be more precise, let it slip."

"Who was the man at whom she had set her cap?"

"Can you not guess?"

211

Randolph Soames put his glass upon the hearthstone and leaned forward in the leather chair.

"Striker?"

"Yes."

"Did the girl actually tell you his name?"

"She did. She was quite infatuated with him."

"I suppose that Striker had plenty of opportunities to take advantage of her feelings for him."

"Yes, but did he have reason to murder her?"

"Ah!" said Randolph Soames. "That's surely another story."

"I believe he may have had a reason."

"Clare?"

"Clare, marriage, possession of Headrick."

Randolph shook his head. "So trivial, so petty?"

"Men have murdered for less."

The minister rose and came to the library table where Galloway was seated. He brought himself close enough to whisper and be heard. "Should we tell Clare?"

"Tell Clare what?"

"Of your – of our suspicions."

"She would not, alas, believe us."

"We could make her believe us?"

"Not," John Galloway said, "if she is infatuated with Striker too."

"I find that hard to swallow."

"Do you? Unfortunately, I don't."

"What if you're right, though, John? We cannot ignore the possibility. We must do something."

"See him hanged?" John Galloway suggested.

"How can we, if he is innocent of any crime?"

"Of this crime," Galloway said.

"Are there other crimes of which he is guilty?"

"None that I can prove."

"John, what are you saying?"

"Only that if anything happens to Clare – "

"What?"

"Nothing," Galloway gripped the minister's wrist. "There is one thing you can do for me, Randolph."

"And what is that?"

"Pray that I'm wrong."

* * *

Luncheon was eaten in restrained silence and, as soon as it was polite to do so, Henri excused himself and set off for the fish-shed to put in a little work before daylight faded.

Frederick was less sure what to do with himself and hung about the drawing-room with his hands in his pockets and a lugubrious expression on his face.

Clare had kept Melissa out of grown-up company as much as possible during the past couple of days. She had warned the servants not to discuss Katy's death in detail in Melissa's presence for fear that it would bring to the surface the strain of morbidity that lurked in her daughter's character. Early that morning Melissa and been packed off with Lizzie and Jen to visit Lizzie's aunt in Kerse, and Clare had fretted on and off throughout the morning about the girls' safety and the harum-scarum tricks that Lizzie might drag them into along the way.

Clare had considerable sympathy for the Gowries in their loss. For all that, it had been a relief to turn Annie over to her grandfather's care after the burial service.

"I have the June tallies set out," Frederick said, "if you wish to go over them with me."

A dull occupation for a dull afternoon; but dullness was itself an anodyne and arithmetic might while away the hours until Melissa and the servants returned from Kerse. Clare wondered what the Gowries would be doing right now. No feast had been announced, no friends or colleagues invited back to the salthouse or to a room in the Neptune to eat and drink and lift the pall with consoling conversation.

"Are you thinking of the Gowries?" Frederick said.

"Yes, I am."

"I guessed as much," Frederick said. "I wonder who'll do the cooking now Kate's gone. Annie's incapable of it. I suppose I'll have to attend to that too."

"Is it not a domestic matter?"

"No," said Frederick. "What affects the Gowries affects our profits. They must be fit and well fed in order to do their work properly."

He sounded peevish, Clare thought, as if Kate Gowrie had drowned just to spite him.

"You have not answered my question, Clare. Do you wish to total the – "

"No, I do not think I do."

"In that case I must find something else to occupy me."

Clare sipped tea. It had cooled in the cup and tasted unpleasantly strong.

"When's the next sale?" she said.

"What sale?"

"At the Neptune," Clare said. "Can you not attend the Harding's next sale and purchase a girl to take Kate Gowrie's place?"

"What the devil!"

"It would hardly matter to the Gowries, would it? Provided they are kept well fed and fit to work, one girl is surely much the same as another."

"I'm sure you don't intend to sound callous."

"Oh, but I do," said Clare. "I'm as concerned as you are about a lapse in salt production. How long shall we allow them to grieve, Frederick? A day, two days?"

"Work is all they know, Clare."

"Put them to work then," Clare said. "You could order them to begin a draught this very evening. Questionable if they'll sleep much, so they may as well be boiling brine as tossing and turning in their beds."

"Clare!"

"Are you not a staunch Son of Apollo?"

"The sales are not lodge matters."

"Is Daniel Harding not in Ireland right now?"

"Really, I have no idea."

"According to Pratie he was seen boarding a collier brig late yesterday afternoon."

"Take your servant's word for it, by all means," said Frederick angrily. "Servants seem to know everything."

Clare put down her cup and leaned her chin on her hands.

"It's unfortunate that Eleanor is so close to her time, otherwise I could have put her to work with the Gowries."

"No!"

"Why ever not?"

"She's not – "

"Not what, Frederick?"

"She's not suited to that sort of work."

"Oh, I'm sure she would soon pick it up. What is there to it, after all? Raking weed, lugging water, cooking, airing beds, washing clothes. Taking a turn with a salt-skimmer now and then. If a poor skinny little thing with half her wits, like Annie Gowrie, can do it I'm sure Eleanor Antrim would be able to cope."

"The point is, in any case, moot," Frederick reminded her. "Eleanor's too large for strenuous labour. In addition, I doubt if the Gowries would accept Tannahill's wife as a day-servant."

"After her baby's born we might persuade – "

"No, Clare. I forbid it."

"Oh, of course!" Clare said. "How careless of me to forget. It's not up to the salt factor to find hands for Bob Gowrie. He must do that for himself."

"Yes, that is indeed the way of it."

"Even so, would it not be a handsome gesture on your part to suggest a suitable replacement? Bob Gowrie may be stubborn and proud but he is also a pragmatist. I've no doubt he would let you choose a girl for him since you have such an eye for it."

"Stop it."

"Katy would not be hard to replace."

"Stop it, I say."

"I'm only trying to be helpful, Frederick."

"You are mocking the dead and I do not care for it."

"Did she mean so much to you, Frederick? Kate, after all, was not a relative," Clare said. "Or was she?"

"So," Frederick said, "you've heard that tale too. From your precious housekeeper, no doubt. Well, it's not true, not one word of it."

"What tale?"

"Stop it," Frederick said again.

His agitation was compounded partly of anger, partly of apprehension. Clare observed him carefully. She had not yet perfected the fine sense of timing that would allow her to goad him to the limit and no further. She had said enough for the present, however, and was on the point of taking her leave when Frederick rounded on her, crossed the carpet in two long strides and swept her into his arms.

Pinning her arms to her sides he kissed her upon the mouth, his lips hard, like worn leather.

"Now will you stop it," he said.

Grey stubble rubbed Clare's cheek, his flesh strangely dry against her own; yet there was a strength to him, a passion that seemed to echo the past, a quality to which she might respond.

He did not kiss her again but continued to hold her tightly.

"I am here in your house as your factor and your guest," he said. "But we both know that I am more than that. Damn you, Clare, I'm doing all in my power to live up to your expectations.

215

I cannot shake off my past entirely and I resent having it cast in my face at every turn."

"Yes," Clare said, "I have been rather unfair to you."

"Do you think I'd have the girl, Katy, dead?"

"The question is, Frederick, did you have the girl when she was alive?"

"*Aaahhh!*" he cried, throwing back his head in disgust. "I admit she was enamoured of me but Kate Gowrie was nothing but a child, a silly little lassie. For God's sake, Clare, do you not realise that I am in love with *you?*"

"I've heard you say it before."

"This time will you not believe me?"

"I believed you last time too, Frederick."

"God in heaven, what more can I do to prove my good intentions?"

He slackened his hold upon her. She could have slipped easily away from him but did not. She placed an arm about him, raised herself up and kissed him sharply, almost impertinently, as if it was more than he deserved.

"Give me just a little more time, Frederick."

"How long, damn it?"

"Until September."

"September," Frederick said. "Do you promise?"

She gave him a smile, inappropriately girlish, and answered, "No, Frederick. No promises."

A moment later, slamming the door behind him, Frederick left the dining-room and Clare sat shakily down at the table to finish drinking her tea.

*   *   *

The Greenock engineer was a jovial fellow by the name of Peter Merkland. He was of an age with Robertson Blyth but small and athletic in build. He relished exploration and had no fear of the dirt and discomfort involved in crawling about the honeycombed depths of Cairns. It was he who took both the lantern and the lead when the cribbing ran out at two hundred and fifty feet and more or less tugged Blyth along behind him to the mouth of the new sinking which lay under Thunder Hill.

Blyth's best hewers had already stripped and banded a small section of the seam. It was, nonetheless, a tight squeeze into the forward room and Blyth sat hunched like a goblin while

Merkland tapped and hammered, measured and made notes by lantern light.

The seam was eight feet thick on estimate, and Robertson Blyth was optimistic that it would yield vast quantities of rich coal if he could reasonably cost its development.

It was Robertson Blyth's intention to brace the haulage tunnels with bolted iron and use steam power and cables to winch the tubs from the cuttings to the shaft. Several of his managers thought him a genius, most thought him mad to contemplate such an ambitious scheme.

At the back of his mind Robertson Blyth had stored the memory of Leblanc's "wand of light", a device which his brethren had regarded as no more than a toy but which he had seen as a tool which might render iron a viable alternative to oak. As soon as Merkland's estimates were to hand he would press Leblanc to demonstrate his advances and, if necessary, bleed more of his own limited resources into securing a share of the patent.

The Frenchman was far from Robertson Blyth's thoughts, though, as he huddled in a corner with his back to a great slabby rake of rock.

The coalmaster had no liking for the pit's infernal depths. There was something too elemental about the compression of water, rock and pungent air, something too primitive about the hewers and borers who laboured there. Sweating, muscular and manly, they constituted a race of creatures to which he would never belong.

In spite of his fear, he went underground two or three times a month just to stiffen his soul and to defy Sarah who, though she would never admit it, was terrified of dark, narrow places.

Mr Merkland and the coalmaster were both dressed in every-day tweeds and half-length riding boots. The only concessions made to the surroundings were hats tied on with string and the sporting of heavy buckram bibs across their shoulders. The hewers who had opened the seam had been sent off shift an hour ago, for Robertson Blyth was secretive in his dealings with engineers, and the pair were alone, a long way down from the last of the open stalls.

They had been pressed in the little space against the seam for less than five minutes when, without a scrap of warning, the whole floor moved.

Robertson Blyth did not even have time to scramble to his feet. He managed a single instinctive movement, a dashing out

217

of the hands to brace himself, before the floor shifted again and he found himself hoisted involuntarily on to his knees. Mr Merkland swayed, legs splayed.

The lantern shook and tumbled from the ledge where it had been lodged. The Greenock engineer caught it by its hook before it struck the rock, a reaction so swift that Robertson Blyth was distracted by it and did not at first notice the rain of stone chips and fine dust that showered down upon him.

"Oh!" said Peter Merkland. "Nasty!"

The sound in the wake of the slump resembled a long, low groan which growled away and away into nothingness through coal and solid rock. From far off, towards the shaft, Blyth heard the *pop-pop-pop* of splitting pit-props and, on his knees, he waited to be crushed like an ant and his soul carried to infinity.

"Unsteady, what?" Merkland remarked, the lantern still swinging wildly in his hand. "Reckon I'd better be sharpish, don't you, sir?"

The floor angle had altered and raked away from the seam. Fissures exposed a line of rock that had not been there before, rock of a pretty reddish colour, like buffed sandstone. No sound or further upheavals disturbed the silence, no shouts of panic or distress from the tunnels.

Robertson Blyth got to his feet.

He licked his lips and tasted rock dust. He spat lightly to one side and said, "Tell me, Mr Merkland, how are you being paid?"

"By the hour, sir."

"And what do you have still to do?"

"Ah, well," said the Greenock engineer. "Measure the angle of slippage, recalculate the prop lengths. That sort of thing."

"How long?"

"Ten minutes, a quarter hour at most."

"Are you not afraid, Mr Merkland?"

"Moderately, Mr Blyth, moderately. And you?"

"The same."

"I have a cure for nervous disposition, Coalmaster, if you will give permission to use it."

"By all means." Robertson Blyth watched the man fish a silver spirit flask from a pocket in his jacket. "Dutch courage, is it?"

"Rum," said Merkland. "Every sailor's friend."

He uncapped the flask with his thumbnail, left the lid dangling from the silver chain, and offered it to Robertson

Blyth who accepted it and, without hesitation, took a long pull from the narrow neck.

Nothing in life had ever seemed so good.

He could taste the Indies in his throat, washing through the mineral dust. The experience of drinking a dram of rum in a moment of extreme danger deep underground snapped his last tenuous link with Sarah. If the shaft fell in, if the rock should thud shut like a great Bible, if he should be crushed like a brown leaf, what the hell did it matter?

He stood there like a man, with a man for company.

He wiped his mouth on his sleeve and returned the flask to Merkland. For an instant their eyes met and there was between them a feeling of rapport that bound them like brothers.

He watched the Greenock engineer knock back a mouthful, heard him sigh and say, "By God, that's better."

"May I ask, Mr Merkland, are you a married man?"

"I am, for my sins."

"Is your wife a good wife to you?"

"She is a wife beyond reproach," Peter Merkland said. "She keeps house for me better than I deserve and she is caring towards our children."

"But?"

"She is dull company, Mr Blyth, very dull company."

"And yet you endure her dullness, do you, for the sake of the marriage?"

"Not entirely, sir." Merkland grinned. "Company that's not dull can be easily found."

"Female company?"

"Of course."

"Where, sir?"

"In my case," Merkland said, "in the Anchor, and its upstairs rooms."

"If you were, say, benighted in this town, in Ladybrook, where would you find such jovial female company?" Robertson Blyth said. "The Neptune?"

"Where else?"

"And the name, sir, of the best of it?"

"Nancy."

"Indeed?"

"Indeed, yes."

In a thin and distant echo the ground shivered and, for a split second, the rock groaned plaintively overhead.

"Thank you, Mr Merkland," Blyth said, "for the rum *and* the advice. Are you game to continue?"

"I am, Mr Blyth."

"By all means then let's do so," said Robertson Blyth and, for no obvious reason, laughed.

*　　*　　*

It was a little after four o'clock on a Thursday afternoon, eight days after Kate Gowrie had been put into the ground, before Clare walked purposefully across the bridge, across the turnpike and down to the buildings by the rock pool.

She'd had daily reports from Frederick, of course, but she had deliberately steered clear of the Gowries until now.

The girnal had been open for the sale of salt to the cadgers and Mr Bartholomew had been paid his dues, but not one grain of fresh salt had been cast for over a week and, Clare gathered, Frederick encountered not grief but truculence from the salters.

No smoke greeted her as she approached the saltings but, a little to her surprise, there was some activity evident both within and without the panhouse.

Billy and Annie were splashing at the edge of the pool. They appeared to be washing salt sacks, though this job was usually hired out to local women at piece-work rate. If the pair saw Clare at all they paid her no heed but kept their heads down and went on with their half-hearted labours.

There was no sign of Frederick within the panhouse but Clare found Bob Gowrie and his father-in-law, in shirt-sleeves and aprons, scouring the smaller of the pans. A bottle-glass lantern, lit, had been placed on the stairs but without the fire glow or faint radiation from bubbling brine the chamber was dark and gloomy.

"Who's that by the door?" Matt Pringle shouted and waved a battered mallet in Clare's direction.

Bob leaned on the pan's rim and squinted at Clare through his spectacles. "Mrs Quinn."

"What the hell does she want?"

"I didn't mean to alarm you, Mr Pringle."

"What are you here for?"

"No need to roar, old man." Bob clambered from the pan and respectfully removed his cap. "I expect Mrs Quinn's come to offer her condolences."

Clare had already expressed her deep and sincere sympathy to the salter but the fact had obviously been forgotten and Clare suspected that, like many a bereaved person, Bob Gowrie would cling tenaciously to the power that suffering had conferred upon him.

She squared her shoulders and said, "I've come to enquire when you might be ready to cast salt, Mr Gowrie."

"It takes a while – a while, you know. She's sorely missed in this household."

"Yes," Clare said, curtly. "It's for that reason that I'm prepared to offer you an allowance to employ another hand."

"WHAT?" Matt Pringle shouted.

He was no more than three or four feet from Clare and his voice rang painfully in her ears.

"Be quiet, Pringle. She's only tryin' to help." Bob Gowrie shuffled forward, a lump of salt-cake held in one hand like a ritual offering. "As you can see, Mrs Quinn, we've got ourselves back to work. But it's a sore time for us, a sore time."

Clare said, "Will I instruct Mr Striker to find a girl to take care of your household management?"

"Annie does all that."

"I see," said Clare. "In that case perhaps you'd prefer to take on a boy to learn the trade. I'm prepared to adjust the rate to compensate for the additional expense."

Before his son-in-law could answer, Matt Pringle said, "Don't think you can buy us off, Mrs Quinn."

"Buy you off?"

"You're makin' this offer for Striker's sake, aren't you?" Matt Pringle said accusingly.

"Pay no heed to him," Bob apologised. "He's got a bee in his bonnet about – I mean, it's been a distressin' time for all of us."

"I'm offering help, Mr Pringle, because Kate's untimely death has left you short-handed."

"Aye," Matt Pringle said, "I notice you're not offerin' help to find out who murdered her."

"What?"

"Don't listen, Mrs Quinn. He's ravin' like an old cockerel. He means no harm."

"Ravin', am I?" said Matt Pringle. "She comes holdin' out hush money exactly like I said she would an' you still think I'm wrong?"

"Hush money?" said Clare. "Why do I need to buy your silence, Mr Pringle?"

"To protect the man who murdered her."

"I see," Clare said, steadily. "You, Gowrie, do you believe that your daughter was done to death?"

"No, I – "

"Tell her the bloody truth," Matt Pringle shouted.

Dropping the salt-cake Bob Gowrie obsequiously touched Clare's arm. "We're not needin' extra help. We appreciate the offer, Mrs Quinn, but we can manage fine, just the four of us."

Clare paid the salter no attention. She was intrigued by the older man, by Pringle. He had folded his arms across his chest and had straightened his back and she saw him fleetingly as he might have been twenty or thirty years ago, tall and broad and arrogant, betrayed now only by half-blind, squinting eyes.

Clare said, "What makes you suppose Kate did not drown by accident?"

"Because she could swim like a fish."

"That's not what Mr Striker told me."

"Then Mr Striker is lyin'."

"Who, though," Clare said, "would want to see her dead?"

"Ask your factor the answer to that one too."

"Enough, enough, for God's sake," Bob Gowrie pleaded. "You and your tongue'll get us all into trouble."

"Are you, Pringle, implying that my factor took your grand-daughter to the pond and drowned her?"

"No, no, no," said Bob. "He's babblin', just babblin'."

"Come along, Pringle," Clare insisted, "do you or do you not have valid reasons for accusing Mr Striker of murder?"

Matt Pringle backed down a little. "I don't know who did it – only that it was done. Do you doubt the Englishman's capable of murder?"

Clare did not answer at once. She had not forgotten the empty bedroom and Frederick's unexplained absence on the night of Kate Gowrie's death. She chose her words with care, for she was suddenly wary of Matt Pringle and the harm that his slanders might do to Headrick.

"Do you, in fact, know that Kate was murdered at all?" Clare said.

"No, but, by God, I intend to find out."

"How will you do so?"

"By ways not known to you," he answered, mysteriously.

"If it transpires that the girl's death was not an accident will you put your evidence before the Sheriff?"

"No," Matt Pringle told her, "I'll take my own revenge."

"Against my factor?"

"If he's guilty, aye," Matt Pringle said. "An' you'd better not try to stop us."

"If he's guilty," Clare said, "I won't."

"Do I have your promise on that score?"

"Yes," Clare said, firmly. "You have my promise. If Frederick Striker killed your granddaughter, you may do with him as you see fit." She held up her hand to prevent Pringle going on. "Now, Gowrie, when may I expect you to get back to making salt?"

"Tomorrow."

"And when will I have something to sell?"

"The week's end," Bob Gowrie answered.

"Good," said Clare and, without another word to either of the men, hastily left the panhouse and set off home.

*   *   *

It would not have been the first time that he had found the maid, Teresa, in her mistress's bed, the pair snuggled under a hundredweight of sheets, blankets and embroidered quilts, whispering and sniggering. Robertson Blyth detested Teresa almost as much as he detested his wife and had no truck with her except when necessity, or Sarah, demanded it.

On that particular night, however, Robertson Blyth was too drunk to give a hoot about female sensibilities.

He was filled with beefsteak and oysters, rum and claret and expensive old port. He had spent the evening with Peter Merkland in the coaching inn at the Thunder Hill crossroads where they had celebrated their brush with death, and discussed women, pro and con, until Mr Merkland had collapsed beneath the table and Mr Blyth had tottered out to find Pranzo and ride home through the airy darkness.

Perhaps it was the rum or his bragging account of his brush with the Irish girl, or the bawdy nature of Merkland's conversation but, somewhere along the banks of the Linn, Robertson Blyth's intoxication transformed itself into lust. He came striding up the back staircase at several minutes past midnight trailing pit-dust and the odour of spirits, ignored Fingal's inquisitive face in the doorway of his room, strode on along the passageway, flung open the door of Sarah's chamber and marched straight in.

223

The room was walled in stone. The huge four-poster, isolated by light from a candle-cluster, loomed under the vaulted roof.

Teresa was not in bed with Sarah but was seated glumly on a gilded stool by the bedside, reading aloud from a novel.

Sarah was propped up on bolsters like an invalid. A compress cloth showed under her nightcap and her frilled nightgown frothed about her like whipped milk. Startled, the women looked up at him. Sarah opened her mouth to protest but Robbie drowned her out by kicking the door shut behind him, making both the women and the candelabrum jump.

He pointed at the maid.

"You," he said. "Out."

Teresa rose. She wore only a thin gown and he could see plum-coloured patches of hair beneath it in the shine of the light, the arrogant bosom. She held the book to her chin and tapped it and glanced at her mistress for instructions.

"OUT, DAMN IT, UNLESS YOU WANT A SHARE."

Sarah sat up straight. She had a cordial glass in her left hand, a vessel so slender and delicate that it might have been spun from sugar. It contained a rose-tinted liquid decorated with a sprig of lemon balm.

"Perhaps you had better leave us, Teresa," Sarah said.

Teresa hurried past him, her eyes bulbous and grape-like, her mouth with a ripe, petulant fullness that made Robbie think of crushed pomegranates. He raised his arms, stuck out his neck, and emitted a loud growl which drove the lady's maid into a run. Her broad rump vanished in a whisk of muslin as she dragged open the door and bolted.

"Now, Sarah," Robertson Blyth said.

She was sitting upright now, sharp as steel.

"What have you heard?" she said.

Robbie wasn't listening.

He stripped off his coat, ripped off his waistcoat and flung both garments to the floor.

Sarah said, "Whatever you've heard, I deny it."

Robbie wriggled out of his breeches.

"All I want to hear," he said, "is the sound of a bed creaking."

At last she was alarmed. She stretched and put the cordial glass upon the bed-table and, in the same motion, flicked away the covers and curved one long leg towards the floor. Robbie was too quick for her. He caught her foot, lifted her and threw her backwards across the sheets. She stared up at him glassy-eyed, and let her nether lip quiver.

In a tiny childish voice she said, "No, Robertson. I am unwell."

"No you're not."

"I am, I am, I tell you."

"Then I have just the medicine for you."

She struggled, but had lost the knack.

Spread beneath him, angular and exposed, she could find no substitute for imperiousness. "Stop it this instant, I say. You are behaving like a brute. Do you not see the cordial and the bandage?"

Habit took hold of him. He hesitated.

"What's wrong with you?"

"My – my head aches."

"Hoh!"

She gasped as he lifted her hips and fitted himself to her familiar angles. She scowled up at him, nose to nose.

"Are you punishing me for something?"

"Don't be so bloody daft," the coalmaster said and, thrusting his face down against her cold cheek, forged on regardless.

*　　*　　*

It had been years since Matt Pringle had strayed further inland than St Cedric's kirk and when he climbed the dyke that separated Headrick from the Leddings he lost contact with whatever rational force had steered him thus far.

The moor was marked only by the *churr* of grouse and the liquid call of a cuckoo saying farewell. Green shapes were perforated by yellow gorse and the late-afternoon sky seemed to have three or four little crescent moons floating in it like the petals of a bellflower. Angrily he slapped his ash stick into vetches and willowherb in search of the path that would lead him through the wilderness to Rose Tannahill's cottage.

He was sweating heavily, the stick stained with sap, his hands stung by nettles and thorns and his anger had turned to half-blind, impotent rage before he heard the voice.

"What are you doin' here, Matt Pringle? Are you for stealin' my cows?"

He stopped dead in his tracks and swung his head this way and that, but he could not locate the source of the voice and had just begun to wonder if it too was a figment of his imagination when she said, "Here I am. Look closer."

She appeared suddenly out of the whins, an arm's length away.

"Man," she said, "you're a sorry sight. Are you lost?"

"Not now, Mrs Tannahill, since it's you I came to see."

"I'm not so easy to find," Rose Tannahill said. "What do you want from me, Matt Pringle? A cure for those cataracts of yours? Has Galloway not seen fit to bleed you?"

"He canna cure crystalline humours."

"I can. A purge of calomel and a hemlock poultice will soften them."

Matt Pringle ignored the offer. "Where's your cottage?"

"Down yonder," the old woman said. "Do you not smell its smoke?"

"Take me there."

"For what reason?"

"To talk in confidence."

"Talk here," she said, "unless you think hares spread gossip."

"I hear you've gifts beyond the natural," Matt Pringle said. "Is it true you can unlock the secrets of the past?"

"What if I can?"

"Our girl died, drowned."

"I heard."

"I want to know how."

"She slipped an' fell."

"No, it was done deliberate."

"So that's how the wind blows, is it?" Rose said. "What do you expect me to do? Summon her poor spirit from the grave? Leave her in peace, I say."

"What if she's not at peace?"

"Have you been visited?"

"No, nothin' of that sort."

Serious talk of spirits and visitations would have brought scorn from his mouth a month ago but he listened now with dread, afraid of his own desperate conversion as well as the old woman's catalogue of mysteries.

"What you require is a powerful sort of magic, an' I canna guarantee an answer at the end of it."

"I've heard you've a crystal – "

"It needs more than the crystal to carry me where you want me to go," Rose said. "It'll cost you much money."

226

"Aye." He brought a leather purse from his pocket. "I thought it would. Twenty pounds, Rose Tannahill. It's all I have in the world. Will that be enough?"

"If it's all that you have, it'll be enough."

"Here." He dug into the breast of his jacket, produced a crumpled garment and held it out. "Kate's shift."

"The one she wore when she passed on?"

"Aye."

Rose Tannahill took the shift from the old man's hand and shook it gently. The scanty fabric billowed and filled, though there was no breath of wind on the moor. He watched the old woman stroke the shift with her knuckles, wring it lightly in one fist, press it to her nose to sniff.

His skin was suddenly cold and clammy and he had an almost overwhelming desire to strike the old woman with his stick. His anger and frustration seemed to have turned him inside out and to encompass everyone and everything.

"What does it tell you?"

"I canna speak to the dead without an ambassador," she said. "Where's your money?"

"Here."

She took the purse but did not open it.

"How soon will you have word?" the salter said.

"Two or three nights from now," Rose Tannahill said. "But it will not be my word and you will have to believe what he tells you for there's no one greater behind him."

"Is this a man? What man?"

She held him by the arm.

Suddenly he saw her clearly. Her skin was nut-brown and wrinkled and the little locks of hair that escaped from her bonnet were white as snowflakes. Her eyes were piercing, so piercing that once more he was possessed of an urge to strike her down.

"Will you take his word?" Rose said.

"If it's honest."

"If he speaks at all to me, he'll tell the truth."

"Who is this man? A warlock?"

When her fingertips touched his cheek a strange, paralysing dizziness overcame him. He clung to her helplessly while she pressed her thumbs against his eyelids and created a wheel of light within which were contained two dark, dark shapes, one of which he gradually recognised.

Matt Pringle let out a cry of terror.

He pushed the old woman from him and turned away and, lumbering through the whins and vetches, ran for the safety of the shore.

*   *   *

Clare suspected that she had kept Melissa out too late and that the long evening shadows had preyed upon the child's mind and fed her melancholy imagination.

It was the first time in over a week that Clare had ventured to the beach with her daughter. She had avoided the salthouse, though, and had taken the back route to the bay.

The evening had been very fine. The bay waters had bustled with coastal craft, and crabbers and clam-diggers had been busy on the rocks and sands. Polite folk, leggy and barefoot, they had murmured greetings to Clare and, with permission, had given Melissa shells or clean crab claws in token of their respect for a land-owner who, unlike most Ayrshire blue-bloods, did not deny them access to the shore.

In spite of the diversions, Melissa's attention had eventually gravitated to the curl of smoke from the panhouse and Clare had known from her daughter's silence that her thoughts had turned to little Kate Gowrie and the fate of her immortal soul.

Melissa did not reveal her preoccupations until bedtime. She had been quiet all through supper and not even Henri's teasing pleasantries had been able to draw her out and only when she was in bed, and Lizzie gone, did she raise herself from the pillows and stare at the slivers of daylight that penetrated the edges of the curtain.

"Mama," she said, "I think I hear the lodge bell."

Clare had been brushing and folding her daughter's clothes, loitering in expectation.

"I don't think so, dearest. It's very calm tonight."

Prim and pale under her nightcap Melissa's face expressed an innocent apprehension. "Do you not hear it?"

"No."

"Is it Papa's handbell, do you suppose?"

"How can it be?" Clare put the child's dress across a chair and came to the bed. "Henri is in Papa's room now and the handbell has been taken away."

"Where?"

"It's in the closet behind the stairs in the hallway, I believe."

228

Clare seated herself on the side of the bed. "Do you still hear it, Melissa?"

"No."

"What is it then?"

"Mama, is Papa burning in the fiery pit?"

"Papa is in heaven, dear, with the angels."

"Did Jesus forgive him?"

"Forgive him for what?" said Clare, dismayed at the unexpected tenor of the conversation.

"His wickedness."

"Melissa! Papa was not a wicked person."

"Did he not know Frederick?"

"Why yes, he did," Clare said. "But *we* know Frederick, and Henri knows Frederick, and we aren't wicked, are we?"

Melissa pondered this problem for a second.

"Papa knew Frederick when Frederick was wicked."

"Oh, Melissa, who's been filling your head with such nonsense?"

"Nobody."

"Have you been listening to Pratie and Mrs Shay?"

"Did you have another baby?" Melissa blurted out.

"What?"

"Did you have a little boy, like me, before I was born?"

Clare had imparted to her daughter many facts regarding her life in Glasgow but she had excised all mention of Peterkin, of her arrest, trial and acquittal. She had promised herself that when Melissa was sixteen, say, she would tell her the whole story but, it seemed, Frederick's return had destroyed that plan too.

"Who told you?"

"It wasn't Lizzie's fault," Melissa said. "She was talking to Pratie on the drying lawn and – and I just happened to overhear them, by mistake." She paused. "Is he in heaven too?"

Before Clare could frame an answer, Melissa sat up alertly and asked, "If he is in heaven will he know my Papa, and will my Papa know him?"

It was on the tip of Clare's tongue to defer this complicated question to Mr Soames's judgement but she could not evade responsibility so easily, for on this occasion there was more behind it than curiosity about the Lord's many mansions.

Clare said, "I did have a child before you, dearest. His name was Peterkin. He died when he was very young. Hardly more than an infant, in fact."

"Like Mrs Deans's baby?"

"Yes."

"Was Frederick your husband?"

"No."

"Was it Mr Purves?"

"Mr Purves was my cousin," Clare said. "He was married to someone else."

She hesitated. She did not know how to answer without leading Melissa into a tortuous maze of questions about marriage, birth and death.

Melissa patted her hand.

"Was he a nice boy?"

"Very."

"Were you very sad when he died, Mama?"

"Yes, of course."

"Why did God take him from you?"

"I really cannot say."

"Was it a punishment?"

"Perhaps."

"Was Papa there?"

"No," Clare said, "I had not met Papa then."

"Was Frederick there?"

Gossiping servants were a hazard in every household. Pratie had a certain sense of discretion and a stubborn loyalty to her late master but the situation within the house had become too highly charged of late for the younger girls to remain immune to it.

"I do not know how God arranges things in heaven, darling," Clare said, side-stepping the question about Frederick. "I believe, though, that all things are possible and that my little boy, my Peterkin, and your Papa will be happy there together."

"And Katy?"

"Yes," Clare said. "Katy too."

Melissa appeared to be comforted and lay back with her head upon the pillows, one hand up beside her ear, the fingers loosely curled. Her blue eyes looked sleepy and Clare, though she continued to sit with her daughter, hoped that the interrogation was at an end.

"Did you do wrong, Mama?"

"When?"

"When you lost Peterkin? When God took him away?"

"Perhaps I did," Clare said, "without knowing it."

"And He punished you?"

"Perhaps."

"I wonder if He will punish me," said Melissa, though with no great show of being perturbed.

"For what reason, dearest?"

"Listening to Lizzie and Pratie."

"Oh, that's such a small thing, I expect God will forgive you."

"Did He forgive you, Mama?"

"I hope He does."

"Frederick – "

"No, Melissa," Clare said firmly. "That's enough talk for tonight. If you have all this still in your mind tomorrow we'll discuss it then. Meanwhile, it's time you went to sleep."

"Will you tell me about Peterkin?"

"Tomorrow," Clare promised.

Melissa smiled. "I'll see him one day, Mama, won't I?"

"Yes, but not for a long time."

"A long, long, long, long time?" Melissa said.

"Longer even than that," said Clare and with infinite relief heard her daughter sigh as she turned her cheek to the pillow and settled down to sleep.

*　　*　　*

Forty-two years had passed since last Rose Tannahill had forged a covenant of salt. She had done it once, and had vowed she would never do it again.

She had been full swollen with child at the time, cramped with pain and frightened for the foetus that quivered and quailed within her. At night she'd dreamed black dreams of writhing sea-serpents, two-headed beasts and humpbacked monsters. And at length she had taken out the implements her grandmother had given her thirty years before, had found the incantation written on parchment and had learned it, syllable by syllable, until she could repeat it without a fault or stumble.

Now, in her ninetieth year, she slid a stone from the cottage wall, took once more from the hidden cavity her grandmother's satchel and unfurled the yellowing parchment.

By firelight she read over the symbolic language in which the spells of summoning and dismissal were couched.

Although it was over forty years since last she'd mouthed the words she remembered them as well as if they'd been graven on her memory; nor had she forgotten the details of the ritual.

As she undressed before the fire, Rose imagined she could hear her grandmother calling out a warning. She had not told Norman what she intended to do but instinct and experience indicated that something was afoot and he had taken Eleanor early to bed and had barred the door of the loft on the inside.

She bathed in fresh warm water, dressed herself in a clean linen gown and tied it about the middle with a rope of hemp. That done, she opened a second little package from the satchel and removed a tarnished silver salt mill and a gnarled black root the length of her forefinger. Putting the mill on the table, she broke off a piece of the root and placed it in her mouth.

The taste was strong and bitter but, eyes closed, Rose sucked the fragment doggedly until every crumb of it was consumed and every drop of bitter saliva swallowed.

Forty years instantly fell away. Senses sharpened, blood vibrant, she felt strong and agile again, like a woman restored to her prime.

She gave a little groan of pleasure and terror and rapidly gathered all the objects that the rite required; the silver mill, a measure of sea-salt in a wooden bowl, a spoon, a bone engraved with strange emblems, Kate Gowrie's garment and, last of all, her talisman, the serpent's egg. She placed them in a straw-lined basket and, barefoot and bare-headed, left the cottage.

On the flagstone outside the door, however, she paused long enough to chase the cats into the kitchen and to lay a thick grey granular line of salt across the threshold of her abode, to keep it safe.

That done, she hoisted the basket on to her arm and set off through the darkness for the spot on the moor where the grass grew tall, a quarter of a mile away.

*   *   *

"What's she doing now?" Eleanor said.

"Nothing," Norman told her.

"She's up to somethin'. Listen to her groan."

"It's nothing for you to bother about."

Eleanor rolled on to an elbow and rested her belly against her husband's flank.

The bed was narrow at the best of times but with her

greatly increased bulk she felt crushed by the sloping roof and suffocated by the proximity of the thatch.

"Has she been an' barred us in?" Eleanor said.

Norman lay on his back with his hands behind his head, staring at the roof, saying not a word.

The attic was usually pitch-dark but tonight there was a faint sourceless sift of light by which Eleanor could just discern her husband's profile. She nudged him with her knee.

"Norman, I canna breathe."

He moved an inch or two. She leaned more weight against him and placed a hand upon his chest. It was hot in the attic, stifling. All the orifices of her body itched. She felt impelled to throw off the clothes, to clamber over him and open the horizontal door.

As if he knew exactly what thought had come into her mind, Norman put an arm across her.

"No, dearest," he said.

"Am I your blessed prisoner?" she protested indignantly. Norman stroked her back with one large hand, kneading her flesh until she relaxed and, sighing, said, "That's good."

"Be still an' never mind about mother," he said.

She put her head down upon his chest.

It was uncannily quiet outside, not muffled like in winter when mists came creeping in from the sea but a wide, glassy silence which, in spite of Norman's reassurance, Eleanor found disturbing.

The door below opened and admitted the almost inaudible scamper of cats. The door closed again.

"She's gone outside now," Eleanor said.

"Aye."

"At this hour?"

"Sleep, dearest," Norman said again. "Sleep if you can."

But Norman did not close his eyes and Eleanor could tell by his ragged breathing and an unusual tension in his limbs that Norman was troubled too.

* * *

In a faint pool of moonlight Rose knelt upon the grass and measured sea-salt into the mill. The grass was moist under her knees though dawn was still three or four hours off. The root had filled her with rash courage and, wasting no time, she cranked the handle of the mill vigorously and recited over and over the sounds of the prayer of invocation.

Last time he had arrived with leaden tread, fettered with chains and carrying a sickle. He had been angry at being disturbed. She spun the handle of the mill, let the salt run fine and free on to the ground and, with eyes wide, scanned the moonlit grassland.

Who or what would come stalking from the netherworld tonight, she wondered, the iron god with his whistling sickle, the dead girl's shade or some other angry entity?

First she would invoke the truth about the Gowrie girl and then put her own urgent questions about Eleanor and Eleanor's child before dismissing the thing the spell had drawn. She must not cause it to tarry too long for with each passing second her power over it would wane. She had no notion what might be done to her if she lost her control, what form its vengeance might take.

She had come too far to retreat, though. She wound the mill's hard handle until its load of salt was spilled upon the ground and muttered the urgent sounds over and over until she ran out of breath.

She felt a little twinge of disappointment that nothing had happened. And then the earth trembled beneath her knees and, looking up, she saw the horseman swoop out of the vale of the Linn.

He was huge, the horse huge.

He came with a roar of laughter, not fury.

She could see his teeth gleaming in his swart face, lips like raw red beef peeled back. Sooty black locks bobbed under a hat feathered like a chevalier's. He did not dismount. He rode round her in a circle, the horse snorting, its massive hoofs shaking the ground but bruising not a blade of grass.

The beast reared, pawing the air, and Rose fell sprawling backward. Shift, crystal and incantation were all forgotten as she waited for Satan's hoofs to trample her to dust. Whatever questions she had meant to ask fled from her mind along with her prayers. She had tried to summon a shade and had got Satan himself, Satan laughing his wolf's roar at her feebleness, her stupidity.

She tried to crawl away but found that she was incapable of movement. It was as if he had pierced her with a lance and pinned her to the ground. She could do nothing but swallow the foul cloud of air that enveloped her, gurgle and gape up at him.

The saddle and reins were studded with black diamonds and the horse wore a cap beaded with opals which clicked and clittered when he shook his head. When he reared above her once more she saw that the belly-band was made of copper, and the stirrups of gold, and that Satan was not hoofed but booted and spurred and ready for the ride.

The horse leapt clean over her.

Rose Tannahill shrieked and buried her face in her hands as the rider swept down from the saddle and scraped the back of her neck with one long fingernail.

And then, still roaring with laughter, he was gone, swirling away towards Ladybrook and Cairns as if he had business there too.

*   *   *

Norman found her in the grey light of dawn. She was lying face down on the grass with the blood-streaked gown twisted about her shanks.

He thought at first she'd been attacked by a dog-fox or one of the wildcats that were reputed to live on the moor but when he stooped and teased back her hair he found that the neck wounds were shallow and had bled hardly at all. She was cold, though, cold as snow. She looked, he thought, as old and gnarled as the black briar in the kirkyard that had been there for a thousand years.

He lifted her gently and rested her head on his lap.

Her eyes were wide open.

When he asked her what had happened she gave no answer. It was as if her voice had been plucked from her throat. She recognised him, though, closed her fist about his fingers as a baby will and gave him a dribbling little smile. He wiped her mouth with his knuckle and hugged her to him. He had seen the shift twisted on the grass, the bone, the mill, the circle of salt; and the serpent's egg, no longer whole but smashed into fragments.

"In God's name, Mother, what have you done?"

She gave him no answer. Never would.

He propped her into a sitting position and gathered the objects into the basket. He brushed his hand over the grass to erase the tell-tale stains then slung the basket from his elbow and got to his feet. He stared away across the moor then, turning, looked towards Ladybrook, hazy under a pearl-grey

235

sky, north-west towards Cairns already marked by heavy little sprigs of pure black smoke.

Norman lifted his mother in his arms and carried her, childlike, home.

Book Four

The Guardian Angel

Headrick House, 23rd August, 1802

Dear Andrew,
Within the next week or two Frederick Striker will make me a proposal of marriage which I shall accept. Banns will be read and the wedding arranged for the end of the month of September, after the Holy Fair.

Many will say I am mad to take on a man of Frederick Striker's reputation and – I flatter myself – others will be disappointed in my lack of judgement. There is no help for it. I cannot at this stage give consideration to the opinion of others. I am sure that you will understand what is behind it.

When arrangements are finalised and dates to hand I will write to you again.

Meanwhile, Adieu!

Your Loving Cousin
Clare.

Seventeen

It was not the first time John Galloway had been summoned to Cairns. He had nursed the younger son through a virulent attack of mumps a couple of years ago and at one time or another had treated many of the household servants for quinsy and croup brought on by dampness. He had even cured Blyth himself of an acute lumbago by administering wine-whey and white mustard along with blistering plasters, a regime which, not surprisingly, had had the coalmaster back on his feet inside a week. Never before, though, had the good doctor been sent for by the lady of Cairns and requested not only to look upon but to touch her noble female flesh.

The Italian-looking maid had brought the letter to his door one evening after dark; a very queer letter it was too, filled with minute instructions as to when he must call and how he would be admitted. Many well-bred ladies suffered from a morbid form of modesty, however, and were pathologically embarrassed to admit that they were ill at all. John Galloway thought little enough of it until, that is, he had completed an intimate examination of Sarah Blyth's icy white body, by which time he knew why she had been so secretive in summoning him to her bedside.

She looked like a flower, a great pale lily, now that she had folded down her gown and had slithered back into bed.

She lay motionless and expressionless while Galloway carefully wiped the instrument he had used upon her and rolled it up in its chamois cloth again.

The spaniel-eyed maid continued to hover by her mistress's feet, wringing her fat hands and crooning something that sounded like a Gaelic dirge.

John Galloway kept his back to the women, sucked in a deep breath and said, "At the risk of flouting decorum, I think it might be advisable to send your maid away for a few minutes."

241

"Have you more to do to me?"

"No, Madam," Galloway said. "All that remains for me to do is to tell you what's wrong with you and administer medicines in pursuit of a cure."

"What is wrong?"

"The maid, Mrs Blyth?"

"Go, Teresa."

Teresa went, gloomily but without protest.

In early afternoon the huge, rambling mansion house was abnormally quiet.

Galloway had no idea where the boys were or the host of servants that danced to the lady's every whim. A shaft of sunlight, eerily wan, lit the vaulted stone chamber. It was not a room he would have wished to sleep in for it reminded him rather too much of the chapel in Stafford where the town's dead were laid out in time of plague. He busied himself at the dressing-table which had been cleared for his use, extracting from the pouches of his travelling bag the jars required to mix the first of his preparations.

"What is it, sir? Am I like to die?"

How could he tell her what it really was?

He had heard the contagion called by a dozen different names, some bravely dismissive, others colourful and euphemistic. Any name he gave it would seem harsh to Sarah Blyth's ears. He chose instead a vague term, a suitable generalisation for the collection of symptoms that the virus engendered and for its treatment.

"No, you are not like to die," Galloway said. "However, the healing regime will be protracted and exceedingly uncomfortable and it will require a deal of patience and commitment from you if you hope to become well again."

"All this for a sore throat and a little hoarseness?"

He had selected a suitable sialagogue, mercuric chloride, which he would cream into an unction for localised relief. Later that afternoon he would make up a bolus of fifteen grains of calomel whose internal action he preferred. His immediate concern was to prevent the poison from tainting the woman's circulating fluids and becoming stubbornly constitutional. He swung round, spoon and jar in hand.

"Mrs Blyth," he said, in the firm, grave, commanding tone he reserved for refractory children and girning old men, "you know as well as I do that it's not your throat that's primarily affected. Swelling of the lymphatic glands is only the obvious

242

sign of something more deep-seated."

"Nonsense. I am uncommonly sensitive, that's all. My complexion is so pale that every small bruise shows upon me. It's nothing, certainly not what you say it is."

"What do I say it is?"

"I am not oblivious to your implication, Mr Galloway."

"In argument and debate, Madam, I may be prone to imply and infer but in matters of medicine I *state*. And what I state is that you have a serious, though not uncommon, condition caused by a contagious infection. Do you wish me to give it its vulgar name?"

Sarah Blyth swallowed.

Movement of the muscles that clad her throat was pronounced and difficult. Once treatment began in earnest, though, with vomiting, purging and sweating, a sore throat would be but a minor irritation.

"Well, do you?"

She shook her head.

"In view of the nature of the treatment, I would suggest you take your maid into your confidence, if, that is, she can be trusted."

"What . . . what will I tell my husband?"

"Tell him you have an inflammation of the uterus which has led to a general infection of the system." The ready-made excuse seldom failed, for men were exceedingly squeamish about female disorders. "You, however, must perpetrate the lie. I will do no more than tacitly endorse the diagnosis."

"If what you say is correct – "

"It is."

"– my husband . . ."

John Galloway advanced to the bed-end with the measuring spoon cocked like a pointer. "Your condition is contagious, Mrs Blyth," he told her sternly. "The infection is commonly acquired by cohabitation and commonly passed on by the same means. Is your husband also sick?"

"He has said nothing to me."

"There is a theory that the poison can be acquired from sucking an unclean spoon, from a glass or cup or tobacco pipe," Galloway said, "but it is not a theory to which I give much credence. I presume that you do not regularly share a tobacco pipe with anyone?"

She glared at him, and swallowed hard.

Sarah Blyth might feign imperious self-assurance but the

243

arrogance had gone out of her and Galloway detected in the colourless pupils more than a hint of fear.

"Has there been another?" he asked.

For an instant he thought he'd misjudged her and that she was about to send him packing, then she said, "I will inform him that I am indisposed."

"Your husband?"

"The other."

Galloway nodded and returned to the table with the jar and the spoon. He hid what he was doing from her with his body, hid too the slight tremor that had suddenly affected his fingertips. As casually as possible he said, "If this person is also ill you may send him to me at my house. It would be foolish, not to say dangerous, to mask his condition out of false sentiment and thus deny himself treatment."

"Do you know who it is?"

Galloway turned from the waist. "No."

The fear in her eyes had been replaced by vindictiveness, the conceit of possessing a secret that he, the doctor, could not force her to share.

"I'll not tell you his name, sir," Sarah Blyth said. "I will, however, see to it that he is informed of your offer."

"It's Striker, isn't it?" John Galloway said.

"Oh, no," Sarah Blyth wagged a forefinger. "If you wish to learn his identity you must wait for it, sir, you must simply wait and see."

*   *   *

Frederick was surprised to find Eleanor in the glen west of the house. She was seated on the steep bank of the Linn out of sight of the house windows and below the edge of the lawn. When she saw him on the wooden bridge she rose and waddled down the path to meet him.

He had been thinking of other things and was weary from an afternoon stint in the girnal. He might have been short with her if she had not looked so appallingly white and exhausted. He glanced around, found no one in sight, then kissed Eleanor on the brow.

"What are you doing here?" he asked.

"Waitin' for you."

"Have you no work to do?"

"Mrs Kerrigan let me go early."

244

"Where's your husband?"

"Somewhere. Busy."

"Stop here," Frederick said, "catch your breath and tell me what you want."

She eased herself down on to the grass at the end of the bridge among bluebell stalks and fern. Frederick crouched on the path, his hands on his kneecaps and looked at her with concern.

Eleanor said, "Have you not guessed yet?"

"Guessed?"

"Look at me, at my size. I'm eight months gone."

"Yes, I thought you were heavy."

"It isn't Tannahill's child, Frederick, it's yours."

The August evening was calm. The dell was filled with dusty sunlight, flocked with insects and grass seeds.

Frederick nodded. "Have you told Tannahill yet?"

"I hoped I wouldn't have to. I hoped somethin' would happen before it comes."

"Hoped that I'd take you away?"

"Aye."

"I can't, Eleanor," Frederick said gently. "Do you not see how it is? I'm on the verge of clinching things here. In a year, less than a year, I'll have everything we ever wanted and could possibly need."

"I can't wait a year," Eleanor said. "Even if Norman will still keep me as his wife, I can't stay here. The old woman – "

"What about her?"

"She's gone queer in the head."

"Queer? What do you mean?"

"She's won't speak. She sits all day in the kitchen, crouched over the fire. She was taken ill out on the Leddings in the middle of a dark night. Norman had to go out and look for her. She hasn't been right in the head since he brought her back. She doesn't cook. She doesn't even eat. Norman's back and forth from the cottage all the day long. He's worried about her. He thinks it's a sickness of age."

"What do you think?"

"I think she has it in for me."

Frederick held himself in balance and with slight, consoling pressure drew her forward so that he could kiss her again. The great mound of her stomach seemed less intrusive now, for he did not for a moment doubt that she had told him the truth. He thought of a boy child, the image of Peterkin, dark-haired, lively and loving. His!

245

"She's very old, you know," he said. "She can't last for ever."

"She'll last long enough to see me drop."

Frederick brought himself closer to Eleanor's knees. He had known women who bloomed in the days of their confinement, Clare among them. Eleanor was not so favoured. But she was still beautiful in spite of the ravages that pregnancy had wrought upon her.

"Are you in love with her?" Eleanor asked.

"Clare?" Frederick shrugged. "She's a means to an end, that's all. I don't feel for her as I feel for you. I never have."

"I thought you'd hate me."

"How can I hate you?" Frederick said. "My intentions haven't changed."

"What about Henri?"

"Him! Oh, Henri will muddle along, I'm sure."

"Could she not marry him instead of you?"

He tried not to laugh. "No, somehow I do not see that as a match. Besides, if I don't marry Clare we'll be poor, you and I. I want the best for us, and our child." He eased himself stiffly to his feet, offered a hand to Eleanor and brought her into his arms, talking all the while. "I'll sell Headrick just as soon as I possibly can. Harding will pay a fat price for the place. And then we'll be off to London, you and I and our little lad, with a great hamper full of banknotes to keep us cosy for the rest of our lives."

"An' she'll be dead?"

Frederick held her tightly. He could rush her to the cliff beside the bridge, have her over, watch her drop into the river below – but the water was shallow and Eleanor strong enough to survive the fall.

"The house and its furnishings, the land, a thriving salt-works," he said. "Eight or ten thousand pounds are ours for the asking."

"If she goes, will the child go too?"

"What child?"

"Melissa."

"Ah!" said Frederick. "No. I'll send her to Glasgow, to the cousin's house. Purves will take her in."

"Penniless?"

"Melissa Quinn isn't *my* child." Frederick placed his hand on Eleanor's stomach. "But this fine, fat fellow is."

She softened. She hadn't energy enough to be cautious and

was more liable to trust in his lies than Tannahill's forgiving nature. She nuzzled her head against his chest.

"Do you mean what you say, Frederick?"

"Every word,"

"And do you love me?"

"More than all the world," Frederick said and knew that, at least for the time being, young Eleanor believed him.

*   *   *

It was a cloudy morning with just a hint of autumn in the air as Clare walked by the long route to Headrick Bay.

She had put on her riding habit and boots for the excursion and had waited until Frederick had left for the saltworks before she in turn had left the house. She had said not a word of farewell, not even to Melissa. It was Henri's wish that she keep their rendezvous secret and she saw sense in the request. As she approached the laboratory, however, she felt a sudden excitement as if at last the pace of events was quickening and she, like a stick in a stream, was caught up in them and was being hastened towards some source or conclusion whether she willed it or not.

Henri was waiting at the door of the laboratory.

The door had been roped wide open, and on the sward before the shed some sort of contraption had already been erected, a structure like a little bridge made of logs crossed by a stout iron bar.

Clare had a vague recollection of paying an invoice from the stock-keeper at Cairns for the purchase of just such a bar and she glanced at it curiously in passing. It had been scraped clean of rust and reminded Clare of one of the rails that ran up the ramp at the Malliston coalhill, which is probably just what it was.

"Madame Quinn." Henri bowed. "It is good of you to attend to my invitation."

"How could I refuse," Clare said, "when it was put so intriguingly?" She gestured towards the trestle. "Is this what you have lured me here to see?"

"It is the one part of it," Henri said. "The lesser part."

"And the greater?"

"Now you are here I will bring it forth."

"Tell me, Henri, are you about to demonstrate the result of your labours?"

"Yes, Madame Quinn, I am," he said solemnly.

He was dressed in a rusty brown suit that Clare had not seen him wear before. The collar of his shirt was freshly starched and his cravat had been ironed. This was Henri without gaiety, Clare realised, Henri acting professionally.

"Pardon me, if you will." He bowed again and backed away into the shed.

Clare waited outside.

She glimpsed Henri as he moved about the laboratory, saw glassware, the furnace, the strange coffin-shaped electrical device and then, to her astonishment, the snout of a cannon-like object which seemed to be emerging from the doorway of its own volition.

Involuntarily she backed away a step or two as the cannon rolled into view with Henri behind it, pushing with all his might. Some three feet in height, the gun was lashed to a two-wheeled carriage constructed from a pair of wheels from a colliery waggon and the bed of a flat cart. The deck was raked slightly downward from fore to aft and upon it was, indeed, a cannon. But what a cannon! Clare had seen nothing quite like it before; an iron and brass gargoyle with rubberised horns, a tubular tail, a snout that narrowed into a tiny brass beak with three taps sticking out from it.

"It's a gun?" Clare said.

"It is not what you had reason to expect?" Henri said and, puffing, leaned upon the carriage and mopped his brow.

"I did not know what to expect."

Henri patted the machine affectionately.

"Since it is all purchased with the money you gave to me," he said, "you are entitled to have me to explain it to you, if you wish."

"I think," Clare said, "a demonstration might be of more benefit."

"We will take a patent order on the device, although the building of it is no difficult matter once the design is presented to the correct craftsman," Henri said. "The gases in the cylinders, how to mix them in accurate measure, that is the secret to the machine. We will take a separate patent on the ingredients of the gases and the process for their manufacture."

"Show me how it works," said Clare.

Henri pushed the machine forward and set it before the trestles. He braced the wheels with wooden wedges and adjusted the angle of the carriage so that the beak – the brass nozzle –

pointed at the iron bar. He took a tinderbox from his pocket, fired it, lit a wax taper and stood back.

"Madame Quinn, if you will be kind enough to make a mark upon the iron bar." He offered her a lump of chalk. "It will show to you that I have not cheated by weakening the bar at any one point."

Clare approached warily, studied the bar and then, a little to the left of its central point, made a guiding mark.

"Will that do?"

Henri waggled his hand as if to say that it made no matter. The taper in his fingers released a final splutter of smoke and then settled to a clear yellow flame.

"If you will assume to a position of safety behind me, please," Henri said, "I will make to proceed."

Clare obeyed the Frenchman's request.

She watched him sidle close to the front of the gun, fiddle with the taps and then, at arm's length, touch the taper to the nozzle.

Clare had no idea what to expect. Would there be a prolonged pause as with a fuse or would the gun emit a sudden explosive roar? She raised her hands to her ears but had no need to do so. A fierce and sustained ripping sound, like a roll of fabric being torn lengthwise, was accompanied by a flame of blinding-white intensity, a flame which, even as Clare watched, gobbled into the iron bar and melted it like a wax tablet.

The process was too controlled and concentrated to be frightening. In three or four minutes the bar had been bitten in half. It did not so much snap as fold in upon itself, the cold ends cocking up like cards.

Henri calmly turned off the taps, the jet diminished, dribbled, spluttered like a liquid and, with a final little hiss, vanished into the spout. Stepping round the gun he tapped the bar lightly with a small stone and split it into two neat portions exactly along the line of Clare's mark.

He spread his palms to the sky, and grinned.

"Do you understand what you have witnessed?" he asked.

"An amazing device," said Clare. "Amazing!"

"Do you wish to have a question?"

"How long will the gas in the containers last?"

"Eighteen or twenty cuts."

"Does the gun not grow hot?"

"Only the nose." Henri pointed. "Here."

"How expensive are the gases to manufacture?"

"In quantity, to my precise direction? Not so much."

A dozen questions clamoured in her brain but she checked her excitement, stepped forward, flung her arms about the Frenchman's neck and kissed him on both cheeks.

"Henri," she said, soberly, "you are to be congratulated. You have delivered to me and to the world a new and valuable process."

"I will show how to make it all work upon the applications for patents. You will have every franc, every sou back with much interest, Clare, as I promised to you."

"Oh, yes, yes, Henri."

He caught her hands and danced a jig around the gun, drawing Clare with him, saying, "I will put up another bar of iron. We will show it to Frederick in this evening. We will show it to M. Blyth and M. Harding. We – "

Dragging on his hands, Clare stopped his capers abruptly.

"No," she said. "No, Henri, you must show your invention to no one just yet. Tell no one that it is complete and functioning effectively."

"We cannot tell even Frederick?"

"Not even Frederick."

"But why is this to be?" He was suddenly crestfallen. "Do you not think I did it with honesty?"

"It's not that at all," Clare told him. "Nor will I expect you to wait long for the praise and admiration that will surely come your way. I ask only that you delay for a month, for my sake."

"For your sake, Clare? I do not understand."

She positioned herself before him and peered up at him with all the earnest authority that she could muster. "I do not want anyone to know that your work is complete. The time is not quite ripe, believe me. Will you keep silent, Henri, for three or four weeks?"

"For you?"

His ingenuousness was touching. How easy it must have been for Frederick to entrap him. Why, though, had Frederick failed to exploit the Frenchman's skills for his own, exclusive advantage?

"For me, Henri. Please."

"I will do it," said M. Leblanc. "One month?"

"Yes," said Clare, "a month will be quite long enough."

* * *

250

Supper was over. A fire burned bright in the grate. Candles shone on decanters and glasses and glinted on the silver teapot that Pratie, at Clare's request, had carried into the drawing-room. Melissa had been tucked up in bed for an hour. At a less than subtle sign from Frederick, Henri had curtailed his inclination to linger and had taken himself off to bed too.

By the stroke of ten o'clock Mr Frederick Striker and Mrs Clare Quinn were at last alone.

Clare had put on her best blue frock and had spent a considerable amount of time on her coiffure. Frederick too had made a special effort with his appearance and had squeezed himself into a pair of cream-coloured breeks that unfortunately, displayed the boniness of his shanks. The coat was full frock, though, and gave him a distinct air of grandeur, though his wig, hand-powdered and curled, made him look rather too sedate for Clare's liking.

"May I pour you a glass of wine?" Frederick said.

He had drunk nothing at all during supper. He stood by the table now with an expression on his face that could only be described as eager.

"No, thank you. I am happy with my dish of tea."

"May I, for myself?"

"By all means."

He poured, sipped, put bottle and glass down again upon the little table. He cleared his throat.

"You know, Clare, summer's almost at an end."

"In the wake of the Holy Fair, winter will soon be upon us, I'm afraid, yes."

"Have we not had a good season?"

"In terms of salt profits, I have no complaint."

"Have I not done what you expected of me?"

"In spite of all that's happened, yes, you have."

"The Gowrie girl's accident was an unforeseen setback, certainly, but we appear to have weathered the storm," Frederick said, with a trace of smugness. "I fancy next year will be even more rewarding."

"I have not given next year much thought," Clare said.

"Have you, however, given thought to our arrangement?"

It was a moment for delicacy, for modesty this side of coyness. Clare lowered her eyes.

"It has, I confess, been much on my mind," she said.

"Are you disappointed in me?"

"On the contrary."

"Have I fulfilled your expectations?"

"In all ways, Frederick," Clare said. "Save one."

"Oh!" He exclaimed in mild surprise. "In what particular area have I failed you?"

"You have not made love to me."

Frederick, nonplussed, took two or three seconds to gather himself. "I – I did not think that my attentions would be welcome, I mean, physically. I mean, did you not make it clear – "

"I did not expect you to be put off by my apparent hesitations." Clare looked up. "I cannot say that I am flattered by your restraint."

"It was accomplished only with the greatest effort of will on my part," Frederick said. "Do you – do you wish me to make love to you now?"

"In what manner?"

"In the – the accustomed manner."

"There is love, Frederick, and there is love-making . . ." Clare began.

He had his hands about her before she could prevent it.

He lifted her from the sofa and kissed her upon the mouth. The frock-coat pressed against her breast. The wig scratched her cheek.

She allowed him to complete his impetuous little exercise in osculation – for it was no more than that to either of them, a phase of negotiations – without flinching. He held her rather awkwardly, her skirts and petticoats crushed by the edge of the sofa.

As soon as he took his mouth from hers, Clare continued, ". . . and there is marriage, which combines love and love-making in perfect harmony."

"Clare, will you marry me?"

"Put me down, please."

"Oh, yes, yes of course."

He lowered her gently to the sofa.

He seated himself by her side, one long leg stretched out in the artificial pose of a suitor. He clasped her hands in his, all perfect and pictorial; except that Clare could feel the calluses on his palms, see all too clearly the tiny grizzled tufts missed by the razor and the livid little rash at the corner of his mouth. In spite of his expensive finery he exuded the neglected air of an ageing bachelor, comical and sad at one and the same time.

"Clare, I beg you to give me a direct answer."

"Do you love me, Frederick?"

"More than all the world."

"Is it me that you love," she said, "or Headrick?"

"You, you of course. I care not a damn about Headrick," he said, "except insofar as it is your place, your home."

"If I came with nothing, if I came to you as I did once before, penniless and without prospects," Clare said, "would you still wish to have me as your wife?"

"Yes," Frederick said. "Yes, yes."

"Ask me again, dearest."

"Clare, will you marry me?"

"I will, Frederick."

"Oh, God!" he cried out. "How happy you have made me. I swear I am the happiest man alive."

"You may kiss me again, if you wish."

He pulled her to him and kissed her passionately. His lips were bruising, his tongue insinuating.

Clare arched her back but her arms about his neck were slack and she did not, not for an instant, close her eyes.

"When shall it be?" Frederick said. "The great day, I mean?"

"In September," Clare informed him. "The twenty-eighth day of the month."

Frederick laughed. He eased his hold on her a fraction but did not release her.

"You planned this, you minx. You trapped me into it, didn't you? Admit it."

Clare smiled. "I admit it."

"But why, why did you keep me waiting so long?"

"To be sure of you."

"Are you sure now?"

"As sure as I will ever be."

He got up, paused, kissed her again, then tilted back his head and raised his arms as if he was about to howl like a wolf at the moon. He uttered no loud sound, however, only a low contented growl.

"Ahhh! I cannot believe my good fortune. This is what I'd hoped for when I came back to find you. But I did not believe it would come to pass, that you would ever find it in your heart to forgive me."

"Are you not a changed man?"

"Yes, yes, I am," he said. "Look, when can I – we – when can we tell everyone the good news? I feel like shouting it from the rooftop. I feel like riding down to Ladybrook and ringing the rescue bell."

"Come now, Frederick: the rescue bell? That hardly seems appropriate," Clare said. "Besides, as a widow lady I am obliged to behave with a certain amount of decorum."

"Of course, of course."

"Mr Soames must be told and banns prepared for crying in the kirk. Then we must decide on the nature of the celebration which will follow. Modest, I think."

"A supper party, perhaps?" Frederick said. "Or we might make a day of it – if you would not find that too tiring."

"No, I would not find that too tiring," said Clare. "But first thing of all I must write to Mr Greenslade and ask him to call upon us."

"Mr Greenslade, your lawyer?"

"Yes."

"Why?"

"If you are to be my husband, Frederick, it is only right and proper that you are apprised of the duties that will fall upon you under Scotch law," Clare said. "And the peculiarities of the right of entail."

"Entail?" He stood by the hearth with one hand upon his chest, fingers spread, as if he had been smitten by a sudden sharp pain. "Is that not a matter best examined after we're married?"

"Better if it is done before," Clare said. "I must confess I do not completely understand the fine points of the law in respect of succession, but Donald was versed in them and had many interesting consultations with Mr Greenslade in the latter days of his life."

"This is – the will?"

"Yes." Clare sighed as if the law of inheritance was nothing but a bothersome trifle. "The substance is clear enough, I suppose. Mr Greenslade will be able to explain the rest of it to you. I will be relieved to be rid of it."

"What is the substance of it, Clare?" Frederick cleared his throat again and struggled to make his question seem casual. "From my scant knowledge of the subject I would assume that, in the absence of issue, you are the sole legatee of all Donald's goods, monies and lands."

"Not so," said Clare.

"What?"

"There is issue, you see."

"But not male, not – "

"Testate succession, in Scotch law, does not require the heir to be male," Clare said. "Melissa is the legatee of Headrick. I am merely her trustee. I can do nothing to diminish Melissa's material inheritance even if I wished to do so – which, of course, I do not."

"Headrick cannot, for example, be sold?"

"No."

"Not even to pay debts?"

"No," said Clare.

"I did not know of this."

"There was no reason for you to know." She got to her feet and came to him sinuously. She put an arm about his waist and leaned her head on his chest. "It will be such a relief to have someone to care for me and take care of the future." She glanced up into Frederick's face, her eyes wide and innocent. "I'm glad that you love me. You do, Frederick, don't you?"

"Of course, of course."

"This silly business of entail will make no difference to our wedding plans, will it?"

"None at all," said Frederick, grimly. "I love you and I want you. And that's enough."

"Is it, dearest?"

"Absolutely," Frederick said and, with all the sincerity he could muster, kissed her on the mouth once more.

*   *   *

Brock Harding lolled in the big wooden chair in the scant light of the over-room. It was early evening. Trade in the Neptune, brisk at dinnertime, had dwindled to a lull before farmers came down from the hills and weavers slid their shuttles and rolled to the inn in search of drink and good company. Above the black-smith's head the Eye of Apollo had been shielded with baize cloth and if Frederick had been a true Mason he would have realised that a degree ceremony was in the offing. He was too agitated to notice the cloth, however, and prowled the hollow room like a wolf in a cage, his voice strident and echoing.

Brock, in contrast, seemed quite unperturbed. He leaned an elbow on the arm of the chair, head on hand, and waited patiently for Freddie to cool down.

At length Frederick paused and Brock had an opportunity to put his question: "She is a-goin' to marry you, though?"

"Yes, in September."

"That's all that matters," Brock said. "To be candid, Fred, I never imagined you'd be able to bring her to heel."

"Not much point in bringing her to heel if she's worth nothing, is there?"

"Who says she's worth nothing?"

"Have you been asleep for the last half-hour?" said Frederick testily. "I told you, she doesn't own Headrick."

"Not yet, perhaps."

Frederick stopped his frantic pacing and seated himself on the edge of the dais, hands on knees.

"Not yet?" he said. "What's that supposed to mean?"

Brock chuckled. "If you ask me, Fred, you've been taken for a hay-ride. Clare Quinn ain't stupid. I'll wager there was no clause in the original will which nominated the kidling as Quinn's successor."

"Oh! So I've nothing to worry about?"

"I didn't say that," Brock told him. "You've plenty to worry about."

"But not the – what's it called – testate succession?"

"If you ask me," said Brock again, "Clare Quinn altered the will soon after you loomed over the horizon. Quinn wouldn't have dreamed of cuttin' his wife off from her inheritance. Aye, it might have been different if he'd had sons, but Quinn had no more respect for daughters than I have myself."

"Perhaps the lawyer, Greenslade, suggested it to him?"

"Nah, nah," Brock said. "Think on it, Fred. First the widow makes you wait and gets her pound of flesh from you in terms of work. Then she takes on a partnership with the Frenchman, steals your thunder there too – "

"What are you implying?"

"She's tied you up, old son," Brock said. "She has you bound hoof-and-tail like a lamb for the slaughter."

"Balderdash!" Frederick shouted. "She loves me. She's infatuated with me. She has told me so herself."

"Aye, in the same breath as she tells you the kidling's Headrick's legatee," Brock said. "Clare Quinn, not her dear departed husband, drafted that deed of entail."

"What difference does it make who drafted it?" Frederick said. "Obviously it's been copied and witnessed and there's precious little I can do about it. I mean, I could refuse to marry her unless the contract is changed."

"Not wise," said Brock. "'Specially when the blushing bride thinks you're marryin' her for love."

"I must say you're taking my news very calmly, Brock," Frederick said. "Come along, tell me what's on your mind."

"Well, I've waited years to lay hands on Headrick, a few more months ain't goin' to make much difference." He tapped his nose with a forefinger. "Patience, Freddie, that's the ticket."

"So – I push on with the wedding, do I?"

"Full sail ahead," Brock said.

"And then what?"

Brock stirred, eased his shoulders then settled back in the chair again, hands behind his head.

"Some things you can do that I can't," he said. "I could never persuade the lady Quinn to marry me, for instance, nor even to marry one o' my lads. Too much bad blood left over from the old days, I expect. But you – you seem to have got around her just like you said you would. Won't be no hardship for you beddin' the lovely widow Quinn, will it?"

Frederick, curiously embarrassed, shook his head.

"Until the Reverend pronounces you man an' wife, though, you'll be butter to Clare Quinn's knife," Brock went on. "Express no interest in meetin' Greenslade. Ask no questions about the daughter's entitlements. You've been told. You accept it. That's an end of it. Right?"

"Until I have my feet properly under the table?"

"Properly an' legally," Brock said.

"I understand," Frederick said.

"Nevertheless, there are things I can do, Fred, that you can't, as has already been proved. Am I right?"

"Yes, you're right," Frederick cautiously agreed.

"If the clever Mrs Quinn has hived off the entail to her sweet wee daughter – well, that can be rectified too."

"Rectified?"

"The problem can be removed."

"I'll not stand by and see the child killed."

"You weren't so squeamish about the last 'un, Fred."

"I didn't know you were going to – "

"'Course you did," Brock said, a sudden hard edge to his voice. "You paid for it, remember?"

"Yes, but I didn't realise you intended to drown – "

"What did you think we was a-goin' to do?" Brock said. "She was a threat to our plans, to your plans. She was too young an' too stupid to listen to reason. If the Gowrie girl had opened her mouth an' sung the wrong song do you think you'd ever have got Clare Quinn to the altar?"

"But to – to drown her?"

"She drowned herself," Brock said. "All Daniel did was help her have an accident. Come to think of it, Fred, you never did thank Daniel for disposin' of the problem."

"All right, Brock, all right," Frederick said. "What happened to the Gowrie girl is over and done with. But I don't want Melissa Quinn dismissed in the same way. I do not want her to meet an untimely end. Is that clear?"

"Scared of what her Mama will say?"

"Clare's daughter will be my responsibility by then."

"Clare's daughter stands between you an' a trim sum of money, remember."

"Brock, I warn you – "

Brock shook his head. "You ain't half the man you used to be, Freddie. Such an attack o' the scruples I never would have believed."

"Whatever happens I don't want Melissa killed."

"Suit yourself," Brock Harding said. "There are other ways of being rid of her."

"What other ways?"

"What comes in with the tide," Brock said, "can go out with the tide."

"What the devil do you mean?"

"She's a bright girl, good-lookin' too, or will be when she grows apiece," Brock said. "She'd thrive in Ireland, I'm sure, if we found a nice quiet billet to tuck her up in."

"Dear God!"

"What's wrong with you, Freddie?" Brock Harding said. "Will you give up a fortune just for the sake of a child?"

"I'll not see her harmed."

"You won't have to see anythin'. You'll be fast asleep in your wife's bed when it happens. You can always blame the gypsies."

"No, Brock, it'll never work."

"After all I done for you, Fred," Brock said, "after all the dirty linen I've got stored in my basket, it's my way or it's no way at all."

"How soon after my marriage will this happen?"

"A decent interval. Six months or a year."

"And then?"

"It's up to you to dispose of the lady," Brock said, "just like you done before."

*   *   *

Three times Matt Pringle had made a solitary trek across the Leddings and three times he had been sent away angry and unsatisfied.

On the last occasion the old salter had admitted defeat and had demanded his money back. Norman had gone to the hiding place in the wall, had taken out the cashbox and, there and then, had counted out twenty pounds. Rose had sullenly observed the transaction but had uttered not a word of reprimand to her son for breaching the sacred box, her holy reliquary, and throwing back money she had justly earned.

"She can't tell you what you want to know, Mr Pringle," Norman had said. "She's sick, as you can see."

"She's mad, if you ask me," Matt Pringle had said and with a final savage glance at the old woman slumped in her chair by the fire had stumbled away into the gloaming.

Norman closed the cottage door behind the salter and stalked back into the kitchen.

Eleanor was on her knees by the hearthstone keeling a luke-warm broth-pot and watching raw stew refuse to bubble in a pan. Nothing had been done in the house or upon the farm that day or for many days. Dust lay thick upon the dresser shelves and the summer's trim of herbs and flowers were scattered, shrivelled, where Rose had strewn them before her illness struck.

Norman put a hand under his wife's arm, hoisted her from the hearthstone and led her to the door.

"Wait ben the house," he told her quietly. "I want to talk to my mother."

The house had a bad smell to it now, an odour of decay.

Pig seep and cats' piss infected the stale air of the kitchen. Eleanor could do nothing to remedy the sorry state of affairs.

She worked her stint at Headrick and toiled home on Norman's arm to find the old woman exactly where she had been left, a bowl of gruel stiff and cold upon the table and nothing touched except the dish of tea, and that barely. Eleanor would cook and clean as best she could but she had no energy for extra tasks and not enough hours in the day to scrub away the invidious layers of dirt that had grown so rapidly since

259

Rose had retreated into herself, into a carapace so seamed and tight that nothing could penetrate it.

Eleanor leaned upon the doorpost.

Dusk was down upon the Leddings, late-summer dusk, drowsy and fecund. The cats skulked before her, their eyes like little yellow moons, watching, waiting to be fed. She could hear the grunt of the sow in the sty, fat with farrow, and Norman's voice, crisp as gunfire and, for once, angry.

"*What did you promise him, Mother? What did you see that night?*"

Eleanor let her weight take her to the ground. She rested her belly against her knees, leaning forward. One cat, a young queen, came stealthily to her side and rubbed an ear against her flank.

"*Did you try to summon a shade, Mother? Is that it?*" Norman shouted. "*Why will you not talk to me? Am I not your son any more?*"

In two days' time they would go to St Cedric's to participate in the annual communion service, the Holy Fair. A thousand would come to the Ladybrook kirk, tramping in to hear the preachers, to drink at the inns, to eat their dinners under the elms and oaks and to queue for the dispensation of bread and wine, the sacred tokens of redemption. Eleanor had told Norman that she wasn't up to it, but he was adamant. Now more than ever, he said, they needed to be cleansed by the Sacrament, their child protected by ingestion of the Blood and the Body. Norman was too strong to be swayed by her girlish tears.

"*What did you see, Mother? What robbed you of your senses? Where have you gone to, Mumma, where?*"

Eleanor stroked the cat's soft ruff and felt its tongue upon her fingertips.

She had seen the strike of this illness before, in Dublin, the mind blown by age, the senses lost in dumb melancholy. There was nothing occult about it, Eleanor thought, only life's pain and terror unravelled and made plain at last in age.

Norman was crying when he came to fetch her in.

Eleanor had never seen Norman cry before. It did not seem right, somehow.

She wondered if he would cry this sore for her when her time came to go.

She offered him her hand but he did not take it. He wiped his eyes with his knuckle, ashamed of his tears.

"She's leavin'," he said. "My Mumma's leavin' me, an' I canna bring her back."

"There, love," said Eleanor. "There, there."

She leaned her head against his knees and let him weep, not for her, for Freddie Striker's whore, but for the loss of the withered old woman who lurked alive indoors.

* * *

The perfume from the roses was almost overpowering. Cloying sweetness caught upon the back of Clare's throat and tasted the tea that John had had brought out to the garden for her refreshment.

There were roses in beds, roses nodding on the south-west wall, roses peeping from the shrubbery, dwarfs and standards and hybrids, a satin dance of petals, flame and shaded apricot, carmine, copper and lemon yellow, while from the borders at her feet, cameos of scarlet and salmon pink peeped coyly up at her. She would swear that she could hear the roses drone like bees in the still, oppressive air of that September Saturday.

She had caught John gardening.

He wore calico trousers and a plain cotton shirt, untied at waist and sleeves. It was not light labour that occupied him that stifling forenoon but hard digging with a spade. He told her enthusiastically that he was cutting a pit to build a new hotbed ready for delivery of a big box frame he had ordered made in Ayr, ready too for the fall of autumn leaves which he would liberally mix with stable straw to ferment a fine spring mulch.

John Galloway had not seemed in the least dismayed at being interrupted and had abandoned his digging as soon as Clare had appeared at the gate. He had invited her to stay for dinner but she had declined the invitation.

She was not at all sure that her friend would wish to share her company after he'd heard what she had to say.

At first Clare confined the conversation to general matters and discussed tomorrow's Holy Fair, sympathising with Reverend Soames and his elders who would dispense the sacraments to a thousand communicants in five separate services that would surely leave the minister exhausted in body, mind and spirit.

After Ishbel had served tea, however, Clare could defer the dreaded moment no longer.

She said, "John?"

He put his teacup and saucer down by the side of the bench and studied her anxiously. "What is it?"

"John, I am to be married."

"I see."

She was sticky beneath her gown, and her bonnet, light though it was, cut into her brow. There was not a breath of air in the corner of the garden between the hedges and not a leaf stirred, not a petal.

"To Striker, I assume?" John Galloway said.

"Yes, to Frederick."

"Will it be soon?"

"Before the end of the month."

He sucked his underlip for a moment, making a little hissing sound. He had not yet shaved for the day and perspiration made the stubble on his chin seem glossy. He was a handsome man in a plain no-nonsense sort of way, and she had hurt him deeply by her sudden, bald announcement.

"If I were to tell you that your husband-to-be is evil, would you take it as pique on my part?" he said.

"I would take it as an honest opinion."

"But my opinion would not make you change your mind?"

"No, John, it would not."

"Why him? Why Striker?" John Galloway said. "Love, is it? Blind as always. What is there between you, Clare?"

"Something left over, something undone."

"He *is* evil, you know."

"Selfish and mercenary," Clare said, "but not evil, no."

"Do you not see what he is after?"

"Headrick," Clare said. "It's obvious."

"Does he mean so much to you that you'd simply hand it to him meekly, like a pie upon a plate?"

"Headrick is not mine to give," Clare said. "Have you forgotten our trip to Irvine? Melissa is the real mistress of Headrick, under law at least."

"Does Striker know it?"

"Yes."

"What was his response to the information?"

"He took it calmly."

Galloway watched a finch alight on the verge and hop listlessly towards the excavation then, losing interest, flutter into the hedge again. At length he said, "Clare, I must warn you again: Frederick Striker's not just a faithless rogue and rantin' boy. He's corrupt in ways you cannot imagine."

"I know a deal more about Frederick than you think I do," Clare said. "It's for that reason I've come today; to remind you of your promise to be my guardian angel."

"With the best will in the world, Clare, I will not be able to come between a man and his wife."

"I do not expect you to," Clare said, "but if anything should happen to me, John, will you personally see to it that Melissa is protected?"

"If anything – " He shoved himself to his feet and stared at her in astonishment. "Good God! Do you mean to say you're willing to risk being murdered just to take revenge upon this man?"

"No, I'm too fond of life, and of my daughter, to offer myself as a willing victim."

"But when Striker has you, when you are conjugally joined to him, how can you possibly defend yourself?" John Galloway asked. "He will poison you as surely as he has poisoned everything and everyone he's touched."

"I've come too far," Clare said, "to pull back now."

"Surely you don't mean you've already – "

"I'm not that much of a fool."

"So you haven't – haven't slept with him?"

"No."

He studied her again for a moment then, without force, put his hands upon her shoulders and kissed her lips.

"Do you know that I love you?" he said.

"Yes."

"But you prefer Frederick?"

"I am already linked to him, John," Clare said. "There's no help for it."

"Can the link not be broken?"

"Only by Frederick."

"Before it's too late?" John Galloway asked.

"I hope so," Clare told him. "I hope so, John, really and truly I do."

Eighteen

Even the most generous apologist would not claim that the Reverend Randolph Soames had a "soul like a star and dwelt apart". His aloofness and serenity were only skin deep and, when aroused by spleen or spiritual passion, he could match any evangelical in railing against the low morals of the times. Mr Soames was, however, prone to stress the all-too-obvious fact that the lapsing of the masses had begun long ago and that neglect of congregational catechising was nowhere more apparent than on the days of the Holy Fairs.

He believed that those great traditional rabbles of preaching and drinking, of sacramental pilgrimage, instant conversion, of flirting and fornication had, by ignorance, idleness and neglect, turned the Sacrament of the Lord's Supper into a disgraceful farce.

It had too long been the habit for folk to flock from kirk to kirk around the parishes for Reverend Soames to put a sudden stop to it, even if he had not been constrained by the guidance of the Presbytery. But he had done everything in his power to ensure that St Cedric's Annual Communion had lost its appeal as a purely social event by banning ale carts from the kirkyard and having the Glebe patrolled to prevent the field being used as a knocking-shop.

In addition he steadfastly refused to allow the Sacraments to be administered except within the hallowed walls of the kirk and would not permit the Elements to be tasted on tubs in tents, however much such open-air exhibitions might appeal to die-hard covenanting spirits.

Soames's strictures, and the regimentation that went with them, deterred casual sermon-tasters and indigent layabouts alike and the hordes of yore had dwindled to an almost manageable thousand or so.

It was still a worthwhile crowd, though, and the kirk

grounds still fêted a fair smack of visiting preachers including "Dandy Danny" Coutts from Auchinmore and the diminutive "Bairn" Braintree, who in spite of his small stature had a voice like a brass trumpet and could make himself heard by passing ships at sea. The local inns still did a roaring trade, courtships were still crowned with sinful acts, and weary pilgrims still slept like sheep upon the grass. But much of the old rowdiness had been swept away, thanks be to God and Mr Soames, and it was safe for Clare and Frederick to come down in the afternoon to book a five o'clock place at the Lord's Table.

Headrick's servants had queued for their share of bread and wine early that morning and Melissa had been left in their care for, in Clare's judgement, her daughter was just too susceptible to brimstone preaching to be subjected to such an onslaught of it all at once.

It was not, in any case, an inspiring sort of day. The sky was layered with coal-black clouds, the air motionless and humid and not a fresh breath of air stirred the scalloped tents and canvas awnings from under whose protection the ministers, in unison and in turn, addressed the multitude.

Sweat rivered Frederick's face and neck. He paused frequently to mop his brow with a handkerchief and Clare was concerned lest he fall in a swoon like some histrionic convert into whose heart God had descended unexpectedly.

There was no blink of sunshine on the surface of the waters and the hills away to the east were dark and featureless. It was a day for drink and snoozing, for taverns not sermons; yet the preachers were hard at it and even away under the elms Todd Greevy was lecturing fisherfolk, pointing to this grave and that and shouting Redemption in sailors' terms.

Randolph's elders were out in force, herding the three o'clock congregation towards the door of the church while the bell in the steeple tolled sonorously and, by the little side door, Mr Ormiston rolled in yet another keg of consecrated port.

"Shall we rest here against the wall, Frederick?"

Clare too was saturated with perspiration. She felt smothered by the carpet-cloth of cloud. She could hardly take her eyes off the horizon. She was not alone. More than one communicant gazed at the wrathful sky with strange anxiety and the kirkyard, for a Holy Saturday, was emptying rapidly.

"Yes," Frederick said. "Unless there's a preacher you particularly wish to hear."

"No, there is none."

"Rain in the air," said Frederick, sniffing.

"Too dry," Clare said. "Taste the sulphur."

"I can taste only brass," said Frederick. "I trust it will be a brighter afternoon for our nuptials."

"A glorious autumn day, yes."

"Will you have flower petals?"

"Hardly suitable, since I am a matron not a maid."

"Yes, I suppose that's true."

Frederick leaned upon the drystone and tipped his hat from his brow. Haggard by the heat, he sucked in breath, mopped his brow and cocked his head to catch a phrase or two from Reverend Greevy's catechism.

Clare leaned, unladylike, upon her elbows and listlessly watched the communicants ebb and flow about the doorway of the kirk, Eleanor and Norman Tannahill, old Matt Pringle with Annie Gowrie clinging to his hand, and John Galloway among them. Friends, enemies and acquaintances; the church swallowed them up indiscriminately.

"We should go down soon," Frederick said, "to stake our places for the five o'clock show."

"Yes."

Neither of them made a move.

In the elms rooks strutted and barked. Travelling inland came a great loose flock of black-head and herring-gulls, flying high over the steeple.

The bell ceased its abject tolling.

"Look," Frederick said.

Clare turned and followed the direction of his gaze.

Dressed in black, Rose Tannahill toiled to the crest of the ridge behind the kirkyard and, struggling, raised herself up.

"I thought she was near to death," Frederick said.

"It certainly does not seem so," Clare said and, as thunder rolled ominously, turned back to stare at the sky above the firth, frowning.

*   *   *

266

Randolph Soames did not take the pledge of communion lightly but even he, that stifling September day, had had to fight an impulse to short-change his parishioners and the visiting strangers who had come in all good faith to affirm the new covenant of Christ and partake of the outward and visible signs of the promise of a life everlasting.

Dripping with sweat, he had twice retired to the vestry to change his linen and allow his robes to dry. Every pore glared. His face, he knew, had assumed the hue of fresh-cut beetroot. He was obliged to crane his head back as he filled the cups from which the communicants would drink. Even so, perspiration was sprinkled indiscriminately into and about the silverware.

He had never been so hot, never so keen for the ceremonies to be over; yet he refused to hurry through the preaching or rush the prayer, the psalm, the toil of dispensation. Manfully he laboured, manfully endured.

"*And Jesus said unto them, I am the bread of life; he that cometh to me shall never hunger; and he that believeth in me shall never thirst –* "

Faces packed row on row below him. Pews and benches, chairs in the gallery all filled. In the body of the kirk, the new wife of Norman Tannahill, swollen like a plum. At the back, Pringle the salter and his grandchild, recently bereaved. John Galloway, his old friend, in the pew to the side of the pulpit.

"*He that eateth my flesh, and drinketh my blood, dwelleth in me, and I in him.*"

I'm not alone in my suffering, he thought. His poor elders were sore pressed too. Robertson Blyth, with a sick wife at home, surely had more on his mind than trays of divine bread and communal cups. As the trays went round, Soames lifted his hands and began his blessing. No matter how often he uttered them, how familiar they had become, the words of the long speech still pricked his spirit with a rapture that humidity and discomfort could not quench.

"*Behold I stand at the door and knock.*"

The growl of distant thunder which he had heard and ignored, broke in a sudden numbing clap just overhead.

In the benches beneath the gallery a woman screamed.

Lifting his eyes, Soames faltered as a fragment of plaster detached itself from among the rafters and plummeted, whistling, to the flagstones below.

*　　*　　*

267

She had taken a piece of oat bread from the big silver plate and held it safe in her fingers while Norman, to her left, bore the weight of the salver and transported it carefully along the row away from her.

In the silence that had come upon the congregation she could hear the minister's words ring out clear and loud, the skliff and shuffle of the elders' shoes as they edged along the aisles. Hear, too, the mutter of thunder beyond the walls, the first flat slap of rain upon the roof high overhead, the first buffet of wind upon the widows.

Chill air brushed her cheek like an owl's wing.

Inside her body the child churned and struggled.

She put the square of bread into her mouth and held it, dry, upon her tongue.

She heard the sudden awful peal directly overhead and at precisely the same moment glimpsed the knob of mortar as it fell from the roof. It seemed to draw a chalk line on the edge of her vision and the noise of its impact was louder than the thunder.

Elder Millar stepped back from the first explosion of dust in the aisle and, with the communion plate swaying in his hands, looked up at the arch of the roof. He stepped neatly back from the second explosion and then, with the communion plate tucked under one arm, ran pell-mell for the main door, scattering bread in a trail behind him.

Someone, a woman, screamed.

Norman caught Eleanor by the arm.

He dragged her past his knees and thrust her towards the aisle a split second before panic gripped the congregation and a wild stampede began.

*   *   *

Clare and Frederick, arm in arm, were making their way down the knoll from the kirkyard when the rain arrived.

It preceded a violent clap of thunder and the first searing flash of lightning by two or three minutes and was announced only by a rushing tide of wind which shook the tents and awnings and made the elm trees tremble.

Clare stopped, riveted by the strange phenomenon.

Sleepers rose like resurrected corpses from between the tombstones and hastily began to gather their belongings. Children ran in search of Mama's skirts and on the ridge beyond the kirkyard wall Rose Tannahill's shawl flapped about her like a tattered winding sheet. The sky was blacker than midnight, the rain a sudden glacial torrent that wetted Clare's skin and soaked her clothes instantly. The hiss of it was almost deafening.

"The church," Frederick shouted. "We'll find shelter in the church."

Holding his hat on with one hand, he grabbed Clare's arm and, in company with several hundred others, headed down the straggling path towards St Cedric's.

They had made no more than a dozen yards before thunder pealed above them, sheet lightning illuminated the sky and the scamper became a charge.

At that moment Elder Millar flung open the kirk's front door and, yelling blue murder, made good his escape.

*   *   *

Pringle's one overwhelming fear was that the girl would be wrested from him. He clung to her with both hands as he was thrust out into the aisle and, on the instant, became locked both in front and behind. He knew exactly what was happening and what it might lead to and, stooping, caught the girl about the waist and snatched her close in against his belly.

She let out not so much as a whimper when he stowed her between his legs and, bent almost double, began to bore his buttocks back against the press behind, against a fearful mass of folk whose one and only thought was to reach the kirk's front door.

They clambered on top of him. They clawed at his ears and eyes. They punched his shoulders and his head. Braced like a bulwark, he kept Annie secure between his thighs even when it seemed that the weight of the whole shrieking congregation was piled upon him, surging and swaying like a high spring tide.

Sweat poured from him. He roared. His voice was lost in thunder and babble.

Blood pounded in his ears and all he could see about him were heads, mouths, ears, staring eyes and Annie's Sunday-best bonnet, knocked askew, at the level of his navel. He smelled their sweat as they squirmed all over him, slid beneath him, clung to his thighs. He felt their limbs writhe against his flesh and slither beneath his feet. He was tempted to let himself go in the hope that Annie and he would not be consumed by the headlong mass but would be propelled along the aisle, swept through the narrow doorway and ejected safe into the daylight. He was too old to depend on miracles, though, and stood his ground even after his arm was jerked out of its socket and his ribs so bruised that breathing itself was a labour almost too painful to endure.

One final blow, quite savage, landed upon his chest, and then the weight lifted.

Raising his head a little he saw bodies piled in the aisle and compressed against the door.

He fished his granddaughter from between his thighs and, keeping a firm grip on her with his functioning hand, he staggered and fell to his knees.

"Pringle, are you injured," a voice yelled in his ear.

"Who is it?"

"Galloway. Are you able to walk, man?"

"Aye."

"Come this way then, you and the girl," the doctor told him. "Come on, I'll see you safe."

*　　*　　*

Even from a distance of fifty yards Clare could see the evolution of the tragedy all too clearly. Bodies packed in the doorway, the exit blocked for two or three fatal minutes by those who had rushed into the church to shelter from the squall.

At first the struggle was childishly selfish, pushing, shoving, shouting, women and half-grown lads involved in it as well as men. Then, as the reality of the situation dawned, there was a falling back from the doorway, a slow, choked, coiling confusion into which the young and the weak were drawn like debris into a whirlpool.

The noise was appalling. Above the thunder, through the hiss of the rain, rang the shrieks of those trapped in the narrow hall.

Now and then a body would be hurled outward, spat on to the grass; a screaming girl in a shredded dress, a chap with the jacket ripped from his back. One man, whose demented strength had carried him through, came rampaging out of the church with arms raised high in triumph. But the mound against the door grew higher and more dense by the second as those who could win no extra inch died where they stood, smothered, crushed and trampled an arm's length away from safety.

"Oh, God! Oh, God!" Frederick exclaimed in horror.

He seemed to tower over Clare, coat, hat, breeches blackened by the rain.

He pointed to the ground. "Stay here."

But Clare followed after him as he fled towards the church for she too had seen Norman Tannahill trapped in the mass in the doorway and had heard Frederick's cry as he ran.

"Eleanor, Eleanor," Frederick shouted, and hurled himself into the throng.

*   *   *

Once clear of the church, Matt Pringle had no thought for anyone. He stumbled away from the side door with his left arm useless, his right hand locked on Annie's shoulder. His only desire was to get as far away as possible from St Cedric's, to make sure that Annie was safe; then he would worry about the damage done to him, what was broken and what was not.

He trudged around the back of the church, heading for the kirkyard and the ridge behind the elms. Now and then Annie would lag a little, turn her head and look back but he did not ask what she saw there, just jerked her hand to keep her moving on.

The kirkyard was empty, the path that straggled over the ridge deserted. He was no longer vague about his direction. Even in sheeting rain he could find his way home by following familiar landmarks. And if his random route had not by chance passed within a yard of her, he would have missed her entirely for she was seated on the summit of the knoll with her shawl cowled over her head, motionless and silent as an old tree stump.

"Who is it? Who's there?" he called out.

Annie answered, "Mrs Tannahill."

He let the girl's hand go, veered off the path and brought the old woman into focus.

She was seated on the wet grass with her head in her hands and hardly seemed to be aware of what had happened in the field below. She rocked back and forth, back and forth, crooning softly to herself. Matt Pringle thought her mad to be here at all, sick and alone in the teeming rain. But he had no respect for madness, none at all.

He stretched out a hand, tore the shawl from her head and pinned it about her neck to make her stop her swaying.

He stuck his face close to hers and said, "Who did it, old

271

woman? Since there's only you an' I interested now, will you not tell me?"

She peered at him, tossed her head like some coy young thing and simpered.

"The stranger," Rose Tannahill said.

And Matt Pringle, having had his answer, turned and blundered away.

*   *   *

When the Reverend Soames was called upon to furnish a complete account of the Ladybrook tragedy, he unearthed many details that had simply not registered with him at the time of happening and many more which had been wiped away by the events which followed hard on the heels of the tumult.

It was, however, incumbent upon him to fulfil his obligations and in due course he produced a report which was to become a standard source for local historians for many years to come.

Never, Randolph Soames wrote, *was exhibited a more singular instance of the direful effects of fear and credulity. Some, believing that a traditional prophecy was about to be fulfilled and that the gallery was falling, threw themselves into the body of the church; some tried in vain to smash windows; and others, conceiving that death was inevitable, rushed upon the outer door only to encounter the exodus from the gallery there. Two or three individuals, whose minds were more collected, ascended upon the communion tables to exhort the congregation to order and quiet; but such was the bewilderment that the scene inspired that, like the others, they soon abandoned their positions and became victims of the general terror.*

So great, indeed, was the delusion, that many, after rushing out into the green, did not dare to look behind lest they be crushed to death by the walls which their disordered senses, further excited by a sudden storm of thunder, led them to believe were falling to pieces. So striking was the grip of the imagination that one man, meeting the minister later upon the ground, swore that the kirk steeple had tumbled, though the steeple and the kirk itself were then, as they still are, perfectly entire and substantial.

In the meantime intelligence of the catastrophe had spread to every corner of the town. All were overwhelmed by consternation. Soon the spot was thronged by hundreds of inhabitants enquiring anxiously about friends, relatives and neighbours. It was only with the greatest temerity and disregard of safety that the doctor of Ladybrook and the coalmaster of Cairns, who had escaped through a side door, ventured into the interior of the church to alleviate, if possible, the agonies of the sufferers. The scene that presented itself to their view was peculiarly distressing.

At the foot of the stairs a mass of persons of both sexes lay wedged together, maimed, dead or dying. When, with considerable difficulty, one layer of bodies was removed from above another, the appalling announcement was made that eleven had breathed their last. Some were so disfigured that their friends could only recognise them by their apparel. The bodies of two of the females were shockingly injured, their breasts being deeply marked by the heavy shoes of an individual, whose "brutal hurry" during the calamity is not yet forgotten.

It was particularly affecting to behold the removal of the bodies from the kirkyard, where they had first been carried, to the homes they had so lately left in all cheerfulness and health. Some were attended by groups of sorrowing relatives and acquaintances; others by only two or three mourners; and, in one instance, a man from a distant parish was observed, unaccompanied, carrying away upon his shoulders the corpse of a beloved brother, and weeping like a child as he went along. Although not all of the dead or injured were of Ladybrook parish, an unusual sensation was created in the community and the gloom of sorrow appeared to deepen as evening approached, and the names of the departed became generally known.

Moreover, the storm of rain and thunder which had accompanied the tragic event had passed over as swiftly as it had come and night came on serene and beautifully arrayed by the beams of a silver moon. But no heart was at ease. Death and distress were the all-engrossing themes; and the voice of mourning was heard not only in the abodes of the widow and the orphan but in many another dwelling where grief had been awakened by the heart-rending occurrence.

Five of the dead were from Ladybrook town and parish and one of the injured, released from further suffering, died soon after.

*   *   *

"Good God, man, I cannot leave her as she is," John Galloway said. "Can't you see she's in desperate straits?"

The girl, a weaver's daughter, had both legs broken and lay crushed against the staircase to the gallery. Blyth and Ormiston, assisted by Cabel Harding, had cleared two corpses from off her and Galloway was amazed to find her alive. The base of the gallery steps had been the site of the worst havoc and all of the dead came from that corner of the entranceway.

"You *must* come, Dr Galloway." Norman Tannahill caught the doctor's shoulder and swung him round. "It's my wife."

Galloway looked up. His hands lay upon the girl, cupped and gentle as autumn leaves, and he shifted position not one quarter inch.

"What about your wife?"

"She – she's deliverin'."

"Where is she?"

"Inside, by the pulpit."

The big man's ear had been torn and his nose dribbled two columns of coagulating blood which he had stanched with strips torn from his shirt. Galloway glanced from Rose Tannahill's son to the coalmaster who, soaked with rain and blood, nodded gravely.

"Go with him, Galloway," he said. "We'll see to this poor wretch."

"Very well. Take her outside then come and tell me where you've put her." Galloway got to his feet. "Has somebody gone for my drug-case and my knives? I told somebody to fetch them. Where is the idiot?"

"Please, please come now," Tannahill interrupted and Galloway followed him into the church which, oddly, was virtually deserted.

Once the vestibule had been partly cleared victims had been removed directly through the front door. Besides, there remained a great residue of fear among the people that the building might still crash down about their ears. Even John Galloway found that he was walking with shoulders hunched and could not resist an occasional glance upward, though he did not for a moment believe that the roof was or ever had been on point of collapse.

On the aisle's flagstones, though, the splash-marks of two little pieces of plaster which had signalled the start of the panic were clearly visible, amid the scattered bread and a pathetic collection of abandoned shoes, hats, scarves and shawls.

The normally reticent Tannahill chattered in his ear, "I lost her in the crowd, y' see. I couldna keep hold of her, y' see, an' she was carried away from me. When I found her, she was trampled. The bairn had started to come an' – "

"All right, all right," Galloway said, testily.

He had already spotted the mother-to-be and, to his amazement, Clare and Frederick Striker. They were huddled by one of the communion tables from which an elder named McGregor, an old man, was clearing plates and cups. He worked with the stunned, disconnected air of a somnambulist and seemed utterly oblivious to the woman who writhed on the flagstones by his feet.

She was already arched, arms spread as if to hold herself on a rotating wheel which spun faster with each new wave of pain. She was lying on a woollen rug and her skirts, stretched taut, still covered her. Her eyes started out of her head and she was drenched with sweat. Tannahill had been right to insist that he attend her immediately. He dropped to his knees and, throwing decorum to the winds, tore away her skirts and underthings and slid his hands beneath her.

"When did her pains begin? Tannahill, listen to me. When did she begin to have pains?"

"I don't – She never told me."

Membranes were ruptured. She had passed through the first and second stages. Her contractions were continuous.

Galloway cleaned her with his hand.

The expulsive efforts of the uterus were massive and appeared to pass from one spasm directly to the next. The infant's head was already engaged in the vulva. He had witnessed swift deliveries before but nothing to compare with this. She released breath, panted, uttered a strange, strangulated cry. With his fingertips, he felt the baby's crown recede and then, as Eleanor arched against his forearms, realised that it was not a head but a shoulder which lay transversely across the pelvis. Obstructed!

He needed instruments, scissors, strong bone forceps, his steel tractator. He needed more light and a place to work. He needed swabbing cloths and water, some form of alcohol, his curved needle, his threads.

"We'll need to move her at once," Galloway said. "But she cannot be moved far, not in this condition."

"Is there a table in the vestry?" Clare said.

"Yes, I believe there is."

"Is – is Eleanor dying?" Frederick Striker asked.

"I'll do what I can to save her."

"An' the babby?" Norman Tannahill said.

"In the hands of God," said Galloway.

*　　*　　*

275

As soon as the squall passed and the rain eased, Elder Millar crept back from his hiding place under a canvas awning and, with confidence restored, began to tour the kirk grounds and to exercise his authority in several petty ways. He appeared to believe that his first priority was not to attend the injured or comfort the bereaved but to clear riff-raff from the vicinity of St Cedric's and to make sure that no one stole from the poor-box or the widows' plate.

When he approached the kirk's side door he was dismayed to find that some presumptuous persons had commandeered the vestry and had flung out into the narrow passageway robes, psalters and two kegs of unblessed port wine. Finger-wagging pompously, he advanced upon the small group of people which had gathered within the doorway.

Outside the door, however, sat one of the young Hardings, sucking a wound upon his arm. The lad, though Elder Millar had no way of knowing it, had been the Mercury who had eventually collected Dr Galloway's accoutrements from the villa and, being a resourceful young fellow, had also located and "borrowed" certain other items which the doctor urgently required.

The wound on Joey Harding's arm had not been acquired in escaping from the kirk. He was too young to partake of the Lord's Supper and too wild to be included in Harding family outings. Along with four or five other boys he had, in fact, been half-way up an elm tree when the squall had struck and had torn a strip of skin from his forearm during a hasty descent.

His sleeve was soaked with blood but he had no fear of reprimand tonight for minor misdemeanours would surely be lost in general gravity and his father would be too busy to whip him for spoiling his clothes. He also had as an excuse the fact that he had been co-opted to assist Dr Galloway and for that reason remained at his post by the side door, awaiting further instructions.

"You, boy," Millar shouted. "What mischief are you up to?"

"No mischief." Joey Harding sucked and spat. "Helpin'."

"Helping yourself from the poor-box, I'll be bound."

"Helpin' them in there."

"Who? Who?" Millar hooted. "Who's in there?"

Joey Harding spat and sucked. "See for yourself."

"Don't think I won't," said Elder Millar. "And when I come out again, you'd better be gone."

"Or what?"

"Or else!"

Millar entered the mouth of the narrow passage with finger poised and a moment later reappeared, retreating backward before the furious Dr Galloway who, with arms already bloody to the elbows, seemed not averse to bloodying himself some more.

"– and fetch me Mr Soames. Wherever he is, whatever he's doing tell him I need him here urgently."

"I – I dunno where he is," Mr Millar stammered.

Joey Harding leapt to his feet. "I do."

"Good lad," John Galloway said. "Find him and bring him to the vestry without delay."

"As good as done, sir," Joey said and sprinted off around the gable with the speed of a young hare.

*   *   *

It was all too soon apparent that Eleanor was beyond medical aid. Galloway removed the little creature to which she had given birth, wrapped it in a blanket and put it below the vestry table. He was considerably shaken by all that had occurred, not least the events of the last twenty minutes, but he refused to abandon the young woman and gave every appearance of being calm as he soothed her.

He fed a quantity of laudanum into her mouth from a communion spoon, gently wiped perspiration from her brow and smiled down at her as she touched his hand.

She looked strangely serene, her brow marble white and her hair, all tangled, black as jet in the light of the four candles that he had arranged about the little room.

She was conscious, though only barely, and he could see the glint of her dark eyes under wet lashes as she stirred and tried to raise herself to look for the child.

"It's being cared for, Eleanor," he told her, quietly.

"What . . . what . . .?"

"A boy," he said. "A fine, handsome boy."

"I . . . I want . . ."

"You'll see him soon, I promise," John Galloway said.

She began to weep.

He was surprised. He did not think she would have strength left or that the infusion of laudanum into her blood would permit it. But weep she did, her head turned to one side. John Galloway

277

felt something tear inside himself and might have wept too if his position had allowed it. It was, after all, better for the Irish girl to die before she learned the truth; and yet he could not bring himself to wish death upon her.

"F . . . Frederick . . ." she murmured.

"Your husband?" Galloway said. "Shall I fetch him?"

"Frederick."

He had braced a chair against the door to keep out intruders for he had not decided what he would do with the poor creature in the blanket, how he would smuggle it out and what would become of it then. It was to help solve that problem that he had dispatched the Harding boy to fetch Soames.

Now another problem had been put before him. Eleanor had asked for Striker to attend her, not her husband and there was something in him that rebelled against yielding to her dying wish. He moistened her lips with water from the corner of a handkerchief, hoping she would say no more.

"P . . . p . . . please," she whispered. "F . . . fetch him."

He arranged the blood-soaked blankets, disguised the mess as best he could and put her arms out, hands folded upon her breast. He cleaned her face with the handkerchief, then he stooped and removed the bundle from beneath the table.

Screening it from Eleanor's sight, he placed it upon a chair where it would not be noticed.

And then he opened the door.

*　　*　　*

When Clare saw John Galloway's face she knew why he had sent for the minister and why he ignored Norman Tannahill's anxious questions. Norman started forward but Galloway blocked the doorway. Behind the doctor Clare caught a glimpse of the girl upon the table, covered like a corpse.

"Eleanor!" Norman struggled to push the doctor aside.

"Is she dead, John?" Clare asked.

"No, but I can do no more for her," John Galloway said. "Striker, she wishes to see you too."

Frederick bowed and turned to Clare, so correct and polite of manner that it seemed like a mockery.

"May I?" he asked.

Clare nodded.

Frederick bowed again and, when John Galloway stepped to one side, followed Norman into the vestry.

278

So intent was she on the scene within the room that Clare did not notice when John Galloway slipped out of the church into the dusk.

Clare watched while Norman lifted his wife into his arms as if his strength, his devotion might be enough to pull her back from the brink. He looked hideously maimed, with his bloody nose and torn ear, and his grief was so passionate and guileless that Clare could hardly bear to watch. Frederick, in contrast, was calm and detached. He stood by the head of the table, arms folded, chin cocked so that his scrutiny had an arrogant and disapproving air.

With all that remained of her strength Eleanor beat against her husband's arms and cried out, "Frederick, Frederick. I want my Frederick. Where are you? Are you not here?"

The movement was sudden and shocking. He reached out with both hands and thrust Norman violently away from the girl then leaned over her and brushed his lips across her brow.

"I'm here," he said, softly.

She twisted her body grotesquely and stared up at him, from the tops of her eyes, her face glowing with a strange dark joy.

"Take me, darlin'," she gasped, "take me away, take me away from here, take me . . ."

"I will, dearest," Frederick said.

He placed his big, ugly hands about her head, his fingers buried in her hair and, smiling, kissed her on the lips.

"Ah, Freddie," she said and, smiling too, she died.

*   *   *

Randolph Soames walked with quick little nibbling steps, hands folded one over the other at chest height, a fussy little frown stamped upon his brow. He *tutted* audibly under his breath as the Harding boy led him away from the desolate scenes on the green to meet John Galloway at the side door.

"What is it, John? I've much to do, much to do," Soames complained. "Haven't time to waste on gardening today."

John Galloway looked at the boy. "You've done well, young man, and you have my thanks but," he jerked his head, "now you must make yourself scarce."

"Don't you need me no more?"

"No. Go home."

The boy gestured towards the minister. "What about him?"

"I'll see to him."

"Suit yourself," Joey Harding said and, hands in pockets, sauntered off a little sulkily.

Galloway hoisted the bundle into the crook of his arm.

He grabbed the minister's sleeve and pulled him out of sight of the crowd, led him to the back of the church and there released him. He stepped back and, without warning, administered a stinging open-handed slap to Soames's cheek which, as intended, brought him at once out of shock.

Randolph cried out and raised his fingers to his face.

"What has happened to us here?" he said. "Why, today of all days, did this happen? What made them think the church was anything but whole?"

"Randolph, are you sensible?"

"Yes, yes. I'm sensible."

"I need your advice, and your aid."

"Yes, yes, of course. I'm sorry." He rubbed both hands down his face. "What is it?"

Shifting the bundle into both arms Galloway drew back the folds and let Soames gape at the object within.

"Oh, God!" Soames said. "What is it? Is this a demon you've found on holy ground, the reason for – "

"No demon, Randolph. It's the Irish girl's child."

"No, it cannot be human."

"All too human, Randolph, I assure you. It's a double foetus, a two-headed male twin. I've never seen one before outside of a jar. See how it's joined at shoulder and hip. Not one, really, but two."

"Hide it away, hide it away. I've seen more horrors than I can stand today. What sort of manifestation is upon us, John? What does the appearance of this abnormal creature signify?"

"It's an accident of nature and, as such, has no significance at all," Galloway said, sternly. "I want you to take it away now and bury it."

"On consecrated ground? Never!"

"Do you not think it has a soul?"

"It has not been baptised."

"It has been born, hasn't it? It's God's creature, however ugly."

"John, don't you see – "

"Don't *you* see? If this poor thing is found today of all days Tannahill will be blamed for all our misfortunes."

"Tannahill?"

"He fathered it," John Galloway said. "As for the mother, it hardly matters now. She's beyond my aid and yours. But I do not wish to be responsible for touching a spark to the tinderbox of suspicion and rage that surrounds us and to see an entirely innocent man suffer."

Galloway covered the little staring pink heads. He tucked the blanket tightly about them and offered the bundle to Soames.

"Please, Randolph, take it away from here."

"What will I do with it? What if I'm caught with it?"

"Take it to my house. Hide it in my garden, under the hedge by the rose bushes. I'll dispose of it later."

"What if Eppie or Ishbel see me?"

"What's wrong with you, man? For God's sake, have you lost your common sense as well as your courage?" Galloway said. "Never mind. Go back to your poor, precious flock. I'll do it myself."

Shamed, Soames said, "No, I'll do what you ask. Give it here."

With an involuntary shudder Soames received the bundle from the doctor's arms. He glanced furtively over his shoulder and then up at the church gable and the long trail of cloud that flowed swiftly over it.

"Oh, God, what's happening to us?" he asked without expectation of an answer; then he turned and hurried away into the gathering dusk to do John Galloway's bidding.

Nineteen

A bleeding wound would have caused weakness but the dry pain of a dislocated shoulder brought to Matt Pringle the same obsessive self-confidence which enables young men to lift heavy weights and run long distances in defiance of suffering.

He hurried back to the salthouse with Annie bustling to keep up, hanging on to his good right hand.

He was not amazed or dismayed by what had happened in St Cedric's. He gave it hardly a thought. It was as if his mind had vaulted backwards over that event to land in balance on the edge of another abyss. When he reached the salthouse he sent Annie ahead of him and, grunting, laboured upstairs after her, hauling himself one-handed by the rail.

The atmosphere in the loft was thick with the lazy reek of coal-smoke, cod simmering in a pot, and beer. Billy and his father had been drinking to while away the long, hot, dreary afternoon. Bob was over by the window studying the text of a bawdy poem that had been given him by one of the cadgers. He toted a pewter mug in one hand and wore a silly expression which told Pringle that he had put sobriety behind him. He peered over the tops of his glasses at his daughter and father-in-law while Billy, who had been lying on his bed, rolled his feet to the floor and held out his arms to welcome his sister.

Annie flung herself into her brother's arms.

Giggling as if it had all been a great joke, she said, "The kirk fell down."

Billy hugged her, grinning. "What blethers!"

"It did, it did an' a'."

"What nonsense is this you've been puttin' into her head now, old man?" Bob said.

Pringle seated himself on a chair by the table and, wincing, hoisted his left arm on to the table-top.

Bob got to his feet, "What the hell's wrong wi' you?"

"I found out," Matt Pringle stated.

With the bawdy pamphlet in one hand and the beer pot in the other, Bob apprehensively approached his father-in-law. Since Katy's death the old man had not been himself. His moroseness was understandable but his refusal to accept that Katy had drowned by accident was, at best, illogical.

"Found out what?" Bob said.

Annie had hauled Billy to his knees and was shuffling round him in a playful way, chanting, "The kirk fell down, the kirk fell down, ring-jing, the kirk fell down."

"I found out who killed her." Pringle said. "Look, I've put my damned shoulder out. I'll be needin' your help to put it back in place, Bob."

"Wait, wait, wait," Bob Gowrie said. "What is goin' on here? She's yellin' about the kirk fallin down, an' you've got a shoulder out of joint – "

"Bruised ribs too."

"The kirk fell down, the kirk fell down – "

"Annie, hold your noise," Billy said.

"Her frock's soaked through," Pringle said. "See she changes it, Billy, before she catches her death."

"Bruised ribs?" Bob said. "*Did* the kirk fall down?"

"The church is still standin'. It was a scare, a panic, that's all," Matt Pringle said. "Here, grip my arm an' pull the damned shoulder back into place. I've got work to do an' I'll need both hands to do it."

"Fixin' a dislocation's a job for the doctor."

"I haven't time to palaver wi' doctors. Come on, you've done it before."

"Billy, fetch the bottle," Bob said.

"Whisky or brandy?"

"Brandy."

Annie's high spirits had not been dampened by her brother's mild reprimand. She went to her grandfather and stroked his hair as she might have petted a dog. What wit there had been in the girl had been dimmed by her sister's drowning and the disruption it had caused in the household's routine. She seemed completely unaware of the magnitude of what had occurred that afternoon or what was unfolding about her now.

"Baw-baw, Grandpa," she crooned; then jerked her hand away as he yelled with pain.

Bob knew perfectly well what to do with an out-of-joint shoulder; a sudden tug, a twist, a push would do the trick.

He caught his father-in-law off guard and had it done before Matt Pringle could brood upon the pain.

Pringle fell forward across the table, sobbing dryly.

Billy brought brandy in a glass and held the medicine until Matt was sufficiently recovered to take it from him. He watched with admiration as his grandfather propped himself up, tested the repair, then downed the brandy in one swallow.

"What about the ribs?" Bob said.

"Damn the ribs," Pringle said. "We've somethin' more important to discuss than the state of my health. I've found out who murdered Katy."

"Somebody saw it?" Bob asked.

"In a manner o' speakin'. Rose Tannahill told me."

"Rose Tannahill! That old witch! She's daft in the head," Billy declared. "I wouldna believe a word she said."

"Who did she say it was?" Bob asked.

"A stranger."

"Huh! Fat lot that tells us," said Billy.

"How many strangers are there in Headrick?"

He looked grey about the gills and his damp clothing had begun to steam a little in the warmth from the fire. The arm, in spite of Bob's sterling treatment, felt swollen and was stiffening by the minute. He worked his fingers into a fist and kneaded the table's edge, enjoying the little rivers of pain that flowed through his body.

He answered his own question. "Two. Right?"

"Mr Striker," Billy said.

"An' the Frenchman."

"Why would Mr Striker want to do away wi' our Katy?"

"Aye, Matt, answer us that," Bob said.

Pringle poured brandy into his glass and sipped it. The throbbing in his left arm and shoulder and the knifing pains in his rib-cage stoked his anger. He considered Bob's request in silence for several seconds then turned to his granddaughter who, with thumb in mouth, had settled herself by her brother's flank.

"Did Mr Striker ever touch you, Annie?" he asked.

"Uh?"

"Did Mr Striker ever touch you – or Kate?"

"Nah."

"Do you know who the Frenchman is, sweetheart?"

"Aye. Henri."

"Henri?"

"He told us we could ca' him Henri. On-ree, he said it. Katy couldna say it but I could. On'ree. On'ree. There!"

Pringle frowned at his son-in-law who stabbed his spectacles hard against the bridge of his nose and crouched down at his daughter's side.

"When did the Frenchie tell you what t' call him?"

"'Fore Katy went."

"Went where?" said Bob.

"Went away," Annie said.

She was uncertain of the nature of the attention that had devolved upon her. Could not be sure whether she liked it or whether, behind it, lurked punishment. She sucked the tip of her thumb and slid closer to Billy as if she could be sure of his protection.

"Where," Bob said, "did you meet the Frenchman?"

"He took us in, the both o' us. He showed us things."

"Into the fish-shed? He took you both into the fish-shed with him, did he?"

She could smell the sourness of beer off her father, the stinging smell of the brandy off her grandfather. Billy smelled of straw, like he always did.

She was not up to explanation, nor to denial.

She said, "Aye."

"You an' Katy together?"

"Aye."

"Did *he* touch you?"

"Aye."

"Where did he touch you?"

Annie did not know how to answer.

Billy said, "Did he touch you down there?"

"Aye."

"Christ!"

"Annie, Annie, tell me the truth now," her father said. "Did he, did the Frenchie ever take Katy away on her own?"

"Aye."

"Out of your sight?"

"Aye."

"What did he do to her? Did she not tell you?"

Annie squirmed. "He – he showed her things."

"What things, Annie?"

"Secrets."

"Secrets – is that what Katy told you?"

"She said I wasna t' tell anyone."

285

"Katy said that?"

"I think so."

"Are you sure it wasn't him said it, the Frenchie?"

"It – it might've been."

Abruptly the men seemed to lose interest in her.

Grandpa sat back in his chair, poured more brandy then handed the big black bottle to Billy, who drank from the neck and passed it on to Daddy.

"Is that good enough for you both?" Matt Pringle said.

"I doubt it would be enough evidence to satisfy a magistrate," said Bob.

"A magistrate! Magistrates don't care about the likes of us. A salter's lassie found drowned. Dead, buried an' forgotten," Pringle said. "Rose Tannahill saw all this in her crystal, ye know."

"What crystal?"

"I paid her for a readin'," Pringle admitted. "An', damn me, if she didn't see the Frenchie."

"I thought she only saw a stranger?" Billy said.

"He's a stranger, is he not?"

Bob drank from the neck of the brandy bottle, holding the vessel in both hands. He lowered it and said, "Must say I never much cared for havin' a Frenchie sittin' on our doorstep. Him an' his furnace an' his fireworks. He never thought to invite *us* to see what devilment he was up to."

"Only our girls," Pringle said. "He went for the girls."

Billy leaned both hands on the table and peered into the old man's face. "What should we do about it, eh?"

"Sort him out ourselves," Matt Pringle said.

"When?"

"Right now."

*   *   *

For Henri the working day had been long, peaceful and highly satisfactory. The Holy Fair had creamed away cadgers and beachcombers and the bay had been for the most part deserted. His work had not been disturbed by stealthy footsteps, by furtive whispers. He had not been obliged to fling open the laboratory door and assume a frighteningly foreign appearance to scare away intruders. He had worked, sweating, throughout the stifling morning, but in late afternoon rain had come crackling

286

out of a pitch-black sky to cleanse and cool his little oasis among the gorse.

By half-past six o'clock the rain had gone off again and Henri was seated on a stool at the long table inscribing into his laboratory book details of the day's experiments.

He had lighted an oil lamp which combined with the smoulder of coals in the furnace to give the shed's interior a strange shadowy effect which Henri found conducive to concentration. The scratch of quill on paper and complex little diagrams drawn in black ink amid coded prose absorbed his attention completely.

He did not hear the men approach.

The first he knew of their presence was when the door of the shed burst open and Pringle, armed with a shovel, stood outlined against the pale evening light.

Henri had no clue what act on his part had brought retribution. Suspicion, superstition, drink, pride or universal ignorance; something had whipped up the Gowries and had directed their hatred against him. He was a foreigner, a stranger and a scientist and, in consequence, a natural, hand-made scapegoat. He had, however, survived the Mob in Paris and had narrowly escaped injury in several other cities, including Dublin, and he was far too sensible to try to debate the issue or sue for justice.

The tilt of the old man's shovel and the blazing tar-brand in the young man's hand told their own story.

The gun was out of reach. In any case, he could never bring himself to turn a tool into a weapon. He was by inclination a bird of passage, doomed to fly not fight.

He cast a despairing glance at the board-and-leather laboratory notebooks stacked on the table before him. He was tempted to grab them and gather them into his arms. Those records of a thousand hours of intellectual labour, of knowledge wrung from nature one drop at a time were worth almost as much as his life.

But not quite.

The brand, splattering tar, hurtled through the air and smashed the chemical jars and network of glass piping on the long bench to Henri's right.

"WHAT DID YOU DO TO HER?"

Pringle shouted and advanced with his shovel towards the flames which already bordered the table-top.

Henri heaved himself to his feet and caught the stool as it

toppled. He had no notion of how many villagers might be ranked behind the salters but he was not deterred by weight of numbers. With all his might, he flung the stool straight at the old man's head.

It clanged against the shovel's edge, rebounded and caught the salter a glancing blow upon the temple. He cried out and staggered back just as the young man, Billy, tossed a second tar-brand into the half bale of straw which Henri kept for tinder.

"MURDERER," Billy Gowrie cried as his grandfather fell to his knees. "LOOK WHAT YOU'VE DONE NOW."

Armed with a skimming pole Billy leapt past Pringle and attacked Henri head on.

"What *have* I done?" Henri said. "Tell me."

The blade of the pole sliced past Henri's nose and noisily dismembered a portion of the voltaic accumulator.

"MURDERIN' PIG! TOUCHIN' MY SISTER."

Billy would have struck at him again if Henri hadn't snared the pole and jerked the boy off balance.

Flames spread along the bench and up the wooden wall, flat, soft-edged flames fed by combustible chemicals. Henri could make out Bob Gowrie in the doorway and he suddenly realised that the salters believed he had drowned the daughter of the household. He opened his mouth to protest but thought better of it and danced with Billy, back and forth, sawing the skimming pole between them.

Broken glass crunched beneath their heels and the old man, though still dazed, was trying to crawl away from them on all fours.

Keeping his distance, Bob Gowrie lit another tar-brand and pitched it underhand into the shed.

"I have done nothing," Henri shouted in desperation. "I am a man innocent."

Guilt and innocence were matters of no apparent interest to the Gowries.

Billy hauled on the pole, his face livid with fury. Henri was surprised, though, at the young man's lack of strength and found that he was able to fend the boy off quite easily. All in all he felt remarkably calm, given the circumstances and the outrageous charge against him.

From the corner of his eye he watched flames lick about the air-gun. He was uncertain how much heat it would take to generate an explosion in the cylinders or even what volume of gases remained within them. But he did not intend to wait to find out.

There was a sudden flare of brightly coloured light behind him as one of the large retorts imploded. Billy, startled, ducked, tripped over his grandfather's shins and, in falling, let go the skimming pole.

Henri crossed his forearms over his head and charged at Bob Gowrie who slashed at him half-heartedly with an unlit brand then meekly gave way.

Leaving everything behind, Henri plunged through the doorway and ran like the devil into the dusk.

*   *   *

Clare did not take Frederick's arm and he did not offer it. Was it, she wondered, fear or sorrow that rendered him dumb?

Neither of them looked back from the crest of the road, but sounds of pain and mourning followed them, hauntingly, through the cool, moist evening air. Along the road limped carts and pedestrians, and at the Thunder Hill crossroads there was a gathering of folk in tears.

Clare fastened her gaze upon the road and matched Frederick's stride as best she could.

Eleanor Antrim had been taken away.

Norman had carried her off.

"Where's my babby?" he'd said.

"Stillborn," John Galloway had answered.

"I want it. It's mine."

"It came too early to be fully formed."

"Did it not draw breath?"

"No, it never was alive."

"Where is it, though?"

"I've taken it into my care," John Galloway had said. "With your permission, I'll see to the remains."

Norman had not protested. He had clung to Eleanor's hand as if the gesture might make her finally and completely his. To Frederick he had said not one word and Clare had watched him lift the girl and carry her out of the vestry with a strange sense of relief, as if the whole incident had been a sinister dream from which she could now allow herself to wake.

"Are you all right, Clare?" John had asked, and had squeezed her arm, leaving upon her sleeve two or three little smudges of Eleanor's blood.

Clare had nodded her answer and, a moment later, John Galloway had been summoned away to render his professional aid to the injured.

Strange now to look out over the firth glinting in the very last of the autumn twilight and to think that sailors on the sea-going ships had no knowledge of the tragedy that had taken place in Ladybrook that afternoon.

Smoke from the foreshore indicated that the pans had been fired and that come Monday there would be salt to be weighed and bagged. She watched the smoke purl up darkly, dark grey on black. In the light of all that had happened her clever schemes seemed petty and inconsequential, but she had come too far with them to abandon them now.

Quite deliberately she looped her arm through Frederick's as they came to the gates of the estate.

He stared down at her, his expression more haggard than ever, the lines bitten so deeply into his flesh that he appeared to be scarred.

"I did not think you would want to touch me, Clare."

"Why not?"

"Because of what you saw. Because of Eleanor."

"I am only sorry that she had to die."

"It must be obvious that I knew her in the past."

"It came as no surprise to me, Frederick."

He stopped within the gates.

"You knew?"

"Yes."

"Did Eleanor tell you?"

"I know that she loved you, Frederick."

"And died for it."

"You must not think like that."

"I am sorry for Tannahill," Frederick said. "He has lost both a wife and a child today."

With a little prickle of surprise Clare realised that he was testing her, that the game between them had not been spoiled but had moved on to a different plane.

"What have you lost, Frederick?" she said.

"Have I not lost you, Clare?"

"What if I had died today instead of Eleanor?"

"Do not dare say such a thing."

"Why did you bring her to Scotland?"

"She refused to be left behind."

"You arranged a strange method of doing it," Clare said.

290

"Of her devising," Frederick said, "not mine."

"Did you owe it to her, Frederick?"

"I suppose that I did."

"What do you owe to me?"

"Everything that I am, that I will be."

"And what's that?"

He lifted his shoulders. His gravity was no longer impenetrable. He was, Clare knew, neither cruel nor evil but he had lived so long with deceit that he had lost all sense of morality. She could not save him now even if she had cared enough to try.

"Frederick, what is that?"

He sighed, shook his head, and then moved on.

Clare followed, not touching now, a safe half-step behind.

*   *   *

They had not quite reached the gravel drive when Henri appeared from the glen. He came swarming up to the top of the path and ran, staggering a little, towards them, clad only in shirt and breeches. He looked so dishevelled and harried that Clare wondered if he had been among the congregation at St Cedric's.

"What is it? What's happened?"

Breathless and worn out, Henri clutched at Frederick for support. His shirt was torn at cuff and collar and stained with tar, his face purple with exertion.

"Fire," he gasped. "My work, all of it is gone in the flames."

"Are you injured?" Frederick asked.

"No, I make a good escape from them." He darted a glance over his shoulder towards the glen. "I think perhaps they will follow me."

"Who, who will follow you?"

"The salting people. Gowries. They attacked me and have burned down my laboratory."

If it had not been for the column of black smoke that she had seen above the tree-line Clare might have been less inclined to believe him. But the madness of the afternoon had left her less rational so that, even as she stared into the night sky and saw the shooting sparks, she was prepared to acknowledge that Henri was telling the truth.

"The house," Henri said. "We will be safe from them in your house, Clare."

Leaning on Frederick, the Frenchman dragged them to the front door and, a minute or two later, they were in the drawing-room and Clare took command.

First she told Pratie of the disaster at St Cedric's and informed her that Eleanor was dead. Next she sent Melissa and Lizzie upstairs with strict instructions to keep away from the windows and not to come down until summoned.

Finally she ordered Pratie to bolt doors and windows and then to bring a bowl of warm water and fresh towels to the drawing-room, together with brandy and a tureen of hot soup. The housekeeper was, not unnaturally, confused.

"What does this have to do wi' what happened at the church?" she asked.

"I do not know yet," Clare informed her. "Perhaps nothing. But the Gowries have attacked M. Leblanc and have burned down his laboratory."

"Hah!" Pratie exclaimed as if she had expected such a thing all along. "Do you think they're comin' here? Just let them. By Jesus an' Joseph, just let me get my hands on them."

"They are, I think, armed."

"Aye, an' drunk too, no doubt," Pratie said and hastened away to make the house secure.

In spite of the heat which remained trapped within the house, Henri was shivering. Frederick stirred the coals in the grate and the Frenchman huddled over them, his trembling hands extended. Frederick had already informed him of the events of the afternoon and of Eleanor's death and it was several minutes before Henri was sufficiently recovered to give an account of the attack upon the laboratory.

"But why, Henri? What harm did you ever do them?"

"It is to pay me back for the girl."

"What girl?" Clare enquired, imagining Eleanor.

"Kate Gowrie," Frederick said. "They believe that Henri murdered her."

"But Kate drowned accidentally."

"I saw her," Henri said, "one time. The sisters, they came to the door of where I was working. I showed to them two, three tricks with fire and fluid electricity. They go away again, happy."

"Is that all that happened?" said Frederick.

"All, I swear to you, all."

"Did you not explain to the Gowries?" said Frederick.

"How could I explain? They had torches. They gave me no time to speak. *Whoof!* I am on fire."

Frederick glanced at Clare. "Pringle's behind this, I'll wager. He hasn't been right in the head since his granddaughter was found. He cannot accept that it was simply an act of God."

"But to torch my property – "

"Everything gone," said Henri, head in hands. "Books, papers, the gun – everything."

"Surely, Henri, you can start again?" Clare said.

Frederick said sharply, "Not here."

"The Gowries won't go unpunished," Clare said. "Believe me. Why should you be forced to flee when you are innocent?"

"No, Clare, Frederick is correct. I cannot stay now."

"What about our partnership, our agreement?"

"Perhaps, I will come back to work for you later."

At that moment Pratie kneed open the drawing-room door and brought in a tray.

She was stiff with indignation, her ginger hair bristling as she put the bowl of water and liniment upon one table and the brandy glasses upon another. She poured spirits and handed a glass to Henri and left again immediately to man her guard post by the hall window.

Frederick said, "I think Henri's right, Clare. He must leave Headrick for a time. Make himself scarce."

Clare paused, then nodded. "I agree."

"You do?"

"I regret all that has happened to you, Henri. We will miss your company and your songs. But, yes, on reflection, I really believe you had better leave Headrick while you can. Tonight, in fact," Clare said.

"Where will I go to? I have nothing."

"I will give you a little money, enough to see you through," Clare said. "As to your baggage, you may leave it here or take it with you, as you wish. I ask only one thing in return, Henri."

"Madame Quinn?"

"On the first day of the New Year I ask that you take up pen and paper and write to me, telling me where you are and how you are faring."

"Madame, I will." Henri kissed her hand. "I hope you do not believe that I leave because I did this crime."

"No, Henri, I know that you did not." Clare kissed him upon the cheek. "I'll miss you, you know."

293

"I did make the machine," Henri said. "I will make another one for you, no?"

"Some day, Henri," Clare said. "Some day, perhaps."

An hour later, with many tears from Melissa, M. Henri Leblanc, surrounded by his luggage, left the stableyard in the gig with Frederick at the reins.

Frederick claimed to know the road to Irvine well enough to navigate it by moonlight and promised that when he had deposited Henri safe and sound in a coaching inn, he would return at once to Headrick to protect his betrothed.

Of that one fact Clare had no doubt at all.

*   *   *

Much to Clare's surprise Melissa was uncommonly matter-of-fact about the day's extraordinary events and after a droll, almost perfunctory little prayer for the souls of the departed, she had nestled her head on Clare's breast and had been asleep within minutes.

No direct threat from the Gowries had materialised – Clare had not expected it – and some time before midnight, quite exhausted, she too had fallen asleep.

It was still and grey when she wakened, not quite dawn. She rose, dressed quietly and, leaving Melissa asleep, tiptoed along the passageway to Frederick's room.

The door, for once, was unlocked. Clare opened it stealthily and peeped into the room.

Frederick lay at an angle across the top of the bed. He was still clad in shirt and breeches, with his stockings wrinkled about his ankles and his shoes on the floor where he had kicked them. The brandy decanter and a glass from the drawing-room stood on the little bedside table with two or three little blue medicine jars.

Snoring thickly, Frederick did not stir and Clare closed the door again softly and stole away down the passage.

Twenty minutes later she arrived at the beach which, at that very early hour, was completely deserted.

Light rain during the night had laid a tarry sheen on all that remained of the fish-shed. Here and there, under charred timbers and broken glassware, embers still glowed. Only the furnace remained intact, its brickwork slicked with soot, its iron parts still warm to the touch. The debris was patched with vivid hues where chemical jars had split open and their contents ignited, the rubberised tubes had melted into the ground like snakeskin.

The air-gun was barely recognisable. Its iron cylinders had survived but the clever little brass nozzle had been blown off and lay several yards away, broken into pieces, and all the rest had been burned away.

Poor Henri had been correct; nothing worthwhile remained. Months, years of patient labour had been totally destroyed.

Clare did not stay long.

She walked through the gorse bushes and along the back of the sand dunes to the salthouse, climbed the outside staircase and pushed open the door to the loft.

The loft, of course, was empty.

Cots had been stripped of bedding, all the furniture, except the table, removed. It had been done in desperate haste, curtain hooks bent, the floor scarred, glasses and salt jars and a dozen or so bottles smashed against the walls and the trap torn up from its hinges.

Clare descended into the darkened panhouse, opened the door to admit grey, grainy dawn light by which she surveyed the devastation which the Gowries had left behind in payment for their years of servitude and security.

Shovels were missing, skimming poles, ladles, all the pan irons. The Gowries had obviously found a carter willing to undertake a long night ride and had crammed on to his conveyance every item that it would hold.

Clare could hardly blame them for that. What she could not forgive her salters was their wanton destruction, for they had taken hammers to the pans, had split all the plates, had loosened the brickwork and had even knocked out the grates. It would cost her dear in money and time to repair the place and put it back into production.

She hurried round to the girnal but here the Gowries had drawn the line. The storehouse was unbreached, the salt sacks safe. Fear of retribution from Excise officers was obviously stronger than fear of her revenge. She might possibly lay them by the heels, if she moved against them quickly. Laden as they were, they could not have gone far. But she would not pursue them, would not make a fuss, for her first loyalty now was to Frederick and he would have no wish to be involved with the forces of law and order.

Henri? Henri need not have fled at all. But she would not try to bring him back, not now. Henri was a gentle soul at heart and better out of Ladybrook until she did what had to be done.

In a single day everything had changed – yet nothing had changed. She was as steadfast in her purpose now as she had ever been.

For several minutes she stood motionless, staring reflectively out to sea, at the brown hills of Arran shaping themselves in the mist, at the silent sea-going traffic of the Clyde, at the soft slapping waves on the rocks of the pond where little Kate Gowrie had been drowned.

Then, gathering her skirts about her, she hurried back home to Headrick to waken Frederick Striker from his sleep.

Twenty

To give them their due the brethren of Lodge Ladybrook flung themselves heart and soul into raising money for the alleviation of hardship among widows and orphans. Charity was something the brothers understood, a visible sign of honourable intent which boosted their stock in the local community and reduced the voice of protest to mere whisper.

Nobody blamed Randolph for what had occurred.

Indeed, Mr Soames was praised by his peers for the Christian manner in which he had dealt with the events of that tragic day and the succour he had provided in the mourning period that followed.

Since a scapegoat was needed, however, and McCracken was far away in Edinburgh, opinion swiftly turned against his lordship, that miserable, grasping, tight-fisted, tyrannical old blue-blood whose refusal to fund the erection of a brand new church had cost the parish dear in life and limb.

On his son-in-law's advice Lord McCracken did not ride post-haste to Cairns to comfort his employees. And poor Sarah, lost in her own miseries, had to survive without paternal sympathy and endure unprotected both John Galloway's fiendish ministrations and her husband's ill-concealed glee at the discomforts of her cure.

Not that she saw much of Robertson these days; he had become more and more occupied with fund-raising and other matters concerned with the welfare of the town's less salubrious inhabitants, and with a colliery business which regularly took him up to Greenock to consult with some stupid engineer named Merkland. What Sarah Blyth did not know was that her husband also did business with Nancy Neptune and, when that was concluded of an evening, he would join Brock Harding in the over-room to drink rum, exchange ungentlemanly confidences and wink, more knowingly now, at the painted Eye of Apollo.

"How was Nancy this dank autumn night?" Brock would say. "Full of love an' affection, I trust?"

"As loving as a man could wish for," Robbie Blyth would say. "I think I'll just wrap her round me for the winter."

"Wear her like a coat, you mean?"

"Buttoned tight, and belted too."

"Is she as much a comfort to you as was the Irish girl?"

"More."

"Still, it's a pity the Irish beauty had to die."

"Oh, well," Robbie would say, "she was lost to me in any case, since Tannahill had taken her over."

"Perhaps Daniel can find you another Irish peach, one to keep for yourself?"

"Sound idea, Brock, sound idea."

It was in the middle of one such bibulous conversation that Brock had made an offer to the coalmaster and had bought from him, for the sum of one hundred pounds, the partnership document for the now defunct enterprise which Mrs Quinn had floated.

Robbie, in his fuddled state, had no idea why Brock wanted an extra share, for the whole of Ladybrook knew that the Gowries had burned the Frenchie out, that the Frenchie, like the coward he was, had legged it and that all that remained of that bright hope of profit was a burned-out stump by the Headrick shore. Robbie, however, was not one to look a gift horse in the mouth, and cash and document duly changed hands.

Brock was elated. He had not, of course, contrived the set of circumstances which had robbed Clare Quinn of her French chemist and, in the same stroke, of her salt income. He was not slow to seize the advantage, however, and had swiftly rejigged and improved his plans, particularly when Frederick informed him that the wedding date had been set for the 28th day of the month.

The banns had been posted in the tiny church at Malliston for St Cedric's was still webbed with wooden scaffolding and would not be reconsecrated before Christmas.

Brock did not care if Frederick's marriage to the widow took place in a lobsterboat, provided the ceremony itself was legal and binding.

Once Frederick was wed to Clare Quinn, Brock would be at liberty to show his hand. He had everything he needed to sink the foundering estate and force its sale; and if the golden-haired daughter stood in the way, that was just too bad. He was confident that in a year's time the Hardings would be the legitimate owners of the Headrick estates and he would not be drinking in the Neptune with a dissolute coalmaster.

He poured a tumbler of rum and held out his glass.

"Well, Robbie, here's health to brother Frederick."

"And to his blushing bride."

"May she bring him happiness."

"When," Robbie Blyth asked, "is this famous wedding actually slated to take place?"

"Friday," Brock answered, "at half-past two o'clock."

"Where? At Malliston?"

"Here, down below, in the Neptune."

"Will you be there, Brock?"

"Oh, aye," Brock answered, grinning. "Wild horses wouldn't keep me away."

*　　*　　*

The last of the harvests had been quickly gathered and the fields gleaned with some haste lest October brought cold rain or even a touch of snow to the high parts of the county, for there were those who saw the year as blighted by the Ladybrook disaster, who took it, as farmers will, as some sort of gloomy omen. In the neat little gardens of the town, though, cabbages were sturdy and apples heavy on the bough and the beds and borders of the villas on the high road had not lost all their blooms, not by a long chalk.

Clare, driving the gig, clicked the pony briskly towards the manse.

There were times, and this was one of them, when she felt she might have been happier as a tenant in one of McCracken's villas rather than clinging on to Headrick. Four or five rooms and a long garden would suit her perfectly – except that Headrick was her charge and would remain so until Melissa came of age.

She was disconcerted to discover that John Galloway was in the manse garden along with the minister.

She had hoped to make one final plea to Randolph to conduct the marriage service and not leave her at the mercy of Reverend Braintree. She had not spoken directly with Randolph since the day of the disaster but there had been between them a sharp exchange of letters in which the minister had refused to perform his pastoral duty on her behalf because – so he said – he did not approve of tavern weddings.

Neither the minister nor the doctor seemed particularly pleased to see her and she was not offered tea or invited into the manse. Her treatment by Randolph Soames was, in fact, perfunctory to the point of rudeness.

"Well, Mrs Quinn," he began, without a greeting, "I believe I can guess why you are here. My answer has not changed, you know."

John Galloway, who seemed more embarrassed than hostile, hung back a step or two, toying with a rosebud.

"If you will not conduct the service," Clare said, "will you at least consent to be present as a guest?"

"I have other business, out-of-town business, to attend to on Friday." Soames fished a watch from his vest pocket and glanced at it ostentatiously. "In fact, I have other business to attend to now, Madam. So if you have nothing further to discuss – "

"Randolph, will you not reconsider?" John Galloway said.

"No, John, I will not."

Clare said, "Do you really disapprove of tavern weddings, Reverend Mr Soames, or do you disapprove of my choice of a husband?"

The minister studied her in silence for a moment then said, "Striker is not the sort of man I would recommend as a husband for any woman of my acquaintance, Mrs Quinn, least of all a friend."

"Why is that, sir?"

"It is not for me to say."

He swung the watch on its chain, bowed, turned on his heel and headed up the front path towards the villa's front door almost at a trot. Clare was left, as she had hoped she would not be, alone with John Galloway.

At a loss, she looked away towards the Glebe and beyond it to the steeple of St Cedric's upon which wooden scaffolding had already begun to grow.

"I will walk you to the gig, Clare." The doctor placed the rosebud, which was browned with frost about the edges, into the vee of his waistcoat and went before her to open the gate. "You mustn't heed Randolph. He is not at all himself these days. Understandably, I suppose."

He opened the gate and let her pass through it. He did not follow her to the gig, though, but closed the gate from the inside and leaned upon it.

Clare hesitated. "Do you feel as Randolph does?"

"About Frederick?" John Galloway sighed. "No, you must do what you have to, Clare."

She had a sudden compulsion to confess the truth but, as if to forestall her, John Galloway placed a finger to his lips and, almost imperceptibly, shook his head.

"Friday?" Clare asked.

"Of course," the doctor answered.

*   *   *

They discussed their future together as soberly as a pair of burgesses in a Glasgow coffee house.

It was agreed between them that no attempt would be made to hire a master salter to replace Gowrie until February had come and gone and the pans, pump and cistern had been repaired and overhauled and the loft made more habitable. Stored salt would be sold off to local cadgers in small packets and bulk contracts cancelled.

Frederick, it seemed, would not be coming into the marriage entirely empty-handed. He declared himself in funds to the tune of forty-six pounds. No profits could be expected from the Leddings, however. Rose Tannahill was seriously ill and Norman, desolate in his loss, had neglected all his obligations. There was no help but time for the mending of that situation and neither Clare nor Frederick pressed the point in their discussions.

Pratie and the other servants were remarkably reconciled to having a new master and the housekeeper had become, if not affable, at least civil towards him.

Outside, upon the hedges, the best of stuff from the linen chests, new-laundered, dried in the late-September breeze; sheets and pillow-cases, blankets, and the big patchwork for the double-bed which had been stripped and aired and restored to pride of place in the master bedroom, now that Henri had departed.

"Why will you sleep there?" Melissa asked. "Why will you not sleep with me, in my room?"

"I must be with my – with Frederick."

"But why?"

"It is how it is with married people, dear."

"Until the babies come?"

"What?"

"And then you have to sleep with the babies, like you did with me?"

"Ah!" Clare said. "Yes, that's right, Melissa."

"Will you have more babies now?"

"No, I do doubt it."

"In case you die, like Eleanor did?"

"Because I already have you, and I could never hope to have such a good and pretty baby as you were."

"If you *did* die, though, would Frederick look after me?"

"Yes."

"I like Frederick, but I would *hate* it if you were not here, Mama."

"I'll be here, Melissa, I promise."

"For always?"

"Until I'm a very old, old lady and you have a husband and children of your own."

"And Frederick won't have to look after me then?"

"No."

"'Cause he'll be dead too," Melissa said with an air of smug and irrefutable logic.

Reverend Braintree had been engaged to perform the service. Victuals had been purchased to feed those guests who had been invited to participate in the celebration.

Clare had chosen material for her gown some weeks ago. She had been measured by a seamstress from Irvine who came on Wednesday for a final fitting of a dress which, though done in ivory or cream, had all the frills and lace-edgings that a bride could wish for.

On Thursday afternoon Frederick would take himself and his box to Ladybrook and, for the sake of tradition, would lodge for one night like a bachelor in the Neptune's very best apartment. He would dine and wine a selection of his Masonic brothers, sleep the sleep of the just and, on Friday morning, would avail himself of the services of a barber and a valet so that he might spring forth, gleaming in silk and velvet, to meet and to marry his beloved.

*   *   *

On Wednesday night Frederick slept hardly at all. His head ached, his eyes smarted and he was disturbed by foul dreams whenever he laid his head upon the pillow.

He rose two or three times to mix himself medicines,

but stinging eyes, throbbing temples and general restlessness defeated the action of the drugs.

He stood, shivering, by the embers of the fire and tried to imagine what it would be like to sleep with Clare again after so many years had passed. Would vigour be restored to him? he wondered. Would Clare find him disappointing? How would he compare to the man that he had been? How, come to think of it, would he compare to Donald Quinn?

Vague stirrings of melancholy dampened his desire.

In all probability Clare was still fertile. What if he fathered a child upon her?

The prospect filled him with both longing and dread. The arrival of a second heir, a male, say, would complicate his agreement with Brock Harding to a ridiculous degree. He would not be able to bring himself to shake Clare off then, to wilfully and calculatingly dispose of her or of his own flesh and blood.

Shivering again, he draped his greatcoat about his shoulders, poured and drank a cup of whisky then hauled from beneath the bed his battered travelling trunk and, kneeling upon the rug, unlocked it and lifted the lid.

So much had been sold off in times of debt that what remained seemed scant reward for all the effort he had put into its acquistion.

Stockings, shirts, shoes and suits, appurtenances of his trade, were all of high quality, however. He had Eleanor O'Neill to thank for that; and for a silver snuff box and a tiny golden locket with a sprig of her coarse dyed hair glued safe inside.

A scarf from Meggie, a pretty Liverpudlian. A pocket knife from Mrs Arbuthnot to whom he had given solace in his youth. An ink-bottle holder from Lord Taradale's daughter. From Sarah Blyth a miniature volume of Herrick's poems, inscribed on the foreleaf in her tiny icy hand. He had a handkerchief of spotted silk from Eleanor Antrim, and a little brass cruet, more ornament than anything, which she had bought for him one bright gay day in Morganstown two years ago.

Of his beloved sister Eunice all that remained were three letters, cross and complaining notelets, faded now with age, and of all strange things, a pair of brand-new kidskin stays which he had bought from a stall in Wallasey and had never got around to giving her before she died.

Below that was the bottom of the trunk, with dust in its corners and a few grains of sand from some forgotten shore.

"Frederick, are you awake?"

Clare opened the door before he could answer.

Caught with all his trade goods strewn about him, he threw himself forward and covered the items with his coat sleeves, as if the trunk was an altar upon which he had abased himself. He squinted up at Clare furtively.

She wore a transparent nightgown with no covering robe and she had taken off her cap and had shaken out her hair. She carried a candle in a scrolled holder which she put upon the top of the tallboy. She did not come forward from the door, however, but leaned against the post and contemplated the little scene before her.

"Possessions?"

"Yes," Frederick said. "I intend to be rid of them."

"No need for that. We'll find a safe place for them," Clare said. "Can you not sleep?"

"No. My head – "

"Is it excitement, do you think?"

"Perhaps," Frederick said.

"On Friday night," Clare said, "it will be excitement of another kind which will keep us both awake."

He was tense with anxiety lest she sidle further into the room to poke and pry about the objects he had scattered around him, enquire into the meaning of this, the origin of that. Tomorrow or the next day he would burn them all, burn everything in a bonfire down by the shore.

Clare, however, remained by the door.

In flickering candlelight at that dead hour she looked, Frederick thought, like a young girl – or the dream of a young girl – or a ghost.

"Will you not hold me, Frederick?"

"Love you?" he said with a trace of alarm.

"Hold me, just hold me. As you used to do."

He got up stiffly. With the side of his foot he scuffed the letters, the book, the kidskin stays half out of sight behind the trunk then, still with the greatcoat draped about him, he took Clare into his arms.

Her body was warm and pliant. She crushed herself against him, nothing between them but two thin layers of fabric, fine as membrane. Frederick was once more engulfed by melancholy and a sense of loss and he clung to her not in hunger but in despair.

She kissed his chin, his cheek, his mouth.

Suddenly she seemed so greedy, so aroused that Frederick was shocked by her passion, as if he was to blame for it, and, with the memory of Eleanor upon him, he gave a little cry and pushed Clare away.

"Do you want me to make love to you?" he said, angrily. "If you do, come straight out with it. Do not tease me in this manner. Do you want me to love you here and now?"

"I do not think that would be wise," Clare said.

"Then, for God's sake, let me go."

"If that's what you wish, darling," she said. "I will."

Without haste, Clare plucked the candleholder from the tallboy and left Frederick alone to scoop up his chattels and make ready, at last, for his wedding day.

*   *   *

On Brock Harding's orders the floor of the long bar parlour had been swept and sanded, the grubby little windows washed, a table with a brocade cloth upon it laid out and a stretch of good turkey carpet. At the back of the room was a bowl of punch and plates of dainty little biscuits to provide refreshment for the guests. Four long benches and ten chairs were arranged in front of the table and forty guests could have been accommodated in comfort, if forty guests had turned up.

In fact there were no guests at all, with the exception of John Galloway and Mr Robertson Blyth, and that condition of emptiness was the first of several shocks for Frederick Striker when, all toffed and titivated, he descended from his first-floor room at twenty-two minutes past two o'clock.

Reverend Braintree had come early from Malliston and had taken dinner with the coalmaster in the snuggery. When that was done he had set out his Bible and had waited, chatting to Cabel, for the bride and her entourage to arrive.

Reverend Braintree had no aversion to private weddings. He would have preferred to conduct the service at Headrick but he understood from local gossip that the circumstances of the marriage were rather unusual and that the bride was acting with decorum in choosing to be wed in the Neptune and not at home.

The minister had no clue that anything was amiss.

The first he knew of it was when the groom appeared in the beamed entrance and, in a flat, clacking English voice, said, "Where the devil is everyone?"

Galloway, sipping coffee from a china cup, answered casually, "This, I think, is it."

"Clare wrote thirty invitations. I saw her do so. She received thirty acceptances too, so she told me," Frederick said. "Where's Greenslade, for example? Where's Kneeble and his wife, and the Bartholomews?"

"My wife sends her regrets," said Robertson Blyth. "She is, alas, unwell."

"Damn it, I know about Sarah," Frederick snapped. Nervous agitation was not uncommon in bridegrooms whatever their age or station. "Did *all* of the rest refuse?"

"Perhaps you had better ask that question of your wife, sir," said Robertson Blyth, huffily. "Your wife-to-be, I mean, who, it would appear, has deceived you as to her popularity."

Brock put a hand on Frederick's shoulder and whispered into his ear, "Be still now, Freddie, there's a good fellow. Perhaps they'll all turn up tonight for the feastin'. We've a quorum of dependable witnesses here, that's all we really need to make it legal."

"An' the bride," Cabel reminded his father.

"Aye, an' the bride," said Brock, still smiling.

None of the Harding clan were present as official guests but they had done Frederick the honour of turning up anyway.

"Where is the lady in question?" Cabel said. "Seein' as how it's already gone half-past two o'clock."

"Late, late," said Frederick. "A woman's prerogative."

He said exactly the same thing again some ten minutes later.

By that time he had joined the others at the front door and, pacing and biting his knuckle, had peered up at the mouth of the turnpike from which direction the party from Headrick would presumably appear.

Harding women and children formed a noisy crowd about the front of the smithy and, on the seats outside the inn, six or eight local cadgers had assembled to wish the happy couple well and handsel them in the old style with scatterings of salt.

Weavers' daughters had emerged from cottages to eat their oat-bread dinners and gawk at the pretty things the ladies wore, and a few fisher-wives had wandered round from the quays on the off chance that there would be free drink or some other charitable dispensation. Nancy Neptune and other inn servants leaned from upper-floor windows ready to cheer when the Headrick team were spotted. Two false alarms had not daunted their enthusiasm.

"Where the devil is she?" Frederick fumed.

"Not eager, apparently," Cabel said.

"Perhaps the gig has tumbled," Robbie Blyth suggested, "and the lady has taken a spill."

"Ten to three, ten to three," Frederick muttered. "Perhaps there has been an accident." Abruptly he beat his fists against his thighs in frustration then, turning, shouted up to the inn servants, "What do you see?"

"Not a blessed thing, sir."

"Galloway, what do you know of this delay?"

"No more than you do, Striker."

"What should we do?"

"Allow her another ten minutes," John Galloway said, "then send a boy to Headrick on a horse."

"I'll not wait. I'll do it now," said Frederick.

At precisely five minutes to three o'clock young Joey Harding divested himself of his leather apron, donned his cocky felt hat and rode out from the back of the Neptune on his uncle's horse.

Groom, guests and other interested parties repaired indoors meanwhile to quaff punch, nibble biscuits and await the pleasure of the lady of Headrick who, some at least were beginning to suspect, did not intend to turn up at all.

*   *   *

Glasgow had altered out of all proportion to the time she had been away. Under the influence of the new commerce it had expanded outwards and upwards and had attained in the process a bustling sort of munificence.

If dear old Glasgow's thriving, striving upward thrust had been carefully planned by the City fathers it did not seem so to Clare. She saw it as random, more organic than architectural, as if, fertilised by tobacco and sugar-cane and now by cotton and dark brown soot, the sedate little town had spread strong roots and was ready to sprout again like a great rank weed.

St Matthew's church was much the same, though, and the kirkyard had not changed at all. It was still a place of soft angles and secluded corners, exactly as it had been on that March day in 1788 when she had stood here last.

Spring had given way to autumn, however, and the shady

307

trees had shed their leaves upon the monuments so that Andrew Purves, grunting a little, had to brush clean the tablet of weathered granite that lay sunken in the ground.

He rose and offered Clare his hand.

She took it, dropped to her knees and read the letters which were carved in the stone: *Peterkin, an Infant, Died Dec. 1787.* She placed a spray of greenhouse chrysanthemums upon her son's small grave and thought how large they looked, too rich and ornate for the simple little soul upon whose breast they rested; and she wondered at the distance, in time not space, that separated her from him now.

She began, not unnaturally, to cry.

Andrew, like the city in which he lived, had expanded and grown more well-to-do. He was heavy about the middle and round-faced. But his eyes had that same calm, watchful expression that Clare remembered so well. In spite of the suede gloves, embroidered waistcoat, powdered wig, the watch chain with its golden seal, he was still the man she had once known, her sad, heroic Andrew, her kinsman.

While Clare's tears flowed Andrew did nothing.

He was not embarrassed by her show of emotion and did not think her foolish or sentimental. When she had wept enough he quietly passed her the big lace-bordered cambric handkerchief that he had brought for the occasion, let her dry her eyes and recover before he offered his hand and gallantly helped her to her feet.

She leaned against him, looking down at the chrysanthemums and gradually heard again the rattle of carts upon the High Street hill, the garrulous chatter of new Glaswegians flowing from the markets across Kentigern Street. She smelled again the ochre smoke of the tannery in Brandon Lane and knew that Peterkin was safe among the Purveses and that soon, very soon, his little debt would be paid and all squared away.

"What time is it?" Clare asked.

"Almost four," Andrew answered.

"He'll know the truth by now."

"But will he understand?"

"Oh, yes," Clare took her cousin's arm. "Oh, yes, he'll understand."

*   *   *

When Joey swung down off the horse, Frederick grabbed him and would have shaken the boy as a terrier will a rat if Daniel had not pulled him back.

"Gone?" Frederick shouted. "What do you mean – gone?"

"Ain't there. Ain't nobody there but her housekeeper."

"A letter, was there a letter?"

"No letter, no nothin'. Ain't my fault, Mr Striker."

"What did she say? What exactly did Kerrigan say?"

"Seems Mrs Quinn and her girl left yesterday. Drove down to Ayr. Went on from there."

"On? On where?"

"Where you can't get them," Joey Harding said. "Mrs Kerrigan told me specific I was to tell you that. Where you can't get them."

"Is that it, is that all?"

"Well," Joey said, "there *was* one more thing."

"What? What?"

"She said – she said you'd understand."

*   *   *

While she had visited the kirkyard with Andrew, Clare had left Lizzie and Melissa in the herb garden behind the colleges, not far away.

Lizzie and Melissa would rather have been turned loose to roam the streets of the Saltmarket or the quays of the Broomielaw but Clare had put a crimp on that suggestion.

Tomorrow she would take them upon a grand tour, show them all the sights that Glasgow had to offer to two young country girls. This evening belonged to Andrew, however, and to those two or three old friends who still worked in the Captains' Bank where, at seven, Mrs Clare Quinn and her daughter would dine with the famous banker and exchange all the news and gossip which had slipped the net of correspondence over the years.

Yesterday Clare and the girls had travelled from Ayr on the afternoon flyer. They had reached the posting yard behind the Tontine Hotel long after the sun had gone down, but flares and brilliant chandeliers and the opulent smell of cooking from the Tontine's mighty kitchens had welcomed them and had taken Melissa's mind off her mother's abrupt and disconcerting change of plan.

Inevitably there had been a flock of whispered questions in the coach.

309

"Are we meeting Frederick in Glasgow?"

"No, dearest."

"Where *is* Frederick?"

"In Ladybrook."

"Are we coming back tomorrow for the wedding?"

"We will be in Glasgow for three days."

"Are you not going to marry Frederick then?"

"No, Melissa. I'm not."

"What will Frederick have to say to that?"

"I really could not say." Clare had put an arm about her daughter's shoulders. "Do you mind very much if we stay as we are, you and I, without Frederick?"

"Don't you like him any more?"

"I do not dislike him but I do not want to be his wife."

"Is he a bad man?"

"He is not 'bad', Melissa, but he is not for me."

"Will he not wait for you?"

Clare had hesitated before she'd given an answer, "That, dearest, remains to be seen."

After a long silence, Melissa had said, "I wish Henri hadn't gone away. Will Henri come back, Mama?"

"He might. Some day."

Two or three minutes had passed while the coach rattled on and Melissa considered the situation.

"Mama?"

"What is it, Melissa?"

"Are we in Glasgow yet?"

Some years before, Andrew had purchased a small country estate some twenty miles from Glasgow and there Edwina was esconsed for a good part of the year along with daughters Margaret and Dorothea.

Servants from the Captains' Bank had been transferred to the rustic seat and a new cook, coachman, valet and maids now inhabited the quarters where once Clare had lived. Of the "old crew" only Mr Shenken, the accountant, remained. He greeted Clare with tears, smiles and much hugging and was, of course, enchanted by Melissa, who was soon seated on his desk demonstrating her skill with pen and ink and being rewarded for her efforts with peppermint candy. The other clerks, a dozen in all, seemed alarmingly young. Although they knew who Clare was and what scandal had surrounded her departure they were too ambitious for advancement to ogle her openly for long.

The banking hall had been extended and made quite grand but the domestic apartments upstairs were much as Clare remembered them.

It was strange to walk along those corridors again. She felt as if a door might open at any moment and she would see Edwina scowling out at her, glimpse young Master William's flying heels as he galloped in search of mischief or old Mr Purves, like an amiable wraith, haunting the halls with his nightcap and lantern. Or Frederick, sensation of the season, craggy, handsome and arrogant, standing by the library door, beckoning her to enter.

The nursery was no more. It had been reappointed as a bedroom, masculine and austere, with a single bed, a single chair and a small bow-fronted bookcase occupying the spaces where once upon a time Maddy and she had reared the three young Purveses and kept them safe from harm.

"I suppose it brings back memories?" Andrew said.

"Of course it does."

"Not all bad, I trust?"

"No, Andrew, not all bad," Clare said.

Clare had hoped that Dorothea and little Margaret would have been brought into town to dine with them but Andrew explained that, as he had made no secret of Clare's visit, Edwina, as was her way, had insisted upon keeping the girls at home with her.

Putting aside her disappointment, Clare ate with appetite. By about half-past seven o'clock, Melissa, wearied by her adventures, began to droop and doze in her chair at the table and finally fell asleep.

Lizzie was supping with the Purveses' servants in the kitchen, and was no doubt being teased for her rustic manners. When Clare suggested sending for the girl, however, Andrew said, "Please, if you will allow me," and lifted Melissa gently into his arms.

Andrew carried the child into the library where, to Clare's surprise, a fire had been kept alight and a cosy little bed made up on a couch. He put Melissa upon it, slipped off her shoes and covered her with a blanket to let her sleep until it was time to return to the Tontine.

Clare thought of the handful of men she had known who looked comfortable with a child in their arms – John Galloway, Andrew, Frederick too, she supposed – and fleetingly recalled her own father, an angry, selfish reprobate who had shown her

311

no affection and had abandoned his family without a backward glance.

"Mama?" Melissa murmured sleepily.

"Yes, dearest?"

"Where am I?"

"In Cousin Andrew's house."

Melissa nodded as if it was the most natural place in the world to find herself. She closed her eyes, sighed, and let the tip of her thumb rest on her underlip.

"Will it disturb her if we take tea in here?" Andrew asked.

"I doubt it," Clare answered, and seated herself in an armchair by the fire in the same snug little room where once, long ago, Andrew and Frederick had carelessly drunk the night away.

*　　*　　*

He had ridden out to Headrick immediately, travelling in a gig borrowed from the Neptune, with Brock Harding at his side and Cabel following on horseback.

Late-autumn dusk had gathered early in the oaks. The rooks were noisy overhead and, even as they thundered up the drive, there was a dead, deserted feeling in the air over Headrick as if the heart and soul had been taken out of it.

Even before he reined the horse to a halt on the gravel, Frederick knew that young Joey Harding had told the truth for outside the front door, looming on the step, was his scarred leather travelling trunk.

He leapt from the gig, lunged at the door and found it locked and barred against him.

He stepped back and gazed up at the front of the building while behind him Cabel pranced his horse and shouted, "Try the kitchens, Striker, before we force our way in."

"No way in," a voice shouted. "All the doors are the same as this one. I'd be savin' myself the effort, if I was you." Pratie Kerrigan leaned from a bedroom window, ginger hair contained within a gigantic mob cap, her sleeves rolled up as if she meant business.

"WHERE IS SHE? WHERE'S CLARE?"

"Gone. Flown. Nobody here but my good self."

"WHEN WILL SHE RETURN?"

"When it suits her," Pratie Kerrigan said. "Needn't go

blamin' me. Everythin's accordin' to Mrs Quinn's orders. But I warn you, Mr Striker, if you try to enter this house by force I'll have the magistrates on to your top an' you wouldn't be wantin' that, would you?"

Hands on his hips, Frederick stared up at the Irish apparition for fully half a minute then he turned to Brock, who had remained in the gig.

"What am I to do? Tell me, what am I to do?"

Pratie Kerrigan answered him. "Take your dunnage an' leave. What's more, Mr Striker, if you heed my advice you won't come back this way again."

"Clare didn't – "

"Aye," said Brock Harding, quietly. "Clare did."

*　　*　　*

Andrew drank gin and water with a slice of fresh lemon bobbing in the glass while Clare went through the ceremony of pouring tea. Her cousin seemed not quite at ease and at length, after a pause prolonged enough to be awkward, he said, "What did you tell him? Frederick, I mean."

"Very little," Clare said. "Nothing, in fact."

"Did you leave him a letter?"

"No, not even that." Clare's turn to pause. "Do you think it was cruel of me not to explain?"

"It's no more than he deserves," Andrew said. "But how did you manage to convince him that all was forgiven and forgotten? I did not suppose that Striker would be naive enough to believe you."

"He believed me, I think, because he loved me."

"Did you love him? I mean, was there some of the old feeling left, some residue?"

"A little, perhaps," Clare admitted.

"I was, I confess, concerned."

"How could I tell you what was on my mind, Andrew, without making it seem – what? – villainous?" Clare said. "He is, in his way, a pathetic creature. But I was as wary about offering pity as I was about offering love. I know what Frederick is capable of, how he can lure and entice."

"Even now?"

Clare said, "Frederick regards me as his best opportunity, his best chance to escape, as I at one time thought of him. Ironic, is it not?"

313

"It occurs to me that is a very female notion of irony," Andrew said. "I'm not as gentle as you are, Clare. I'd like to have been there today to enjoy his humiliation."

"I do not know what he will do now."

"Do you care?"

"Yes, I suppose I do."

"Do you, perhaps, hope that he will not let go?"

"It would make matters very awkward."

"Not the point," Andrew said.

"I know what the point is," Clare said. "I'd be touched – no, flattered – if Frederick stayed. But he won't. He'll do as he always does when the tide turns against him. He'll vanish into thin air."

"You sound unsure," Andrew said.

"Rose Tannahill once told me that Frederick would never leave Ladybrook again. She said she saw it as a prophecy in the serpent's egg."

"Surely you set no store by such superstitious stuff."

"Part of me – the Purves part, perhaps – scorns it. Yet I cannot help but glance over my shoulder from time to time and wish that it was true."

"Does Striker know what you're really worth?"

"No, I led him to believe that Headrick was sinking into a financial quagmire," Clare said.

"And he believed you?"

"Without doubt. I think he wanted to believe that I was as helpless and unprotected as his last wife or as his sister used to be. He wanted me to need him, to be malleable and under his control. He could not bring himself to believe that I was not and never would be again."

"He has no knowledge of your investments?"

"None," Clare said.

The banker rose and stepped to a little cabinet in the corner. He slid open a drawer and removed a ledger bound in half brown calf. He opened the book with his forefinger and held the book towards Clare so that she could scan the column of figures entered below her name.

"So much," Clare said, with a strange little sigh.

"Thirteen thousand pounds, give or take," Andrew said. "The money is at your disposal, Clare. You may do anything you wish with it."

"I do not know what I wish," Clare said. "I haven't given much thought to the future, to tell the truth."

314

"Will you be happy when you are rid of him?"

"I am rid of him."

"Are you sure?"

"Yes," said Clare. "I'm sure."

*　　　*　　　*

No one remained in the Neptune's parlour to keep Frederick company except Blyth and the Hardings and they all had been drinking steadily for at least an hour. Whisky was the tipple, a raw and fiery malt made palatable by the addition of warm water and raw brown sugar.

The spirits had calmed Frederick's agitation but had in the process fogged his reasoning. He had received such a blow to his pride that he was for a time too shocked and empty to do more than rest upon the consolation of his companions. Before it occurred to him that Brock and the others were deliberately trying to make him drunk he was too drunk to care.

When he tried to rise his legs buckled beneath him. He was pushed off by Blyth, handed on by Daniel and finally found himself supported by old Brock, by the old blacksmith himself.

"Wha're you doin' t'me?" Frederick mumbled. "Wha's goin' on here?"

"Time for bed, Freddie," Brock said.

"I sho' go ho-ome."

"You ain't got no home, Fred, remember," Cabel said.

"No home, Fred, an' no friends," Daniel said.

"'Cept us," said Cabel.

"Carry him upstairs," Brock Harding said.

He fell twice on the staircase, sprawling. He was picked up, hauled along the passage into his room and, just as he was, tossed on to his back on the bed.

He lay there, gasping. The unfamiliar ceiling swam in and out of focus. He tried to draw a bead upon the faces but they were blurred too. He tried to make excuses for his condition and to fashion apologies but his tongue was no longer under his control.

He flopped a forearm over his face to hide his tears and moaned incoherently, "Clare, Clare, Clare," over and over, while one of the Hardings sniggered.

"Sleep it off, Fred. We'll be back for you real soon."

Then the room was as dark as a pond and, still mumbling Clare's name and sobbing, Frederick passed out.

*   *   *

Andrew said, "It'll certainly be amusing to dine at the Tontine tomorrow night. Have you been recognised yet?"

Clare shook her head.

"But you have, I'll be bound, drawn some admiring glances?"

Clare smiled. "I think it is my little daughter's blue eyes and endless chatter which draws the attention."

"Tomorrow night," Andrew promised, "will be an entertainment for both of us. Not only will I have an attractive young woman upon my arm to set the gossips a-buzz but some of the old school in the dining-room are bound to put two and two together."

"If you would prefer – "

"Certainly not," Andrew said. "When a man reaches my august age he is entitled to display his indiscretions in public. Do my stock good, shouldn't be surprised."

"What will Edwina say?"

"She'll huff and puff and rattle away," Andrew said.

"Shan't you mind?"

"I have, of late, developed a deafness in one ear, the ear that happens to be turned in my wife's direction." He held up a forefinger. "I do not wish you to suppose, Clare, that I spend my life slandering poor Edwina or that she is perpetually the subject of my scorn. I give her all the respect that she is due. But you – well, you know her too well to be fooled. I'll never leave her, you know. Not now."

"Have you ever been tempted?"

"Once, just once."

"By Eunice?"

"Yes."

"I guessed as much," Clare said.

Andrew put down his glass, scratched his earlobe and then said, "Actually, I'm not telling the whole truth."

"Oh?"

"I had a cousin once, not a real cousin, a cousin-german. She was as pretty as a picture and I was more than half in love with her."

"Do you think she knew it?"

"How can I tell?"

316

"I suspect she may have been half in love with you too, Andrew. Was it wrong of her not to tell you?"

"No, it would not have been proper. She was, you see, a servant in my house."

"That would not have stopped many men taking advantage, you know."

"Ah, but I loved her more than I desired her, so the solution would not have been an easy one."

"You were too cautious in those days."

"Too cautious for my own good, perhaps."

"I wonder what happened to that girl?" Clare said.

"She married a merchant down in Ayrshire and became, I believe, quite wealthy," Andrew said.

"It's unfortunate that you set your cousin such a sterling example," Clare said. "Caution and a sense of honour are not necessarily virtues in a flighty girl."

"We Purveses – too sensible by half."

"Agreed," said Clare.

He looked at Melissa who, purring in her sleep, lay all unaware upon the quilted couch, her half-clenched fists upon the pillow by her head.

"Did your daughter take to Frederick?"

"Yes, she did," Clare answered. "But she much preferred Henri Leblanc."

"What about this doctor fellow, this Galloway," Andrew said, "are you fond of him?"

"Very fond," Clare answered.

"Would he not make a suitable husband?"

"John has not declared an interest in marriage."

"Oh, I suspect he is – interested in marriage, I mean."

Clare smiled and shook her finger at her cousin. "You know him, you devil! You've known him all along."

"He's a customer here, yes."

"Why did you say nothing?" Clare said. "Do you talk about me behind my back?"

"Of course we do."

"What, may I ask, does he tell you?"

"All the things you do not see fit to put in your letters."

"What things, pray?"

Andrew was smiling now. "Oh, he tells me how you are, how well you look, how much regard he has for you. I warn him off, of course."

"You do not."

"Indeed, I do."

"Do you think you've dissuaded him?"

"I doubt it," Andrew said then, soberly, added, "I could not, unfortunately, tell him what you would do when Frederick Striker came back into your life."

"I did not know myself," Clare said. "At first I was afraid I wouldn't be able to go through with it."

"Striker is corrupt, Clare. He carries corruption with him like a taint. In my opinion, you have done absolutely the right thing."

"By taking my revenge?" Clare said.

"It is also revenge for what he did to Eunice," Andrew told her, "and to Peterkin. The fact that Striker is no longer young does not mean he deserves to be absolved for all the harm and hurt he caused in the past."

Clare was silent for a moment, then said, "Everything you say is true, I admit, but I still have some sympathy for him and I hope I have not destroyed him."

"The Strikers of this world are indestructible," Andrew assured her. "He's a coward, Clare. He'll scuttle off with his tail between his legs and this time he will not return. You've shown him that you are his equal and he'll not dare risk a confrontation with you again."

"I would like to think that you are right," Clare said. "I'm weary of enmity and retribution. Strange as it may seem, I'm glad that Frederick came back."

"Do you regret what you have done to him?"

"No," Clare answered. "I do not think I do."

"In a month or two, Clare, you'll find a new direction. You have money, a decent piece of land and, what's more important, you have earned your own freedom."

"If, that is, Frederick has indeed left Ladybrook."

"You'll see no more of Frederick Striker, Clare," Andrew told her, "not in this world and certainly not in the next."

"Andrew, are you sure?"

"Believe me, Clare, I'm sure."

Twenty-one

If the lodge bell tolled a summoning Frederick did not hear it. He lay sprawled in his wedding finery on the bed in the glum apartment in the Neptune, mouth open, long legs trailing over the side of the mattress. He would have snored the night away in that position if a wave of icy cold water had not suddenly drenched his head and shoulders and the shock of it jerked him from sleep.

He shot upright, spluttering and shouting. A canvas hood was dropped over his head, wrenched down and fastened tightly with a cord about his neck. Bubbles of air, trapped within the fabric, muffled his cries as he was flung on to his belly on the bed and the coat and shirt were torn from his back.

By now he perceived that his attackers were entities of flesh and blood not phantoms, and he kicked and writhed frantically while his arms were forced behind his back and lengths of cord wound round his wrists. He yelled again when he was hitched upright, lifted like a corn stook and dropped to the floor. He fell to the side and struck his forehead upon the bedpost as he scrambled to find his feet. He could do nothing to defend himself except lunge and lash about like a poled steer blinded by the slaughtermen.

Shuffling feet, stifled laughter, the stink of the stacking in his nostrils, the taste of oatmeal not salt upon his tongue.

"Hoist him up, for God's sake. Daddy's waitin' to get started," Cabel Harding hissed.

Frederick was jerked to his feet.

Fingers cupped his neck. He was pressed down and forward so violently that pain flowed up his spine into his skull and, bent double, he was steered out of the bedchamber, along the passageway and upstairs to the over-room.

"God, but I've seen pigs more sensible," Daniel Harding said, butting Frederick on the backside to urge him along.

"Who's there?" Frederick shouted. "Are you there, Brock? Is this your idea of a joke?"

"No joke, Freddie," said Brock from a distance. "Listen hard, you'll hear none of us laughin' now."

An arm locked about his shoulders and Cabel's voice said in his ear, "How d'you like it, Mr Striker? Ain't this how it was when they topped my poor old Uncle Jericho? Think on him when you're swingin' from the rope."

Frederick shouted again but there was no sense to his clamour.

He heard Brock say, "Take off the muffle, son, an' let him speak. Let's hear what the Deceiver has to say for himself before we nominate Apollo's punishment."

Frederick felt the cord being loosened, the hood dragged upward over his chin and mouth and cinched again below his nose, leaving him still blind.

He gulped air, spat out crumbs of oatmeal. "So this is supposed to be lodge business, is it? What am I then? A meek apprentice that you'd treat me so?"

"You're a liar, Brother Striker, that's what you are."

Frederick recognised the coalmaster's voice.

"When have I ever lied to you, Blyth?" he shouted.

He felt steadier now, not on sure ground but approaching it. They might strip him and stripe him, humiliate him, cause him pain but surely they would do him no lasting harm. The oaths of the lodge might seem fierce and Satanic but they were all just bluster. He felt better now that he'd learned he was not alone with the Hardings.

"You're not even an initiate," Blyth told him. "You've deceived the brotherhood and have stolen our secrets and that, sir, is a dire crime in the eyes of Apollo."

"I have not lied." Someone struck him a numbing blow across the back of the head. Frederick staggered but did not fall. "I have *not* lied, damn you!"

"Careful now, Freddie," Brock Harding said. "You don't even know what the punishments are."

"Oh, come now," said Frederick. "You aren't going to sear my flesh with hot pokers and tear my tongue out by the roots, are you, Master Harding?"

"What do you take us for, Freddie, barbarians?" Cabel said.

"If you were really one of us," Brock said, "you'd realise that our oaths are symbolic. But then you aren't one of us at all, are you, Fred?" Frederick gave no answer. How had Brock discovered that he was not a brother-by-degree? In fact, he had purchased Masonic secrets from a drunken cabinet-maker in Liverpool and had added to his knowledge by reading several condemnatory pamphlets. The issue at stake was not one of fraternal deception, however serious that might be, but one of broken promises. Fear had cleared the whisky fumes from his head and he felt suddenly sharp and cunning.

"What are you going to do to me then?" he asked.

"Hang you," Brock said. "Try you first then string you up from a crossbeam."

"After which," said Daniel, "it'll be me for the boat and you, Fred, for deep water off the Nebbocks."

"Too many witnesses, Brock," Frederick said. "You'll never get away with it."

"You got away with it," Brock said, "when you had my brother hanged."

"I told you, I had nothing to do with the verdict against your brother."

"I hope you make as good an exit as Uncle Jericho," said Daniel Harding, "but I doubt it. I've got you marked down as a squealer."

"Hold on," Frederick said. "Aren't you getting somewhat ahead of yourselves with all this talk of hanging? I haven't been found guilty yet. What, first of all, are the charges against me?"

"Fornication," Robertson Blyth said.

"Well, we've all been guilty of that, surely."

"Not with my wife, we haven't."

"Your wife?"

"Take off the hood, son," Brock said.

The hood was removed from Frederick's eyes.

He blinked and peered about him.

The room was lit by firelight and two fat flickering candles in the bracket by the dais. Cabel and Daniel were on his left. On his right Robertson Blyth occupied an empty bench while Brock lounged in his chair beneath the painted Eye of Apollo.

There was no one else in the room.

Frederick gasped and struggled, plunging this way and that. He would have flung himself straight at the little side door if Daniel hadn't pinned him with a knee in the small of the back.

"What's wrong, Freddie?" Daniel said. "Ain't four witnesses enough for you?"

"I reckon it's the rope he don't like," Cabel said and gripping Frederick's chin, tipped back his head. "See."

The noose already hung from the crossbeam, its shadow pasted by candlelight to the long wall.

On the edge of the dais perched two heavy sacks, filled, Frederick guessed, with sand. The drop was no more than four feet and he, Frederick, was long in the leg and body. He had a sudden shocking vision of his hanged body, head cocked close to the crossbeam, feet, kicking and twitching, just three or four inches from the floor.

"How do you like it" Cabel asked.

"I don't think he likes it at all," said Daniel. "Look, he's gone a bit white about the gills."

"Be whiter yet before we're through."

Frederick forced out the words, "The charges?"

"Fornication," said Robertson Blyth again.

The coalmaster was stone cold sober now. He had put on a plain black coat and arranged a white lace cravat in his collar, and swung his pocket watch lightly between his finger and thumb.

"Who told you such a thing?" Frederick said.

"She did."

"I do not believe you, sir."

"Are you accusing my wife of purveying untruths?" Blyth said. "If you imagine that this is some sort of calumny that my wife has devised out of malice, let me tell you that she did not betray you willingly." He swung the watch and caught it deftly in his left hand. "I had to wring it out of her, sir, positively wring it out."

Brock got lazily to his feet. "Do you hear what our honourable brother has to say, Fred? We're quiet folk in this town, you know. We go decently about our business and attend our own affairs with discretion. We didn't ask you to come back here. Didn't invite you to desecrate – is that the right word, Mr Blyth?"

"That *is* the right word, Mr Harding."

"To desecrate our gentlewomen an' spread – "

"In Christ's name," Frederick shouted, "dispense with all this pious claptrap and get on with it."

"Now, now, Fred, surely you wouldn't deny us our bit of fun," Brock said. "We prefer to show some respect for the law, even if you never did."

"But that won't stop you hanging me, will it?"

"Certainly not," Brock said. He brushed the noose aside and placed a hand on Frederick's shoulder.

"Think how lucky you are we can't go callin' all the witnesses who deserve to be here. Think how lucky you are that Bob Gowrie took it into his head to depart these shores just when he did. Think how fortunate for you that Tannahill's so occupied with his sick old mother that he can't be with us tonight. Think what it would be like for you, Frederick, if we were able to bring the O'Neill family over from Dublin or dig up the bones of poor Eleanor Antrim to put evidence on the table."

"Your hands aren't clean either, Brock. What about Kate Gowrie, just for a start to the list?"

"Kate Gowrie?" In a tone of injured innocence, Brock enquired, "Do any of us here know anythin' about Kate Gowrie?"

"We can go further back, if you wish," Frederick said.

"I'm sure we could, Fred," Brock said. "But we aren't goin' to. I'm goin' to ask you just one question. If your answer's right, you walk out that door a free man. If your answer's wrong," he raised his hand and gently tugged the noose behind him, "you dance."

"What is the question?"

"Just this." From his side pocket Brock extracted four sheets of legal paper, each one bearing a small round waxy seal. "Can you pay me what's due?"

"Due?"

"On agreements made in the spring, to compensate me for my loss on my investment."

"How much?"

"Well, since I bought out Mr Blyth's share, it comes to just four hundred pounds."

"But it isn't my debt."

"Oh, and whose debt is it?"

"Clare's, of course."

"Mrs Quinn's?"

"Yes," Frederick said. "For God's sake, Brock, you can't hold me responsible. Clare's your partner, not mine."

"And who is your partner, Frederick?"

"What?"

"If Clare Quinn isn't your partner, who is?"

Trapped, he opened his mouth but found no answer there, no point of argument, no clever verbal trick which would extricate him from his predicament. It wasn't Brock who had deceived him but Clare. Nature, female nature, had won.

He stared straight into Brock Harding's face and answered, "No one."

"No one." Brock sighed. "Therefore you must be the one to carry the can. Am I right, Freddie?"

"You're right, Brock. Absolutely right."

"So, can you pay me? Can you settle your dues?"

"No, I can't."

Brock sighed again and turned away. He held the papers up in his right hand.

"Time to vote, gentlemen. All those who think Mr Striker's innocent?" He looked around expectantly. "Well?"

"Nary a one," said Cabel. "Ain't that odd?"

"All those in favour of a guilty verdict?"

"Three," said Daniel.

"Well, well, it seems I don't even have to use my castin' vote," Brock said. "Poor old Freddie Striker's been found guilty by a jury of his peers."

"Now what?" Frederick asked.

"We hangs you," Brock answered, "right here an' now."

*   *   *

Fortunately Mr Henry Nock had been more successful than Henri Leblanc in applying for a patent. It was also fortunate that the officers of the Staffordshire Militia had seen fit to present their departing surgeon with a half-stocked shotgun with a pair of thirty-two inch barrels and a Nock patent breech. At the time John Galloway had been a mite less than impressed for he was not fond of shooting. He had, however, carried the gun off to Scotland with him and, because it was a handsome object, had kept it on display in the library, upright between two bookcases.

The Nock shotgun may not have impressed Dr Galloway but it certainly impressed the gentlemen who were gathered in the Neptune's over-room.

The gun's purposeful quality somehow transferred itself to its handler. Aided by a cocked hat tipped back from his brow and a coal-breaker's hammer stuck into his belt, the doctor did not look like a man to be tampered with. He had brought along the hammer not to crack skulls but to demolish a panel of the over-room's door which he had expected to find locked. The fact that it had not been locked, added to the fact that he had been able to lurk undetected in the ground-floor passage, indicated a quality of conceit in the Hardings which Galloway found contemptible.

He had heard enough of the conversation to realise that the room was not full of lodge members, that the trial was not a hollow Masonic ritual and that the Hardings really did intend to execute the Englishman.

He was no longer play-acting when he kicked open the door with the sole of his shoe and stalked forward with the shotgun primed and loaded, his fingers twitching upon its triggers.

"What the devil do you want?" Brock shouted. "You've no right to be here."

"Cut him down," Galloway said.

"He ain't strung up yet," Cabel said.

"Release him then."

"Dad?" Daniel Harding enquired.

"He's a doctor an' he won't dare fire," said Cabel.

"This business doesn't concern you, Galloway," Brock said. "Leave alone what you don't understand."

"I understand that you intend to hang a man."

"A guilty man."

"Guilty? In whose judgement?" Galloway said. "In any case, I'm a doctor not an advocate."

"You've been treating my wife, sir, haven't you?" said Robertson Blyth and slowly and methodically got up from the bench.

"I question if this farce has much to do with Mrs Blyth's state of health," Galloway said. "Come now, send Striker down to me."

"Why are you doing this? You, of all people?" Brock said. "Wouldn't it be better for you if Striker was put out of the way?"

"Why would it benefit me?"

"With Striker gone," Brock said, "you might enjoy the widow's exclusive favours once more."

Galloway had fired the shotgun before and recalled its percussion foibles well enough to brace the stock against the soft flesh of his upper arm and to assume a broad stance before pulling one of the triggers. The explosion boomed out in the confined space of the over-room. Fumes spread in the wake of the shot. Rather to his surprise Galloway saw that he had all but obliterated the Eye of Apollo upon the gable wall.

"It will not have escaped your notice, gentlemen," he said, "that I have, still primed, a second barrel."

Unlike his sons Brock Harding did not fling his hands over his head at the roar of the shot. He swayed from the splash of pellets and gripped the edge of the dais with one hand but otherwise he did not appear to be intimidated.

"Striker," John Galloway said, "step down."

Hands still fastened behind his back, Frederick crabbed to the end of the platform, crouched and dropped to the floor below. He staggered, found his balance and swiftly took position behind the doctor.

Brock watched impassively as Galloway, preceded by the Englishman, backed towards the open door, and then he said, "You're a dead man, Freddie, mark my words."

Frederick only laughed and, turning away, pattered down the staircase while Galloway, and his shotgun, followed on.

*   *   *

Norman rose some time after midnight. He climbed down the ladder and entered the kitchen. Nothing definite had disturbed him but he had not been able to sleep and had gradually become aware that a subtle alteration had taken place in the quality of silence in the cottage kitchen and had dutifully come down to investigate.

His nightshirt was no longer clean. His hair was matted, his chin unshaven.

Cows and calves might fend for themselves, the sow trample on her farrow, the cats turn feral; Headrick's lawns might grow shaggy, its vegetable garden sour; he was bound now to his mother and dedicated to her welfare for as long as she might last, and grief manifested itself as indifference to all other obligations.

Clare Quinn had left him alone. She had her lover to occupy her attentions; Striker, who had brought Eleanor to Headrick and, in some mysterious way which Norman could not understand, had managed to take her back. He did not hate Clare Quinn or the Englishman. He had no feeling for them, except a certain vinegary dislike, quite mild in comparison to what he felt for his mother, that venerable confusion of love and loathing which faded as she faded and which would go from him only when she had gone.

He was, he knew, only waiting for her to die.

She was seated in the old chair, propped on shuck pillows and with her feet upon a bolster. He had left a slice of candle burning in a dish for she no longer found darkness tolerable. In it she hissed like a cat or cried with her eyes wide open, vacant as the sky. She made noises but did not speak. Sometimes she seemed to recognise him and a wee smile would crimp her cheeks but for the most part he was as much a stranger to her as she was to the world.

He had not summoned Galloway and he administered no herb, no potion drawn from the dusty jars and bottles whose contents were mysteries to him. He fed her pap from a spoon and beaten egg from a cup. He weaned her and wiped off her dribble with his cuff. He bathed her hands and face with warm water. He changed her soiled stockings and damp skirts and, when there was no linen left, laundered the garments in the Linn and dried them on a bramble bush.

Hour after hour he would sit motionless at the table, watching her, waiting for her to say his name or to slip silently away from him, one or the other; yet during the dazed and tedious hours of devoted attention he hardly spared a thought for Rose at all, thought rather of Eleanor, and all the hours of happiness she'd brought him and how he might capture them again.

He lit the lantern and set it upon the table.

A brown mouse sat up upon the cheese board, a crumb of bread caught in its tiny paws. It stared at him indignantly then scurried and leapt and was lost, scratching, under the footboard of the dresser. Ash slumped in the grate.

The air in the kitchen was stale with age.

"Mother, did you call for me?"

She gave no sign of having heard.

Something had changed, though.

Norman kneeled on the stone before her and took her weightless hands in his.

"What is it?" he whispered. "What ails you now?"

She stared past him as if something lurked in the shadows. No longer taken in by her fantasies, Norman did not glance round. It shocked him to realise that she had moved her eyes again, that she was looking at him now.

"What?" he said. "What? Tell me."

"Bo-ok."

"What?"

"Bo-ok." She struggled suddenly and pointed. "Book, book, book."

327

Rising, he opened a drawer of the dresser and took out the leather-bound Bible which had lain there as long as he could recall. It was too hefty a tome to carry to kirk and Rose had never been much of a one for prayer, not even when the boys were small. Names were penned on the fly but they were not revealing; no ancestral tree, no paternal line, only her name and the names of her sons, descending unevenly to his name printed at the bottom of the page.

He held the Bible up to her in both hands, nodding his question. "This?"

She gave no sign that he had understood her wishes but he went forward, nonetheless, and gently laid the Bible on her knees. He knelt by her feet, supporting the weight of the book on his hands. He watched her press her forearms upon the dusty leather binding and waited for her to speak again, to furnish him with a final meaning, something profound.

He could see the dark funnel that her tongue made but no sound came. He was crushed by disappointment.

They sat together, motionless and mute, for four or five minutes, linked only by their contact with the book; then quite distinctly his mother said, "The stranger's gone."

"What do you mean, Mumma?" Norman asked.

She shook her head slightly and, easing her position in the chair, slid back against the pillows, closed her eyes and said no more to him, not that night or ever again.

*   *   *

Frederick fingered the soft lapel of the robe that John Galloway had given him. "What is this stuff?"

"Mohair," the doctor told him. "From goats."

"Expensive?"

"Moderately so," Galloway said. "Are you warmer now?"

"Yes, but I cannot seem to stop shivering."

"A natural reaction."

"May I have a little more brandy?"

"By all means," Galloway said. "But not just yet."

"Moderation in all things?" said Frederick.

"Quite!"

Frederick drew the robe about him and huddled over the small fire that smoked in the grate of Galloway's study. He stretched out his hands to the inadequate flames and watched his fingers shake. He did not attempt to hide his physical failings from the doctor who, he gathered, had already deduced the nature and extent of his infirmities. Out of the corner of his eye he glanced at the shotgun which Galloway had restored to its place in a niche between the bookcases.

"Odd," Frederick said. "I did not have you marked as a sporting gentleman."

"The gun is a relic from my past."

"Would you have used it?"

"On Harding? Yes, if I'd had to."

Frederick shifted his weight. The fire gave no warmth and the brandy had been absorbed into his bloodstream too quickly to bring more than a temporary flush to his skin. He felt cold through and through, cold to the very marrow of his bones.

"Did you know that Clare intended to humiliate me?"

"What makes you suppose that?"

"Your appearance at the Neptune tonight seemed somehow planned, too opportune to put down to luck."

"I've been in Ladybrook long enough to realise that the Hardings are ruthless and vicious. I returned to the inn only to make sure that they didn't harm you."

"So Clare had nothing to do with it?"

"Nothing at all."

Frederick straightened.

"Where is she?" he asked.

"With her cousin in Glasgow."

"Purves?"

"Yes."

"I might have known he'd be involved in all this."

"Come now," Galloway said, "surely you do not imagine that Clare is at the heart of a conspiracy against you?"

"What else am I to think. What Clare did this afternoon was obviously intended to put me in a difficult position."

"Were the difficulties not, perhaps, of your own making?"

"Have you met Purves?" Frederick asked.

"I cannot say I know him well," Galloway answered.

"Take my word on it," Frederick said, "Purves is even more ruthless than the Hardings."

"Banking does require a certain cold cast of mind, I suppose," Galloway said. "Why, though, would Andrew Purves wish to do you harm?"

"Did Clare not tell you?"

"I am not her confidante, Striker," John Galloway said. "Nor am I involved in this imagined conspiracy against you."

Frederick hesitated. The house was silent. The fussy sisters who served the doctor had been packed off back to bed. He should have felt secure in Galloway's villa but his relief was tempered by strange fears. He felt as if he had passed from one deep moment of danger into another, had descended into a darkness more smothering than that of the hangman's hood. He had a vague suspicion that he had not been rescued at all but, rather, saved to face some other sort of fate.

"It all goes back to something that happened years ago," Frederick heard himself say.

"At the time of Clare's imprisonment?"

"About that period, yes. Purves was my sister's lover. He used her and abandoned her. It was because of Purves that my Eunice hanged herself."

"And it had nothing to do with you?"

"Very little."

"I see."

"It's clear at last," Frederick said, "that I've been set up as a scapegoat all along, that it's Purves who has plotted to bring me down."

"Not Clare?"

"She has been used and manipulated, that's all."

"Do you not think her capable of plotting revenge."

"Clare loves me. Clare has always loved me."

"Is that why you came back to Ladybrook in the first place?"

"To find Clare, yes."

"Did it not occur to you that you would be in danger?"

"It hardly mattered."

"Love is blind, hmmm?" Galloway asked.

"No, no, at my age love is as clear-sighted as it is possible to be," said Frederick.

"Did Sarah Blyth also contrive against you?"

"Sarah? Ah, so you've been treating her silly female ailment, have you? What lies has she been telling you?"

Galloway did not answer at once.

By lifting his head Frederick could see the man, calm and obscure, in the shadow behind the oval table to his left. In the panes of the book cases and in the leaded glass front of the druggist's cabinet Galloway's reflections seemed more colourful than the reality of flesh and blood. Frederick could see his own face too, haggard as a carving in the candlelight, scraped white as whalebone.

"Was love not blind for Eleanor Antrim?" Galloway said.

"Eleanor?"

"Or for little Kate Gowrie, perhaps?"

"Why," Frederick said, "do you link me with Eleanor and with the salter's lass? They, poor creatures, are dead and gone."

"Perhaps I do so *because* they are dead and gone."

"What do you mean?"

"I mean, you too will soon be dead."

"Murdered by the Hardings? No, no, not now."

"You are seriously ill, Striker."

"Who told you that?"

"I do not have to be told. I've a regrettable amount of experience in recognising the signs which attend certain incurable diseases."

"Incurable? Is Sarah . . .?"

"No. She will, with care, recover."

Frederick pushed himself to his feet. In the squared panes of the cabinet his bone-white features became blurred and were lost in the halo from the candles. He steadied himself against the chairback.

"How long do I have?"

"A year, I would say, at most."

"Are you sure?"

"I cannot say with absolute certainty." Galloway shrugged. "But, because of what is in you, it will be sooner rather than later, I expect."

"Can you not cure me?"

"Too late for that, alas."

"Is it because of my illness that Clare . . .?"

"Clare renounced you for other reasons, reasons of her own. I do not suppose you will have to search your soul too deeply to discover what they are."

"She loves me, Galloway. She has always loved me. Her marriage to Quinn was a desperate aberration, a means of keeping as close to me as possible."

"I doubt that," Galloway said. "Clare married Quinn because he was caring and reliable."

"Like you?" said Frederick. "Do you see yourself as the next master of Headrick?"

"I like to think that I might one day marry Clare."

"In that case why didn't you let Brock hang me?"

"Because I am not a barbarian," Galloway answered. "But make no mistake I didn't save you out of sympathy. If you must

331

know I gave Clare my promise that I would not let you come to harm."

"Did you, indeed?" Frederick said. "And was it to protect me or to protect Clare that you kept your mouth shut about my association with Sarah Blyth?"

"I will not betray a patient's confidences."

"What about Eleanor, though?"

Galloway paused. "Was it your child, Striker?"

"It may have been."

"Why did you bring her – the Irish girl, why did you bring her to Scotland when your sights were set on Clare?"

"I felt I – I owed Eleanor something. We were – friends for so long, you see. I could not leave her behind."

"And yet you would have gone through with a marriage to Clare?"

"Yes, damn it."

"In spite of your illness?"

"Clare's love would have kept me alive. She would have restored me to health and strength."

"If you believed that," Galloway said, "then you're a fool, an ignorant fool."

"I did not intend to harm Clare. You must believe me on that score."

"How much do you owe to Harding?"

"What?" said Frederick, put out by the doctor's sudden change of tack.

"Harding seems to be of the opinion that you owe him several hundred pounds."

"What does money have to do with it? Good God, Galloway! In one breath you tell me I'm as good as dead and in the next you quibble about money."

"I'm not talking about money. I'm concerned about what you owe and what you would have owed if you had become Clare's husband this afternoon?"

"I'd have paid off my debts, never fear."

"And what of your debt to Clare?"

"How can I be expected to pay her debts when Headrick is entailed?"

"So Clare told you?" Galloway said.

"Yes, her daughter is the nominated inheritor."

"If you knew that the estate was already entailed why did you enter into a transaction with Brock Harding and make promises that you could never hope to fulfil?"

"So that I could remain in Ladybrook. If I had not come to an arrangement with Harding he would have murdered me long ago."

"You promised him Headrick, did you not?"

"I may have led him to believe . . ."

"What did you plan to do with Melissa?"

"Raise her as my own."

"And your other children?"

"I have no other children," Frederick said and then, with a little swagger of arrogance, added, "none, that is, that I have been obliged to acknowledge."

"No family, no relatives?"

"Fortunately not."

"So, when you slip out of Ladybrook this morning and take to the road again where will you go and what will you do with the time that remains to you?"

"Slip out of Ladybrook?"

"Surely you realise that you cannot stay here?"

Frederick spread his hands. "Why not?"

"For one thing Harding will have you killed."

"Does that matter now?" Frederick said. "You're quite right, Galloway. I *have* no place to go. If I'm to die soon I may as well die here in Ayrshire, don't you think?"

"Not with Clare?"

"No."

Frederick pulled the robe about his shoulders. He looked to the doctor like a great brown cormorant, sly and unrepentant, as if he had in mind the rudiments of a scheme which would rescue him from extinction.

"I do not believe you," Galloway said.

"That is your prerogative."

"Far too many people have taken you on trust, Striker, and most of them seem to have died or lived to regret it."

"You want Clare for yourself, don't you?"

"What if I do. You have had your chance and failed."

"And yet, it seems, I still stand in your way."

"Leave here, please. Leave Ladybrook."

"Leave Clare to you, is that what you mean?"

"You have nothing left to offer her, Striker, nothing more to give."

"I would not be too sure of that," Frederick said.

There was no obvious explosion, no reddening of the cheeks, no shrillness entered in the voice. Only a sudden swiftness of movement indicated that anger had taken possession of John Galloway.

When he whirled and darted towards the bookcases Frederick's first thought was that Galloway was reaching for the shotgun. In spite of his resolve, Frederick flinched and drew back towards the fireplace, groping for the protection of the leather armchair; then he caught the glint of a ring of keys on a short steel chain jerked so violently from one of the doctor's pockets that it seemed to spin in mid-air for a moment.

Squatting, Galloway fitted a key to the lock and flung open the cupboard's knee-high door. He reached into the dark recess with both hands and emerged a second later with a large glass bottle in his grasp. He hoisted it into the crook of one arm and got to his feet again.

Even before the vessel was set upon the table and the candlelight illuminated its contents, Frederick had begun to tremble once more.

The specimen, if that's what it was, swayed a little and bobbed within the confines of the glass. It had been folded neatly to fit the space, its tiny hands, like the claws of a newt, were linked before its chest with a strand of wire or cord. Soft, rubbery knees were fasted in a similar fashion so that the infant seemed to be kneeling quietly in its own little ocean of preserving fluid, eyes closed, and both heads nodding drowsily.

Frederick drew closer and leaned forward from the waist, his breast against the table's edge. He was mesmerised by the sight of the creature which, even as the liquid shivered and settled, seemed to generate motion, to have a life and vestigial will of its own. As it swung and drifted towards him he saw eight limbs not four tucked and neatly bound to fit the swell of the glass; twin boys fused at hip and shoulder, not two at all, but one.

"Eleanor's child," Galloway told him.

"No, no, it's a monster."

"Your child, Striker, your monster."

Magnetically drawn, Frederick leaned even closer, until his forehead touched the ice-cold glass and his face was no more than inches from the faces of his sons. He could see fine silky black hair, curled lashes, pursed lips, the perfect little noses, everything about them perfect and whole, except that nature had knit them together in the bone, had made them inseparable, and freaks.

Frederick cupped a hand gently upon the crown of the glass and soundlessly began to weep.

"Why?" he sobbed. "Why have you preserved it?"

"Because it's yours, Frederick."

"God, oh God!"

"I kept it for you to keep."

*   *   *

The room was more cheerful now. The coals had caught and flame from the hearth warmed the brown outlines of the books and brushed the leaded panes with leaf yellow and rivulets of russet, the colours of an autumn twilight. It warmed too the volume of wood alcohol and tinted pink the soft dead flesh and glazed the glass redly so that Frederick's hand upon it seemed youthful and wholesome and steady now that tears had drained him of his rage.

He had shouted, had shaken the table, had raised his fists to heaven. He had implored Galloway to take the thing away; but Galloway would not, Galloway could not. This was his, Frederick's, legacy, something that he could not shrug off and leave behind him; an infant, a two-headed heir, too tender and frail to rattle in his trunk, to put on show in inns and taverns, to survive the shock of further escapades, of voyages and escapes. Here it must stay, and he with it.

With the acknowledgment that he was no longer free the last wisps of ambition shrivelled and blew away. All he had left were dead sons and a sister, widows, wives and children hardly out of frocks; and he, Frederick Striker alone in a strange room with a foetus in a bottle and nothing else with which to console himself save longing for all that he had lost, for Eunice and Eleanor, for Peterkin, and Clare.

He had lived too long with the pleasure of scheming for it to desert him completely, though. He grinned to himself as he heard Galloway's tread descending the staircase.

He had professed himself willing to discuss flight, had put on a convincing show of negotiating for a loan of money. He had asked if he might borrow clothes and have a late supper, or early breakfast, to see him on his way.

And Galloway, being a decent chap, had left his servants to their slumbers and had gone down into the kitchen to boil a kettle, cut bread and scramble eggs, leaving Frederick alone in the study to contemplate the babe in the bottle and sip a second glass of brandy, generously dispensed.

Patting the shoulder of the glass lightly, Frederick whispered,

335

"Hold on," and, when he heard the kitchen door open and close again deep below stairs, pushed himself with alacrity out of the chair.

He lowered himself to his knees before the empty cupboard and, with the deftness of a sneak thief, plucked out the ring of keys that Galloway had left hanging from the lock. Squinting, he sorted through the keys, found one that appeared as if it might fit and, shifting the candle to the table's edge to provide light, tried the key in the cabinet's tight brass lock, and heard it click.

The heavy lead-paned door of the druggist's cabinet swung open of its own accord. Six deep shelves lined with jars and bottles confronted him, each container conveniently labelled in the doctor's copperplate script.

Frederick removed the set of little brass scales that barred access to the rear shelves then, one by one, extracted the bottles and jars, some of plain glass, others stained dark blue or emerald. He read the label on each, put each container to the side, ranking them neatly along the shelf which fronted the bookcase.

He wished that he'd had his own tray of medicines to work with for he knew the properties of the substances well. But he was pressed for time and could not risk delay, a change of heart, the onset of wheedling selfishness or the seductive illusion that he might somehow survive and somehow prosper.

Arsenic would not do the trick. Aconitum was too slow. Chloride of Mercury would only make him vomit. Strychnine's delayed convulsions might encourage Galloway to try to revive him. He was momentarily confused as he ransacked the shelves and then, in the darkest corner of the cabinet, he discovered a small, amber-coloured, stoppered bottle and even before the read the label, knew that he had found the stuff that would cure all his ills. Prussic; a single drop of which would paralyse his heart instantly.

Cautiously he carried the bottle to the table and held it up to the light. He eased the stopper and sniffed the colourless liquid greedily. The almond-like odour, bitter and stringent, pleased him for it meant that the oil was pure. He placed the vessel by the brandy glass and glanced around the study in search of ink, pens and paper. He found them easily enough in the first drawer that he opened and took them to the oval table.

He shed the robe, seated himself, and wrote a few words in ink across the foolscap.

336

Time was pressing now. He paused to listen, afraid that Galloway would return too soon.

He had the same peculiar mix of feelings in him now that he'd had before he'd administered the first small batch of poison to his wife; mischievous excitement, apprehension, determination and a liking for the power that the substance gave him. He moved the candle-holder to the far side of the table and let it cast its halo through the bottles. Brandy, wood alcohol, Prussic, shed individual filaments of colour upon the paper, very clear and pretty.

He drank the brandy and cleaned the measure with his forefinger. He poured the contents of the amber-coloured bottle into the glass and, without hesitation, drank it too in one long swallow.

Frederick looked at the creature floating before him.

"Are you ready, son?" he said and, writhing a little, fell backwards on to the floor.

*   *   *

They arrived home in the middle of Friday afternoon in a carriage which Clare had hired from the coaching inn at Irvine. The two horses had made fast time through the soft autumnal haze that enclosed the Ayrshire hinterlands and transformed the sea to a pale blue chalk line.

It had been hazy in Glasgow too that morning and the streets had smelled of horses and cattle and river mud. Clare had left the city, and her cousin, with strange pangs of regret. Melissa, being still a child, had wept and even Lizzie had snuffled away into one of the new lace handkerchiefs that had been Clare's present to her, to accompany Andrew's generous gift of a guinea. There were also presents in the luggage for Jen, Mrs Shay and Pratie but not, as Melissa had rather embarrassingly pointed out, for Frederick.

In Clare's baggage, tucked safe away, was a leather wallet containing four hundred pounds in banknotes which she had withdrawn from her account with the Captains' Bank.

For twenty or thirty minutes after the carriage had deposited Clare and the girls at the front door of Headrick House there was such a fuss and bustle that neither Clare nor her daughter seemed to have time to spare a thought for Frederick. Not until gifts had been distributed, dusty gowns exchanged for plain wear and tea was about to be served in the drawing-room, did

Clare realise that she was waiting, tensely, for the Englishman to appear in the doorway.

Pratie brought in the tea things at half-past four. Sensing what would be required of her, she closed the drawing-room door behind her with her heel.

"I take it," Clare said, "that Mr Striker is no longer lodged in the house?"

"No, Mrs Quinn. He's gone."

"His boxes too?"

"Everythin', put out as you instructed."

"Did he collect them in person?"

"Aye, he arrived in the Hardings' gig."

"Was he angry?"

"Very angry. He'd have done damage to the house if Brock Hardin' hadn't calmed him down."

"Have you not seen Frederick since then?"

"No, I have not."

"Did he not send a message?"

"Not a word," said Pratie.

"So you have not heard how he is?"

"I heard a rumour that he left Ladybrook yesterday mornin'," Pratie said, "which, if you ask me, Mrs Quinn, is the best thing that could happen under the circumstances."

"I suppose it is," Clare said. "But somehow I did not think he would – "

"Leave you?" said Pratie. "But why would he stay when there was nothin' here for him?"

"Frederick's gone?" Melissa put in.

"Yes, dear."

"Gone for good, Mama?"

"That remains to be seen," said Clare.

Twenty-two

For the best part of October there was considerable awkwardness between Clare and John Galloway. Clare could not be sure whether she had offended him by her deviousness or disappointed him by her outrageous behaviour.

On her only visit to the church at Malliston what a buzz there had been when she made her entry, what a drawing away. Mr Braintree had been frosty and Randolph Soames, who was also in attendance, reserved in his greeting. But Clare was unconcerned about public opinion which, she knew, waxed and waned with each shiny new scandal.

What did concern her was John Galloway's disapproval, if disapproval it was. He was guarded and uncommunicative and held himself back from her, as if he had somehow lost trust in their friendship. She did her best to bring him round by teasing him about his secret acquaintance with Andrew Purves but, for once, the doctor did not rise to her bait and seemed to regard her remarks as unnecessarily flippant.

When she asked him about Frederick, he told her very little, only that there had been trouble with the Hardings and that Frederick had been fortunate to make good his escape.

"Did he leave nothing with you?" Clare asked.

"What, for instance?"

"A note, a letter?"

"To the best of my knowledge, Striker stole off quietly under cover of darkness," John said. "I take it that you have heard nothing from him by means of the mails?"

"No, I have not."

"Is it not a trifle unreasonable of you to expect him to write to you after what you did?"

"I suppose it is, yes."

"Your rejection of him was exceedingly emphatic and exceedingly public, you know."

"I know it was."

"I find it hard to imagine that you didn't know exactly what you were doing and what the consequence would be."

"I did. Of course, I did."

"Do you regret his departure?"

"I'm curious, that's all."

"There's nothing to be curious about," John told her. "Striker's gone. You paid him back, Clare. He got no more than he deserved. Why should you feel sorry for him now?"

"Yes, I suppose that's true."

"Put him out of your mind. You're well rid of him."

"I wonder what he'll do, though?"

"Marry someone else, probably," John said, a novel thought that taunted Clare for the best part of the month.

Now that the nights were drawing in and the curtains were pulled early the house seemed quiet and almost sullen with Henri and Frederick gone.

There was a staid quality to the passage of the days of which even Melissa seemed aware. She was moody, and less garrulous than Clare had ever known her to be. She would talk now and then of Henri and confess that she missed him but she said not one solitary word regarding Frederick. It was as if Melissa had grown sufficiently mature to grasp something of the intricate, adult nature of the events which had enlivened the long and arduous summer and did not quite approve of them.

There was one last nip left in the autumn, however.

Several days before the end of the month Norman Tannahill appeared at the kitchen door at Headrick to inform the mistress of the house that his mother had passed away.

It came as no great shock to anyone.

Unsure of her welcome, Clare had avoided the Tannahills since the day of the disaster at St Cedric's. She had, however, sent Lizzie across the Leddings every two or three days with a basket of food and had gleaned from the girl the true state of affairs at the cottage. Consequently, Clare had had Pratie hire a boy, Tommy, from the farm at Kerse to see to the pony and take up the vegetables before they rotted in the ground.

Rose Tannahill was buried in St Cedric's kirkyard side by side with her daughter-in-law, with no watch or wake, no funeral celebration and nobody at the grave except Mr Soames and Norman and, behind the wall, young Lizzie to shed a tear for the departed.

Two days later, while Clare was leading Melissa in her lessons in the small parlour, Pratie came in, summoned her to the dyke by the kitchen garden and pointed out the column of smoke that wavered over the Leddings on the breeze.

"What's he doin' now?" Pratie asked.

"Burning his mother's things, I expect," Clare said.

"What a waste."

"Who would want them?" Clare said.

"Aye, that's true," Pratie said. "Will I send Lizzie over to see if he needs help?"

"Why not?" said Clare.

The shape of the smoke slithering on the wind and the faint pungency of burning herbs made Clare think of the serpent's egg. She wondered what Norman would do with it and was half inclined to try to redeem it and keep it for herself. But she knew that she lacked belief in the old ways, that she was too modern and rational to coax predictions from the crystal, to distil dreams and fashion longings from the cold heart of the glass.

That afternoon Clare ordered Tommy to run out the gig and, dressed in her winter cloak and a feathered hat, drove down to Ladybrook. It was time, high time, that she did a little house-cleaning of her own.

There was much activity about the blacksmith's shop. Two huge plough-horses waited to be shod and a hay-cart, balanced on its shafts, was having a wheel rerimmed. She glimpsed within the forge the glare of the furnace and sprays of sparks, heard the ringing of hammer on iron and above the din someone cheerfully whistling.

Hardly had Clare drawn the gig to a halt, however, before Brock, red-cheeked and sweating, appeared in the doorway. He wiped his hands on his leather apron and regarded her with a certain wary curiosity.

"So it's yourself, is it, Mrs Quinn?" he said. "What can we be doin' for you today? Does the pony need a shoe?"

"No, I've come to pay my debt."

Clare leaned from the gig and offered him the wallet.

"Well, well," Brock Harding said, "I hadn't thought to see my money again, certainly not so soon."

"When, Mr Harding, is the next lodge meeting?"

"Lodge meetin'?" he said, surprised. "That's not somethin' I could tell to you, Mrs Quinn."

"Whenever it is," Clare said, "I would be obliged if you would see to it that Mr Blyth is paid his money too."

"I'll see that it's done," Brock said, "an' that you receive a signature for receipt, unless you feel like takin' it up to Cairns yourself."

"That would not be prudent," Clare said, "since Mrs Blyth remains unwell."

"She's on the mend, I believe." Brock stretched out a muscular arm, took the wallet, opened it and, raising his brows, said, "Banknotes, Mrs Quinn?"

"They are, I assure you, legal tender."

"Aye, from Purves's bank," Brock said, "they would be." He stepped closer to the gig and pressed the wallet of notes to his chest. "Whose debts are you payin', Mrs Quinn? Your own or Freddie Striker's?"

"I know nothing of any debts that Mr Striker may have left behind," Clare said. "If Frederick owes you money, Mr Harding, then you will have to pursue him for it."

"No need to pursue him," Brock said. "He'll come back of his own accord. This year or next year, he'll be back."

"Did he say as much?"

"He didn't have to."

"And when he does – come back, I mean?"

"He'll not have you to protect him next time, will he?"

"No, Mr Harding, he will not."

"Aye, you did for old Freddie thoroughly, Clare Quinn. An' if I'd had my way you might have had the satisfaction of doing for him permanently."

"What stopped you?"

"My tender heart," Brock Harding said.

She felt a little leap of relief in her breast. Something in the blacksmith's expression indicated that he was telling her the truth.

"Will you be quittin' Headrick, by any chance?" Brock enquired.

"Most certainly not."

"In that case you'll be needin' the saltpans repaired."

"Yes, Mr Harding, I will."

"We do good work, my boys an' me."

"I know you do," Clare said. "At a price, of course."

"Oh, aye, always at a price," Brock Harding said and for some reason laughed aloud. "We'll do business again then, Mrs Quinn, will we not?"

"I expect we will, sir," Clare said. "Yes, I expect we will," and, pleased with the result of her afternoon's excursion, rode off home.

*   *   *

For the first time in weeks John Galloway's gloom had been relieved by optimism. As he had no patients to attend to that day he spent the afternoon attending to his appearance and even permitted Eppie to apply her little curved sewing scissors to his sidelocks and eyebrows before choosing his clothes for the evening's excursion. He plumped for a scarlet coat with sweeping tails which he hadn't worn for years and he was gratified to find that it still fitted him without letting out the seams. Ishbel had polished his waistcoat buttons and, with a silk handkerchief and matching cravat, he felt himself well set up to pay court to the most desirable woman in the county.

Clare's invitation to join her for supper at Headrick House had come as a vast relief to the doctor. Norman Tannahill and the servant Lizzie had walked down together from Headrick to deliver Clare's letter and to carry back the doctor's reply.

John Galloway still did not understand why Clare had been so cool towards him upon her return from Glasgow. He wondered if she had somehow stumbled upon the truth, though how that could be was a mystery since he had been exceedingly careful to disguise his actions. Clare, of course, had chided him about his friendship with Andrew Purves; that was to be expected. But her attitude to the mild deception had seemed almost hostile as if Purves had made her aware of flaws in the doctor's character so similar to her own that she was alarmed by them.

The arrival of the hand-written invitation, however, put paid to John Galloway's doubts and he sealed the letter of reply not just with blue wax but with a stealthy little kiss. Only flowers, he decided, would suit the tone of the occasion. Although it was November four or five roses still remained in a sheltered corner of the garden and he prayed that they would remain intact long enough to make a dainty posy for his love.

There was little he could do to protect the blossoms from the winter's chill but he knew that the stems would imbibe whatever subtle air of summer remained locked with the minerals of the wall. In mid-afternoon, he finally went out to cut them.

There had been no rain of late and the ground was soft and dry. He picked his way into the sheltered angle of the wall and, with stitching scissors, clipped off the yellow roses and a few green leaves. He stepped carefully back with the blossoms cradled in his palm, then stopped. Where he had dug the pit for the hotbed was now a mound of grass sods lightly strewn with autumn leaves. An unmarked stone from the beach was set flat upon it as if he'd intended to lead a pathway from the spot but had somehow changed his mind.

For a moment John Galloway felt almost irreverent in his dashing coat and silk cravat, as if he had stolen a little of the character of the man who was buried there, had robbed him of vestiges of his boldness and his charm. He glanced towards the house, little of which could be seen from the secluded corner, then he crouched and brushed the scattered leaves from off the unpolished stone.

When he'd left the Englishman alone in the library it had not occurred to him that Striker would have the gall to do away with himself. Naturally he had been shocked to find Striker's body on the floor, not quite dead but so deep in coma that he was beyond aid and had, in fact, passed away within minutes.

It did not seem to be in Striker's character to take his own life; yet there was a kind of courage in such an ending, defiance rather than cowardice. Even so, Galloway would not have done what he did if it had not been for Striker's last letter. *Bury me,* Striker had written, *and do not tell Clare. Let her think that I am gone away or she will blame herself. And that, of course, would never do.*

Indeed, in that sentiment at least Striker was correct. It would never do for Clare to learn the whole truth; nor would it be fair to expect him to compete with the dead.

Hunching his shoulders, Galloway patted down the grass with the flat of his hand. He had bedded the pit with quick-lime and had put more on top of the corpses and by springtime nothing much would remain of Mr Frederick Striker and there would be no trace at all of Eleanor's poor, ill-wrought love-child who lay cradled in his father's arms.

Sighing, John Galloway got to his feet.

He looked down at the blossoms in his hand then, on impulse, separated one from the others and gently placed it on the mound of grass. One rose, after all, would hardly be missed. Satisfied with the gesture, he wiped his hand upon his handkerchief and, with the posy held against his breast, set off for Headrick to begin his wooing in earnest at long last.

* * *

Now it was November and the sea was grey, Arran stark and black and patient as if the island waited for the first snows to score its rugged peaks and give it grandeur. It was no day to be out upon the shore for the dry wind had a keen, cutting edge but, on impulse, Clare had taken Melissa to the beach for the first time since their return from Glasgow over a month ago.

They walked to the fish-shed and stood for a few minutes by the greasy ruin which was all that remained of her imprudent investment. The ground was streaked with lurid chemicals but the brickwork remained upright, testament to the Hardings' workmanship. Precious little was left of Henri's marvellous devices for the site had been plundered by beachcombers and fisherfolk and everything salvageable had been removed.

The spot was too sad and ugly to tempt Clare to linger long and she led Melissa quickly away through the gorse bushes to visit the salthouse before dusk came sweeping in from the horizon.

Mr Bartholomew had kept a weather eye upon the girnal for there were still several bushels of salt in store but the salthouse remained untended, just as the Gowries had left it. In a month or so she would contract with the Hardings for repair of the pans and cisterns and would see to it that the loft was refurbished. Then she would instruct Mr Greenslade to employ another family of salters to bring the Headrick pans into production by the spring.

Clare locked the salthouse doors, put the keys into her pocket and, taking Melissa's hand, turned towards the track.

Behind her the pool lay restless and unchanging, impervious to all that had happened. The rocks would still be here in a thousand years, long after Headrick had crumbled into dust and her line, if line there was to be, had been obliterated and forgotten.

On the summit of the dunes Clare paused and looked back at the salthouse shore where, out of the winter gale, Frederick had stepped into her life again less than a year ago. She wondered, wistfully, if she would ever see him again. Somehow she doubted it.

"Mama?"

"What is it, dear?"

"There's nothing out there, Mama."

"I know, I know."

What her daughter said was true. There *was* nothing out there, nothing to covet, nothing to fear.

345

From this small piece of coast she had made her first beginnings and from here, one day, she would make her final endings. Suddenly she felt centred and complete.

It was, Clare realised, a very comfortable feeling.

"Mama, have you forgotten?" Melissa said impatiently. "Dr Galloway's coming to supper."

"How could I possibly forget such an important engagement?" Clare said with a smile. "What are you trying to tell me, Melissa?"

"I'm trying to tell you I'm cold and I want to go home."

Clare laughed and putting an arm about her daughter's waist set off across the turnpike for the house.